branded

cat mccaughey

branded

ISBN-13: 979-8-9914566-0-9

ISBN-10: 8-9914566-0-9

The following story is a work of fiction. All names, characters, places, and events are the product of the author's imagination. Any resemblance to places, events, or persons, either living or dead, is entirely coincidental.

Cover art: Catherine McCaughey (designed with Canva)

Cover font: TAN-PEARL

Book layout: Catherine McCaughey

Map art: Catherine McCaughey (designed with Canva)

wordcraftnovels.com

IG: @wordcraft_novels

dedication

To Mom and Dad

for everything.

To Bridget, Michael, Mary, Eleanor,

Patrick, Kilian, and Keenan,

and to Ryan, Marc, Margaret,

Elizabeth, and Holly.

And to the Lord of Life,

the first Word

Who gave me the gift of words.

I've done my best,

and You will make it what it ought to be.

In the evening of this life, let me stand

before You with empty hands.

~St. Thérèse of Lisieux

pronunciation

Alteva – uhl-TAY-vuh

Cilia – SEE-lee-uh

Chiara – kee-AR-uh

Dwyn – DWIN

Ensyth – EN-sith

Felwen – FELL-wen

Fhír – FEER

Jeka – JEH-kuh

Lacar – lah-KAHR

Lassari – luh-SAHR-ee

Laera – lay-AIR-uh

Ondural – AHN-dur-uhl

Tegea – teg-EE-uh

Tegid – TEHG-id

Tivore – teh-VOOR-ay

Tonitrus – TAHN-ih-truhs

Tsuru – SOO-roo

Vanha – VON-uh

Vastil – vahst-EEL

Vikur – VEE-kur

Encyclopedia of Vanha

The world of Vanha is home to five primary species of sentient beings, each with a unique Gift. The following are brief excerpts from the *Encyclopedia of Vanha* that outline each species' Gift, their primary physical and social characteristics, and any subspecies.

଼

Tegids

Tegids make up the largest percent of Vanha's population. They dwell in the middle country of Tegea, primarily in larger cities, well-developed towns, and surrounding farmland, and are governed by an elected republic. Their primary religion revolves around the worship of Arva, the Maker, whom they honor in both household and public shrines.

The Tegid Gift is physical perfection and accelerated healing. Tegids appear humanoid, standing anywhere from five to seven feet, with pronounced muscle definition in both males and females. All Tegids receive symbolic tattoos as markers of their physical feats and accomplishments. They are fast, strong, and impervious to illness, and heal within seconds when injured. However, they are susceptible to high doses of certain poisons, and they cannot heal from burns, so they greatly fear fire.

଼

Nousk

Nousk are the second-largest species in Vanha. They dwell in the western country of Noskia, primarily in smaller city-states and farms, and are governed by democracies. Their primary religion revolves the worship of Arva, the Maker, and they rely heavily on prophecy and blessings. Nousk are the most likely of all the species to adopt superstition and false crafts.

The Nousk Gift is mental prowess. There are three subspecies of Nousk, each exhibiting a different aspect of the Gift. All Nousk appear humanoid, but their skin pigmentation can change based on their moods, a characteristic they learn to control as children. Also, each subspecies has certain distinguishing physical features that are non-humanoid. All three subspecies are genetically compatible, and mixed marriages are not unheard of. However, the children of such marriages are rarely born with more than one Gift. Although uncommon, there are some Nousk born with two Gifts, and these are referred to as "doua." Doua cannot exercise both Gifts at the same time.

- ❖ **Jeka** are capable of reading others' thoughts and projecting their own thoughts into others' heads. Their ability requires training to reach proficiency, and their Gift is limited by distance and visibility. All Jeka have unusually large ears of a unique shape, which function as an identifying feature similar to fingerprints.

- ❖ **Ensyth** are capable of experiencing others' emotions and projecting their own emotions into others. Their ability requires discipline to temper and control, and their Gift is also limited by distance, although not by visibility. All Ensyth have a set of horns or antlers on their heads, and older Ensyth have been known to grow multiple sets.

- ❖ **Telk** are capable of performing telepathy on objects and other living creatures. Their ability requires training to strengthen concentration, although they are not necessarily limited by the size of the object. A Telk cannot perform telepathy on himself. Highly trained Telk can manipulate certain objects that are not visible to them, although this technique is limited by distance. Of all the subspecies, the Telk Gift is the most physically taxing when used for extended periods of time. All Telk have double thumbs on each hand.

◌

Beast-skins

Beast-skins are generally nomadic, so their exact numbers are difficult to estimate. There are five subspecies: Kithsa, Dwyn, Felwen, Vikur, and Selkies. Most Beast-skins establish law and order via the head of their individual clan or family, who establishes strict codes of behavior. They generally acknowledge Arva, the Maker, but most religious practices focus primarily on honoring their First Ancestors and clan founders through rituals of passage and sacred hunting and burial grounds.

All five subspecies are vaguely humanoid in form, but not features: they have the tails, ears, teeth and claws of beasts, as well as furred limbs and heads. They can stand on two limbs or four with ease. The Beast-skins' Gift is possession of the senses and abilities of beasts, which differ for each subspecies. All Beast-skins can shift to a more beast-like form at will, but only Dwyn and Selkies can shift fully into beast form.

- ❖ Kithsa are cat-skins. On two legs, Common Kithsa stand between three and four feet, while exotic Kithsa stand anywhere from eight to twelve feet. They are nomadic, but Common Kithsa have often been known to live in Tegean cities.

- ❖ Dwyn are bear-skins. On two legs, they stand anywhere from five to ten feet. Dwyn are one of the two Beast-skin subspecies that can shift fully into beast form, although that is not a common occurrence. They are nomadic and are rarely found in groups larger than three.

- ❖ Felwen are wolf-skins. On two legs, they stand between six and seven feet. In physical features, they normally appear the most beast-like of the Beast-skins, although none of them can shift fully into beast form. In behavior and habits, they are considered the most beast-like of the Beast-skins. They are nomadic and live in large familial clans.

- ❖ Vikur are fox-skins. On two legs, they stand between three and five feet. They are nomadic and live in smaller familial troupes anywhere from three to a dozen in number.

- ❖ Selkies are seal-skins. On two legs, they stand between six and eight feet. Selkies are the second Beast-skin subspecies that can shift fully into beast form, and they generally prefer to remain in beast-form. They are the least nomadic of the Beast-skins, residing in sea caves and cliffs in large, multi-generational familial colonies.

ᛨ

Tsuru

Tsuru are the third largest species in Vanha. They live in colonies on cliffsides and mountainsides, typically close to bodies of water, and rarely mingle with the other species. They are most often governed by a matriarchy. Their primary religion is an ascetic worship of Arva, the Maker, and incorporates water rituals such as purification rites and sea pilgrimages.

The Tsuru Gift is flight and stamina. Tsuru are feather-winged humanoids, standing between three and five feet tall. They sport feathered crests, not hair, on their heads. They have keen sight and hearing and can fly great distances at a time.

ᛨ

Lacar

Lacar make up the smallest percentage of Vanha's population. They live in the tiny northern country of Laera, in a network of small kingdoms under either a sole monarch or a married pair. Their primary religion is a ritualistic worship of Arva, the Maker, and a high honor of the Handmaid, and involves elaborate traditions that incorporate fire, such as sacrificial offerings of livestock and crops.

Lacar appear the most humanoid of all Vanha's species. Their Gift is fire, which they can summon from within at will. They can also manipulate existing natural fire, as well as summon light and heat independently of each other. Highly skilled Lacar can even summon colored fire or light. Lacar have been known to exhibit glowing limbs, hair, eyes, or even freckles when exercising their powers. They cannot be burned by any fire or heat, save the internal fire which they summon themselves.

map of Vanha

Laera
Lassari Mountains
Lassari Sea
Prescot
Noskia
Tegea
Vasill Forest
Onaford Mountains
terra incognita
Tonitrus River
Belkar
Onaford River
terra incognita
key
borderline
city
N
W
E
S

map of Tegea

N
W
E
S
Laustrul Mountains
Ondurul Mountains
Crescor
Daret
Tegea
Noskia
Vastil Forest
Talin
Grede
Tonitrus River
Belkar
Ondural River
Riften
key
borderline
campsite
flood
bandits
Tivore
outpost
Ora
Arsonists

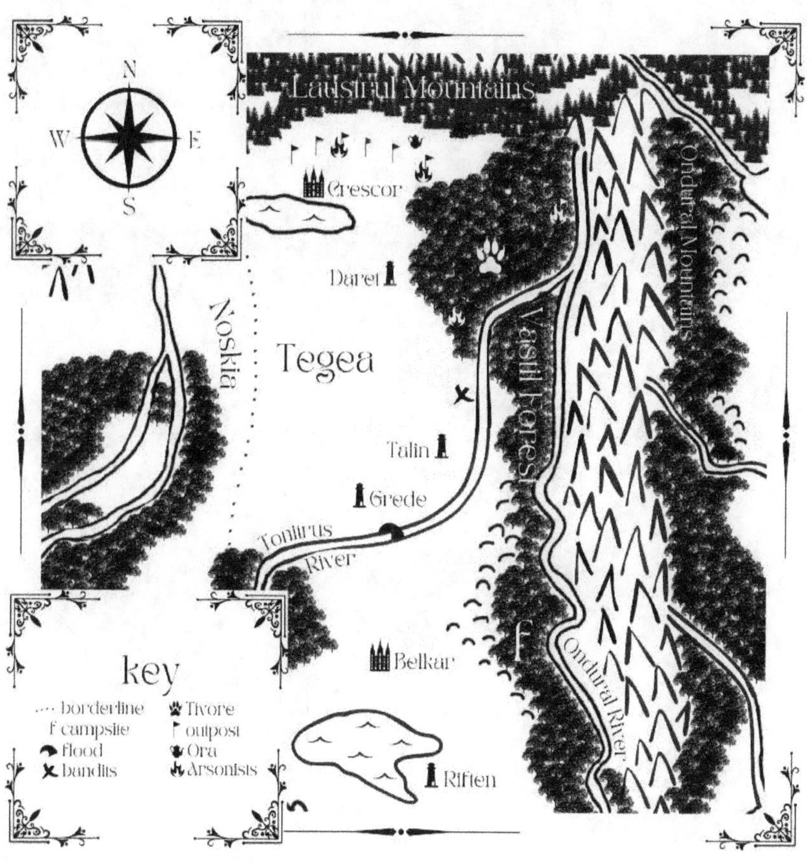

1

"Trust me on this ... it's worth at least meeting the Ringmaster."

"I don't know, Zelie ..." Chiara pressed her lips together, tracing an absent-minded finger across the burn scars on her left jaw. Four welts, ridged flesh, running down along her neck. Covered with makeup, yes. Practically invisible to the naked eye. But she could still feel them.

"Chiara." Zelie turned a bright blue gaze on her, stretching upward to make eye contact. She was a Common Kithsa; her head only came to Chiara's waist. "You deserve a life outside of ... this." She flicked her ears toward the field in front of them.

They were leaning in the shade of the trees against the iron fence, staring into the field beyond as it baked in the heat of the afternoon. Sunlight was filtering down through the leaves overhead.

On the other side, the scattered stones were watching them.

Chiara shifted and looked away, grass crunching underfoot. "This *was* my whole life, Zelie." *And now it's done.*

Zelie's ears flattened. "Not your whole life. You're still here."

Here? Maybe. But not all of her. Something had died that night, three years ago.

"You know …" Zelie began slowly. "It's not just my idea. The Ringmaster wanted to meet you. He asked me to tell you about a duo trapeze act—"

"A *duo*?" Chiara glanced at her friend sharply. "Zelie, I can't do that!"

Not a duo.

A dry, hot coal pulsed in the pit of her stomach, a lump of heated iron, flaring, cooling, over and over again.

"Chiara … he's not a Tegid," said Zelie softly. "He doesn't care about—"

"That's not why." Chiara closed her eyes. "Isak was my only catcher." *And he's gone now. How could I replace him?*

Zelie said nothing.

Regret twinged in Chiara's chest, and she exhaled slowly. "Sorry. That was harsh." She offered Zelie an apologetic glance.

Zelie shook her head. "It's fine." She pressed her lips together.

Silence, for a moment. Then Zelie placed her furred hand gently on Chiara's arm. "For what it's worth … he would've wanted you to have more than this. He would've wanted you to have a second chance."

True. But Chiara wanted Isak to be there for her second chance. And he wasn't coming back.

She looked away, eyes stinging. "I never wanted more than what I had."

Her arm twitched, and Zelie's hand fell away.

We've been through this. Too many times to count. Every time Zelie came back, they had the same conversation. *You could join the circus with me … Cirque du Fhír. It's a mixed circus … They'd be happy to have you …*

Zelie, I can't. Not anymore. Not after Crescor.

It wasn't entirely Zelie's fault. Zelie had never been a flier, never had a catcher. Chiara couldn't blame her for not understanding.

A breeze trickled through the clearing, lifting the dead summer air for a moment.

"I'm sorry," Zelie murmured softly. "You can make your own decisions. I just … I don't want your life to end like this." Her black tail laced back and forth.

Silence. Silence, except for the underlying buzz of the insects, the invisible watchers in the trees around them.

Chiara let out a slow, tense breath.

It wasn't easy. None of this was easy. Not Zelie joining a circus, right after what happened at Crescor. Not Zelie being mostly gone for the last three years. Not Zelie trying to reconnect anytime she came back to visit.

You could try. You could talk to her about why you're turning her down. You could tell her you still want to be a flier. You could tell her it would still feel like betraying his memory.

Chiara pushed the little voice away. "Thank you, Zelie. It … it means a lot to me. Really," she added, trying for a smile.

Zelie pattered her claws on the rail insistently. "I *do* still think you should come watch us practice tonight. Just to see! You live there, anyway. I solemnly swear that nobody will give you grief."

"Arva forbid," Chiara muttered. "Like we need another gym patron being jumped."

Zelie looked deeply offended. "What did you expect me to do? Let someone talk dirt about my best friend?"

Best friend … There was a tiny, awkward pause before Chiara mustered a smile. "No … no, I don't. But I don't think Master Rothgar would be satisfied with that reason. I don't think anybody's ever been attacked at his gym before. He almost had a conniption when he heard about it."

"I regret nothing," Zelie sniffed. "And I'm serious, by the way. You should think about coming tonight. Doesn't running away to join the circus sound fun?"

Chiara laughed. "Fun? Weren't you just complaining earlier about having to set up the stage tonight?"

Zelie's ears and tail shot upright. "Claws and teeth, I forgot about that! Oh, Mishkil's going to tan my hide! I gotta go, sorry."

She threw her arms around Chiara's waist in a tight hug. "Come tonight! I'm serious!" And then she was bolting off toward the gravel road behind them.

"Good luck!" Chiara called. Then she turned back to the fence, breathing in deeply. The air was heavy and thick in her lungs.

The gate was a few yards down, but she didn't feel like walking. She vaulted over the fence, landing on her feet with ease.

Grass crackled under her boots as she weaved slowly between the stones, making her way toward the massive oak tree that sprawled out in the far corner of the field.

Softer, and slower, until she found the stone she was looking for.

Not a gravestone. "Grave" meant somebody had been laid to rest, asleep beneath the earth. "Grave" meant the name in the stone wasn't the only thing left.

All the other stones were gravestones. Not this one.

Chiara knelt down and began brushing the loam aside, sweeping away acorns and dead leaves. "I'll bring a rake next time." Sweat dripped down the nape of her neck, dampening her short-cropped curls. She dusted off her hands on worn canvas pants. Then she stood and crossed her arms over her chest.

"Hey … It's me."

Branches creaked above her head. She paused, searching for words. "I'd say the weather's nice … but it's not. At least the crepe myrtles are blooming." She stopped, swallowed. Even now, her throat was prickling, the coal in her stomach starting to burn.

Start over. She tried again, tried to talk past the tightness in her chest. "Zelie's in town. With the circus. She … she keeps telling me to join. But … without you …"

Choking, choking. Heat in her lungs and her mouth, like the smoke that night. The scars on her face were throbbing. Her fists clenched, fingernails digging into her palms.

Not without you. Not after you.

The stone in front of her was silent still.

A breath of wind stirred the oak, fanning her hot skin. She cleared her throat roughly. "I have to go. But I'll be back tomorrow, okay? Tomorrow."

She traced the letters on the face of the stone. She knew them as well as if they were engraved in her own flesh, engraved like her own scars.

Isak.

That was all she had left of him. His name, and the scars on her neck.

And regret. All unfaded. Carved in stone or skin — what difference did it make?

The words hung in the listening air. Breathing did no good today. Not when the air was as hot as her own skin. Chiara rose slowly to her feet, wincing as pins and needles seized her leg. She touched a hand to the stone.

"Tomorrow," she whispered. Then she loped away, leaped the fence, and broke into a swift jog along the road.

ᴄ⳼

Breathless, legs shaking, Chiara slid in the gymnasium side door, straight into the acrobatics arena. "I am so late …" She braced herself for any sign of her mentor. But Master Rothgar wasn't anywhere in sight. *Thank Arva.*

The shrine to Arva the Maker was right by the door. Chiara dipped her hand into the scented oil pot and swiped it across her forehead, the prayer running through her head mechanically: *Arva, grant me strength for the work ahead.*

Then she got her first good look at the arena itself. The indoor arena was situated inside the largest room in the entire gymnasium. The enormous sandy circle was full of cavorting figures and shouted instructions. Horses trotted around the circumference, carrying carefully balanced riders. Cirque du Fhír, already hard at work.

But it was the aerial acrobats who drew Chiara's eyes. High up on the trapeze bars, flying back and forth, slinging their bodies weightlessly through the air.

Chiara let out a soft breath, goosebumps tingling across her arms. She still remembered it — the rush of adrenaline, the pull of the fall, the euphoria as her fingers wrapped around the bar. It was years gone now, but she still remembered it.

A grim twist curved her lips.

"You're here!" Zelie bounded up, snapping Chiara out of her thoughts. "Come meet Mishkil!"

She tugged Chiara's arm and pointed toward a massive figure in the middle of the ring. A male bear-skin, towering head and shoulders above everyone else. He was practically eye to eye with the riders on horseback as he gestured commands.

Chiara pulled back with a nervous laugh. "Your Ringmaster's a Dwyn?" His claws looked large enough to crush her skull between them. "Uh, maybe not today, thanks," she stammered, extricating herself from Zelie's grip. "I have way more chores to do now that you're all staying here."

"Does Rothgar pay you extra?" Zelie rolled back and forth on the balls of her heels. Even in normal conversation, she could never stand still for long. "Can I help? Ooh! Will he pay me if I help?"

"Not if I'm late, no, and definitely not. Besides, don't you get paid to perform?"

Zelie pouted. "Not nearly enough. Your dad got us a nice commission, though."

"I heard." Chiara fell silent, staring at the lively arena.

Dad. Known throughout Belkar as Torva Alteva, First Foreign Relations Officer. Traveling across Tegea and even to other countries, gone for weeks on end. He'd seen Fhír at some point — who knew when — and somehow, he'd convinced the Belkar Low Council to commission them as one of the Midsummer Festival's main events.

"Didn't he get the Council to pay for all this?" Zelie waved a hand around.

"Sort of. He got them to fund the gym for hosting you."

Zelie grinned. "Nice. That means you get a raise, right?"

Chiara shrugged. "I dunno. Seems kinda selfish to ask for one. I already get free room and board." And a mentor.

"Chiara Alteva!" a loud voice boomed behind her. "You're late."

Speak of the devil ... "Fesht," Chiara muttered, spinning around to face the grizzled Tegid who was standing behind her.

"I'll be going now," Zelie whispered, scampering off.

"Master Rothgar." Chiara stood stiffly at attention. "Reporting for duty. Apologies for being late, sir."

Even with her back ramrod straight, the top of her head was barely at a level with her mentor's barrel chest. For someone his height and weight, Rothgar was surprisingly light on his feet. She should've been paying more attention.

He stared down at her with dark, impassive eyes. "Seven years, and I still have to remind you to be on time?"

He crossed powerful limbs across his chest. Every inch of his skin was covered with a thick pattern of navy runic tattoos, the Tegid record of past feats. He probably had more tattoos than months Chiara had been alive.

She risked a glance at his right shoulder. It was semi-immobile from a burn injury he'd received years ago, and it was a flawless barometer for his mood. Tension … not a good sign.

Chiara wanted to wilt. *I let him down.* "Apologies, sir. I was … visiting."

It was not a good excuse. Not when they were hosting Fhír, which was more a burden than an honor for Rothgar.

His face didn't soften, exactly. But the wrinkles around his eyes seemed less tight. "Very well. See that you aren't late again."

"Yes, sir."

Rothgar jabbed a thumb over his shoulder. "Extra assignments on the wall in my workroom — cleaning instructions for you. Double-time. Get a move on."

"Yes, sir." Chiara trotted past him to the door in the corner. As soon as she walked into the workroom, she spotted the long paper on the opposite wall. It was an extensive list.

She gave it a rueful glance. "This would be so much easier if I was a Telk." She'd give an arm and a leg to lift things with her mind.

The Tegid Gift wasn't much compared to some of the other races. So what if Tegids were strong and fast and never got sick? Telk could manipulate objects with their minds. Beast-skins had heightened senses. Tsuru could *fly*, for Arva's sake. *That* would be a useful Gift.

But even mere physical strength was an eternity better than being born Stunted.

Chiara's breath hissed through her teeth. She grabbed the cleaning trolley and headed for the lift on the other side of the arena.

The whole sprawling building was four stories, but they'd closed off all the other wings except the one with the arena. Here, all the upper floors ran in a wide rectangle around the center arena, leaving room for the trapeze bars and aerial silks.

The whole place was filled to the seams with movement and shouts. It was a nice change. Normally, Mum and Dad were the only ones who came religiously. And Zelie, too, whenever she was traveling through.

The second floor brought Chiara almost at a level with the lowest set of trapeze bars. She hesitated a moment, chills running across her skin, watching Zelie fling herself down a set of aerial silks.

She wanted you to join. That could be you.

Chiara breathed in deeply, smelling the sand and wood shavings and chalk.

No, it couldn't. Not without Isak. She turned away from the railing.

A few minutes later, she'd fallen back into the familiar rhythm of cleaning. Fhír were excellent houseguests. There wasn't much to clean. Still, it took much longer than normal. Any other week, it would've been just her room on the fifth floor and Rothgar in the ground floor workroom. This time, it was thirty extra people, plus four trained horses.

But Chiara couldn't really complain. Rothgar kept her employed, fed, and sheltered, and he taught her everything he knew. True, he was tough as nails, and he didn't give her an inch. But if he hadn't chosen her, she never would've been apprenticed. No one else would have taken the chance.

Not on her, or him. He was burned, and she was Stunted.

They weren't supposed to be that way. All Tegids were born perfect. Perfect health, perfect healing, perfect performance. Nobody was supposed to be "Stunted." Rothgar would've healed from any other injury in seconds … but not a burn. No Tegid could heal from a burn. And Chiara was supposed to perform as well as any other Tegid acrobat.

But Rothgar's burn would never heal, and Chiara had never healed properly to begin with. So the Tegea National Military had quietly dismissed Rothgar to "retirement," and Belkar Acrobatics Academy had expelled Chiara two years shy of apprenticeship. Now here they were … a broken mentor and a broken apprentice, holed away at a gym nobody visited.

At least, not anymore.

Isak had. He'd come with Chiara every day to rehearse, even after she'd gotten expelled. If he hadn't, she never would've learned to be a flier — not that she'd ever be allowed to perform publicly, but the secret duo trapeze practices were as close as she ever came to a performance.

And even those were over now.

Chiara thrust the broom against the floor with slightly more force, and the handle suddenly snapped in her hands.

A laugh escaped her lips. "Oh, great." *So I'm not strong enough to do anything useful, but I'm still strong enough to break something useful.* She shoved the broken pieces onto the trolley with a sigh. "Guess I'll have to get a new one."

Ironic — being strong, but never strong enough.

☙

Chiara dangled upside down in a knee hang, feeling the muscles in her thighs begin to ache. The breath hissed between her teeth. She curled upright and wrapped her arms around the ropes.

Technically, she wasn't allowed to use the trapeze equipment. She wasn't a registered acrobat in Belkar. But Rothgar adamantly vetoed that. *It's my gym,* he'd growled. *If the Council wants to stop it, they should come to the gym themselves.* So Chiara and Isak had practiced there for years under his watchful eye.

Now that Isak was gone, she did solo trapeze. It would never be the same as a duo routine. But at least she was on the bars. That was the closest she'd ever get to him again.

Chiara gripped the bar between both hands and lifted herself up, balancing her legs out behind her. Breathe in, breathe out. Suspending her weight … aching, aching …

Expelled at thirteen, two years before apprenticeship age. She never got an apprenticeship. She got a diagnosis. "Declared Stunted by official examination." As if years of colds and slow-healing scrapes and an ever-high temperature weren't enough proof of that.

Physically unable to complete the minimum requirements. Seven words was all it took for her to be expelled from Belkar Acrobatics Academy.

Chiara swung her legs down, flipping herself over the bar. Her arms shook; she gritted her teeth and tightened her fingers around the metal. Once, twice—

Isak had disregarded it completely. He'd brought her to Rothgar's gym the very next day. He was the reason she was still here, instead of rotting somewhere in a factory.

Thank Arva Rothgar had allowed it. She and Isak were still able to practice every duo routine from the Academy. Even three years on, she still knew them inside and out.

One last swing. Air rushed into Chiara's chest; she pushed up slowly on the bar, extending her legs in sideways splits.

Of course, Isak would've been invited to any gym anywhere in Tegea — and he could've had any flier he wanted. Only the best for a gold-winning student.

But he never wanted anyone other than Chiara. Even though she could never heal like a Tegid. Being a flier was everything she'd ever wanted, and he was the only catcher in Tegea who would have picked her. No one else would ever take the chance — her own risk of injury was too great.

Chiara swung backward and her legs shot up. Curling her toes around the bar, she rolled her body up into a standing position. She wrapped tight fingers around the suspension ropes, feeling her lungs burn. *Breathe. Breathe.*

For the last seven years, the gym was all she had. No official graduation documents. No formal entry into society. And now, at twenty years old, no First Tattoo … at least, not that anyone else knew about.

Any other Tegid would be graduating from their apprenticeship, receiving their First Tattoo, proudly carrying that mark of their talent as they entered society. But Chiara hadn't graduated, so she wasn't legally allowed to get a First Tattoo.

She wrapped her legs around the ropes and began inching her way up, feeling tension coiled in every limb. She panted for breath.

Rothgar had declared it a load of horse manure, and he'd given her the First Tattoo himself: the Acrobat mark, a circle surrounding an interlocking pair of S-shapes. *You earned it, just like the rest of them,* he'd insisted fiercely.

Chiara opened her hands and slung forward until she was upside down. She slid down the ropes, feeling the blood rush to her head.

Of course, nobody could know about her First Tattoo. She would've been punished for carrying a tattoo she hadn't formally earned. Rothgar knew that as well as she did. He hadn't tattooed her between the shoulder blades, as was customary. Instead, he'd placed it on her lower back, where no one else could see.

Chiara's feet caught on the bar, and she swung around, curling up underneath it, snatching it in her hands again.

Her only tattoo, supposedly a mark of prowess, and it was invisible to the rest of the world. All anyone else saw was Stunted. A failed-out flier. Of course, nobody quite said that to her face. People still respected her father for being on the Low Council.

But Chiara and Isak, his adopted cubs? Polite company would never talk about them. As for impolite company …

Chiara unhooked her feet and unfurled herself, letting her legs swing downward. She dangled from the bar. Gravity pulled at her feet, begging her to fall.

Stunted! What's wrong *with you?*

Nobody knew. Chiara had been that way her whole life — she was born like that, most likely. For years, Mum and Dad tried to figure it out, until finally she convinced them to let it go. Instead, she learned how to cover it up. Illness, bruises, her temperature, anything that marked her out as different.

But the failing marks weren't something she could hide. And the scars from three years ago … those never healed, either. Makeup was the best way to avoid staring eyes. Another cover.

Chiara swung forward, back, forward, back, feeling the momentum build in her limbs. She fixed her eyes on the bar across from her, visualizing the leap in her mind.

One, two, three …

There. The golden sliver of a second. Her hands released; her body curled; she arced through the air — and she caught the bar.

A bone-deep ache ran down her arms. Gravity was winning. A sharp cry of frustration escaped her as her muscles shook, threatening to give. She tried to pull herself up, but she dangled in place, unable to move.

After all this time — after three years of solo practice — she still jumped like a flier.

"Come *on!*" she roared, wiggling forward slightly, trying to squeeze the last bit of strength from her shoulders.

She could never be a flier again. No one could ever know about this. About any of it. Her weakness, her tattoo, her nighttime practice sessions in some old gym. Hidden, always hidden.

Isak was the only good thing about being a trapeze flier, and now he was gone. And all she had left was a set of scars that wouldn't heal, like some kind of horrible reverse tattoo.

A mark of failure.

Failure. A desperate snarl escaped; her fingers gave; she was plummeting toward the ground, ten feet below.

She barely made the landing. Her foot buckled beneath her, sending her sprawling onto the ground; pain twinged up her leg and she bit off a sharp cry.

Twisted ankle. She extended her leg carefully in front of her and tapped the offending ankle gingerly on the ground. It was tender, but not terrible. She'd done worse.

"Fesht," she cursed softly, spitting sand out of her mouth. Any Tegid with a minor injury like that would heal in a matter of seconds. No need for bandages or splints. But Chiara needed them, more often than she liked to admit, and Rothgar had taught her how to make her own.

Of course, a healthy *Tegid wouldn't have fallen in the first place.* Chiara spat again. She clambered to her feet and began limping slowly out of the arena.

It could've been a lot worse. *Thank Arva Rothgar wasn't here to see that.* She bit her lip roughly as her bad foot came down too forcefully on the stone floor. She set her teeth and straightened her back, trying to walk faster.

You're not a failure. Isak would've said so if he was here.

He was right, in a way. One sprained ankle wasn't a failure.

branded

Being Stunted … *that* was a failure. Being Stunted was the world's worst curse, and she couldn't change it.

It was bad enough that she'd never really perform. Now her only catcher was gone, because she wasn't fast enough to save him.

2

*H*ome. It was a strange word, no matter how Chiara tried to define it. Strange enough to make her pause where she stood on the steep front steps of her parents' three-story house, the evening after her trapeze mishap, with more than her ankle twinging.

Where is home, really …? Belkar, where she'd never really have a place? The gymnasium, where she would never be a flier again? Or the house she didn't live in anymore — the house she hadn't even been born in, but brought to, with Isak?

Isak, who wasn't here anymore. But here was the closest place to peaceful that she'd probably ever have. Here, with Mum and Dad and Dad's mum Nani.

Is it still home without Isak?

Chiara's eyes drifted over the worn stone beneath her feet, and then the red painted door in front of her. From the street, it looked pristine, but up close, she could still spot the carefully repaired scuffs and scrapes in the wood, reminders of past years when she and Isak were more careless.

The potted plants along the steps were wilted from the summer heat. A glimpse around the side of the house told Chiara that the garden was in a similar state of exhaustion. *Poor Mum.* The garden was her passion project, and she always worked so hard to keep it maintained.

Chiara felt a pang of guilt. *I should come more often. I could help* ... Most of the time, like tonight, she was only there for family dinner. One night a week, every week, ever since she'd moved to the gymnasium. Mum and Dad's place was several blocks east of the gymnasium — almost at the outskirts of Belkar, far from the hubbub of the train stations and First Circle at the heart of the city.

Dad preferred it like that. Quiet, out of the way. *Private life and public life shouldn't mix,* he always said. To the rest of Tegea, he was the First Foreign Relations Officer — a prestigious office in the Tegea republic. But at home, he was just Dad. No public life, no work talk — just spending time with his family.

For most of her life, Chiara had been grateful for that. The only thing worse than being Stunted in a Tegid city was being the Stunted daughter of a public official. As soon as she'd been old enough to understand that, she wanted nothing more than for Dad to keep their private life to himself.

Until he left us out of it, too.

Chiara exhaled softly and rapped the door with sharp knuckles. "Mum? Dad? I'm here!"

No reply. She frowned at the frosted glass panes on the front door. *I am a bit early ... but they're normally home by now.* She stooped to the potted crepe myrtle by the door and sifted through the soil until she found the key.

One last knock, unanswered. Then she turned the key in the lock and stepped inside.

The long front hallway ran down the length of the house in front of her, its wooden floorboards covered with worn woven carpet. Doors opened up on either side — dining room to the right, parlor to the left; sitting rooms and kitchen toward the back. Near the end of the hallway, on the right-hand side, was a grand spiral staircase that led up to the second and third floors.

She turned to the small alcove in the wall next to the door. The house shrine to Arva, the Maker. Every Tegid family had one. Freshly cut flowers in vases, a jar of scented oil, a small painted-glass image of two hands holding a hammer and chisel.

Chiara dipped a finger in the oil and swiped it across her forehead. *Grant peace, protection, and prosperity to this house.* That was the prayer Mum had taught her to say, ever since she'd been old enough to speak. Right before leaving and right after coming home.

Chiara walked a few feet into the hall and peered into the dining room. Empty. "I'm here," she called again. No response. Not a sound, except her own breathing.

Slowly, she walked down the hall, her steps muted by the thick carpet underfoot. The walls on either side were lined with portraits and photographs. The family all together … Dad receiving some award from the Crescor High Council … Mum performing in the Crescor National Ballet, the very night she and Dad had met.

That one was quite the story. Dad had arrived in Crescor on official Council business, and he'd left head over heels for Cilia Giadro, a nationally acclaimed ballerina.

How'd it happen? Chiara and Isak used to ask Dad about it all the time. They knew the story by heart, but they never got tired of listening.

I was at some party right after the ballet ended … "some party" being a formal banquet put on by the High Council. *And I was trying to find my seat. I saw the number at my table, and I was walking over, and then I looked up … and there she was.*

There she was. They'd been seated next to each other. A month later, Dad returned to Crescor to court her formally, and they were married in less than a year. It made quite the headline: "Belle of the Ballet Becomes Blushing Bride," or some other ridiculous alliteration.

Mum had left her stage career behind without once looking back, much to the chagrin of her company and the press. *I'm not sorry,* she'd always say, lifting her chin, and even after twenty-two years, Dad still looked at her with eyes so fiercely proud and adoring that it gave Chiara chills.

The hallway ended, and Chiara began walking up the staircase. "Mum? Dad!" After several steps, she reached the second-floor landing and began peering into a few of the bedrooms. *Nani might be sleeping …* although, knowing Dad, he had probably persuaded his retired mother to accompany him, just to keep her out of trouble.

Nobody knew what Nani did before retirement. Most of her tattoos were unrecognizable symbols. Chiara's personal theory was that Nani had been a spy, or maybe an assassin, since she seemed to know way more about poisons and injuries than any Tegid should. She'd taught Chiara first aid even before Rothgar, in addition to seven different ways to kill a Tegid … although Chiara had never yet found herself in a situation where that knowledge would be helpful.

Nani wasn't in. Chiara withdrew her head. Nobody would be on the third floor. Besides the attic, the only other rooms up there were Chiara's … and Isak's. His face was in all the third-floor photos.

She turned back around to face the second-story landing, and her eyes drifted across the far wall. More photos. Dad and Mum at their wedding, their dark, silky hair and olive skin making them a picture-perfect couple. The two of them again, standing on a pier in front of a sailing ship. All the aunts and uncles at the family reunion in Crescor.

And then came the photo of Mum, cradling two bundles with tiny, wrinkled faces.

That was the story Isak loved the most. *How'd you find us?* he'd ask excitedly, and Mum's eyes would go misty.

It was only a few months after Dad and Mum's marriage, and they were traveling to Crescor to visit Mum's family. *We met a friend who was taking care of you, and we were asked if we could care for you … and I started to cry.* Mum was the one telling the story, but Dad would always seem on the verge of tears himself.

But you never *cry!* Isak would protest. It was true. Mum was all poise and elegance, ever calm, ever measured.

But she cried for you! Dad would exclaim, ruffling Isak's hair. *She saw you both, and she said, "I can't leave without them."*

Mum was never able to have cubs of her own. The window for childbirth for female Tegids was narrow, and Mum had been trained since childhood to spend her life in the Crescor National Ballet. She never expected anyone to fall in love with her. After all, what Tegid would end a professional ballerina's career by marrying her?

Well, Dad had, and Mum called it the happiest tragedy of her life. But when they married, her time for cubs had ended. Dad knew that, and they were still happily married. But they both wanted cubs.

So you found us! Isak would crow excitedly.

My friend needed help, Mum would explain softly. *We knew we couldn't leave without you. So we adopted you.*

That had also caused quite the uproar in the press. Rumors were flying that the cubs brought home by Torva Alteva and his wife Cilia had been *abandoned.* But Dad put an early end to the gossip with a public announcement that their new cubs were "children of a dear friend no longer with us."

Chiara asked Dad about that a few times when she was little. Who was the mysterious friend? Why were they taking care of two Tegid cubs from different parents? What happened to their biological parents?

But Dad never said more than what he'd already told the rest of the world. *Our friend asked us to keep our silence, and we gave our word that the truth would remain with us.* And he always promised Chiara that he had done it for her and Isak's sakes as much as for the sake of the mysterious friend.

Eventually, she'd stopped asking about it. He'd done it for her ... but was it just to spare her from the truth? Were her biological parents really dead?

... Or had they left her on purpose?

Chiara moved on from Mum's photo.

Maybe her birth parents had known about her condition. Maybe they hadn't wanted her. She used to wonder about that, sometimes.

But what did it matter? Mum and Dad wanted her, from the very first moment they met her. That hadn't changed, no matter how many times she was injured or sick. Even after the Academy.

And after Isak ...?

Chiara's feet stopped, just like they always did, in front of the last photograph. The one right next to Dad's study.

A close-up portrait. No matter that it was black and white — she could see the colors easily in her mind's eye.

Chiara and Isak, side by side, seven years old. Neither of them looked a thing like Mum or Dad.

She spared a glance at the much younger version of herself. Large eyes, fuzzy curls, an uncertain smile. Skin without scars.

Before.

Her eyes flicked to Isak.

He was the photogenic one. His smile beamed out of the frame. Blonde, curly hair, dimpled cheeks, eyes like bluejay's feathers. Even in grayscale, he looked ...

Alive. Chiara turned abruptly away, the knot in her stomach starting to burn.

"Dad?" She tapped the study door hesitantly, then tested the handle. Unlocked. She paused for a moment, and then pushed the door open.

The familiar scent of the study washed over her even before she could see the room itself … something sharp and almost sweet, like cloves. The smell of Dad's pipe smoke. He'd never smoke inside; Mum didn't like it. Instead, he'd stand on the little second-story balcony just outside his study.

Chiara took a step forward, and the door swung inward silently to reveal a somewhat disheveled room.

Two bay windows with the curtains drawn. Dad's desk sat in the middle of the wide, cluttered floor, both covered with heaps of papers and books. Floor-to-ceiling bookshelves lined each wall, full to overflowing, with small pillars of books clustered at the foot of each shelf, patiently waiting their return from exile. A large map of Tegea hung on the left wall, right above a long wooden table filled with knick-knacks. A globe, a compass and sextant, an old typewriter, a much newer telegraph …

Our table. Her and Isak's table, the one they'd used as cubs when Mum taught them history and reading and arithmetic and politics, and all of Vanha's different races and their Gifts.

Chiara's favorite book was always the *Encyclopedia of Vanha*, a large collection of volumes with big colored pictures and tiny print. It had been huge and heavy in her tiny hands the first time she picked it up, and opening it was like seeing the entire world at her fingertips.

Mum would read it to them like a storybook. First the Tegids, with their Gift of strength and healing; then the Nousk with their mental prowess; then the Beast-skins; then the winged Tsuru; and lastly the fire-summoning Lacar.

That was the shortest entry in the encyclopedia — a mere mention of the Lacar Gift, followed by a brief paragraph about some treaty. It was very dull, and Chiara would pester Mum for more information, but Mum would only close the book with a sigh. *The author of this book is Tegid, and Tegea has no ties to Laera.*

Not forbidden knowledge — simply little knowledge. The Lacar country was remote as it was, and apparently, that boring treaty had severed the two countries permanently. There were some complicated politics on the surface, but Chiara always half-wondered whether the real reason might be because all Tegids feared fire. With good reason — they couldn't heal from burns.

Pieces of that fear could be seen all over their cities. Wood was avoided in construction whenever possible. Even their lanterns and streetlights were fireless — Tegids used glowworms, or fireflies, or even bioluminescent algae in globes of water. Cooking was done only in specialized ovens.

The only exception to their excess of caution was fireworks, possibly because those exploded in the air — but even that was sometimes considered too risky. A nation of fire-fearing Tegids attempting to mix with a nation of fire-gifted Lacar was a recipe for chaos.

Chiara touched a finger to her scars. *The one thing we share in common.* Fear of fire. She might be the only Stunted Tegid in the entire country, but when it came to fire, all Tegids were just as vulnerable as her.

Once again … ironic. The only equalizing factor, and it was the very thing that had taken Isak.

But what was possibly most ironic of all was that Chiara was still drawn to fire. She always had been. The light, the song of the flames, the dancing sparks. Even now.

She sighed and shook away the memories … and her eyes landed on the right wall of Dad's study.

What little space had been left between the bookshelves was now filled up with news clippings and photographs. Pins and thread ran between some of the articles.

Chiara scowled. *So that's what he's been doing for the past three years? All the time he's spent in here …*

Dad hadn't always been so busy. He'd started traveling more often after Isak … staying away from home longer. And he'd return with crates of old books or journals, newspaper clippings, or photographs of people and places Chiara didn't recognize.

And he never talked about any of it. Not where he was going, or what he was doing, or why. He still spent every evening with Mum and Nani, and Chiara — dinner and reading aloud, novels or sometimes the papers. He cherished his time at dinner with them, upheld it almost fiercely. But the rest of the time he was home, he was holed up in his study.

All for a bunch of newspaper clippings. Heat prickled across Chiara's skin. She didn't like being angry. But she was angry just the same. *What's so important about all this?*

She took a few steps forward, scanning the wall with narrowed eyes. There were a few dozen articles. Dad's handwriting in red or green ink was scattered throughout the margins, interspersed with his own notes he'd tacked up.

Some of the headlines looked the same — something about city fires.

A chill ran down her spine. *What—?*

Then there was a bang and a shout downstairs, and voices drifted up to the second floor. Dad, Mum, and Nani.

Chiara darted out of the study and shut it quietly behind her, face burning guiltily. She hadn't been trespassing. Dad had never forbidden her from anything in his study. Still … *I don't want him to know I was in there.*

"Chiara?" Mum called from below the stairs. "Are you home?"

Chiara took a deep breath. "I'm here!" She went to the second-floor balcony and leaned over, putting a smile on her face. "I came early. Where were you?" She began trotting down the staircase.

"The market, darling," said Mum, meeting her halfway with a tight embrace. "We're a little behind today, I'm afraid. Your father got called to a meeting this afternoon." She sighed. "And he has to go to another one tomorrow … an hour before the acrobat show, if you can believe that."

"Oh," Chiara sighed. The unexpected meetings. That was another thing that had changed. Dad was called out unexpectedly so often that even their weekly dinners seemed precariously kept.

Mum took Chiara's hand and led her downstairs. "How was your week? Did you get to chat with Zelie?"

Chiara nodded distractedly, glancing down the hall. Dad was just disappearing into the kitchen, carrying two large bundles of groceries. She turned back to see Nani still stooping by the shrine, still clutching her massive walking stick.

A smile broke out on Chiara's face. "Hello, Nani!"

"Chiara! You're a sight for sore eyes!" Nani rose to her full height and wrapped her in a bear hug.

Chiara could've sworn she heard her ribs creak. "Missed you too, Nani …" she gasped as Nani set her down.

"You should've seen the market today!" Nani exclaimed, tossing her walking stick on the rack by the door. She didn't need it for walking. She was a Tegid; she was in perfect health. The stick was useful for other things, like whacking any pedestrians unwise enough to shove past her. She'd gotten one for Chiara, too, but Chiara always made sure to forget it when they were out.

"Oh? Was it very busy?" Chiara asked. Midsummer Festival lasted several days, and the street markets were always swollen with tourists. It was so crowded that some of the locals would travel out of the city walls to the calmer country markets.

Mum tsked. "Far too busy. It's the Midsummer Festival … I should know better; I should've gone to market out of the city. Everyone and their mother-in-law is out buying food. It was all I could do to find anything for a decent meal …"

Nani snorted. "I'd say we did just fine. Too bad all the other mothers-in-law didn't bring their walking sticks. They might have gotten better bargains." She stumped toward the kitchen. "Torva! I'm coming to help!"

Chiara waited until Nani had disappeared before asking, "How was she?"

Mum lifted her eyebrows. "Not too bad. Only a few barked shins … though I suspect she's saving up her energy for Midsummer's Eve tomorrow."

Tomorrow — the final day of the Midsummer Festival. Fhír would be performing in First Circle, at the heart of Belkar, and Chiara's family had a front-row seat on Dad's office balcony overlooking the Circle.

If any day was the best day for Nani's mischief, it was tomorrow. "I'll keep two eyes on her, then," Chiara joked, and Mum wrapped an arm around her and kissed her on the head.

Then Dad appeared in the hall, dusting off his hands. "There's my girl!" He beamed at her before turning to Mum. "Darling, could I trouble you to begin dinner? I'd like to speak to Chiara a moment."

Chiara noticed a look pass between them. They must have already discussed this ahead of time. "Of course!" Mum gave Chiara one last peck on the cheek and then trotted down the hall.

Chiara looked at Dad expectantly, and he gestured up the stairs. "My study?"

"Of course." *What now …?* She went up the stairs, her feet strangely heavy, and Dad followed behind, pushing open the door for her.

"It's a mess in here — I've got to clean it before your mother sees—" He began pushing aside stacks of books, and a few minutes later, he extracted a chair from the mess. He dragged it over and placed it across from his desk chair. "Shall we?"

Chiara nodded and took up her spot, and Dad sat across from her, the leather creaking beneath his strong hands. His bright green eyes flicked across her face, and she read disquiet in them.

"Is something wrong?" she asked softly.

"No! No," and he gave a small laugh. His fingers twisted together in his lap, and Chiara watched the tattoos writhe on the backs of his hands.

"You saw Zelie yesterday, I hope?"

"Yeah. We were visiting."

A brief smile flickered across Dad's face — brief, but genuine. "I'm glad."

Chiara fidgeted in her chair. "Thanks …"

That same worried look flashed through his eyes, but it disappeared a moment later. He folded his hands across the arms of his chair, and his tone became all business. "I won't keep you too long, my dear. As you know, Fhír is performing for the Festival tomorrow."

Chiara blinked. Whatever she'd been expecting him to talk about, it wasn't that. "Right … they're at the gymnasium."

Dad nodded and turned to his desk, shuffling through papers. "I've been in contact with their Ringmaster — organizing the event and all … and I had the chance to talk with him about the circus …"

The Ringmaster. The Dwyn from the gymnasium. Chiara watched with growing unease as Dad lifted a letter out of the unruly pile.

Then he turned to her again, and she was shocked to see distress in his face. *Is he nervous?* Or was it something else …?

Dad tapped the letter in his hand and leaned forward slightly. He seemed to be searching for words. "He mentioned that he was looking to recruit new talent."

Chiara tensed. *I know where this is going …* "Dad …"

Dad held up a pleading hand. "Please … let me explain?" The businesslike tone from earlier was gone; all that was left was tension, like he was delivering grave news.

Perhaps that was the reason Chiara said, "Okay … I'm listening."

Dad breathed softly through pursed lips. "I asked what positions he was looking to fill, and he said they want to incorporate more trapeze acts."

Her pulse beat fast in her ears, anxiety, anticipation all swirling together. "More trapeze acts?" she repeated. *Has he been talking to Zelie?* "What did you …?"

Dad's eyes softened. "I told him about you — your accomplishments, your skill level. Chiara, he wants to meet with you after the performance tomorrow."

"He what?" Chiara's head began to spin. "Dad, I can't …" *I don't want this. I can't do this … I told myself I was done … I promised I was done …*

"They're a mixed circus — not a Tegid troupe. You'd be able to perform, really perform, the way you always wanted to."

He was right, but the words were grating on her ears. *How could I? After everything …?* Chiara's hands were shaking. He wanted the best for her — she never doubted that … but this?

Dad was still talking, his voice beginning to tremble slightly. "You could have a future. You could leave Belkar — leave all this behind — do what you've always wanted to do. No more staring eyes or prying ears. You could escape this place, leave the past behind you — You could have a life — you could start new—"

Leave the past behind … Chiara's teeth clenched. She closed her eyes, trying to swallow down the frustration.

She knew Dad resented her diagnosis almost more than she did. That was the past he was talking about. But all she could think was, *Leave Isak behind you.*

"I can't." The words tumbled out of her mouth, tight and angry, cutting into Dad's words.

He fell silent, and his face became drawn. She hadn't seen him look like that since … since the diagnosis.

A pang went through her. *He's not trying to hurt me. He's trying to help me.* He believed she had a future. He wanted her to actually perform trapeze … and if she was being completely honest, she wanted that, too.

But she didn't have the same faith.

Chiara bit down on her lip, hard enough to draw blood. "I'm sorry," she said softly. "I just don't think … I could leave here. Not … now."

"Are you worried about injuries?" Dad asked, his voice subdued.

"It's not just that." Chiara's eyes flicked away. "I have a life. I love the gymnasium. I'd have to leave you and Mum …" *And Isak.* "… And Rothgar wouldn't have anyone anymore. I can't do that."

Dad pressed his lips together. "I'm sorry," he said at last. "I don't mean to push this all on you. You don't have to join them. You don't even have to meet with the Ringmaster. I just …" His shoulders tensed. He sounded as though he was delivering bad news to a friend.

And then, unexpectedly: "There's only so much time. I don't want you to miss the chance to live again."

Miss the chance …

She'd missed it three years ago. All this was just limbo, the post-mortem haze.

"I know," she whispered. "Thank you for telling me." She closed her eyes, feeling her lids burn.

When she opened them again, Dad was looking at her, brow twisted with worry.

"You don't have to do a thing," he said again. "But …" He lifted the envelope. "This is for you. Some … notes I took. The contract … other details. Can I ask you one favor?"

His eyes pleaded with her, supplicating.

"… Of course," she said softly. *He wants me to live … he wants me to do what I love.* He was sincere about that; she knew he was.

He held out the envelope to her. "Before we see the performance tomorrow … could you read this? It … explains everything."

Explains everything? Chiara took it hesitantly. The handwriting on the envelope was his. *To Chiara.* She gazed down at it for a moment, and anxiety tightened her stomach.

Why does it feel like there's more going on here?

She took a deep breath and looked up at Dad again. "I'll read it."

"Thank you." The lines on his face eased slightly. He reached out a hand and brushed the side of her face, where her scars were, his fingers unflinching.

Chiara closed her eyes.

"Thank you for listening, my dear," he said quietly. "It … means the world to me."

"Of course." Her throat went tight. *I mean the world to you … but where have you been? Why all this? Why now?*

Dad rose. "I'll … give you a minute." Just before he left the study, he turned to her, that same pleading look in his eyes. "If you'd like to talk tomorrow … after the performance … I'm here."

Chiara nodded wordlessly, and then he closed the door behind him.

She stared at the letter in her lap. It felt almost as heavy as the encyclopedia. Another world at her fingertips.

I don't want you to miss the chance to live again.

The circus contract was in her hands — safe passage to freedom. A door to a life she'd abandoned years ago.

Tears blurred her vision, and she allowed them to drip down her face, hot on her cheeks, her scar.

It's not a world I know how to live in anymore.

3

"Remind me again why we're watching Fhír from the Tower?" Chiara sighed. "Why can't we live and breathe among the people?"

"Oh, darling." Mum squeezed Chiara's hand. "We're an ambassador family. We uphold our duties — no matter how tedious they might be. And besides," she murmured, tapping Chiara's chin, "you have every right to be there."

Chiara glanced sideways at her mother. Even in the afternoon heat, Mum was perfectly composed, a habit ingrained by her ballet years. Her graceful build was a far cry from Chiara's lean limbs and wiry muscles. Anyone who had working eyes in their skull could tell that her nut-brown coloring and bronze curls didn't match her parents. It had made for some painful social interactions in the past.

But today was a better day than usual, because today, there was far too much excitement for anyone else to notice or care. Today, it was Midsummer's Eve.

Midsummer's Eve was the final day of the Midsummer Festival, and the celebrations were reaching a fever pitch. Bright strings of banners, streamers, and flower garlands swung gaily from every balcony and archway of the multi-storied houses and markets. Younger Tegid cubs scampered across the sidewalks, hawking newspapers emblazoned with "MIDSUMMER FESTIVAL" and "CIRQUE DU FHÍR."

"She's right!" Nani shouted energetically over her shoulder. She was forging ahead of them, followed closely by Dad.

"Mum, could you slow down a moment?" he pleaded. "We don't want to cause a ruckus."

"Speak for yourself!" Nani waved her formidable walking stick. She was using it a lot today. The streets and sidewalks were crowded with tourists. Clumps of families and shouting cubs filled the street from end to end. Besides the locals, there were dozens of Dwyn and Kithsa and Vikur, the most common Beast-skin visitors in Tegid cities.

Chiara even caught glimpses of all three Nousk subspecies — Telk, Ensyth, and Jeka. Their bodies shifted colors in rapid succession, reflecting their excitement. Even their clothing was elaborate: bright, bejeweled layers, a far cry from the Tegids' practical working clothes.

The distant rumble and clatter of the Belkar Central Train Station drifted through the air, signaling the arrival of even more tourists. Whooping Tegids flew past on the overhead ziplines, far above the crowded streets of non-Tegid tourists.

Chiara glanced up at them ruefully. *That'd be useful right about now.* They'd get to First Circle way faster than just taking the streets. The ziplines could take Tegids anywhere in the city.

Every Tegid except Chiara. One broken arm was all it took for Mum to declare them a pedestrian family. Hence their long trip on foot, inching along with the rest of the tourists flowing to First Circle. Cirque du Fhír wouldn't be performing for another two hours, but the streets were so crowded that it might take that long to get there.

Chiara had never seen them perform before. She'd seen some of their practices, of course, and Dad had talked about them before … and then there was last night.

Guilt pricked at her chest. She hadn't read Dad's notes yet. She couldn't even bring herself to open the envelope. She'd left it somewhere in her room at the gymnasium.

Chiara pushed the twinge away. *I'll read it after.* Right now, she didn't want to think about it.

There was a crack and a yelp ahead. Chiara's gaze darted to a young male Tegid scampering away, clutching at his elbow. Nani's latest victim.

"Mum, we've talked about this!" Dad winced. Nani merely made a rude gesture — at him or at the injured Tegid; it was unclear — and kept walking.

Dad's shoulders slumped. He fell back to Mum's side, defeated. "She's going to get herself labeled a public menace."

"I'll talk to her, dear. At the Tower." Mum squeezed Dad's hand affectionately. "Have some sympathy for her. She doesn't have much to do after retirement."

"That's exactly what worries me!" Dad winced again as Nani twirled her stick at a male Dwyn. The massive bear-skin turned with a scowl, but she stared him down, undeterred, until he huffed and went on his way.

"Maybe I should walk with her," Chiara offered. "See if I can distract her."

"Oh, thank you, darling," and Mum gave her a grateful look.

A clock tower chimed somewhere, and Dad came to a halt. He squinted up at the sky, and his expression grew distant. "I've got to go … the meeting's in twenty minutes."

Mum tsked. "I'm sorry to see you go, darling. A shame they need you today. It's a holiday!" She had a reproving look on her face. She could be as fiery as Nani when she was cross.

Dad gave her an apologetic look. "I'm sorry, my dear. It couldn't be helped." He glanced up. "I'll have to take the ziplines. I'll meet you at the Tower later."

He kissed Mum and placed a gentle hand on Chiara's back. "Save me a banner, eh?"

"Sure," Chiara murmured, and then she trotted up to Nani.

"Ah, good! You're here. Where's your stick?" Nani fixed her with a sharp, hawklike eye.

"No stick, Nani," Chiara explained, trying to hide her laugh. "I … must have left it at home."

"Fesht!" Nani cursed loudly, ignoring the shocked glances of passersby. "I gave you that stick for a reason! It's no good lying around at home! Where's your friend?" she asked abruptly.

"Who?" Chiara glanced at her, bewildered.

"Cat-skin? Spunky?" Nani laughed. "I like her."

"Oh, you mean Zelie!"

"Aye. What's she up to? Ain't she supposed to give us some grand tour?"

"Uh, I don't think she's *supposed* to …" Chiara scanned the street signs. They were two blocks away from First Circle. Technically, no one was allowed inside the courtyard — it had been blockaded for a week while Fhír set up and rehearsed inside. Zelie, of course, didn't give a hoot about that, and insisted that Chiara come watch a dress rehearsal.

"Chiara!" A piercing shout cut through the noise. Zelie's voice. Chiara and Nani both stumbled to a halt.

"There!" Nani's hand shot out. Her eyesight was still keen at fifty-five. On the far side of the street, a tiny, scarlet figure was leaping up and down, waving vigorously. Chiara and Nani waded through the flow of traffic, dodging clusters of loudly dressed pedestrians.

"You're here!" Zelie was practically hopping with excitement. "How d'you like my hair? Isn't it marvelous?" Her silky, dark hair was wound up in an elaborate knot of braids and ribbons.

Zelie couldn't do her own hair to save her life. She'd come by the gym earlier to get Chiara to put it up for her. "It looks great," said Chiara. "Did you tip the hairdresser?"

"No, but I'll do you one better! Follow me!" Zelie turned tail and shot down the sidewalk. Nani crowed excitedly and jogged after. The street here was very crowded, but one look at Nani's snapping eyes and large stick sent most people hurrying out of her way.

Finally, they made it to First Circle. It was a huge courtyard, five blocks in diameter, ringed in by towering lampposts, walled archways, and the twelve Low Council Towers. Echoes filled the air — merchant booths, set up around the outside of the wall, traders setting up their wares for the influx of sightseers. But First Circle itself was nearly empty, save for Fhír and a few sturdy-looking Belkar officers.

Zelie was already vaulting over a temporary barricade in one of the archways. "Come on!" she cried, waving to them from the other side.

Nani whooped and ran forward.

"Nani, wait—"

But Nani had already thrown her stick over the rail. "Wait?" she scoffed. "Torva lives in that building there half the time, don't he? We've got more right to be in there than Fhír!"

"Well, yes, but—"

Too late. Nani leapt down beside Zelie, and the two of them trotted off. Chiara sighed. She clambered onto the other side and squinted toward the other end of the Circle.

An elaborate metallic structure was now standing at the base of East Tower, looking like a skeleton of needles. Hanging on the tower wall behind the whole thing was an enormous red banner emblazoned with a golden "F."

"Hurry up, Chiara!" Zelie's voice was small in the wide-open space.

Chiara jogged to catch up to them.

"Do you like the banner? I hung it myself!" Zelie exclaimed.

"Nice job." Chiara brushed Zelie's shoulder. "Listen, we should probably get back to Mum. We left her a few blocks behind."

Nani waved a scornful hand. "Why wait? She's coming here anyway!"

"Not *here*, Nani," Chiara corrected. "We're supposed to be in South Tower."

"You're watching from one of the Towers?" Zelie clapped excitedly. "You'll see everything from there!"

"From where? The snotty seats?" Nani said mockingly. "No thanks! Give me a nice crowd any day of the week!"

A nice crowd of victims. Chiara sighed.

"Or, you could see everything *now*," Zelie added, a sparkle in her eye. "We're running another dress rehearsal in a few minutes."

"Don't tempt me with a good time." Chiara smiled. "Honestly, though, I don't want you to get in any trouble for letting us in here."

A shout drifted across the Circle, and Zelie's ears pricked. "Speaking of trouble … they're calling me. Find me after the show, okay? I'll see you later!" She waved and dashed off.

Nani sniffed. "I like her." She turned on Chiara. "Why don't I see you two visiting more often?"

"Because …" Chiara gestured helplessly. "She joined a traveling circus. It's not exactly like she lives in the gym anymore."

"She's got a good heart." Nani tapped her stick on the ground pensively. "You need her in your life."

Sure. Only she left three years ago. Chiara sighed, ruffling her hair. Her curls were woefully frizzy from the heat and humidity. "Okay, Nani."

Nani rapped her knuckles sharply.

"Ow!" Chiara tugged her hands behind her back, annoyed. "What was that for?"

Nani gave her a hard look. "Don't 'Okay, Nani' me. I mean it. That cub stuck by you through thick and thin when you were young'uns. What happened to that?"

What happened? Isak died. Dad started traveling more, gone for weeks on end. Zelie joined the circus.

And you never really talked about that, did you?

"It's not my fault," Chiara murmured. The excuse sounded thin even to her ears. She tried to justify it. "Sometimes, people just … drift apart."

"Horse dung!" Nani struck Chiara's knuckles again, faster than Chiara could pull away.

"Ow! Would you *stop* that?"

"I'll stop when you stop throwing pity parties for yourself." Nani folded her arms sternly. "If you don't talk to people, they won't talk to you. Simple as that."

She was right. Chiara knew that.

But talking about Isak, or joining the circus … where to even begin?

Hi, Zelie. You remember how we went to Crescor with Isak and came back without him?

Hey, Zelie. You remember how I wanted to be a flier my whole life, until my only catcher was gone?

Hi, Zelie. You know how I visit the not-grave every day because I don't want to leave him behind?

Heat pooled in Chiara's stomach, and she turned away. "Come on, Nani. We should go."

℘

The last rays of sun were just sinking below the rooftops. Chiara stood at the corner of Dad's balcony, looking out over the Circle as Mum chatted with Nani.

She only turned half an ear in their direction. The courtyard itself was packed from end to end with throngs of locals and countless other visitors, waving banners, decked out in festive clothes. It was like the people themselves were steeping in the spirit of Midsummer.

It was beautiful … but it didn't draw Chiara's eye quite as much as the circus stage did. Her heart skipped a beat as she gazed down at it. Three arena rings, crowned by a structure of trapeze bars. The whole setup was decked out lavishly in pennants, ribbons, banners, all reds and golds.

Dark figures scurried around the setup — a Belkar stage crew making final preparations. None of the acrobats were to be seen. Doubtless they were waiting patiently in the Tower behind the stage.

Chiara was not so patient. She drummed her fingers on the balcony rail, breathing in deeply, sensing the electricity in the air. The gleaming structure in the twilight sent fire through her veins.

She didn't even have to close her eyes to imagine the swings, the dives, the momentum. The feel of the bars, the feel of empty space. Her heart thudded painfully in her chest.

I miss it … I miss it. She still wanted it. Even after all this time. It was the closest to Isak she'd ever be again …

"Here! So sorry I'm late." Dad's voice interrupted her thoughts.

"Oh, hello, darling," Mum called happily. Dad gave her a kiss and then came to stand beside Chiara.

"Are you excited?" He was smiling — his real smile, not the tired smile he had so often after long trips away.

"Yes." Chiara smiled at him. "Yes, I am …"

"You're going to love them," he promised. "It's like nothing I've ever seen before." He shifted. "Were you able to read …?"

Chiara's face went warm. "I—"

She was saved by an annoyed cry from Nani. "I still don't like this! Why'd we have to sit here among the hoity-toity of the world? I want to be with the *people!*" She gestured dramatically over the railing.

"Mum, you'd hate it down there," Dad sighed. "Everyone would be pushing and shoving."

Nani waved him away. "That's what the stick is for, Torva!"

"Mum, we've talked about this. Physical assault on the public is against the law."

"Physical harm to a senior citizen is against the law!" Nani shook her stick defiantly. "If they're gonna push and shove the elderly, I'll push and shove right back!"

Dad crossed his arms, ready for battle, but Mum interrupted them. "Darlings, please. Now is hardly the time to debate the nuances of public law and custom."

Dad planted a kiss on her lips. "Right as always, love."

Shouts and laughter from the neighboring balcony drowned out Nani's protests. A group of Tegids were crowding there. Young twenties, nice clothes — children of the Low Council families, newly-minted graduates taking liberties with their parents' positions.

The back of Chiara's neck prickled. Someone was staring. She didn't even have to look to know that. It wasn't just the Academy rumors … anybody with working eyes in their skull could tell she didn't look a thing like her parents.

Even if Dad wasn't in the Low Council, she would never be just another face in the crowd.

Her jaw set. *Stare at me? I'll stare right back.* She turned her head deliberately and made eye contact with the staring one — a male Tegid. She watched him, unblinking, and he looked away quickly.

That's what I thought. Chin high, Chiara turned back to the stage. She hated the stares, but she wasn't going to let *them* know that.

Suddenly, the stage lamps flared up. Thousands of voices faded into breathless silence.

"Quiet! It's starting!" Nani hissed, shaking her cane threateningly at the noisy balcony of graduates. They quailed under her gaze.

Chiara pressed close to the railing, both elbows on the heavy wood. One moment stretched by, then another — then finally, a thunder of drums and a blast of horns. A solitary light blazed out above the crowd, illuminating the very highest bar.

A murmur of shock rose as the crowd watched the tiny figure on the bar, dangling effortlessly upside down, dark tail whirling. Even from that distance, Chiara recognized Zelie.

Zelie flung her arms out, and a pair of shimmering red aerial silks rippled down on either side of her, billowing slightly in the evening breeze. Silks in hand, she swung her whole body up and over the bar and plunged down to earth. A large, thick cloth unfurled behind her as she fell — a red field, embossed with large gold letters: *FHÍR.*

Inches before striking the earth, she tugged the silks together and made a nimble twist, landing neatly on both feet. She stood ramrod straight, scarlet skirt floating around her, gold-clad arms outflung as cheers of the crowd echoed deafeningly between the buildings. She looked exotic, almost unreal.

"Good thing her feet are as fast as her tongue!" Nani clapped approvingly as Zelie vaulted from one end of the arena to the other, bowing to the crowd on every side. Whether on four legs or two, she still had all the effortless elegance of a cat.

"VELCOME!" boomed a loud voice above the applause. A large Dwyn stood in the arena — the Ringmaster. He too was dressed in red and gold. The noise quieted as he continued in a thick accent. "Many thanks to the grand city of Belkar for embracing us vith open arms!" His voice was deep and resonant, ideal for his role as master of ceremonies.

Cheers rose from the crowd as he continued. "Ve had heard legends of your Midsummer Festival, but never vitnessed the beauty that flourishes inside your valls … until now." Louder cheers; flowers, banners, and handfuls of colorful rice and glitter were thrown encouragingly toward the arena.

"And now"—he made a sweeping bow—"allow us to introduce ourselves! Ve are *FHÍR*! Most talented traveling circus in Tegea! Hailing from all corners of the earth and every species! Superior in skill — elegance — strength—"

Screams and shouts practically drowned him out as a new acrobat appeared with every word he listed. A scarlet Jeka, a Vikur, an Ensyth with curlicue horns, Tegids, another Dwyn … all dressed in red and gold.

Chiara squinted down at the stage again, trying to pick out their faces. She frowned. *That's … strange.* Something about their faces under the stage lights …

Not the stage lights. *Paint.* Their faces were painted. Bold masks of whites, golds, reds, hiding their expressions.

A sick feeling rose in Chiara's stomach. *Painted faces — faces in the flames* … the nightmares rushed back over her, all those horrible dreams, Isak dying as grotesque masks floated overhead.

She squeezed her eyes shut and turned away. *Snap out of it.* Just nightmares. Not real. There hadn't been any faces that night in Crescor. Only Isak's.

The Ringmaster was reaching the end of his extensive list. Ten more performers were standing on either side of him in the center of the ring.

"Ve are honored to perform here on the final night of your Festival!" he proclaimed. "And now …" His voice grew dramatically quieter. Sensing his intensity, the audience hushed, hanging onto his words.

"Vithout further ado … FHÍR!"

4

Tegid troupes paled in comparison. Cirque du Fhír was like nothing Chiara had ever seen. Every act was structured around the Gift of each species. The aerial silks showcased Zelie's small size and cat-like balance as she tumbled from multi-story heights into perfect landings. The Vikur was a ribbon dancer, cavorting around as her thin gold ribbons wrote patterns through the air. One of the Dwyn was the circus strongman, lifting up his fellow performers and hoisting them easily in the air.

There was even a fire-breathing Ensyth, earning a chorus of nervous gasps from the Tegids in the crowd. But he was clever and careful, playing with his flames until they flashed and burst in a cloud of fireflies, dispersing above the heads of the astonished onlookers.

But by far one of the greatest highlights of the show was a Tegid-Telk duo. The Tegid vaulted from the high bars, flinging himself out above the crowd. On the ground far below, the Telk lifted both hands in elaborate gestures, suspending the Tegid's body in flawless somersaults and flips, eliciting astonished shouts and cheers from the viewers below.

Chiara's hands locked around the railing as her heart stampeded in her chest. She could practically taste the energy pulsing across the stage. Act after act — leaps, jumps, tumbles; music that struck at her, hawklike, relentless.

She'd lost count of the acts when the Ringmaster once again took center stage. "A great thank you to you, dear Belkar, for being such a marvelous crowd! Ve are nearing the end of our show, and the grand firevork finale!"

Suddenly Dad stiffened next to her. "I've got to step out for a minute. I'll be right back." He stood, his jaw tight.

"Now?" Mum asked softly.

Dad leaned down and kissed her. "East Tower. I'll only be a minute. I promise."

They exchanged a long look, and Mum kissed him again. Then he turned and strode off the balcony. Chiara's eyes followed him until the balcony doors shut behind him.

Where are you going now?

She turned back to the railing, heart sinking. *Why did you want me here, anyway? If you're just going to leave …*

"Another round of applause … for our FIREVORKS SHOW!" the Ringmaster cried. He lifted the female Vikur with ease in one massive paw. Zelie scampered up his side and perched neatly on the Vikur's shoulder. She whipped out a sparkler and it flared to life in a blaze of scarlet.

The final show of Midsummer was always a fireworks display. In an instant, the sky was filled with spiraling colored flame, sparks blooming like flowers in the silky darkness above. Green, red, blue, purple, so bright that the crowd below was illuminated in a strange quasi-daylight.

Fireworks. She used to love them so much. Listening to the fire, the soft song whispering in the embers, the song she'd heard as long as she could remember. She'd never been happier than when she was sitting in front of a fire.

And Isak had loved it, too.

And it ruined us both.

The hot coal in Chiara's stomach flared. The palms of her hands were growing warm. Never, never had she thought she would wish she hated fireworks, or fire.

But I do. I do. I want to hate it. The sour, choking smoke; the sting of sparks on her face …

The scar on her neck burned.

Deafening cheers brought her back. One of the Telk performers flung out his arms dramatically. Small black shapes whizzed toward him from every balcony: sparklers, firecrackers, descending like a flock of birds into the center of the arena, shaping themselves into a pyre-like structure.

One of the unlit fireworks hovered by Zelie. With a flourish, she lit the fuse. It shot into the sky, bursting above First Circle in a blaze of gold and red. Screams and applause shook the windows of the buildings.

"It's gorgeous!" Mum applauded loudly, a beaming smile on her face.

Chiara opened her mouth to agree when a flood of tingles burned through her body. She winced, white-knuckling the railing. Tiny pinpricks of heat jabbed beneath her skin as though her hands had fallen asleep.

What in Arva? She shook her hands vigorously to get rid of the tingling. But that only made it worse. Irritated, she lifted a hand to her mouth and nipped at the skin—

—and then a high-pitched wail grated across the air, a knife-blade that turned her blood cold.

Chiara craned her head around wildly, trying to find the source of the scream.

"What's wrong, darling?" Mum was at her side in a moment.

"Someone's screaming!" Heart thundering, Chiara scanned the crowd, but there were too many people to pick out a distinct voice.

Mum was shaking her head. "What screaming?"

Another bloodcurdling cry sliced through the air. Chiara winced, covering her ears. "That scream! You don't hear it?"

"Everyone's screaming! I can't hear a thing!" Nani was next to them now, peering over the balcony.

Mum's eyes flashed with alarm. "What does it sound like?"

"Like someone's …" The word *dying* faded on Chiara's lips.

I know that sound. Dread crawled up her body. That was the sound she'd heard the night Isak died. "No … no …" *This isn't real …*

Then a dull orange flare exploded below — far too low to be a firework. Chiara whipped her head over the railing, and that was when she saw the fire.

Angry flames burst from the third-story windows of East Tower, just behind the circus stage. The horrible screech reached its fever pitch, and the windows erupted in showers of molten glass. Fire burst outward, crawling up the side of the tower like some shapeless spirit of hunger. The stage tapestries and garlands fluttered weakly in the heat, smoldering above the flames.

Different screams rose, screams of alarm and terror as the Festival dissolved into a nightmare. People began shoving away from the arena, trying to escape … but everyone was so close that the scrambling masses of people became locked into one swaying body of terror.

First Circle wasn't a gathering place — it was a prison. Bodies pressed together as people rushed to escape. Even the Belkar officers couldn't keep order.

Fire began licking against the trapeze structure, feeding on the tapestries, sending up clouds of smoke.

"Off the balcony, now!" Mum snatched Chiara and Nina by the arms and practically dragged them toward the door.

"Dad!" Chiara screamed in Mum's ear. "Dad's in there!" She tore out of Mum's grasp and sprinted down the staircase. Flight after flight, until her throat was burning and she was gasping for breath.

"Chiara!" Mum and Nani were right on her heels. Then Chiara landed on the ground floor. She charged through the halls, heading for the entrance.

"Chiara, wait!" Mum shouted, as Chiara reached the front doors. Just then, a horrible rumbling noise echoed above the screams outside, louder by the second.

Chiara's heart stopped.

"No. *No!*" The scream ripped from her throat. She flung open the doors. She knew that sound. That was the last thing she heard before—

"Chiara!" Nani grabbed for her arm, but Chiara was faster. In a heartbeat, she'd flung herself down the front steps into the mass of panicked people streaming by.

She was right in the thick of the press, beating against the living flood, clawing her way under arms, jabbing both elbows madly into anything blocking her path.

Desperation burned in her lungs. One building after another — inch by agonizing inch, around the outside of the Circle.

Dad. Dad was in East Tower. It was going to collapse. She knew it, she knew it … Crescor all over again … *I have to find him — I have to find him — I have to find him—*

Flames were springing up in every street she passed. The fire was spreading. A burning flag floated down onto the pavement. She skidded to a halt and shied away as the letters *F-H-Í-R*, half-destroyed, rippled past her vision.

Her heart skipped a beat.

Fhír. The painted faces. The fire in the building. Something horrible was climbing up her throat.

But there was no time. "Dad!" she screamed again, coughing. The smoke was making her hoarse. The heat was becoming worse — she was getting closer.

Terror lent flight to her feet. "DAD!" *Just one more corner — one more street* — her lungs were burning — there—

She didn't even feel the heat. Smoke blanketed her vision; she hacked and spat, eyes stinging as she stared up at the crumbling building. Creaks and snaps burrowed into her brain, deafening.

"*DAD!*" Suddenly she was seventeen years old, careening through the backstage halls, flinging herself toward the door—

She was twenty feet from the entrance when the fire exploded outward, flinging her backward across the rough stones. Smoke — darkness — her head struck something hard—

☙

It was pain that brought her back. Fresh wounds, stinging across her body. Disoriented, Chiara staggered upright. A dull roar was echoing through the abandoned street.

She lifted her head, and an uncontrollable shudder racked her body. "No … no, no …"

Where the Tower had once stood was a massive inferno, leaping skyward out of the charred mountain of rubble that now filled the courtyard.

Then a deafening *CRACK* split the air — the roof. It tumbled inward slowly, agonizingly, sending up plumes of fire and debris as it collapsed. Thick, acrid smoke filled the street.

"DAD!" The cry ripped from her mouth as she plunged straight into the wreckage. Waves of blistering heat rolled over her; the air was almost unbreathable.

Find him … find him … at least something to bury … She kicked aside the rubble senselessly, heedless of smoking metal and shattered glass. She was hacking, spitting, trying to get the smoke out of her throat and nostrils. *Hurry — hurry …*

Never fast enough … never fast enough …

Please … just his body … just a body to bury. Another voice ripped through her head, turning her blood cold. Time slowed, through molasses; some sick, twisted dream.

Only it wasn't a dream. It was just as horribly real as the first time.

A bestial cry of rage escaped her, piercing the air. Tearing through the last few piles, she lunged toward the ruined building — only to be yanked backward off her feet.

"Are you insane?" screamed an unfamiliar male voice, right in her ear. A vicelike grip encircled her from behind, pinning her arms to her side.

"NO!" Chiara threw her full weight against her captor, clawing viciously at his arms. It worked — he staggered and she tore away; a black figure rose in front of her; a shove sent her sprawling back. She hadn't even seen him move; only an acrobat could be so quick—

Fhír. Black hatred roiled up. Chiara struck out with a cruel kick; her foot connected with solidly with his chest. She could hear the *whoosh* of air as his breath left his lungs. He gave a ragged gasp; she darted around him—

Then another black figure appeared, clamping a hand on her arm, jerking her off-balance. The same iron grasp locked around her arms — he had her again. The second figure was lurking just in front of her.

They killed him. Chiara screamed, clawing even more fiercely at her captor as he dragged her backward once again. Mad with rage, she bit down on his arm. He gave a cry of pain.

"Chiara! Chiara, wait! It's me!" Zelie's voice was barely audible over the roar of the fire.

"Zelie …" Chiara recoiled, dazed. *Zelie? Zelie's … one of them? How—?*

The smoke was growing worse. Black shapes were dancing in her eyes. *How many? How many of them?*

Voices swirled through the smog.

"Sedate her!" yelled the male, somewhere behind her.

"No!" Zelie's voice.

"We have to go *now!*"

Zelie's reply was inaudible. The smoke was nauseating. Chiara's head spun, a maelstrom of thoughts and memories and images, all jumbled together.

I'm being kidnapped. They're taking me … they're taking me away from him— She lashed out again — far too weakly; her foot was batted away easily.

The next moment, a rough hand clamped something over her mouth. A cloying scent filled her nostrils, and she instinctively held her breath.

Too late. Her head became unbearably heavy, and her joints turned to rubber. She sank to the pavement, staring up as two vaguely two-legged shapes loomed over her, spinning away into blackness.

5

Pounding, pounding, relentless in her skull; bitter dryness in her mouth. Every limb felt like lead. She was thirsty … so, so thirsty. A bird chirruped. She could feel warmth on her face — sunlight. Early morning.

Chiara opened her eyes to an unfamiliar ceiling. Canvas, draped overhead, shifting gently. The roof of a tent. Her hands were gripping the frame of a narrow cot beneath her.

This isn't home. Heart skipping a beat, she tried to sit up — but she couldn't. Something was strapped across her chest, looped under her armpits, pinning her down. *No, no, no …*

Sedate her. Someone had brought her here; tied her here.

Fhír. The fire. *Dad.*

Chiara jerked and twitched as the memories crashed over her. Fire coursed through her body, but she couldn't move at all.

Her heart was thrumming in her chest. *Dad … I didn't say goodbye … I didn't even read the letter …* What if that was it? What if that was the last time she'd ever—?

Panic rose in her throat; she swallowed it back. *That's not going to help.* She forced herself to breathe as deeply as her bonds would allow. Sharp tugs of her arms, legs, and feet confirmed the worst. Every limb was bound; there was even something tied across her midriff.

Breathe. Just breathe. Examine the surroundings. Chiara did her best to look around. She was at the back of what appeared to be an empty tent. Folded cots and heavy chests were tucked neatly against the sides. An unlit lantern stood in the center of the floor.

She didn't really have any idea where she was, or how far from home. She could've been unconscious for any number of hours. Judging from the sounds outside, she was in the middle of the woods. No sound of a crowded city nearby. Nowhere near Belkar.

Or Dad. If he was even alive — *please, please, Arva, let him be alive. Please, I can't lose him, too. Not like that …*

Breathe. Breathe.

I have to get out of here first. That was the only way to get back. But if she couldn't undo the knots …

She tested each limb again, this time more carefully, waiting for some sign of give. No such luck. The bonds were loose enough to allow circulation, but only just.

She craned her neck to the side and caught a glimpse of the tie around her wrist. It was red, a little shimmery. *Aerial silks.* Just like the ones Zelie used.

branded

Ice gripped the pit of Chiara's stomach. Her body was burning, but that didn't matter now. *They kidnapped me? Why did they kidnap me? Where am I now?*

Pieces shifting, shifting inside her brain. All those fires, suddenly flaring up all down the street. How did one fire spread so quickly? How did a fire start in the East Tower? Nobody should've been there except the circus. Like that night in Crescor …

Some kind of accident, said all the investigations. *Unusual circumstances* …

The same kind of fire, the screaming flames, like nothing else she'd ever heard.

Suddenly the red flag, the gold "F," was blazing in her brain. She'd seen that "F" before … on a poster, hung up in Crescor during Nationals.

Fhír had been there, too. Performing in the same city—

Her breath was fast and shallow in her throat. The East Tower. The Crescor East Gymnasium. *Fhír.*

It wasn't an accident … it wasn't an accident. They even had a fire-breathing performer.

The fires … Chiara was racking her brain. Dad's office walls. All those old newspaper clippings, tacked to the wall … She squeezed her eyes shut, trying to remember the headlines.

"Strange Inferno." Always the word "Inferno." Grede … six years ago. Talin … five years ago. Crescor, three years ago.

And now Belkar.

"No … no, there's no way," Chiara muttered aloud to the empty tent. "I mean … *Zelie?*"

An almost-hysterical laugh burst out of her. It was absurd. Zelie could be impulsive — even practically feral, sometimes. But never in a million years could she possibly be the kind of person to set fire to buildings.

Especially not Crescor.

And Belkar? *Dad?*

No. There's no way. Not at the price of his own son.

"Okay, so not Zelie." Chiara began muttering to herself. "Maybe someone else in Fhír, working on their own?" How hard could it be for one performer to sneak off and set a fire while the rest were on stage?

And … only a dozen performers were on that stage. But almost thirty of them were staying at Rothgar's gym. *What were the rest of them doing?*

Any one of those people could've done it — maybe more than one, judging by how fast the fires appeared in the other streets.

But … *Zelie.* Chiara's head was throbbing. She kept circling back to that. She couldn't get past it. How could Zelie willingly join a group of arsonists? Or if she didn't know about it before she joined, then how could she possibly not have found out about it afterwards?

But what's the motive? Chiara squeezed her eyes shut, trying to calm her headache. Why *would Fhír set fire to Tegid cities?* And why would they choose to appear publicly as a circus? Did arson really need a cover-up? Why not just do it all in secret, never reveal their identities?

None of it made sense.

One thing was certain. Fhír *had* kidnapped her. Who else would use aerial silks?

Chiara continued wiggling around, trying to strain the silks. *Fesht.*

Her kidnapper must have been very clever. Aerial silks were incredibly durable, and the knots were meant to sustain a body in midair. There was no way they'd come undone, especially not while she was lying flat on her back. Even gravity couldn't help her.

Maybe I can wiggle around enough to flip the cot on its side—

A twig snapped outside. Then another.

Chiara froze. Footsteps — footsteps approaching the tent. She shut her eyes and held her breath, willing her heartbeat to slow.

Canvas rustled. Someone was in the tent with her. *Please, Arva, let it look like I'm still unconscious …*

Fingers pressed against her wrist.

Oh, Arva, it's touching *me …* A new fear flooded the pit of her stomach, a cold, grasping fear.

Then the hands were tugging at her wrists. Untying the knots. First one wrist … then the other … then down to her ankles …

Adrenaline was surging through her limbs, making her dizzy. *He hasn't seen me awake.* She might have a chance. If she could get out — if she could get back to Belkar, back to Dad — *As soon as I'm free, I'll—*

There! The last rope fell. Someone was hovering over her; she could feel it. She got a whiff of some herb … rosemary.

Now! She shot upright — and immediately cracked her forehead against something hard.

Stars exploded in her skull; she gave a cry of agony, shrinking away. There was a twin shout of pain — or was that just the ringing in her ears? Through squinted eyes, she thought she saw a dark shape — maybe two; everything was blurry — stagger away from the cot.

They weren't attacking her, at least. She slumped backward. *That was an enormous mistake.* Fire was coursing through her muscles, heating the inside of her skull. She gripped the frames of the narrow cot, fighting the urge to vomit.

"*Fesht!*" A masculine voice, tight with anger and pain.

Chiara knew that voice. It was the male kidnapper. *Pain be damned.* She struggled upright and tumbled off the cot, thrusting it away, a barricade between her and him.

He was only one person, still doubled over at the front of the tent. She snatched at the nearest thing to a weapon — the heavy lantern —

and kept her eyes pinned on him as she backed up against the canvas wall behind her. Her head was spinning so fast that she could barely stand upright.

Finally, the figure rose to his full height, and she got a real look at him. A Tegid in rough traveling clothes, sleeves of tattoos lacing across the muscles of his bare arms. He looked at least a head taller than her — not quite a fully grown Tegid, but close. Probably around her age.

Then he turned on her, both hands clamped across his mouth. "You—!"

Chiara swung the lantern, more out of instinct than any effective strategy. "Get the hell away from me!" she snarled.

It seemed to work. The Tegid stopped in his tracks, still clutching his face. Something red was dripping down his fingers.

Blood? Chiara frowned. Then it clicked. The thing her forehead had smashed was his face. She'd given him a bloody nose. It was so absurd that she almost laughed.

His dark eyes were flashing. "Whad in *Arva* d'you thing you're doig? You broge my node!" He probably meant to sound furious, but the voice coming from his pinched nose was so ridiculous that Chiara wasn't fazed.

"And I'll do it again if I have to!" she shot back, gripping the lantern handle. "Who are you? Where am I? Why did you take me?"

"Oh, for Arba's sage! You're with *Fhír*! Torba told you we were cobing, righd?"

Torba … Torva. Dad.

Blood roared in Chiara's ears, and she rose to her full height. "What?" Her lip curled in rage. "You mean the Tegid you killed in East Tower?"

"Whad the hell? No!" He glared at her. "Why would we gill your fader? Didn'd he tell you anythig? He's one ob us! And he's *fide*! He wasn'd eben in the buildig." He frowned. "You *are* Chiara, righd?"

He examined her carefully, eyes lingering on the left side of her face.

Chiara angled her head away. The makeup was definitely gone. No hiding the scars now.

Her whole body was trembling. She let out a slow, shaky breath.

Assess the situation. She'd been kidnapped ... but her captor hadn't killed her. And apparently Dad knew him.

And Dad was ... alive.

Is that even true? Or was it just another trick, a sedative to keep her calm?

She tightened her grip on the lantern handle. "How do I know I can trust you?" she asked tightly, fixing her eyes on his face. "I don't even know you!"

A pair of intelligent hazel eyes stared back at her, framed by long lashes. "I promise you can. I'm Cor ... Coren Ascolta. ... Your dad really didn't tell you about this?" His voice was returning to normal. His nose must've healed.

"About what?" Chiara asked cautiously. Maybe Dad knew these people, and maybe he didn't ...

Cor lifted his hands gingerly, revealing a striking set of cheekbones and a firm mouth. "He didn't talk to you," he said, realization dawning on his face.

"No! That's what I've been saying! He barely told me *anything*," Chiara cried in frustration. "All I know is that your Ringmaster was interested in recruiting me — and that *you* kidnapped me! Who the hell are you people? How do you know my father?"

Cor winced and wiped the blood from his face, leaving a small smudge on his cheek. He examined the blood on his fingers and shot her a wry glance. "Nice hit."

"Answer the question." Her voice was dangerously quiet. "How do you know my father?'"

He lifted his hands slowly, palms out. "Please … just hear me out. You are Chiara Alteva, no?"

She gave a sharp nod.

"So your father *is* Torva Alteva?"

"Yes, and? Did he tell you to kidnap me?"

Cor scowled. "Of course not! He told me to save you!"

"*You* were supposed to save *me*?" Chiara jabbed a finger at his chest, then hers.

"Oh, for the love of — *yes*! That's my *job*!" Cor ran his hands through his unruly brown hair, and it fluffed up in haphazard waves. "Your dad told me to run after you!"

"Your … job?" Chiara's shoulders tensed. So … Dad knew about the fire?

Did he know about Crescor? Her heart thudded painfully in her chest.

"*Yes*," Cor huffed. "He'd just finished clearing the Tower when you ran straight into that fire. He was *furious*—"

Chiara cut him off. "He could've died. You expect me to stand there and watch? I'm not letting that happen—" She bit her tongue. She'd almost said "again."

A shadow crossed Cor's face. "No. No, I don't expect you to do nothing." He pursed his lips. "Look, he's fine. He's safe. I swear it on my life. He actually suspected the fire would happen. That's the whole reason he called us to Belkar. And he was supposed to tell you about us *before* all this went down, but …" He sighed. "I guess he didn't get that far."

"Yeah, no kidding," Chiara shot back. "And what do you mean, *us*? Who's *us*?" Suspicion sharpened all her senses.

"Us …" Cor gestured around the tent. "Fhír. We're not actually a circus. Well — technically, we are, but—"

"—But what? You spend your free time running into burning buildings?" Chiara narrowed her eyes at him. "Again. How do I know you didn't set the fires yourself?"

For the first time, real anger crossed Cor's face. "You think we *started* the fire? Are you *insane*? Your *father* helped us get people out of the Tower before it collapsed! Of course we didn't start the fires! We don't set them, we *stop* them!"

"Oh, really? How's Belkar doing?" Chiara snapped.

Cor's eyes darkened, and she felt a twinge of guilt.

"Nobody's dead," he said at last. "Including you."

He had a point. Still …

Chiara folded her arms. "You sedated me."

Cor threw his hands in the air. "Yes! I sedated you. You were running into a burning courtyard, and when I tried to pull you out, you practically broke my nose." He winced, touching a hand to his face. "I guess that's a habit with you."

Chiara glared at him. "I didn't need to be sedated!"

"Look, it wasn't my idea, okay? I hated doing that. But Torva would have killed me with his bare hands if I hadn't gotten you out of there somehow. So can you please put the lantern down and trust me?" He lifted his eyebrows, pleading with her.

Chiara opened her mouth, but she didn't know what to say.

She was alive. And if Cor was really telling the truth, Dad was alive, too.

He wouldn't have saved my life if he was the one who set the fire. If he wanted her dead, he could've killed her without even untying her from the cot.

Chiara let out a terse sigh. "Okay. I believe you."

The tension visibly left his shoulders. "Thank you."

She lifted a warning finger. "Don't get comfy. I still have questions. Who are you, what is Fhír, how is my father part of it, and how did he know the fire was going to happen?"

Cor nodded. "Understandable. Okay … let me start again. I'm Coren. I already said that, I know. You can just call me Cor. Can we sit down? This is going to take a few minutes to explain."

Chiara hesitated for a long moment. Voices battled in her head: *Trust him, don't trust him, trust him …*

"Why did you tie me up?" she asked softly.

Cor sat down cross-legged, keeping a safe distance between himself and her lantern. The anger had left his eyes. His fingers were in constant motion — tracing patterns along the ground, tapping his thighs, drumming on his knees.

He spoke quickly, like he was running through a list of facts. "You were unconscious when I carried you out. But when we got to base, you had some kind of fit. I don't know what caused it. And I think you had some kind of fever."

Chiara pressed a hand to her forehead. Unusually warm … even for her. "A fever …?"

"Yeah. Your skin was hot." He frowned. "Almost … too hot to touch. Zelie was worried you might injure yourself. She and I still had to go back to Belkar and keep putting out fires, but we didn't want to leave you like that. So Zelie tied you down."

A pained expression crossed his face. "Probably not our brightest moment. Anyway, when we told Talia — that's our chief medic — she was absolutely furious. But she still had to stay in Belkar to treat injuries, so she sent me back to untie you."

Chiara watched carefully for dodging eyes, a change in tone — anything that might betray a lie.

Nothing.

"Okay," she said, and sat down slowly across from Cor, still holding the lantern. "I believe you."

Cor looked relieved. "Great."

"Tell me about Fhír."

A flicker of pride crossed his face. "Fhír is a traveling circus. We perform all around Tegea—"

"—And save people from fires?" Chiara lifted an eyebrow.

"Well … yes. Partly. We're not just a circus. We're … well, I guess you could call us a spy ring."

"A spy ring," Chiara repeated slowly. She tried to keep a straight face. *What in the fresh conspiracy theory …?*

"Yes, a spy ring." Cor looked faintly annoyed. "You think that fire was an accident?"

Unusual circumstances … just an accident.

"No," said Chiara. "No, I don't."

Cor nodded. "Right. Neither do we. Neither does Torva." He gave her an odd look. "Did he say anything about that?"

"… We didn't get that far." Chiara pressed her lips together. Another pang of guilt … the letter she never read. *Maybe that would've explained more than just a circus position …*

Cor sighed. "Okay. I'll do my best to explain. Your dad discovered us about three years ago. Somehow, he got in touch with Skipper — our founder, the one who runs the show. His real name is Torin Ferrolto."

"The Ringmaster?"

"No." Cor grinned, a dimple appearing on his cheek. "That's Mishkil. He's great. But Skipper's our real leader. He doesn't perform. He only works with the street crew. He stayed backstage the whole time. That's who your dad went to meet."

"Last night?"

Cor nodded. "Right before all hell broke loose."

And that was when it all clicked.

All the trips. All the meetings. The newspaper clippings … the last-minute business trips … the distant expressions … that look he'd exchanged with Mum, right before he left the balcony.

"Oh, Arva." Chiara ran her hands through her hair. "Oh, Arva … this whole time …"

Dad…and Zelie, too. All the things they said about Fhír …

"What's wrong?" Cor looked alarmed. "You look really pale."

Chiara lifted her gaze to him. Her eyes were starting to burn with tears. "All this time …"

They were trying to tell me …? They were fighting for Isak … and I just kept pushing them away.

For three years … for three years …

"… I just … I didn't know," she finished hoarsely. "You mean he was with Fhír? This whole time?"

"Yes … are you sure you're okay?"

If she didn't calm down, Cor would keep asking. And he was the last person she wanted to open up to.

Breathe … just breathe. She exhaled slowly. "It's just … a lot to take in."

Cor looked at her sympathetically.

She blinked back the tears. "Did … did Mum know, too?"

Cor shook his head. "I don't know. But if I could take a guess, I'd say that she didn't know many of the details. Your dad probably didn't want her … at risk."

"Right …" Chiara took another shaky breath. "So, Dad is one of you? Since when?"

Cor nodded. "Three years ago. Apparently, he was there during one of the fires — Crescor, I think."

Chiara's heart stopped. *Isak.*

Cor was still talking. "He suspected foul play, but the local authorities never found anything." He sighed irritably. "They never do. Anyway, that's when he started searching for answers. After a while, he figured out what we figured out. For the past two decades, there have been a series of unexplained fires in major cities around Tegea."

Chiara was only listening for Isak's name. But Cor never said it. Her heart began to beat again. *He doesn't know … he doesn't know.*

If he knew, he would've asked her about it … and she didn't think she'd be able to explain it. Any of it.

Cor's tattooed hands kept moving, fingers drumming his thighs, tapping his knees. "And he — and we — believe that those fires weren't accidents. We think they were deliberate. Sounds like you guessed that already, though."

"So I was right," Chiara whispered. Some cloying dizziness was rising to her head … elation? Or horror? "It's arson. Arsonists?"

The corners of Cor's mouth turned down. "Unfortunately. At least, that's what we think. Skipper began Fhír years ago as a way to investigate suspected arson attacks. He believed a traveling circus was the perfect way to travel anywhere and learn anything quickly."

"So," Chiara began slowly, "you're a non-Tegid circus … that is also an undercover espionage ring … that is tracking down a group of arsonists."

Cor was nodding. "That about sums it up."

"Well … I guess it makes sense," she admitted. "As weird as it sounds …"

A circus in Tegea could go anywhere, perform for anyone. They were the perfect eyes and ears for gossip, and they could show up or skip town whenever they needed to.

"But why not report it?" she asked. "I mean … tell the High Council, tell someone official. Get them to deal with it? We're talking *fire* here. How has there not been a huge investigation?"

Cor shook his head. "Skipper tried, and he got nowhere. Every single one of those fires was dismissed as an unfortunate accident — basically because there's never been any hard evidence or any eyewitnesses of any suspicious activity when the fires began."

"*What?* How is that possible?" Chiara demanded.

"They're really good." His lip curled. "They've been doing this for twenty years. Fortunately, some people believed Skipper — people like your dad. People who know people … people who hear things. Skipper relies on them for the intel, and then the circus shows up to try and stop the attacks — or if we can't stop them, we save as many people as we can."

"And that's who you're spying on," Chiara realized aloud. "*Serial* arsonists?"

"Yeah. And it's not just some lunatic or a bunch of dumb adolescents." Cor's mouth formed a grim line. "We think it's a whole group of people … extremists, maybe, or terrorists."

"How do you know? What's the motive?"

He shook his head again. "We still can't pin it down completely. There's kind of a pattern between the arson attacks and big events. Festivals, celebrations … things like that. We've been guessing their next targets based on that. But"—he frowned— "it's not totally consistent. Sometimes they attack government buildings, and other times, it's random factories."

Chiara looked at him, her hands turning clammy. "They attacked a government building during the Midsummer Festival."

And Crescor … attacking the East Gymnasium, during the Tegea National Acrobatic Competition.

She leaned in, swallowing. "How? How did they do it without being spotted?"

Cor shrugged. "We know they use some kind of accelerant, although we don't know what it is. And we don't know how they start the fires without anyone seeing them light the place up." His eyes became dark, angry. "But there's only one way they'd get in and out of Tegid cities without any suspicion. They're Tegids."

Ice curled up Chiara's spine. "Our own people?" she whispered. "How is that possible? We *hate* fire …"

A poisonous look flashed across Cor's face, so quick she almost missed it. "Exactly. They're terrorists. Fire is the perfect weapon."

Fire is the perfect weapon.

Chiara sat back, blood roaring in her ears.

Tegids. *Tegids* had brought about Isak's death.

And they'd do it again.

They almost did it to Dad. Fury racked her limbs, burning a hole in her chest.

Dad had never given up after Isak died. *Of course* he never gave up. How could he? That was exactly why he joined Fhír.

Atonement.

Isak wasn't coming back. But maybe … maybe … she could do something about the past.

Redemption … a life in exchange for a life. His life lost in the fire … her life spent in fighting it.

That was the future Dad had wanted for her. It wasn't just about trapeze. *He wanted me to live again …*

"Chiara?" Cor was repeating her name. "Are you sure you're okay?" He looked even more worried. "You look feverish. Maybe you should lie down."

She took a deep breath and looked him in the eye. "How do I join?"

"What?" His eyes went wide.

"You heard me," she said, louder. "Dad and Zelie wanted me to join for years. What do I need to do to be part of Fhír?" She'd never be an acrobat. But it sounded like they had a street crew. She could do something. She'd do anything … anything.

Cor blinked a few times, looking confused. "I … uh, okay. Wow. I mean …"

"Did I stutter?" Chiara demanded. "Tell me what I need to do!"

"Right — right, yes! That's … good! I mean—" He sighed and ran a hand through his hair, leaving it even messier than before.

Chiara lifted her eyebrows. "What's the holdup? Dad wanted me to join. Zelie wanted me to join. *I* want to join. Am I missing something?"

Cor gave her a sympathetic look. "I'm not sure how much your dad explained, but it sounds like it wasn't much. If you join us, you'd have to leave Belkar. You'd live with the circus. You wouldn't be able to see your family very often, or talk to them much."

"I guessed that much from Zelie …"

"It's not just that." He went on, sounding apologetic. "You won't even be able to say goodbye to them right now. We pulled completely out of Belkar, and we can't just show up a day after disappearing. If the Arsonists are still there, we'd risk compromising our operation … and your dad can't come with us. He has to stay in the city and maintain his cover."

Chiara bit her lip. "I know." A pang tightened in her chest. *I won't be able to talk to Dad.* Not face to face. She hadn't even read his letter. And now — right as she began to understand everything — she couldn't go back to talk to him about it.

"I can live with that," she said at last. "As long as my family is safe."

"They're safe. We made sure of that before we left."

The knot in her chest loosened a bit. "Alright. Then I'm joining."

A smile broke out on Cor's face. "Well … that's good enough for me. Welcome to the circus! Skipper will be happy to hear it."

Skipper will be happy to hear it. What had Dad said? *They're not a Tegid troupe.*

"Wait." She chose her words carefully. "Are you sure Skipper is fine? With me, I mean?"

It wasn't a Tegid circus … but it was still a circus, and she was a Tegid who couldn't heal. *They have to know I'm Stunted … don't they?* Cor himself had said she had a fever. Surely he knew based on that alone.

But did Skipper know? Had Dad told him that part of her career?

Cor gave her a puzzled look. "Of course he is. Why wouldn't he be? He agreed with your father. They both wanted you to be a trapeze artist."

"Does he know … about my condition?" Chiara asked warily.

"Your *condition*? What ab—?" Then Cor's face fell, and his eyes flickered angrily. "You mean Stunted." He practically spat the word.

So he definitely knew. Chiara lifted her chin, steeling herself for what she knew would come. "Yes."

"Okay, look." Cor fixed her with a fierce gaze. "I'm only taking you to join the circus on one condition."

"What is it?" she asked cautiously. She could already imagine what he would say. *Never get on the trapeze … stick to groundwork …*

"Swear to me that you'll never call yourself Stunted again."

"What?" Chiara stared at him, baffled. *Is he serious?*

Cor didn't break her gaze. "Did I stutter?" He threw her question back at her. "Swear it. Saying you're Stunted is a load of horse dung. Don't carry it around. This is Fhír. We don't give a rat's tail about your past, just as long as you care about stopping the Arsonists."

His eyes were burning.

Chiara looked away, chewing her lip. *So … they don't care.*

For the first time in three years, she wouldn't be imprisoned anymore. She could leave that behind her.

I could finally do something about Isak.

And that was why she looked Cor in the eye and said, "I swear it," with all the confidence she could muster.

Cor leaned back with a lopsided grin. "Good. And if you break your word, I'll kick you out."

"I'd like to see you try," she fired back.

"I'm glad you're in better spirits." He rose to his feet and offered Chiara a tattooed hand, pulling her up easily.

Energy coursed through her body, fighting off the weariness in her hands and feet. "So … when can I start?" she asked excitedly.

Cor lifted his eyebrows, amused. "Whoa, there. Your fever still hasn't broken. You won't be doing anything until you're completely recovered." He turned to the tent door. "But I'll let Talia know that you're awake, at least."

Chiara followed him. "I'm coming with you."

But just as Cor opened the tent flap, direct sunlight struck her eyes, and a wave of dizziness slammed into her.

She winced and squeezed her eyes shut. When she finally opened them, Cor was facing her with a skeptical look on his face. "You're not fine. Please, lie down. Talia will be here soon. I promise."

"But I—"

"No buts!" Cor shook his head and left the tent.

Chiara peered out curiously after him. They were in the woods, just as she'd guessed. The tent apparently had been set up in some kind of small clearing surrounded by trees. Cor was already a few yards away.

"Wait!" Chiara stepped out of the tent.

He turned, spotted her, and came back. "What's wrong?" His eyes looked almost green in the sunlight.

"Thank you. For … saving me. And … I'm sorry … about your nose," she finished awkwardly. Her cheeks began to burn with something that wasn't fever.

Cor *had* saved her life, but saying it aloud sounded stupid. Not to mention she'd broken his face in return. *Way to make an impression …*

The dimple in his cheek winked at her. "Zelie helped, too."

"Barely."

He laughed. "I … can't really argue with that, actually. You're welcome. Now please, go lie down!"

$$6$$

Chiara slept for most of the day. It was late afternoon when she woke up to someone else coming into the tent — someone new.

"Hello, hello, my dear." A female Nousk was bustling around inside the tent, every step punctuated by a soft, musical clinking. Chiara watched her curiously.

She was tall and strong-limbed, with purple skin. Dark, curly hair tumbled down to her waist, tied back with an orange bandana. Her clothes were just as colorful — a patchwork of brightly patterned cloth and gold jewelry, with bangles, earrings, and tiny chains and charms hemmed into her layered skirts.

"Now, how are we doing today?" she asked, turning around with a smile.

Chiara's eyes widened.

An Ensyth's ridged horns curled back above her forehead, and her Jeka ears were shaped like butterfly's wings. She was a mixed Nousk — a doua.

Chiara hadn't seen many of those before. "Uh …" she stammered. "Fine, I guess …?"

The doua clasped her hands together, gazing at Chiara with sparkling green eyes. Bangles clinked on her wrists as she sank into a graceful curtsey. "That is good to hear! Welcome to Fhír. I am Talia Zoiros — call me Talia." She had a lovely accent — rolling "R's" and soft "T's."

"Well met, Talia." Chiara dipped her head. "I'm Chiara."

Talia nodded. "I must begin with an apology. Coren — that foolish boy — he left you tied here. It was not wise of him. I have had words with him." She tossed her mane of hair, eyes flashing, and Chiara caught a glimpse of something fiery beneath the pretty skirts and bangles. Talia was not, it seemed, to be trifled with.

"I'm fine, really," Chiara repeated, half-hoping to spare Cor from an impending tongue-lashing. "I probably would've done the same thing, honestly."

Talia shook her head imperiously. "It is not acceptable. Please, receive my apology on his behalf."

Chiara had to stifle a smile. "Of course I accept your apology."

"Thank you." Talia curtseyed again. "Now, let us see about your fever." She pressed a hand to Chiara's forehead and *tsked*. "You are too warm still. You will need some time. I will make you a tea. You must drink it."

There was another rustle at the entrance of the tent, and a much smaller figure slipped in … a familiar face.

"You're awake!" Zelie cried. She barged across the tent with wild abandon and crashed into Chiara, wrapping her in a tight hug.

When she drew back, her eyes looked shimmery, like she'd been crying. "I'm so sorry — I wanted to tell you — but your dad wanted to tell you — and — and—"

Chiara shook her head. "It's not your fault." She twisted her fingers awkwardly in her lap. "I'm sorry. After all this time … you kept trying to tell me. I should've listened."

There was so much more she wanted to say. *I didn't know … Dad left a letter … Please, tell me what I missed.* But she didn't even know where to begin.

Talia clapped her hands together, startling them both. "I go for the tea. Zelie, watch our patient." She vanished before either of them could say a word.

Chiara glanced furtively at Zelie. "So … the circus."

Zelie curled up excitedly at the foot of the cot. "It's amazing! Well…actually, I take that back. It's been *really* boring without you. Nobody understands my jokes! But now you're here!"

"Your saving grace …" Chiara attempted a laugh. "Listen, Zelie …" She sighed and chewed her lip. "We should talk. There's a lot I wanted to tell you …"

"I know." Zelie put her small hands on Chiara's. "Let's go for a walk—"

Then Talia brushed back inside the tent with a kettle and a tin cup. "Ah, Miss Zelie! What is this you say about walks? Not today!"

"But Talia—"

Talia shook her head imperiously. "You are on guard patrol soon, no? You must go. Let Chiara rest."

Zelie huffed. "Alright. Fine. Tomorrow, then?" She turned pleading eyes on Talia.

"Ah." Talia sighed. "I see that if I tell you no, you will still come. So I will say yes. Very well."

"Yes!" Zelie cheered. "Okay, I'll see you tomorrow! I'll bring you some food, I promise!"

"Not if it's dead mice, you won't!" Chiara called as Zelie whisked out of the tent.

Talia swept over to Chiara and handed her the steaming cup. "Here! Drink."

Chiara took it carefully. A faintly earthy aroma rose from it. She took a small sip. It was hot, and tangy — almost bitter — but she kept drinking it.

"Now." Talia settled down on the floor next to the cot. "You are Tegid, but you have fever. That is hard to treat. I have done my best."

"Thanks," Chiara murmured, her face turning warm.

"You must not be embarrassed," Talia said insistently. "Fhír is not like your city. You will be part of the circus now. You must perform."

"That's what Cor said," Chiara murmured. The idea of *actually* performing …

"You were a trapeze artist, no?"

Chiara set down her cup. "Well … yes. I mean, that was my original path. But …" She sighed. *How many times will this come up?*

"You are distressed." Talia looked worried. "I have offended you. Forgive me."

"No, it's okay. It's just…" Chiara pressed her lips together. "… I wasn't advancing. I ended up working with a mentor on my own."

Talia's face creased into a bright smile. "Rothgar, yes?"

"You know him?" Chiara asked, surprised.

"We met years ago. It was for a mission. He is a good soul."

"Sure, when he's not yelling," Chiara muttered, but there was a twinge of sadness in her chest. *I didn't get to say goodbye to him, either.*

Talia's gaze was warm. "He spoke about you. He said you gave him purpose."

"He did?" Chiara asked softly. *Purpose?*

Talia nodded. "He said you kept him there."

I kept him … "Oh. I never …" Chiara swallowed. "I mean … he never told me that." She fidgeted with the cup in her hands.

Talia shrugged. "It is no surprise. You have strong heart. He has strong heart. You are both fighters, no? That is your purpose. That is what matters. The Gift does not matter. What is a Gift with no purpose? Pah. Rubbish." She waved a scornful hand in the air.

A Gift with no purpose … Chiara's gaze fell to the floor. "I guess so," she murmured.

"Finish your tea. Then you must rest." Talia stood and smoothed her skirts. "I come tomorrow. You will walk with Zelie, no?" She sounded much more pleased with the idea now that Zelie wasn't there.

"I think so. I mean, I hope so."

Talia nodded. "That is good. You have much to say."

☙

True to her promise, Zelie came the next morning. "I'm taking you to the creek!" she said excitedly, waving around a bundled-up towel. "Best place for a bath!"

"Oh, thank Arva," Chiara murmured, pushing her way out of the tent. Talia had given her a change of clothes, but she hadn't bathed in almost two days, and she reeked of smoke.

She stepped out of the tent and took what felt like her first real breath of fresh air in days. Trees stretched in every direction. The summer heat hadn't quite penetrated the tree cover, so the air was relatively cool. Zelie was already cavorting toward the treeline a few yards away.

Chiara peered around curiously. "Where are we?"

"The infirmary tent!" Zelie skipped around in a circle. "Base camp is that way." She pointed into the woods. "I'll show you all that later! Hurry up, slow-paws!"

"No, I mean where are we *exactly*?" Chiara persisted, following Zelie's lead. "What forest is this?"

The Vastil Forest was the only name she knew — the largest wood in Tegea, several miles east of Belkar.

"No idea!"

"Zelie, how do you not know where you are? Isn't this your base camp?"

"It's not about *east* and *west*!" Zelie turned to make a dopey face. "It's about the *feeling*. The *smells*. The thrill of the *hunt* …" She was scampering around now, waving her arms.

Chiara watched her antics with a resigned sigh. "How long are we staying here?" She scanned the woods curiously. She had no idea how the circus traveled, but she didn't imagine they'd be camping.

"Oh, a few weeks," Zelie sighed, slowing down. "Skipper wants to be sure we weren't followed. Some stuff went wrong at Belkar … we're just keeping our heads down until we're sure it's safe." She shook her head. "But let's not talk about that now. Come on! I can hear the creek!" She dashed off.

Chiara broke into a jog. Her muscles were protesting. *Ooh. I haven't worked out in* … She frowned. Two days? Three? It didn't matter. She needed to stretch. "Zelie! Slow down!"

But Zelie was already out of sight. Chiara sighed. She didn't mind the jog alone. It gave her time to think.

I have to ask her about Fhír … and explain about Isak. Why she hadn't wanted to leave … why she turned away every time Zelie brought up the circus.

Easier said than done …

Running water interrupted Chiara's thoughts. The stream. She began following the babble, and it took her vaguely to the left. After a few minutes, she found it: a wide, smooth-flowing stream, edged in muddy sand.

"Zelie?" she called as she knelt on the bank. She dipped her hands in with a sigh of relief and splashed the cold water across her face, feeling it trickle pleasantly down her neck.

Then there was a loud splash downstream. Startled, Chiara turned. "Zelie?"

But there was no cheerful reply. She crouched down among the bushes. *What kind of animals live here?*

Or *was* it an animal? Zelie said they weren't far from base camp. Maybe it was someone else from the circus. Chiara peered out cautiously and glimpsed a two-legged figure moving through the water, several yards away from her.

She leaned forward, careful not to tumble headlong into the stream. The figure was bending over double now, facing away from her, dipping its hands into the water.

Not a Dwyn — it wasn't tall enough. Probably not a Beast-skin, since there were no ears or tail that she could see. Not a Nousk, either. No color-changing skin.

Then it stood, and she saw that it — he — was stripped to his waist, a stick in hand. Tattoos covered his arms — a Tegid, then.

Chiara almost laughed aloud when she realized what he was doing. *Fishing? There's no way he's fast enough—*

Suddenly, he struck the water. There was another loud splash, and he straightened again, lifting the stick in triumph. Impaled on it was a writhing, silvery shape.

Impressive ... Chiara squinted closer and frowned. There was something about his back ... his skin looked odd. Splotched, somehow. *Tattoos?*

They weren't like any tattoos she'd seen before. No recognizable patterns. And they looked ... red.

Then a furred hand clamped over Chiara's mouth. Biting off a scream, she wriggled around to find Zelie's wide blue eyes staring at her.

"Are you crazy?" Chiara hissed, pulling Zelie's hand away. She did her best to scoot back up the bank. "What were you thinking, jumping me like that?"

"What were *you* thinking, you peeping owl?" Zelie snickered. "That's Cor!" She tossed down the bundled towel and pointed dramatically upstream.

"Peeping owl?" Chiara sputtered. "How was I supposed to know it was Cor?"

"With those shoulders? How could you not?" Zelie wiggled her eyebrows. "Didn't you spend some quality time in the infirmary tent? I thought for sure you'd know it was him!"

"Zelie, are you insane?" Heat crawled up Chiara's neck, and she tried to ignore her embarrassment. "It wasn't 'quality time!' It was barely fifteen minutes! Not to mention I wasn't exactly conscious! Why in Arva would I remember his *shoulders*?"

"Whose shoulders?" Cor materialized behind them, eliciting screams, mostly Zelie's. His shirt was mercifully on, and his spear-stuck fish was still in hand.

"Nobody's shoulders," Chiara coughed awkwardly, right as Zelie exclaimed, "Cor! You're here! We were just talking about you!"

Chiara glared daggers at her.

"Oh, really." Cor lifted his eyebrows. "So … *my* shoulders?"

"No!" Chiara interrupted, just as Zelie opened her mouth. "Sorry we bothered you. Zelie brought me here for a bath. We can leave, if you want."

"Please." Cor gave a neat bow, extending an arm toward the creek. "Say no more. I will leave you in peace." He began walking away from the creek. "I'll be sure no one bothers you," he called over his shoulder. "Come find me when you're done — I'll bring you to Skipper."

☙

The water was perfect. Chiara sank into it with a sigh. She washed, and Zelie curled up in a branch somewhere, hidden by the leaves, keeping an eye out for any unsuspecting visitors.

And they talked.

It was easier to talk about, somehow, when they weren't face to face. Chiara kept her eyes on the water as Zelie told her about life in the circus.

Camping, traveling between cities, performing, hunting the Arsonists. Fhír, it turned out, was more a vagrant gypsy caravan than a formal organization — not very surprising, given the nature of their mission.

"Was it hard? Being away from Belkar?" Chiara asked at one point.

"From Belkar? No. From my best friend? Yes."

Chiara looked down at the water, stirring little circles in it. "I should've listened to you when you asked me to join."

"You're here now!" Zelie said happily. "That's all I care about."

Chiara dug her toes into the sandy bottom. *I could've done this so much sooner …* The weight on her shoulders was almost crushing.

"Zelie … there's more. About why I didn't listen … why I didn't talk."

The branches overhead grew still.

Chiara tried to keep talking, not looking up. "I know it's been … a while. And I know we talked about Crescor. But I never really … talked about it. After."

"You didn't have to."

Chiara swallowed. Even in the water, her body felt too warm. "I should have. You're my best friend. I should've talked to you about it."

"I'm listening," Zelie promised.

And Chiara floated on her toes in the water, and she fought back the heat and the choking in her throat, and she tried to speak.

"I'm … I'm sorry." She looked up at the sky. Her eyes were stinging. "I mean, I know you wanted me to join Fhír — and I guess I wanted to, but …" She swallowed. "Everything stopped three years ago, and every — every time you talked about the circus — every time I thought about joining — it felt like I was betraying—"

Her throat closed up.

Betraying his memory. Leaving him behind.

Still, the branches were silent.

Chiara wiped her eyes with wet hands and waded to the edge. She clambered slowly out of the creek and picked up the folded clothes. A leather belt-like strap, a pair of worn trousers, and a button-down shirt that smelled faintly of dried rosemary. They were too big for her, but at least they were clean.

She dressed and cinched the strap tightly around the waist of the trousers. That would have to do. "I'm decent," she called, pushing damp hair out of her face.

Leaves rustled overhead, and Zelie jumped down. She came right up to Chiara and hugged her. "It's not your fault," she promised.

Hot tears filled Chiara's eyes. "It was my fault. If I was faster …" She cleared her throat hoarsely, and a tear dripped down her face.

"Chiara, stop." Zelie looked up at her with stern blue eyes. "It's *not* your fault. It's not *anyone's* fault. There were thousands of Tegids there when the fire started. They couldn't have stopped it."

"But I was so close — he might still—"

"Chiara, look at me." Zelie pulled Chiara down by the sleeve and took Chiara's face in both little hands. "Do not blame yourself." She emphasized each syllable with a little shake.

Then she let go and folded her arms. "You can't live like that. It will crush you. You have to let him go."

I can't let him go. Not when the scars were still on her face.

"Please … trust me on this one." Zelie's eyes grew dark. "You fight. Sometimes … sometimes people don't make it." She blinked a few times. "It's happened to me, too. But you *cannot* blame yourself. It will eat you alive."

Eat you alive. Heat was burning in Chiara's chest.

"Isak wanted you to live." Zelie's blue eyes searched hers. "He *wanted* you to perform. He'd be furious if you spent the rest of your life at that gymnasium. After all that practice? You know he would!"

She almost coaxed a laugh. "I know," Chiara managed.

"*Promise* me you will do your best to let him rest." Zelie squeezed Chiara's hand. "Promise me you take this chance, and you run with it. For Isak's sake *and* for yours."

For Isak's sake.

"… I promise."

"Good." Zelie gave her hand another quick squeeze. "We should probably go find Cor," she added, glancing over her shoulder.

Chiara let out a shaking breath. "Okay. Just … give me a minute." She wiped at her eyes.

Zelie nodded, and the corners of her mouth turned up in a smile. "Thank you for telling me that."

"Thanks for listening."

"I'm so glad you're finally here." Zelie threw her arms around Chiara's waist. "I'm here whenever you need to talk."

Chiara stooped to hug her back.

☙

It was almost noon by the time Chiara and Zelie arrived at base camp proper. Zelie led her back the way they'd come, past the infirmary tent, along a thin deer trail through the trees.

"Almost there! This way — watch the roots!" Zelie scampered forward down the trail.

Chiara followed her, noticing the trees beginning to fall away. Suddenly, the trail sloped down, and she gave a murmur of surprise as the ground rolled away, revealing a slim valley lying at her feet. Zelie was already loping down the grassy hillside.

Chiara picked her way down, and a few minutes later, she was standing on the valley floor.

Fhír sprawled out in front of her. Four grazing draft horses, a vaguely circular setup of mismatched tents, a few firepits, and six covered gypsy wagons with faded paint. A handful of people were milling around the wagons and tents — some Beast-skins, some Nousk, and a few Tegids. Hammocks were swinging from the nearby trees.

It wasn't much to look at — not for a circus nor an espionage ring.

Zelie was standing in the grass, waiting with a grin. "Welcome to camp! Isn't it neat? I'm gonna find Leo and Fleur. They can't wait to meet you!"

She dashed off before Chiara could reply.

"Okay …" Chiara gazed around curiously. The whole thing looked no different than any other gypsy camp. But as she watched the people moving back and forth between tents and wagons, she began to notice signs of conflict. Pistols holstered on hips, blades strapped to backs, hints of leather armor on shoulders and chests.

This isn't just a circus. For the first time, the idea of "fighting terrorists" began to sink in, and a tingle ran up Chiara's spine.

Fhír was ready for combat.

A figure peeled away from the circle of tents. Cor — she recognized the tattooed arms.

"Chiara!" He jogged up to her with a wave. "There you are! Nice shirt." His dimple was showing.

"Uh … thanks." Chiara glanced down and gave it a tug. She'd knotted up the side and rolled the sleeves back as much as she could, but it was still two sizes too big. "I have no idea whose this is."

Cor squinted at it. "I think I've got a shirt that looks like that." He shrugged. "We'll find you clothes that fit, I promise. Wardrobe options are slim here — that's a pun; don't laugh, it wasn't funny — but I'm sure we can find you something."

Chiara opened her mouth awkwardly, but he was already turning around. "Come on! You're meeting the Captains next."

"Captains?" Chiara repeated, trudging through the grass after him. "As in military captains?"

"Oh! No," Cor laughed. "That's just what we call them. It's Skipper, Mishkil and Talia. They keep things organized around here. I'll show you around."

He began walking, matching Chiara's pace, and pointed as they passed the grazing horses. "That's Ria, Toby, Norik and Nin. They're our performance horses. All smart as a whip. They know every trick in the book."

He led her past the wagons toward the circle of tents, pointing out people as they went. "The Dwyn over there are Yati and Orek. She's a gentle giant and he's … well, he's quiet. But a great fighter."

Yati, the female Dwyn, waved, and Orek, the male, gave a gruff snort. Chiara waved back with an uncertain smile. Dwyn were way bigger up close.

Cor went on. "That little scamp climbing the wagon over there is Ludni. He does object manipulation — juggling knives, that kind of thing. OI! LUDNI! Get down before you break the wagon!" The little Tegid looked over with a start and jumped down.

Cor pointed again. "Those two Tegids messing with that wagon axle are Oxys and Mykzi. They're our self-proclaimed engineers. They also occasionally do groundwork." Chiara waved hello, but the two males were so busy arguing that they didn't notice.

They entered the circle of tents, and a cluster of Vikur looked up from one of the smoldering firepits. Cor waved to them. "That's Faye, Rye, Nadir, and Zenith. Faye and Rye do ground acrobatics. Nadir and Zenith do tightrope. They're twins." The Vikur bobbed their heads in greeting. They went back to talking as soon as she passed.

Chiara's head was spinning. "Is that everyone?" *There's no way I'll remember all that …*

"Uh, no." Cor grinned, flashing his dimple. "There's probably twenty more of us you haven't met yet. Most of them are foraging right now, but you'll meet them all at dinner. Come on! This way." He led her toward the biggest tent.

As they passed more and more people, an unsettling feeling began to settle on Chiara's shoulders … anxiety, like she was waiting for something that hadn't come yet.

"There's Mishkil!" Cor exclaimed, darting ahead. "Wait here!"

Chiara looked after him and spotted another male Dwyn leaving the woods.

She began to jog forward and almost crashed into a ruby Nousk. "Oh, I'm sorry—"

But he was already shaking his head, inky dreadlocks bouncing. "No worries. Welcome to camp. I'm Milio."

He shook her hand, and she noticed his double thumbs. "Chiara," she said. "Well met."

"Well met. I'll see you around!" Milio turned and trotted away … and that was when Chiara figured it out.

Her scars were on full display, and nobody had given her a second glance.

A massive weight lifted off her shoulders.

Belkar was a lot of things … a lot of eyes, a lot of ears. A lot of tongues. But few places to rest. Rothgar's gymnasium. Mum and Dad's house, maybe. But nowhere else. Everyone knew, or knew someone who knew.

But no one knows here. And they didn't care, either. Suddenly, Dad's reasons for wanting her here became a lot clearer.

He knew I'd be free. It wasn't just a career opportunity. It really was a second chance at living — the life he wanted her to have.

"Chiara!" Zelie burst between the tents, followed by two other Kithsa, a male and a female. "This is Leo, and this is Fleur!"

The two diminutive cat-skins offered polite handshakes to Chiara. Leo, the male, was a lanky gray tabby slightly larger than his female counterparts, and Fleur was a dainty calico. "It's a pleasure to meet you," she said in a tiny, musical voice. "Zelie's told us so much about you."

"Thank you. I …" Chiara paused. She couldn't exactly say *I've heard so much about you.* She changed tack. "It's a pleasure to meet you as well. Zelie wanted me to meet you all in Belkar. I'm sorry I didn't," she finished with an awkward smile.

"Well, you're here now!" Leo grinned cheerfully at her. "Seeing as that Cor's abandoned you, we'll finish the tour for him."

The three Kithsa scampered around, pointing to tents and people. From their excited chatter, Chiara managed to gather a little more information. The Beast-skins slept outside for the most part. Everyone else slept in tents or hammocks. Some of the tents were for she-folk, and others for he-folk. One of the tents, larger than the rest, was the Captains' tent … but apparently only the Skipper stayed there.

"Everyone brings their own tents and bedding and things," Fleur explained, "but Lopia knows how to make a tent that is also a hammock. She is very smart!"

"And really pretty," Leo added. "She's not here right now, but you'll meet her soon!"

Chiara must have looked a little overwhelmed, because Zelie said, "I'll take it from here! Thanks, guys." Leo and Fleur waved goodbye and headed into the forest.

Zelie brought Chiara out of the circle of tents and sat her down in the grass. "You looked like you were about to fall over," she laughed.

Chiara shook her head. "I'm okay. Really. Just … it's a lot to take in." She looked around. "I mean … I'm sure I'll get used to it."

"Don't worry!" Zelie exclaimed. "We're the tiniest circus ever. You'll get to know everyone in no time!"

"Yeah …" Chiara glanced back at the tents. "It seemed like there were a lot more of you at Rothgar's gym. How many …?"

Zelie shrugged. "Only thirty or so — give or take. At least …" She trailed off, staring out into the grass.

"What is it?"

Zelie gave a little shake of her head. "Well, it … changes a bit. Sometimes we … well, it can be … dangerous."

What had she said, earlier at the creek? *Sometimes, people don't make it … it's happened to me, too.*

Chiara put a soft hand on Zelie's head. "I'm sorry."

Zelie turned, blinking. "Thanks," she said, a small smile on her face. "It … you know, it happens. Part of the risk." She flicked her ears. "Although — it hasn't happened in a while, thank Arva."

This is a combat mission. Chiara wondered how many people Fhír had lost on missions.

… Am I replacing someone?

Zelie looked somber.

I should talk about something different. Chiara cleared her throat. "So … you camp. In the woods."

"Most of the time!" Zelie said cheerfully. "No showers, no public amenities … living the high life."

"Thrilling," Chiara sighed. "Do you ever stay in cities when you're not performing?"

"Oh, sure. Just … not as Fhír. We split up and stuff to avoid being tracked." Zelie plucked a long blade of grass and placed it between her thumbs. "No trains, either." She blew hard on the grass blade, succeeding only in producing a sad, ducklike quack.

"So it's all on foot?" Chiara asked, incredulous.

Zelie looked affronted. "No, you heathen! We've got wagons!"

"Right. Of course," Chiara snorted.

"Chiara!" Cor walked up behind them. "There you are! I found Mishkil, but when I turned around, you were gone."

"The Kithsa got to me first," Chiara grinned. "Where are we going next?"

"The Captains' tent! They're already waiting for you."

Chiara got up, straightening her shirt. "Wish me luck!"

Zelie waved her off. "You'll be fine!"

7

If any tent could be said to have a military air, the Captains' tent was it. Clean canvas, tight cords, perfect folds, almost like it had been ironed. But there was no emblem or flag to mark it out.

Standing in front of it were two people. The first was Talia, who offered Chiara a curtsey and a warm smile. The second was a male Dwyn — huge, powerful shoulders, furry limbs as wide as Chiara's body, and a thick, braided beard streaked with gray. He was the one who had come out of the woods … Mishkil.

"Chiara Alteva!" he boomed. "Vell met!" He grinned from ear to ear, flashing deadly canine teeth as he offered her a massive claw. She took it timidly and was surprised to find that his grip was quite gentle.

"Well met … uh, Captain," she said uncertainly.

"Please, it is Mishkil to you!" His blue eyes twinkled merrily under bushy eyebrows.

"Skipper is inside." Talia pointed to the tent behind them. "He is almost ready. How was your bath? Did Zelie cause mischief?"

"Fine, thanks." Chiara smiled.

Talia reached forward with a frown and brushed firm hands across the shoulders of Chiara's shirt. "Tsk! Coren, you are chivalrous boy. Still, it is not fitting. Chiara must have her own shirts, not yours."

"I'm sorry, his *what?*" Chiara exclaimed.

"I didn't give …" Cor began, and then he trailed off.

"Zelie," they said in unison, glancing at each other. Mishkil burst out laughing.

"I'm so sorry," Chiara stammered, face turning warm. The linen was suddenly itchy and uncomfortable on her skin. "She brought—"

"Don't worry about it," Cor assured her, but he was pink in the face. "She probably thought they would fit you better than her own clothes."

"I'm sure," Chiara sighed. That was far too kind a guess. She knew Zelie too well. *She definitely planned this.*

She glanced at Cor, tugging uncomfortably at the hem of the shirt. "I'll return them to you as soon as possible."

"Oh, you don't have to," Cor said, and then seemed to realize what it sounded like. He snapped his mouth shut and ran a hand through his hair. "Just — whenever you do is fine. Anyway, I've got chores, so — um—" He began walking backward, jerking a thumb over his shoulder. "See you later?"

"Sure!" Chiara waved after him as he turned and loped away.

Mishkil was still chuckling. Talia swatted his enormous arm, apparently unbothered about chastising someone three times her size.

"Mishkil! Shame!" She shook her head, eyes sparking. "That Kithsa! She has caused mischief, the imp. I will talk to her myself."

"Please don't," Chiara said hurriedly. "She doesn't mean any harm." *Probably.* Her cheeks still felt warm.

Mishkil shook his head. "No, no. She is good soul. Coren, too." He looked Chiara in the eye. "Young, yes. But he has good soul. I heard he gave you fright?"

"Fright?" Chiara blinked. "Oh — you mean the infirmary tent?" She gave a sheepish laugh as her face grew hot again. "You could call it that. I mean, I gave him a bloody nose, so … I guess that makes us even."

Mishkil threw back his head with a booming laugh. "Bloody nose? This is good! Good. He is in need of hard lesson sometimes. Good for heart." He pounded his chest.

"Mishkil," said a calm voice, and they all turned to see a Tegid emerging from the Captains' tent.

He was simply dressed — worn linen sleeves, a leather breastplate, a glove on his left hand — but the clean cut of his beard and the tilt of his head was almost fiercely formal. Authority was etched in every line of his face, every angle of his shoulders and limbs.

Chiara knew his name without any introduction. The Skipper … Torin Ferrolto.

"Chiara Alteva." The Skipper came forward and extended his hand. "Well met."

She accepted his handshake, studying him curiously, noting the edge of the tattoos that appeared just above his collar. He held himself without aggression, or even assertion. But there was something a little too poised, too keenly observant, to be safe. A weapon, held at the ready.

"My name is Torin Ferrolto, but you may call me Skipper." He let go of her hand, studying her with a steady gray gaze. "I have waited many years for this moment." His gaze flicked to the scarred side of her face, and the lines around his eyes hardened. "I was told you wish to join Fhír."

Chiara's heart skipped — the moment of yawning void, right as her hands released the bar. "Yes, sir."

Here we go …

CR

Skipper wasted no time. As soon as the four of them were in the tent, he gestured to the worn rush mats on the ground. "Please, sit."

Chiara obeyed, glancing around curiously. An unlit lantern sat in one corner, and a folded cot and bedding in the other. The only sign that this was a meeting tent were the sitting mats laid carefully on the ground.

Mishkil settled his bulk in the far corner, easily taking up a quarter of the tent. Talia sat opposite him, and Skipper sat across from Chiara.

The other two Captains remained silent and still while Skipper talked. "Welcome to Fhír, Chiara. How much have Cor and Zelie told you?"

"Not much, sir," Chiara admitted. "I knew already from my father and Zelie that you're a small traveling circus. And … an espionage ring," she added, watching Skipper's face carefully.

He simply nodded, so she continued. "And he said that you're hunting … arsonists." Her neck felt hot under the collar of Cor's shirt.

Skipper placed his hands on his knees. "That is correct. We three"— he gestured to himself, then Talia and Mishkil—"began Fhír several years ago, when we first suspected that the fires in Tegid cities were deliberate. We have been hunting the Arsonists ever since. It is the sworn mission of Fhír to find them, to stop them. To end the fires and the deaths."

The temperature inched up in Chiara's body with every word Skipper spoke. At the word "deaths," her hands twitched into fists.

Skipper looked at her with hawk-like eyes. "If you choose to be part of Fhír, that will become your mission as well. But before you pledge your service to us, you must know that you will not be simply a circus acrobat. You will be part of a Clan of fighters. You will be asked to fight for a greater cause — even possibly to die for that cause. Are you prepared to accept such a risk?"

A life for a life. Chiara took a breath, ready to answer, but Skipper held up a hand.

"Before you speak … our mission does not allow the luxury of doubt. You must consider the choice carefully. Remember that you have a family who loves you dearly"—his eyes darkened—"and your death is a thing that will happen to them, as well. I will understand completely if you decide not to choose this. I promise we will get you back safely to your family."

Chiara was already shaking her head. *Go back? To what? I might have a chance here. I might be able to do something with my life.* "No, sir. I won't be going back. Zelie and my father believed in your mission." She lifted her chin. "And they believed that I would have a future here. I … I believe it, too."

If there was any point to that night — her life since then — any of it — she'd find it here. Nowhere else.

Skipper nodded. The lines around his eyes relaxed. "Your father told me you would speak with conviction. That is good to hear. And … truth be told…it is a relief. Had you decided against joining, we wouldn't have kept you here a minute longer than need be … but I'm afraid Fhír is now the safer option for you, implausible though that might sound."

Something about his tone sent a strange chill up Chiara's spine. "What do you mean?" she asked, tense.

Skipper's mouth pressed into a thin line. "Hours before the Arsonists attacked your city, your father discovered evidence that he was being watched."

"Watched." Cold hands grasped her heart. "You mean … by *them*?" She remembered the unexpected talk in the study; the last-minute meeting; Dad's anxiety. *He knew … He probably already knew something was wrong.*

"We suspect so. Your father is likely a target, Chiara."

A target. Her hands were shaking. *First Isak … now Dad …?*

Skipper leaned in. "It was too great a risk for him to stay. As soon as he knew you were safe with us, he left the city with your mother and grandmother. He's taken them to a safe location."

He held up a hand, stifling the question already on her lips. "I know Cor told you otherwise. Outside of this tent, no one else even knows that he left. Including Cor. I can't tell you where he went. Even if I knew, I'd be unwilling to risk compromising him. But you and I both know him well. I think we can say with confidence that he is more than capable."

"I know," Chiara whispered. She twisted her hands together in her lap. *No goodbyes.*

Arva knew when she'd see him again. Not in Belkar, surely. And it was unlikely that he'd meet with Fhír anytime soon, if he was a target …

"Why do you think he's a target?" she asked shakily. "I mean … he works in trade. What kind of a threat could he possibly be?"

"I have my suspicions … but I can't speak with any certainty." The lines around Skipper's eyes became hard again. "We're trying to determine any patterns between the attack on Belkar and the previous fires — anything that might shed light on your father's situation. Two of our members are in Crescor as we speak. Scatha is our chief intelligence operative there, and Kaito is our chief courier. We are expecting him to return with news from Scatha in a few weeks."

He paused. "It's possible that when Kaito returns, we might be able to send your parents a message … if you so wish."

"I'd … like that a lot."

"Then I will do my best to see to it." He offered her a smile.

Maybe I can at least put it on paper. She clenched and unclenched her hands. The knot in her stomach was eating away inside her. "So … what do we do now?" Her entire body was on edge. The air in the tent was suddenly oppressive.

"We train," Skipper replied firmly. "We track. We run espionage drills. We prepare for street combat. And we prepare for the circus stage. You, and I, and every able-bodied fighter in this camp. When the time comes, we will be ready to end the fire for good."

Mishkil gave an affirming grunt.

Chiara's heart hammered desperately in her chest. "What can I do?"

Skipper nodded. "That is what we will discuss next. Your father informed me that you were trained as the flier in a duo trapeze act."

"That is … correct, sir." Chiara's heartbeat quickened. All the plans she'd made with Isak … all ended, three years ago. She'd never been a flier since.

And without him … *Could I even* want *to do it without him?*

Skipper nodded. "He also told me that you have had some training as a solo artist."

"Yes, sir. I would … prefer that."

Skipper nodded. "I understand — but I was asked by your father to pass on his request. He wanted you to perform as a flier with Fhír."

Chiara's heart dropped into her toes. *If I'd read the letter …* She was certain by now that Dad had written more than just job details. *He might have even written about starting over with* this.

Skipper kept talking. "Cor is our resident solo trapeze artist, but he has also been trained as the catcher for a duo act. I believe you saw him at the performance in Belkar?"

"Cor …" Chiara remembered the Telk and Tegid pair. *So that was* him.

Duo trapeze. With Cor … with someone else.

Her stomach dropped. *He would replace Isak …*

Little voices were screaming in her head. *This is your chance! This is your chance! A chance at life! A chance at redemption …*

But the cost? Forgetting Isak?

I don't want to leave him behind. All the old fears came crawling up her throat. *There's no future here. You're losing him again, just like you did before …*

"Chiara?" Skipper prompted softly.

"I … I see, sir. But …"

Skipper was watching her carefully, seemingly aware of her hesitation. "Is there a problem?"

What if I just don't do trapeze …?

Chiara breathed out slowly and met his eyes. "Sir, I … I don't know what my father told you about me, but …" Her scars burned along the side of her face, unpainted, exposed. "… I don't heal properly."

Stunted. Stunted. Stunted. She went on doggedly. "It's been like that ever since my parents adopted me. I was expelled from the Acrobatics Academy after my … formal diagnosis. I can't professionally perform solo or duo trapeze. The risk is too great."

The worst part about that explanation was that it was completely true. The words were beginning to choke her. "If I was to fall and — and be injured, or die …"

Skipper leaned back, his face hardening. "So. You consider yourself a liability. Is that what they told you? The … Belkar Acrobatics Academy, was it?"

"Yes, sir." Chiara had to force the words from between her teeth.

"That's a pile of fesht."

Chiara jumped; she hadn't expected Skipper to curse like that. "Excuse me … sir?"

"You heard me." His eyes never left her face. "Your father never stopped telling me about everything you've done. He told me you were born for the act. When Belkar didn't want you, he knew that you would have a chance beyond that. You have every inch of the talent."

He leaned in. "And you have the heart of a fighter. *That* is what we need. The Tegid Gift is *useless* here if you don't care about fighting for the cause."

Chiara swallowed, then swallowed again. Heat was washing through her body — hope and anger, regret and desperation. *All this time … Dad wanted me to be a part of this. He wanted me to start over new.*

"Sir, I want to be part of Fhír …" *More than I can begin to express.* "… but I can't … I can't perform as a flier. Not anymore. No catcher would …"

Skipper's eyes glinted with something that was almost humor. "No catcher, eh? You can put aside any practical safety hazards. We've had many trapeze artists in the past, several of whom were not Tegids. I know the risks, believe me. Our Telk keep our performers safe. And besides … you're not the only one."

"Sir?" Chiara frowned, confused.

Skipper held out his left arm. He pulled off the worn leather glove and rolled his sleeve up to his elbow.

Chiara bit off a gasp.

His left hand was polished wood … clamped to his wrist by a leather cuff.

"They declared me Stunted, too," he said quietly, contemplating the hand.

The words *What happened?* fell dead in her mouth.

"Fire." Skipper rolled down his sleeve and replaced the glove. "I survived, but ..." He flicked the false hand in a helpless gesture. "My hand never recovered. I wear it for more formal meetings like this, but I find it cumbersome for practical work."

Chiara stared at him, speechless, ears ringing. The ground rolled beneath her.

Skipper went on. "Stunted has no meaning here. Not for our catchers, not for our fliers, not for anyone else. You are a talented gymnast, and — what's more important — you love the work. Your father said I would be a coward and a fool not to let you perform trapeze."

Start over new ...

And then the battle was finished.

"Sir ..." Chiara's voice shook. Skipper's face was becoming blurry. "... If my father truly wanted me to work as a flier, then I'd be ..." *Not glad.* "... ready and willing to do so."

Skipper had something like pride in his eyes. "He would be so proud to know that. I will tell you now that should there be any trouble, or any reason for concern, you have no obligation to remain a flier. There are many other roles in Fhír, and I have no doubt you would excel at any of them."

Then Talia spoke up. "Skipper, if I may." She waited for a nod from him before she went on. "Chiara, you are worried about duo, no? Remember you have trained. Year after year. You chose the fight. You have not lost it yet. You chose this fight; you will not lose."

You have not lost it yet.

But other things would be lost. Relearning a routine? With someone else? *As if Isak never existed ...*

Chiara's eyelids stung. *But I have to try. If this is the only chance ... I have to try.* Find Isak's killers. Find out why Dad believed so much in this mission that he'd spend three years of his life fighting for it.

Find a meaning.

She could never go back and undo the past. Isak was gone. But the future …

One last breath, steeling her nerves. Then she met Skipper's eyes. "Alright. I'll be a flier."

Skipper's mouth lifted in what was almost a smile. "Very well! I have no reservations about your decision to join us. Captains?"

Mishkil shook his great head. "You have good heart, like your friend Zelic. I hear you fight in street. Already you are saving people. Even before Fhír. Ve vant *you*." He folded his massive arms across his chest emphatically.

Already you are saving people …

Talia looked at her proudly. "Coren told us what you did at the Festival — how you went to find your father. He had great astonishment. He said you are a wonder. I need no other word."

"Cor … said that?" Chiara almost laughed. *He didn't seem that excited when he told me about it.*

"And, for what it's worth," Skipper interjected, drawing Chiara's gaze back to him, "I have known Cor his entire life. He would not hesitate for a moment to work as your catcher. He is one of the best catchers I have had the privilege to lead."

"Thank you, sir," Chiara said quietly. "I … appreciate that."

He isn't Isak.

"Of course. All that remains is your solemn pledge to Fhír. Are you ready?"

"Yes, sir."

Skipper gestured for them to rise, and the four of them stood. Mishkil's head and shoulders brushed against the tent roof.

Skipper lifted his voice. "Captains of Fhír," he announced in a clear voice. "You have before you a new recruit — Chiara Alteva, daughter of Torva Alteva of Belkar. Is it your intention to join our Clan?"

Chiara was trembling. "Yes. That is my intention."

"I call on the Captains as a witness." Skipper stepped forward. The words pounded against her like waves on a cliffside. "Raise your right hand, and answer 'I am.'"

Chiara nodded. *This is it … this is it.* The plummet — free-falling through air. Her heartbeat was roaring in her ears.

"Are you willing to be trained in the techniques of combat, performance, and espionage, following orders, trusting your Captains, and employing your Gift, your mind and your will, to the mission of Fhír?"

"I am." *Your Gift … what Gift?*

"Are you willing to live among us as a fellow Clanmate, companion in food and drink, during travel and fight, in street and on stage, lending your shoulder to all our labors?"

"I am," she repeated, more loudly this time.

"Are you willing to sacrifice, if necessary, all that is rightfully yours, should this mission so require it?"

All that is rightfully mine …

"I am."

"Chiara Alteva, our mission is twofold: protect the innocent; combat the Arsonists. You have pledged to uphold that mission. Do the Captains accept her pledge?"

"We accept," Mishkil and Talia echoed back.

Skipper nodded. "Very well. Chiara, you are now a clanmate of Fhír, dedicated to our mission in life and in death."

Life and death … life and death …

It was done. Chiara lowered her hand and took a shuddering breath.

Something like fatherly pride had appeared in Skipper's face. "Welcome to the Clan. Captains, dismissed!" He bowed, and Chiara returned it.

Mishkil clapped her gently on the shoulder, and Talia clasped her hand, eyes shining.

"Come," said Skipper. "I will show you out." He went to the door of the tent and held open the flap for her.

He paused just as they came outside. "Chiara … I know you are worried about the duo act. But your father said to tell you this: 'The fire in you will always be stronger than what haunts you.'"

What haunts you— Chiara's head jerked up. Her heart was thundering in her chest. *Did Dad tell him—?*

But Skipper was already talking. "Cor will find you a weapon. Zelie will show you your things and help make you comfortable. If you need anything, just ask." For the first time that day, he smiled.

"Thank you, sir." Chiara blinked in the noon sunlight, watching him reenter the tent.

It's done. Belkar was over. Fhír was beginning.

Isak, I wish you were here.

8

As soon as Chiara left the tent, she spotted Cor sitting on the open back of one of the nearby wagons. He was tapping some kind of stick on his thigh. She began heading his way, and he leapt to his feet when he saw her.

"How'd it go?" he asked excitedly as she walked up to him.

A smile broke across her face. "I'm in."

Cor's face lit up. "Amazing! See, I was right! They wanted you!"

He whirled the stick in the air, and Chiara saw that it was actually a long knife in a sheath. "So, what's your act?"

She let out a slow breath. *Moment of truth.* "Trapeze. I'm … your new flier."

"Yes!" Cor leapt to his feet, throwing a tattooed arm in the air. "Finally! I can't wait to get started! It's going to be the best — I just know it!" His dimple was practically dancing on his cheek.

"Yeah …" Chiara forced a smile. *It should be the best, shouldn't it?* It was a second chance at life — the life she'd always wanted.

But not at the cost of erasing Isak. *I'm here because of him. I can't ever let go of that.*

Which meant that Cor couldn't be part of her past.

"Are you okay?" Cor asked.

"Fine, just … nervous." She decided to change the subject. "So, you're supposed to be giving me a weapon?"

"Right!" He unsheathed the knife he was holding and held out the hilt. "This is yours."

Chiara took it with a frown, examining it. A ten-inch kitchen knife, blunt on one side, with a wooden handle.

"A sax?" She looked up at Cor. "You actually use this to fight with? I've only seen these used as kitchen knives …"

"We use them for both," Cor explained. "I mean, most of us use other weapons, too, but everyone without claws gets one of these. It helps with hunting and camping and stuff. Have you used them before?"

Chiara tried not to laugh. Memories of Mum's kitchen with its rows of sharpened saxes drew out a smile. "Yes. Just … not for fighting, exactly." *Not real fighting, anyway.* "Rothgar — he was my mentor — he's a melee fighter. He taught me some hand-to-hand combat. We used saxes sometimes."

She and Isak always got in trouble for stealing Mum's saxes to practice with Zelie. Eventually, Isak convinced Rothgar to teach them, since Rothgar knew melee fighting. But the old Tegid agreed only on the condition that they wouldn't ask him to teach them lethal moves.

"Wow." Cor lifted his eyebrows. "A melee fighter? And he was your mentor?"

Chiara shrugged. "Unusual case."

"Well, he sounds like an amazing mentor. How long have you been doing that with him?"

"Ten years."

Cor whistled. "Impressive. Well, that's good to know. You'll have to spar with Crovus sometime. He's one of our horse trainers — he's taught most of us hand-to-hand."

"Oh … okay," Chiara said slowly. "That sounds … fun …" *Squaring up with an expert?* She didn't love that idea.

"It'll be great," Cor grinned. "He can teach you every lethal technique there is. Not cheerful, but it's an occupational necessity. Here."

He handed her the sheath. "Strap it onto your belt — nope, not your hip — the front of your waist — sharp side up — there you go."

Chiara fingered the knife at her waist. It rested across her abdomen, running from hip to hip. She'd never needed to carry one around permanently before. *This feels … different.*

Not pretend. Not anymore. This was real.

"If you don't like it in front, you can always switch it around to the back," Cor suggested. "That's what I do." He drummed tattooed hands on his thighs, and then his face brightened. "You know, if you want, *I* can teach you some things."

"Oh … sure, I guess."

"Any other weapons?" Cor asked.

"Well … Dad taught me how to shoot a pistol. But I'm out of practice." Truthfully, Chiara hadn't fired a pistol in almost three years. But she didn't feel the need to mention that.

"That's fine," Cor said quickly. "We don't use pistols that often, anyway. They're not much good in a fire — hard to tell what you're hitting." He scanned her with a critical eye. "Let's try a short sword for you."

"A short sword?" Chiara tried not to sound skeptical. "I don't know—"

"Don't worry!" Cor turned and climbed farther into the wagon, rummaging around. "It's just a longer sax. You won't have to change too much. I can teach you that, too."

He clambered back out and handed her another longer weapon, about twenty inches from pommel to tip.

Chiara took it reluctantly. "I'm not sure …"

Cor must have heard the hesitation in her voice. "Too soon? Alright, we'll wait on that. We should probably assess your fighting style first, anyway."

He took it back and tossed it into the wagon. "So, you've got your standard-issue sax, and we can start training as soon as tomorrow. Now all we're waiting on is Zelie. She was supposed to set up your bedding and hammock and things."

"Are you sure we can trust her?" Chiara attempted a joke, but her face warmed slightly. "I mean, she's already pulled something funny …" She picked at the loose shirtsleeves.

"Oh — true," and Cor gave a sheepish laugh. "She, uh … knows better than to take my hammock, if that's what you mean."

"I'm sorry about her," Chiara sighed. "She's a troublemaker, but it's mostly harmless. She means well …" She trailed off.

"Believe me, I know." Cor cleared his throat. "Seriously, please don't worry about it. I don't care if you don't."

Chiara shook her head. "I don't care."

"So, you and Zelie … you're pretty close, I'm guessing?" Cor looked at her curiously.

"Yeah. We grew up together." Chiara smiled a little. "We met when she was a kitten and I was a cub. We've been friends …" *Can I say our whole lives? What about the last three years?* "… pretty much our whole lives," she finished. "I … missed her a lot when she joined you."

"I bet." Cor smiled. "Are you sure you weren't a little relieved, though? You sent all the trouble to us!"

Chiara had to laugh. "What about you, then? When did you join?"

Cor looked away, drumming his fingers on the wagon bed. "A while ago. I was … pretty young. My aunt knew Skipper. She's the reason I'm here." He didn't say anything else.

There's more to that story … Chiara decided not to press it. *He might press back.* And she knew she wouldn't answer.

He can keep his secrets.

"I'm here! I'm here!" Zelie panted behind them, interrupting the awkward silence. She pulled at Chiara's hand with a smile. "I set up your hammock next to where I sleep! Come see!"

෬

Zelie had strung the hammock between two maples, right above the twisted roots, where a bed of leaves was already gathered — her own nest.

She clucked admiringly at Chiara's new knife. "Oh, he gave you one of the nicer ones. That was sweet of him."

"Yeah … a lot sweeter than you giving me his clothes!" Chiara turned on her, hands on hips. "What were you *thinking?*"

"My clothes wouldn't fit you!" Zelie protested, trying to look innocent. "You know that!"

But Chiara could see the glint in her eyes. "You're the absolute worst!" She swatted out at her. "I'm trying to make a good impression here!"

Zelie danced out of reach. "*You* broke his nose within five minutes of meeting him," she shot back. "Good impressions can only go up from there!"

"Yeah, and it doesn't need help from you!" Chiara decided not to mention that she'd be Cor's new flier. Not just yet, anyway. *No need to add fuel to* that *fire …*

◌

Chiara spent the rest of the day settling in. She went through the bag of clothes Zelie had given her, checking all of it carefully. None of it *looked* like Cor's, at least. Dried lavender sprigs had been folded into every piece — apparently that was Fhír's way of keeping clothes smelling fresh.

She played with the sax, getting used to its weight in her hands. It was fairly plain, without any engravings. But it was balanced and sharp. Zelie was right — it was a well-made knife.

Isak would be so jealous. She almost smiled. After testing out the sheath both ways, she decided on keeping it at the small of her back. It was less in the way — although she had to practice a few times to reach back and grab it. *I guess I'll get used to it.*

Dinner that night was a jovial event. Most of Fhír was gathered around a handful of firepits, laughing, talking, eating together. The Beast-skins hunted and everyone else knew how to forage, so every meal was a group effort. Only a few people were missing — guards on patrol, keeping an eye on the surrounding woods.

At some point, Skipper called on Chiara to stand, and he introduced her as "our new flier."

For one horrible second, Chiara felt all eyes on her. Her face — her scar.

But then Cor sprang up beside her, and cheers and clapping brought her back to the present.

They … want me here. A slow, hesitant smile crept out, and Chiara sat down, flushing.

She didn't have a moment to enjoy it before Zelie gave a deafening squeal. "You're *partners?* And you didn't *tell me?*" She shook Chiara's arm vigorously.

Chiara winced. She glanced sideways at Cor, who offered her a sympathetic grimace.

Zelie flung her arms around Chiara in a tight hug. "I'm so proud of you!"

"Thanks …"

After dinner, most of Fhír came up to meet her. There was Lopia, the nimble female Tegid who performed object manipulation with Ludni and Milio. There were the stage-fighting experts — Rosc, a gruff-looking male Tegid, and Tara and Nadia, two beautiful female Nousk. The four Vikur from earlier introduced themselves individually now, each offering Chiara a handshake.

Then there was the rambunctious fire-summoning pair. Kojni was an Ensyth and Jarza was a Telk, and they were practically kids. Kojni introduced himself and Jarza with great pomp, and then tossed something into her campfire that turned the flames purple.

"Kojni, you scamp!" Cor reached out to swat the Ensyth, but the two of them were already scampering away, quickly joined by Ludni.

Cor shot them a thunderous glare before turning back to Chiara. "Sorry. They're a handful."

"That's fine." She did her best not to laugh at his perturbed expression.

Lastly were Ness and Arli, two of the four horse trainers. "Crovus is the third, and Tagg's the fourth," said Cor with a grin. "Tagg's also my spotter, and my best friend. He's the worst."

"Where is he?" Chiara asked, glancing around curiously.

"Oh, he's on guard duty right now, but you'll meet him tomorrow."

"Tomorrow?" She shot him a confused look.

"Yeah! When we begin practicing."

Her heart did a strange little flip in her chest. "Right … tomorrow."

That night, she lay in her hammock, Zelie's soft purring breaths rising from below, and she stared up at a crack of dark sky between the leaves. She'd tucked her sax by her side, and now she unsheathed it, running a finger along the metal.

Duo training began tomorrow.

Isak, I swear I'm not forgetting you.

He would've wanted her to do this. And still, guilt plagued her.

The sharp tip pricked her finger, drawing blood.

I swear I won't let you go.

〜

"Rise and shine!" Zelie's voice shattered through a cloud of deep sleep. Chiara shot upright, almost tumbling off the hammock. Her hand instinctively closed around the sax. She whipped it out, staring around wildly. The sky was still dark out.

"Arva!" Zelie yelped. "Why are you sleeping with that?"

Chiara blinked, eyes slowly adjusting to the dark. The Kithsa's alarmed face appeared a few inches away, eyes reflecting in the dark.

Chiara lowered her knife and rubbed a hand across her face. *Of course.* "Why are you startling me awake? It's barely light out!"

"I know! Perfect way to start your first day of training!"

"I emphatically disagree." Chiara let out a breath and sheathed her knife.

"Don't be a sourpuss! Here — I brought food." Zelie held up a satchel and twirled it around her wrist. "Fruit. Cured meat. And … well, you'll have to get your own water. I couldn't find my canteen."

Chiara disentangled herself carefully from her hammock and stepped out. The ground was damp under her feet. Cool air drifted past her, heavy with woodsmoke. She stretched stiff arms above her head, trying to shake the grogginess from her limbs.

"Come *on*!" Zelie skipped back and forth around her. "Eat your food!"

Chiara settled herself on a tree root, snatching the bag from Zelie's paw. "As long as it isn't a dead mouse."

"Oh, please. That was *one time*! And I was five! How was I supposed to know—"

"That *one time* scarred me for life!" Chiara shot back, trying her best to sound annoyed.

Zelie sniffed. "I am wildly underappreciated. I hope you're not so rude to Cor while you're training."

"As long as Cor doesn't bring me the bloody corpses of rodents, I'll be the nicest flier he's ever had." Chiara rolled her eyes.

"Mm … and the *cutest*!" Zelie cackled. "I bet he's happy about that!"

Chiara shot her a baffled look. "Did you get hit on the head or something? What in Arva is wrong with you?"

"What's wrong with *you*?" Zelie shot back accusingly. "Don't tell me you don't think he's cute!"

"I—" Cor's crooked dimple flashed through her head. "I have nothing to say about that," she finished shortly, biting into an apple.

"Oooo." Zelie's tail was flicking lazily from side to side. Never a good sign. "How delicious. He rescues you from a burning building — carries you to safety — guards your tent while you sleep—"

"While I was unconscious, you mean," Chiara corrected through bites of apple.

"Surely you dreamed of him!" Zelie warbled.

"You are delusional."

"And then — you awoke! Face to face at last with your rescuer!" Zelie sighed dramatically. "Surely you were swooning! Those hazel eyes are hard to resist! And that crooked smile—"

"You missed the part where I broke his nose," Chiara interrupted, "and the fact that he scared the living daylights out of me. What story are you even telling?"

"So you're telling me this is a romance between *rivals*?" Zelie crowed.

"Rivals? Why in Arva would we be *rivals*?"

"It's the perfect beginning!"

"Zelie. *Zelie.* Look at me." Chiara swallowed a mouthful of food and fixed her friend with a hard eye. "This is a terrible, terrible idea. This is worse than the dead snake."

"No it isn't!" Zelie protested. "This is even better than that! Mathew was just a poor test subject. I should've known he wouldn't appreciate you killing a snake." She sniffed haughtily.

"Zelie, *you* killed that snake. And Mathew was *ten*! Are you even surprised?"

"Yes! I can't believe he never spoke to you again." Zelie tsked. "Doesn't matter. You were too good for him, anyway. And Cor is so much cuter," she declared.

Chiara threw the apple core at her, and she yelped. "Fine! I'm leaving — but rest assured, this conversation isn't done yet. Finish up, you ingrate!" Then she trotted off into the woods.

Chiara snorted as she chewed on a piece of cured meat. *Leave it to Zelie to play matchmaker with someone I haven't even known for three days ...* not to mention someone who was her partner in a professional circus. *That's just a disaster waiting to happen.*

And no matter what Zelie said, Cor was still Tegid. Tegids didn't marry Stunted.

Chiara's lips twisted wryly. *I suppose that's my saving grace. What a consolation.* Standing, she tossed the satchel into her hammock and began heading toward the stream.

ᘓ

"Morning!" Cor walked up behind Chiara just as she finished washing her face in the water.

She flicked the dampness from her cheeks, fingers sliding over the raised scars. "Morning," she sighed, standing up. "Barely." The sun was up now, but the air was still cool, and there were still stars overhead.

She squinted tiredly at Cor. He was dressed in loose pants and a sleeveless practice top that left his tattoos on full display. He was carrying a large bag on his shoulders. He looked perfectly well-rested — another benefit of Tegid regeneration.

"You look chipper," she muttered. "So … where do we practice when we're …" She gestured around them. "… out here? Not much gym equipment." *I am really not thrilled about this.*

He laughed. "True. Well, you and I can't do as much as everyone else, but there are a few things we can still do out here. Come on. There's this great spot we found farther upstream …"

After almost a mile of walking, they reached it. A sandy clearing, sprawling out beneath a short cliff, split in two by a tumbling channel of water — the source of the stream. Cliff and clearing were framed by towering oaks, their branches interlaced in a web of foliage.

Some of the oaks were dead, almost completely stripped of their bark. Hanging from a few of the limbs were trapeze riggings.

Chiara froze in her tracks. "Oh, no. Absolutely not."

"What's wrong?" Cor dropped his bag at the edge of the sandy patch and pulled out hand wraps. "Here." He tossed a set to Chiara.

She didn't even unwrap them. "You practice on *trees?* Are you—" She bit off the word *insane. Dad, what were you thinking?!*

Cor nodded emphatically. "Sure! Remember Oxys and Mykzi? Arguing over the wagon? They designed those. They do most of our equipment. They've never failed me yet."

What even …? Chiara rubbed the palms of her hands in her eyes. "Sure. Okay. Why not?"

"Plus, don't forget we've got Tagg!" Cor added. "He's been my spotter for years."

Chiara began winding the wraps around her knuckles in a daze. *I'm going to die out here.*

If she could go back to the previous day, she'd run into the tent with Skipper and yell at herself, "Don't do it!" But it was too late for that now.

Here goes nothing. "So … what are we doing today?" she asked, feigning calm. Every limb was tingling.

"Just a warmup routine. No bars today. Pretend like it's any other day at the gym. What do you normally do?"

No bars. *Thank Arva.* "Um, normally …" Chiara listed off her routine on her fingers. "Cardio, upper body, core work, flexibility stretches …"

"Great." Cor gestured to the sandy space. "Have at it. I told Tagg to show up in an hour — he's your catcher, too, now, so you should probably meet him at some point."

All of it put Chiara on edge. Working out in the woods; conditioning with someone else; trapeze bars in *trees* … but the strangest part was that it wasn't Isak next to her.

She knew Isak, and she knew training alone, but *this* …? *What have I gotten myself into?*

Cor kept up an almost steady stream of conversation. Of course, he could — he was barely out of breath after an hour.

Me, on the other hand … Chiara could manage a few monosyllabic answers, but not much else. *That's probably for the best. Fewer questions.*

"So," Cor grunted from his plank position. "You trained for duo and solo trapeze both? You said Rothgar is a melee fighter, right? How did he teach you trapeze?"

He didn't. Isak did. "Like I said … unusual case," Chiara panted. Her abdomen felt like it was on fire. Normally she wasn't in so much pain so soon. *It's been way too long since my last workout.*

"How's that?"

"Academy … kicked me out. Rothgar … took me in. I … taught myself."

Technically, that was true. She *had* taught herself … for the past three years.

"You *taught yourself?*" Cor asked, sounding shocked. "And they kicked you out anyway? What a load of horse manure! You're clearly a natural!"

"What?" *That* took Chiara by surprise. She collapsed to the ground, gasping for breath. Sand stuck to her damp limbs.

She propped herself up on her forearms, looking at him carefully. "What makes you say I'm a natural?" *Did Zelie say something? Or Dad?*

"I—" Cor pressed his mouth shut, looking suddenly embarrassed. "Well … when Fhír was at your gym … one night, I heard someone yell, so I came out to the balcony, and … there you were."

That night in the gym. The night she'd fallen and turned her ankle.

Chiara looked away. *He saw that? And he's calling me a natural?*

She got to her feet, dusting off her pants. "If you saw me there, then you know I botched the landing."

She began walking toward the stream.

"You were reaching for a catcher."

That stopped her short. *Not now. Not like this. I don't want to do this …*

Footsteps crunched through the sand as Cor walked up behind her. "Zelie said you were solo for three years. How long were you a flier?"

Chiara didn't turn around. "Five years." That much was true. She'd had formal training … until they kicked her out. *But I'm not, anymore. I'm not.*

She never was, really. Only because Isak taught her, and that was breaking every rule in the books.

She began to walk forward again.

"Wait." Cor ran in front of her, putting himself between her and the stream. "Five years? You were a flier for *five years?*"

"Yeah? What about it?" She shot him a cautious glance.

Cor was shaking his head. "It's just — your jump was incredible. I definitely would've guessed that you've been a flier for longer …"

Chiara pressed her lips together. *He's going to guess.* "I appreciate the compliment," she said quietly.

It was bad enough not being with Isak. *If he keeps bringing this up, we can't do this together.* She kicked a boot irritably through the sand.

"Hullo. Am I interrupting something here?" said a gruff voice from behind.

Chiara spun around. Standing there scowling at her was the tallest Jeka she'd ever seen. He was easily two or three heads above her, with mottled beige-yellow skin and large, rabbit-like ears that drooped down onto his shoulders. His clothes hung oddly on his narrow frame.

"Hey, Tagg!" Cor jogged past Chiara and clapped the Jeka on the shoulder. Even he looked absurdly short next to his friend. "Chiara, meet your new spotter!"

"Hullo, Chiara. I see you've met our resident basket case," Tagg said without missing a beat. "Arguing already? On your first day of practice?" He had a clipped accent, with tall vowels and swallowed "R's." His face seemed set in a permanent frown.

Chiara glanced at Cor. "Didn't you say he was a Telk?"

"I am." Tagg held out a hand, and Chiara saw the double thumbs.

She took his hand, astonished. "Nice … to meet you … You're a doua, too?"

"Yep. Helps with spotting." He had a strong, stiff grip. "What's Cor done this time?"

"Nothing." Chiara shot a sideways glance at Cor. "We were just … talking about my experience."

"Talking? Or arguing?" Tagg's ears twitched. He examined Chiara with mud-brown eyes. "I'm hearing a bally lot of buzzing."

Chiara eyed him cautiously. *How much can he hear?* Jeka weren't allowed to read thoughts directly without permission. But … that didn't mean they couldn't guess.

"Whoa! Easy, there, mate." Tagg held up both hands. "I can't tell exactly what you're thinking. But I can still hear the noise, and your thoughts are"—he waved a finger toward her head—"rather tense."

"It's … nothing, really." Chiara looked away, cracking her knuckles. "We were just talking about how I was a flier."

"The best flier I've ever seen," Cor interjected.

"Really?" Tagg gave Chiara a reassessing look. "He tell you about his idea for the Riften performance?"

"The what?" Chiara asked.

"Not yet," said Cor. "The First Harvest Festival at Riften. It's happening in a few weeks, and I had a routine for us."

"A few weeks?" Chiara's head began to spin. They'd just been paired together, and now they were supposed to be planning a professional performance?

Solo performance would've been another story. But … *A few weeks to rewrite everything with Isak?*

"We can't do that," she said shortly. "Duo acts take a while to practice. And I *just* met you."

Cor looked at her with surprise. "Why not? I wouldn't suggest it if I wasn't completely confident in your abilities. You're extremely talented."

Chiara narrowed her eyes.

Tagg's scowl grew deeper. "Oo. That was a lot. Whatever *this* is"—he pointed to the two of them—"you need to figure it out. Duo act or no. Trapeze bars don't have room for you *and* your problems."

Chiara pressed her lips together. Tagg was right. There was no room on the bars for distraction.

I want to do this. And I don't want to lose Isak. But where would she even begin to explain all that?

So … she decided not to. "Well … I could give it a shot."

"That's the spirit." Tagg nodded approvingly. "And don't mind him, eh?" he said, leaning in with a look at Cor. "He can get a bit ahead of himself sometimes."

"Hey!" Cor protested.

"Keep your shirt on, mate." Tagg rolled his eyes. "He's not a bad chap. Just a little enthusiastic sometimes. Learned that the hard way when he dropped me."

"I never—!" Cor sputtered in disbelief.

"Liar," Tagg cut in immediately. "He did," he added to Chiara. "Don't worry, though — he never did it again."

"Oh, for Arva's sake!" Cor threw his hands in the air. "We were *six years old*, and it happened *once!* How many times—?"

"You broke my arm," Tagg interrupted.

"It was a *fracture!*" Cor yelled. He looked more annoyed than Chiara had ever seen him. She had to fight the urge to laugh.

"Doesn't matter. A bone's a bone." Tagg crossed his arms, which looked perfectly fine and not-broken. "Sorry you got stuck with this knucklehead." He made a face at Cor, who returned it promptly. "Word to the wise — don't let him drop you. You might end up friends for life."

Chiara lifted her eyebrows at Cor. "So you broke his arm? That's how you know each other?"

"Yep." Tagg's frown lessened somewhat. "First time we met. Idiot wanted me to be a flier so he could practice catching."

"Sounds like you're both idiots," Chiara snorted. "Why'd you agree to it?"

"Eh." Tagg shrugged. "It was a slow day."

"Alright, enough backstory." Cor looked flushed and irritated. "We have to practice."

"Oh, no." Chiara folded her arms. "He just told me your origins as a catcher. You *dropped* him! You really want me to do a duo act with you after that?" She lifted an eyebrow.

Tagg's frown broke for the first time as he gave a short, barking laugh. "I like her!" He clapped Chiara on the shoulder. "You're alright, mate."

9

They didn't practice any moves that first day. Instead, Cor hung upside down from one of the low bars, and Chiara held onto his arms, while Tagg stood a few feet in front of them, calling instructions.

"Chiara, lift your legs parallel to the ground. Now Cor, you lift up … and hold … and down … good. Again … good."

It was strange, dangling there with her arms stretched above her head, muscles aching. Cor's hands were rough and calloused against her skin. His grip was incredibly strong, but not painful.

Like Isak's.

"Okay, now Cor, lift Chiara up — Chiara, inch your hands up to his shoulders … there. Good."

Cor's muscles were hard and tight beneath Chiara's fingertips. The green of his tattoos hovered in the corner of her vision.

"Bally good, you two. Now, Cor, lower Chiara to the ground. Chiara, do a plank position. Great. Now, I'm going to lift you …"

Chiara gasped, arms twitching as some unseen force pulled her from the grass.

"Now, Cor, hands around her waist. I'm letting go in three … two … one …"

Nothing changed. Cor gripped her firmly. She held her body out stiffly, trying not to think about the feel of his hands on her waist.

This isn't Isak … this isn't Isak.

The idea of doing a new routine turned her stomach. What was more uncomfortable? Starting over with a catcher who wasn't Isak? Or starting over with a catcher who was very much like Isak?

"Easy, Chiara," Tagg called. "Stay focused."

Another benefit of a Telk-Jeka combo. Tagg could hear the mental noise, so he could always tell when one of them was losing focus. And he never missed a beat.

They did much of the same — hanging, holds, even a small spin or two — before Tagg was finally satisfied. "I've got a feel for both of you now," he said afterward. "But you'll need more of a feel for each other. We need to do this at least an hour every day."

A feel for each other. Chiara's heart twitched in her chest. *I'm glad Zelie isn't here.*

And still … *This isn't Isak.* Cor was strong, like Isak. But not the same. He was bigger, more solid. *I don't like this …*

Then Chiara and Tagg practiced lifting. Only this time, Chiara would stand still, a few feet away from Tagg, and then he would hold out both arms, and then Chiara would feel that same invisible tug on her body, and then she would slowly begin to levitate.

Which was totally normal and not terrifying at all.

"Doing fine?" Tagg would ask once her feet were on the ground again.

"The adrenaline rush … could kill an elephant," she'd gasped once.

Tagg only chuckled. "Let's try it again."

They practiced with him standing in front of her, and then behind her, and then she stood on her hands and they practiced it all over again. By noon, Tagg had her climbing up a tree and jumping from the lowest branch.

He caught her every time.

Cor watched, every now and then giving a shout of encouragement. "I told you he's the best!" he exclaimed proudly.

By noon, Tagg was panting and sweaty. He hadn't moved his own body around much, but telekinesis on two other people must have been draining. Still, he seemed satisfied … or at least, his frown was fairly light. "Well done, Chiara."

"That was great!" Cor exclaimed, offering a hand to Chiara. She whacked it, hoping she looked more excited than she felt.

"Maybe we could try some moves tomorrow?" There was a hopeful look on his face.

Chiara's stomach tightened. "Um …"

Tagg interrupted. "Alright, alright." He wiped sweat from his forehead and shot a glance at Cor. "Figure that out later. Don't you have somewhere to be?"

Cor made a face. "Yeah … I've got guard patrol. I'll catch you later!" He waved and jogged off.

Chiara shook her head. The last-minute save added to her adrenaline from the last jump.

"What do you think?" Tagg said, turning to her.

"What do I think?" she repeated, feeling her pulse rushing through her body.

Air streaming past her face, ground rushing up to meet her; then suddenly suspended in midair a few feet above impact.

I can actually fly now.

"I … never thought I'd be able to do this," she said quietly. "No matter how good I am, nobody would ever take the risk. And now …" She trailed off, gazing up at the trees around them. *I always, always wanted this. More than anything.*

But it would cost her. All the routines, all the patterns, the years of sweat and tears and triumphant cheers with Isak …

Tagg played with his water canteen, screwing and unscrewing the cap. "But …?" he prompted.

She pressed her lips together and attempted a look of ignorance. "But what?"

He lifted an eyebrow. "Something else is going on in there." He pointed to her head and wiggled his droopy rabbit ears. "You don't wanna do a duo act. Is that it?"

Chiara looked away. "Well …" She tried to think of something plausible. Vague, but true enough that a Jeka wouldn't question it. "It's … been a while since I've been a flier. And I'm not sure … I'm ready."

Tagg nodded. "Trust is a two-way street, mate. You have to take a chance on Cor, too."

Chiara twisted her hands together uncomfortably. *Take a chance … take a chance …*

"Your first time as a flier …" Tagg began, and Chiara's shoulders tensed.

He must have noticed; he went on slowly. "Why did you take that jump?"

Because it was Isak.

"I … trusted him," Chiara whispered at last.

"Is that why you won't take it now?"

"I …" She rubbed her hands across her face, feeling the grit of dust and sweat. "I … don't know."

"Well, for what it's worth, trust takes time." Tagg tilted his head up to look at the sky. "I dunno what's going on in your head — and you don't have to tell me. But my grain of wisdom is, you should probably sort it out. Sooner rather than later."

The bar doesn't have extra room for your problems.

He stood, stretched, and offered her a hand. "Come on. Let's get food."

ଓଃ

The noon hour, and the hour after that, were filled with camp chores. Even under the tree cover, the day was hot, so Fhír didn't practice any circus acts around noon. Instead, they cleaned clothes and gear, tidied up the tents, collected firewood, foraged, and slept.

That was how Chiara met Bakhita. She'd just gone back to her hammock with a pile of clean clothes when she spotted a large shape sprawled out a few feet into the trees, emitting soft, rumbling snores.

It wasn't large enough to be a Dwyn, but it seemed too large to be a Tegid. Chiara took a few tentative steps forward and had to clamp a hand over her mouth so she wouldn't gasp aloud. It was a Kithsa — an Exotic Kithsa. A female lion-skin.

Her long, serpentine tail twitched in the grass, fighting away the gnats. Honey-colored fur ran up her arms and legs, deepening to a bronze around her neck and head, and her face was dark.

"That's Bakhita!" Zelie whispered from her spot under Chiara's hammock.

"You have a lion-skin?" Chiara spun around, eyes wide. "How did I not meet her at dinner?"

"She was on duty last night. You can introduce yourself later."

Chiara didn't feel like napping after that. Of course, Bakhita was a clanmate now. But the idea of resting so close to claws and teeth that large … She was reluctant to get too close. It was the same way with the Dwyn.

She decided to put her sax to some use and began whittling in the shade.

About midafternoon, Cor came to find her. He was holding a pair of long wooden sticks. "Practice with Crovus! If you're up to it." He noticed the stick in her hands. "What did you make?"

"A whistle. Well, I tried, anyway." Chiara tossed it into the grass. "I'm not very good at whittling." Isak made the best whistles, but she never could get them quite right.

She stood up and sheathed her sax. "Where do I go?"

"Behind the tents. That big grassy space."

They began walking side by side around the outside of the tents.

"So … listen, about earlier, you did great." Cor sounded excited.

"Thanks," Chiara murmured. She didn't look at him.

"Why were you worried about the routine?"

Please, don't press it … She shook her head. "Just … not a lot of time to adjust."

"I guess that makes sense." He paused. "For what it's worth, we're already off to a good start. I have a lot of confidence in us."

"Thanks …" Chiara glanced around at the empty grass as they arrived. "He isn't here yet?"

"Oh." Cor frowned. "I bet he's on guard patrol. He'll be back in a few minutes, I think." A glint came into his eye. "But while we're waiting … do you want to spar together?"

Sparring wasn't trapeze. Sparring was different. It was technique, and precision, and focus. Chiara liked sparring.

"I'm game," she said with a smile.

Cor tossed her one of the sticks, and she gave him a confused look. "Just sticks? No saxes?" She twisted the stick in her hands. It was hard, cured wood, smooth with long use.

Cor winced. "After what you did to my face? No thanks. A stick is fine enough for now. You can use your sax on some other victim." He slid his foot back in a fighting stance and gave her a wicked grin. "Don't hold back. You ready?"

"Am I ever." Chiara rolled her shoulders back and slipped into a defensive stance. "You'd better not go easy on me."

◌

He didn't. After one round, Chiara had four new bruises. She was spared a second beating when Crovus the horse-trainer appeared with a shout. "Coren! Ya scamp!"

Crovus, as it turned out, was a wizened Ensyth who sported a white walrus mustache and donkey-like ears, with an attitude to match. His only volume was loud. "Nice of ya to join us! Seeing how you've got nothing better to do, how 'bout ya help me teach the lady some skills?"

The rest of the afternoon passed in a blur of sweat and grass and sore limbs. It wasn't just the workout from that morning; it was the bruises. By the end of several bouts of sparring, Chiara was the not-so-happy bearer of several ugly purple marks scattered across her arms and legs.

When they finally called it quits, she practically collapsed with relief. But she'd gotten in a few good blows, and Cor seemed impressed. "Not bad!" he muttered.

Then Crovus stumped up to them. "Sloppy. Inconsistent. Poor defense," he snapped.

Chiara's face burned. *I didn't think I was that bad.*

Then he leaned in and looked her in the eye. "As for *you*, Chiara … not bad." He sniffed fiercely through his mustache.

Chiara could feel Cor stiffen next to her, but his only response was, "Yes, sir."

"Do better next time," Crovus barked at him. "Now, get outta here. Go take a wash." Cor threw a salute and loped off.

"Now." Crovus sniffed again. "Here's my thoughts. You've a quick eye and a good defense. But ya hesitate. Ya don't strike unless ya know ya can make it."

Chiara glanced at him, startled. *Isak used to say the exact same thing.*

"Is … that a problem? Sir?" she asked cautiously.

"Problem! I'll say so!" Crovus huffed through his mustache. "It could getcha killed out there. Ya got good form, but street fighting ain't about form. It's about life and death."

Life and death. Tingles ran down Chiara's arms. She'd sparred thousands of times with Isak, and not once was it about life and death. "Sir, Cor said I needed to learn … lethal combat."

Crovus nodded with another stern sniff. "That ya do. I'll teach ya myself. But ya got a bad habit of waiting for the perfect moment. We gotta break that. No perfect moments when ya fight. This ain't like performing. Ya gotta keep yer head on straight and take the risks as they come."

branded

So … exactly the opposite of the trapeze artist mindset. "Great," Chiara sighed as Crovus turned and kept walking. "That should be easy."

☙

By the end of the first week, she and Cor were up in the air on the highest trapeze bar. Tagg wanted them to just practice swinging. "Get used to each other. You'll be up there a lot."

Chiara's heart was pounding in double-time. And it wasn't just because of Tagg's telekinesis lifting her up to where Cor was already hanging. It was something else.

The first time. Five years old. Grabbing Isak's hands as he hung upside down. *I promise to catch you.*

"Oi, Chiara! You good, mate?" Tagg called.

"Fine … fine …" she called back, trying to narrow her thoughts. *Focus … focus on the swing … the pull …*

And then Cor's hands locked around her wrists, and suddenly she was up in the air, swinging, connected for the first time in three years to another living body.

Just him, and her. The world sharpened, and narrowed, and came down to one painfully clear point.

Fingers clasped around wrists.

One … two … three …

"Just keep swinging!" Tagg called.

Back … forth … back … forth … the tug of gravity in her feet; weightless everywhere else. It was intoxicating …

… Chiara closed her eyes.

And her body moved of its own accord—

"Chiara!" Cor yelled as her hands slipped from his, and for one horrible moment she was grasping at air, gravity yawning beneath her—

—and then Tagg caught her. He brought her carefully back to earth.

"You alright?" He was scowling darkly. "What happened up there?"

Chiara almost couldn't hear him, her heart was thundering so loudly in her ears. "I lost focus," she gasped, clutching at her chest. Her body felt hollow.

Cor climbed down and came over. His face was sheet white. "What was that?" He stared at her, wide-eyed.

"I … I lost focus." Chiara shuddered, rubbing her hands over her eyes.

Tagg was shaking his head. "Let's break for now. Pick up tomorrow."

"Cor, I'm sorry," she said as they began walking back to camp.

"You almost — I couldn't …" He didn't finish.

Chiara saw that his hands were shaking. She wanted, more than anything, to promise that it wouldn't happen again.

But she couldn't promise.

She knew what she'd done.

That was Isak's routine. He was gone … but her muscles still remembered.

ʘ

Days blurred together until Chiara had been living with Fhír for almost three weeks. Every hour was defined by routine. Wake up; breakfast; conditioning and practice with Tagg; lunch; rest and chores at noon. Then, in the afternoon, sparring with Crovus, camp chores, and dinner.

Crovus apparently thought that Cor and Chiara were well-matched. He had them spar together daily. His compliment on the first day must have been an anomaly — he wasn't interested in sparing Chiara's feelings any longer. He corrected her gruffly, chastised her for mistakes, and insisted that she strike every blow hard enough to kill.

It was like Rothgar all over again.

Chiara didn't realize how much she missed it. *I wonder what it would be like if the two of them met.* Either they'd kill each other or they'd get along famously.

Most nights, once dinner was finished, one of the Kithsa would take her out into the woods to practice stealth tracking or foraging. Whenever Zelie couldn't make it, Leo or Fleur stepped in, or Bakhita — who turned out to be tranquil and even-tempered, belying her lithe muscles and terrible claws. Between day training and evening training, Chiara was asleep at night before her head hit the hammock.

The only consistent measure of time seemed to be the steadily growing collection of bruises, scrapes, and sprains throughout her body. She spent a lot of her noon rest in the infirmary tent, getting patched up by Talia.

It wasn't a total waste of time. Talia was an excellent multitasker and taught Chiara about salves, ointments, tinctures, and all kinds of makeshift remedies.

"Of course, the infirmary at a proper town is best," and Talia would click her tongue. "They have many more supplies. But we make do." She and Chiara compared notes between Nani's instructions and Talia's own experience, and Chiara was surprised to find how much Nani knew about healing, despite never having needed it herself.

"This matriarch, she taught you well," Talia said approvingly. "I am glad of this."

"Thanks. Me too." Chiara traced a finger along a newly applied bandage. Her throat was suddenly tight.

I wonder what Nani's doing right now. If she knew that Chiara had joined the circus without her, she'd have an absolute fit. *I wonder how they're doing now … I wish I could send a message.*

But what would she even put in it? The rescue? The training? There was enough for pages and pages …

But she didn't need pages for what she really wanted to say.

I love you. I'm sorry …

"You miss them, no?" Talia's eyes were gentle. "I am sure they are proud of you."

"I hope so," Chiara murmured.

◌

By the end of three weeks, she was more than exhausted. At the gymnasium, Rothgar had worked her hard physically, but being part of Fhír was testing her mental capacity.

Especially when it came to Cor. They were trying to learn his choreography for the Riften performance, but Chiara couldn't seem to rewrite the old patterns and habits she'd learned. Isak had been gone for three years, but he was still engrained in her muscle memory.

And when push came to shove … she didn't want to unlearn that. Not at all.

The incident during the first week was only a taste of what would come. Every time she got on the bar, she felt like she was splitting in two. She was living her dream … and losing the last shreds of what had kept Isak alive.

Every time she was up in the air, her instinct was still to close her eyes … feel Isak there, as though it was just the same.

But it wasn't.

Cor was taller. Bigger. He held her differently. His body moved differently. And every time she closed her eyes—

"Chiara! Focus!" Tagg's shout sliced through her haze.

Her hands twitched — she was clawing at air — and then Cor snatched her around the wrists, yanking her arms.

She felt bricks in her stomach — the horrible, halting feeling of stumbling just at the lip of a cliff.

"Cor, let her go!" Tagg shouted. "I'm taking her down."

Chiara heard Cor exhale heavily above her. But he didn't say a word. After three weeks of blunders, he still hadn't said a word.

Tagg brought her down to the grass. "What's going on?"

"Lost focus," Chiara muttered. Then Cor dismounted the tree, and she turned as he walked toward them.

Chiara was already bracing herself.

This time, he was angry. "Okay, what was *that*? Every time we're up in the air, it's like we're on point, and then a few minutes later, it completely falls apart! What's going on with you?"

Chiara bristled. "Nothing's going on with me! I'm trying my best, okay? This isn't easy!"

Cor folded his arms. "That's not an answer. But let's see if I've got one for you. You used to have a lighter catcher, didn't you?"

He's gonna find out … he's gonna find out … "What difference does that make?" Chiara glared at him. "You're the catcher! Why are you letting go?"

"Don't give me that!" Cor glared right back at her. "This goes both ways, Chiara! If you're releasing, I *need* to know about it. We each need to know exactly what the other is thinking."

"Oh, really?" She was hot and tired and sweaty, and there was no point snapping at him. But she didn't care. "Do we? How about you tell me who *your* last flier was. Let's start there."

"I haven't *had* a consistent flier!"

"Oh — that explains it." It was a completely unfair thing to say. *I don't care.* "I was wondering why you were so stiff up there. Is three weeks not enough time for you?"

Cor drew back, anger flickering in his eyes. "That's not the problem!"

"So what's the problem, then?"

Cor opened his mouth and then checked himself. "Something's distracting you. Tagg said so himself." He was clearly holding back a much longer tirade.

Chiara turned a black look on Tagg. Cor looked at him, too. "Tagg?"

But Tagg was shaking his head, so hard his ears flopped over his shoulders. "Oh, no. I'm not solving this for you. Here's an idea: tell each other the truth. You're not gonna get anywhere before you do."

He jabbed a finger up at the empty trapeze set. "Bar's only got room for you *or* your problems, not both. You figure it out. I'll wait." He swung on his heel and stalked over to sit beneath one of the trees.

Chiara swiveled back to Cor. "Well? You heard him! What's the truth?"

"You won't like it."

"I already don't like it!" Her hands were becoming warm.

"Fine!" Cor huffed. "You're distracted. We're screwing up on the bars because you can't get out of your head. I don't know who you trained with before, but he's not me and I'm not him, so stop reliving that routine!"

Chiara drew back, tears stinging her eyes. "No. You're not like him," she whispered. *Not at all.*

"Is that or is that not the truth?" Cor demanded.

"You want the truth?" Chiara stepped in, voice shaking. Heat was roiling in the pit of her stomach. "You wanna know why this isn't working? Because I don't trust you. *That's* the truth." She brushed past him and began marching off down the trail to camp.

10

The tension didn't lift for the rest of the day. Chiara did her best to avoid Cor. She watched Rosc, Tara, and Nadia practice their knife-throwing routine. She listened while Oxys and Mykzi had an argument about how to adjust the suspension on the wagons. She tried to listen while Kojni and Jarza attempted to teach her sign language. Of course, Jarza couldn't speak, and Kojni's explanations didn't help much, so by the end of their lesson, Chiara felt like she knew less than she had before.

Finally, she wandered out to the horses, stroking their glossy sides as they grazed quietly in the shade. They were used to her presence by now.

There were a few friendly nickers, and Toby, the inquisitive Clydesdale, came searching for treats.

"No, Toby," she murmured, rubbing his nose. "Not today." Toby was Crovus' horse, and probably the only creature who'd received a soft word from the grumpy Ensyth.

The other gelding, a Punch called Norik, lifted his head with a friendly snort, and Toby trotted back to his side. Nin the Shire horse lifted her head as Chiara walked past her toward Ria, who was grazing a little farther off.

Ria was a Gypsy Vanner, and she was Tagg's. Tagg had introduced her and Chiara during the third day of camp, after which Ria had promptly lifted her hoof to shake.

"She likes you," Tagg said, sounding pleasantly surprised. Chiara had visited her almost every day since.

Now, she stood by Ria's side, absentmindedly braiding her mane. "I know Tagg is right," she murmured. "And I shouldn't've yelled. But ..."

There was no in-between. Either she could hold on to the last thing she had left of Isak, or she could train with Cor. But she couldn't have both.

And she didn't want to choose.

I don't trust you.

"Do I have to trust him?" she murmured. "Does that mean I lose Isak? I don't have to tell him everything, right? We can still work together ..."

Ria nickered, sounding disheartened.

"It should be fine," Chiara said, more to herself than Ria. "It'll be fine."

It had to be fine. She was supposed to be sparring with Crovus and Cor in a few minutes. "See you later, pretty girl," she said, giving Ria a farewell pat.

☙

It was not fine.

As soon as their practice weapons connected, Chiara knew that Cor was still frustrated about earlier. He was saying less, attacking more.

For a second or two, she almost felt bad about yelling at him — and then he cracked her across the shin.

She stayed angry after that.

Crovus was irate with both of them. They were sloppier, more reckless, and, in Chiara's case, at least, so irritable that her mood was skewing her judgment.

They hadn't gone more than a few bouts when the training session came to an ignominious end. Chiara saw an opening and thrust forward, but she overstepped her reach. Cor trapped her arm and tugged her forward, and her ankle turned sharply beneath her.

"Ah!" She buckled with a pained cry, and only Cor's quick reflexes kept her from plunging face-first into the dirt.

"Chiara, are you okay? I'm sorry—"

"I'm fine! Just — get off me!" She struggled out of his grasp and stood upright, straightening her clothes. "I'm fine."

"Test yer ankle!" Crovus snapped. "That don't look so good."

As soon as Chiara stepped forward, her ankle gave out again, and she stumbled forward. Cor caught her and helped her to her feet, but she didn't meet his eyes.

"Agh." Crovus spit on the ground. "That's enough foolery for today. Only reason I don't send ya both running sprints is that ankle. Go see Talia."

"Yes, sir," Chiara managed through gritted teeth. Her ankle was throbbing. "Can you let me go now?" she muttered to Cor.

133

"Can you walk by yourself?" His voice was quiet. He sounded completely subdued now. "Do you need me to walk you back?"

"No. I'll be fine," she replied shortly. She refused to meet his eyes and began limping slowly away.

☙

"Hoo, hoo, *hoo!*" Zelie poked her head into Chiara's hammock with a playful grin on her face. "I heard we had a little lovers' spat this morning, hmm?"

Chiara sighed and put an arm over her face. Dinner was still half an hour away, and she wanted nothing more than to fall asleep and forget the entire morning. "Who told you?"

"Oh, honey," Zelie clucked, crawling up into the tree above. "Nobody needed to tell me. Practically the whole forest heard you two."

"Ugh … really?" Chiara rubbed her hands across her face. *That's just great …*

"No. I'm just teasing. I heard you because I was hunting. I came just in time to see the tail end of things." Zelie peered down at her from the branches. "Wanna talk about it?"

"Not really," Chiara muttered. She sat up in the hammock and ran her hands through her unruly hair. "Oh, Zelie. It was the worst. *I* was the worst. I said he wasn't a good catcher. But he is. He *is*, and I know it."

"Okay, and? You can still apologize, right? It's not unfixable!"

Zelie, ever the optimist. Chiara shook her head. "It's not that easy," she whispered. "He knows my catcher was different. He thinks I'm still reliving …" She swallowed.

Reliving the past. The bars were the last thing she had. "See, that's just the thing," and the words began tumbling out. "He's right. I still remember everything … exactly the way Isak taught me. And I know — I *know* it's dangerous. But if I … rewrite all that …"

"Oh, Chiara." Zelie nuzzled her shoulder. "You're afraid he'll be gone. Is that it?"

Tears stung Chiara's eyes. She bit her lip and nodded. *I don't want to cry today.*

"I know what to do." Zelie sat up straight. "Let's go tell Talia."

"What? Why? I don't ..." Chiara protested, but Zelie was already pulling her out of the hammock.

"She always knows how to solve these things! Come on!"

☙

The ankle wasn't as bad as it seemed. Talia wrapped it as Chiara recounted the argument with Cor. Zelie stationed herself outside to ensure that no unwitting visitors interrupted. Talia didn't speak, merely nodded along, her jewelry clinking together.

The ankle was finished long before Chiara was done. Talia sat back on her heels and tilted her head to the side, contemplating the new bandage. "I see. You are finding this challenging, no? Training with someone new. A duo routine. Coren is smart boy. But ... young." She tsked. "It takes practice."

"Practice? Practicing what?" Chiara rubbed her face in her hands. "We've been at this for *weeks*. My techniques are fine. Cor said so himself!"

Talia shook her head, earrings swinging violently. "That is not what I am talking about. Technique is important, yes. But you tell me that you do not trust him. *Trust* takes practice. It is *trust* that you need."

"So ... I have to trust him?"

Talia lifted her eyebrows. "You must practice trust. It is part of the mission, no? You must swing together. You must fight together. You must live together. So, you practice trust. It is like practice with techniques."

"How am I supposed to do that?"

135

A twinkle entered Talia's eye. "I have an idea."

"I told you!" Zelie sounded muffled from outside the tent. "Talia always has answers!"

"Ah!" Talia shook her head. "No. Not always. But today — yes, today I have an answer." Her eyes were dancing. "Trust exercises."

"Oooo …" Zelie exclaimed.

"Hush, Miss Zelie," Talia ordered.

Oh, no. Chiara's heart sank. "Oh … Talia, no. I don't think — I mean, I'm sure if we just keep practicing, we'll—"

Talia was shaking her head. "No. It is not about practice. Practice only gets you this much." She held her hands an inch apart. "But you are not just body, yes? You have heart. Soul. So does Coren. That is not like a body. You need a different kind of exercise for that. Otherwise … *pfft.*" She snorted. "No use practicing. Either you trust, or you fall."

"But …" Chiara twisted her fingers together in her lap.

Trust exercises meant telling Cor things. Things she didn't want to say. Sooner or later, he'd find out that she wasn't really trying to let go of Isak. He'd say she had to. And if she didn't …

I might never get on the bar again.

She shoved the thought aside. *That won't happen. I can't let it happen.* Isak would never forgive her if she chose the past over the future.

All I have left … all I have left … losing him twice …

"Chiara." Talia was watching her carefully. "There is something more, yes?"

Maybe there's still a way out. Chiara made a last-ditch effort — the closest to the whole story she'd ever come. "I've done duo before. I … had the same partner for years. I'm just … afraid I can't unlearn that. And I … I don't want to unlearn it," she finished in a whisper.

Talia shook her head. "You do not unlearn. You learn more. You learn different. Look. I am not Zelie, yes? And she is not me. Do you trust her?"

"Yes …?" Chiara said, confused.

"Do you trust me?"

"… Yes."

"See?" Talia lifted her hands. "Different person, different trust. You learned with your first catcher. You learned with Zelie. Now you must learn with Coren."

"I don't know if I can." Chiara looked up at her, pained.

Talia's eyes were cool. "You must try. It is about letting go. Either you trust, and he catches, or you fall. Which?"

Dad wanted me to do this. He wouldn't have wanted it if he thought she couldn't do it.

And Isak would've wanted it, too. "Okay … I'll try."

"YES!" Zelie exploded into the tent, dancing in a wild circle.

Talia ignored her. "Very good." She nodded firmly. "I will give to you and Coren list of trust exercises. Every day — you practice. Together. You will tell me whether you complete your exercise or not."

"The ship sails!" Zelie was still hopping around. "Talia, you're a wonderworker!"

"I'm glad to see your investment in my professional growth," Chiara muttered.

"Ach!" Talia swatted at her. "Shoo! You are Kithsa? No. You are *underfoot.* If you stay, you must clean, or I will cook you in a pot!"

"Yes, ma'am!" Zelie vanished out of the tent with alacrity.

Talia gave Chiara a wink. "She is nuisance. Do not worry. Go rest. I will give Coren exercises. No training tomorrow. You practice trust."

❧

There was an air of awkward silence in the sand arena the next morning. Cor was already there when Chiara arrived. He was sitting beneath one of the oaks, whittling a piece of wood.

He sprang to his feet when he saw her, but he didn't approach. As she got closer, she saw that the expression on his face was somber.

"Hey," he called.

"Hey." Chiara folded her arms uncomfortably across her chest.

"How's the ankle?" He glanced down at her bandage.

She shrugged. "Not as bad as it looks. Talia said to take a day."

"I figured." He looked away, scuffing lines in the sand with his toes.

Chiara sighed. *Okay, Talia … Here goes nothing …*

"I'm sorry," she began, right as Cor said, "Chiara, I'm sorry."

There was a pause, and then Cor gave an apologetic smile. "I lost my temper yesterday. I had no idea what you were thinking. I should have just asked you what was going on instead of throwing around accusations."

"I'm sorry, too." Chiara exhaled. "I was unfair yesterday. You're an amazing catcher. I shouldn't have said that you weren't. It isn't true."

"I forgive you." Cor rubbed his knuckles. "And you were right … I *was* stiff. I was worried the same thing would happen again."

"You were right, too." Chiara wouldn't look at him. "I was … remembering an old routine."

Cor nodded and bit his lip. She braced herself for the response: *What routine? Time to let it go.*

But all he said was, "He must have been a great catcher."

He was. Arva, he was. Chiara had to change the subject before she started crying. "Did, um … did Talia tell you? About the—?"

"Trust exercises," Cor laughed nervously, just as Tagg appeared from the trees.

"Oi, you two!" he called. "Nice to see you're patching things up. What's the order of the day?"

"Trust exercises, apparently," Cor said. "Talia said you couldn't help."

"Excellent." Tagg seated himself on the ground. "It's about time."

CR

And that was what they did for an hour — trust falls. Hands across her chest, Chiara would fall backward, stopping only when Cor's large hands pillowed her shoulder blades.

He was a lot heavier than her, so she had to squat when she caught him. Not impossible, but difficult. By the end of an hour, she was pretty winded.

But Tagg was satisfied. "Look at that. You two working together. Well done." He got to his feet. "I've got guard patrol in a few minutes. Play nice, or I'll tell Talia."

"He would," Cor murmured under his breath as they watched Tagg leave. "He's done it before."

Chiara glanced at him uncertainly. "So … should we keep going?" The tree branches overhead twitched and rustled in the still air. She glanced up, suddenly suspicious.

Cor shrugged. "How does your ankle feel?"

Chiara gave it a tentative twitch. "Sore. But not as bad as yesterday."

"How about you go back to camp? Sit down or something?"

"What about you? What will you do until noon?"

He grimaced. "I have to go talk to Crovus. He wasn't kidding about sending us on a run. I'm supposed to ask him what form of disciplinary action he's chosen for us."

Chiara made a face. "Good luck." That didn't sound fun.

The branches stirred again, and she glared up at the leaves. *Oh, I'm going to* kill *her* …

"Thanks," said Cor. "Can I walk you back?"

"Uh …" She looked back down at Cor. "Um, no, actually. I'll be fine! It's not bad in the shade. You go ahead!"

Cor looked uncertain, but he waved goodbye and began jogging off.

As soon as he disappeared into the trees, Chiara turned back to scowl at the branches overhead. "What do you think you're *doing?*"

A dark shape dropped from the tree and leapt to its feet. Zelie. "How was the first day? Any progress? What's the assignment for tomorrow?"

Chiara sighed sharply. "Fine, maybe, and I have no idea. Why are you spying on us?" she demanded.

"Gotta keep an eye on you two! It's important," Zelie grinned. "Think of me as a spotter. Like Tagg, but more *personal* instead of professional." She wiggled her eyebrows.

"I refuse to get involved in your little schemes," Chiara muttered.

"*Schemes?* They're hardly schemes! This is a significant milestone for you!"

Chiara ran her hands through her hair. "The guy's supposed to be my catcher, we've done nothing but argue, and now you're trying to set us up?"

Zelie made a pouty face. "Aw, don't be a sourpaws! Who doesn't love a good rivals-to-lovers?"

"*We are not rivals!* And we aren't *lovers,* either!"

"Of course not," Zelie snorted. "You're not at the emotionally vulnerable stage yet. Don't worry, you'll get there! That's what the trust exercises are for."

"If you keep talking, I'm going to start throwing my shoes at you."

"Don't abuse your spotter!"

Chiara sat down as quickly as her ankle allowed and whipped the shoe off her foot.

Zelie dashed out of range. "Alright, fine! I'll come back when you're in a better mood, Miss Unromantic!"

"The odds of shoes being thrown are increasing exponentially," Chiara called after her.

11

Unfortunately, Cor's prediction was correct. Five days later, Chiara's ankle was pronounced "good" by Talia, and Crovus sent Chiara and Cor on a dawn run. "Six miles," he declared. One for each bout they'd fought poorly.

Chiara winced as a thorny vine whipped across her face, but she didn't break stride. It was barely morning, and the overhanging plants were easy to miss in the half-light. *If only my ankle had twisted sooner.* There would've been fewer miles to run.

Her feet thudded along the narrow trail. Cor was a few yards ahead, tattooed arms pumping in a steady rhythm.

Chiara was a decent runner, but Cor far outstripped her. Even if he wasn't a Tegid, he would've been faster than her — he had the ideal build for it.

"Where … are we headed … again?" Chiara called out breathlessly.

"You'll see," Cor called over his shoulder. "Don't fall behind. Don't want you getting lost."

Crovus didn't care where they ran, as long as they ran the full six miles. But Talia had suggested they go somewhere peaceful for their next trust exercise — back-to-back conversation — and Cor said he knew the perfect place, three miles out from camp.

"How are you this good at cross-country running?" she panted.

"My aunt used to make me do sprints whenever I didn't listen to her."

Chiara managed a laugh. "I bet … your parents … appreciated that."

He didn't answer.

So his aunt disciplined him … not his parents. *They're out of the picture, then?* Chiara tried a different question. "Did they … want you … to join?"

"I always wanted to join," Cor called back. That wasn't exactly an answer. "My aunt's been a part of it since the beginning. She's in Crescor now."

"Wait …" Chiara panted. "Is your aunt … the spy … in Crescor?" *The one Skipper mentioned? What was her name …* "Scatha?"

"Yeah, that's her. As soon as I was old enough, she let me leave Crescor with Skipper and the rest."

"You … grew up … in Crescor?" Chiara's throat was burning, but her exhaustion hadn't outstripped her curiosity yet. "What … was that … like?"

Again, he was silent. She thought he hadn't heard her, and she was about to repeat her question, when he finally said, "Fine. Not as interesting as Fhír. We're almost there. How soon are you gonna catch up to me?"

How well are you gonna handle watching me vomit? But Chiara was too breathless to reply. She pumped her arms faster, lungs burning in her chest. A yard closer … another yard …

The deer trail was beginning to widen, dipping through rocky formations and divots in the ground. *If I'm not careful, I'll twist both ankles.*

After about five minutes, or possibly several hours, Cor rounded a rock overhang and gave a sudden shout. Chiara sped up, rounding the same corner — and Cor was nowhere in sight.

She slowed to a trot and paused, hands on her knees as she caught her breath. Cor had completely disappeared. She glanced bewildered at the rock overhang. Thick stems of ivy poured over its top, clinging to every surface like fur on a living beast.

Her heart, still pounding from the run, sped up with a different kind of adrenaline. She stepped forward, tense. "Cor?"

"Behind the ivy, you goose."

Chiara jumped. His voice was surprisingly close. She put out a tentative hand, brushing it against the leaves — and yelped as something seized it, pulling her forward.

Tickling leaves brushed heavily across her face and arms, and she found herself in a narrow tunnel. Dim light filtered through the other end of the tunnel — sunlight. She blinked, eyes adjusting to the shadows.

Eventually, she could see Cor in front of her, grinning like a kid. His hand was still around her wrist.

She snatched it away and glared at him. "What was that for?"

"Did I startle you?" he laughed.

"You could've warned me before grabbing me!" Chiara crossed her arms.

"Sorry." He stopped smiling, but the dimple was still there. "I like seeing people's reactions to this place. Yours was definitely worth it."

"Glad I'm such a source of entertainment for you," she muttered. "Where are we, anyway?"

"Tagg and I found it when we were on guard patrol last week." Cor gestured elegantly in front of him. "Ladies first."

She didn't budge. "No more surprises."

"Cross my heart."

She eyed him carefully. He seemed sincere enough. "Fine. Where are we going?"

He pointed. "Follow the sunlight."

It was a dirt tunnel a few yards long. The ground was lined with dead leaves. Chiara couldn't tell if it was natural or hewn by hand. As they approached the far end, the sunlight grew steadily brighter, until—

"Whoa," Chiara breathed. They were standing on the floor of what must have been a wrinkle in the valley, a tiny divot, fenced in on all sides by walls of stone. The air was completely still. Vines clambered up the rock faces — morning glories. The sunlight hadn't touched them yet, and the delicate blue petals were still open.

The whole place was so still. Chiara suddenly realized how loudly she was breathing, and she did her best to quiet it.

"You and Tagg found this?" She turned around in a circle. Besides the tunnel itself, there was no other entry into the place.

"Yeah. We were jogging up there"—Cor pointed to the lip of one of the cliffs—"and I almost fell. We wanted to explore it, so Tagg lowered me down. Then I saw the tunnel."

"It's … beautiful." She turned to him. "Nice choice."

"Thanks. So … should we get started?"

☙

They sat facing away from each other, backs just touching, as per Talia's instructions. *Sometimes, is easier to speak when eyes are not watching,* she'd explained.

The exercise was to find out more about the other person by asking each other questions. The catch was that if one of them didn't want to answer a question, they'd have to say something else that was equally personal.

Chiara wondered briefly if either of them would say anything at all, or just sit there in dead silence for an hour, but Cor quickly put that doubt to rest.

He began talking almost as soon as they sat down. "How long have you done duo trapeze?"

Chiara let out a slow breath. *I should've expected that.* "Five years. I told you that already." Her turn. "What was it like growing up in Crescor?"

"Like I said …it was fine. Not as interesting as Fhír. Who was your catcher for those five years?"

"… Someone from the Acrobatics Academy." *That's all he needs to know.* "Were your parents happy that you joined Fhír?"

"I don't know." He paused. "Why did you decide to join Fhír? I mean, I know your dad wanted you to — but why leave the city?"

"Do I really have to answer that?" Chiara rolled her eyes.

"I mean … no, but you'll have to say something else."

"Fine." She pressed her lips together. "I … didn't have a future in Belkar. I think that's why my dad wanted me to join." *That's partly why, anyway.* "Why did *you* want to join? I know your aunt is part of Fhír, but ten-year-olds don't normally leave home to become circus spies."

"What do you mean?" His tone was joking. "Every ten-year-old I know wants to become a circus spy! How do you think we got Kojni and Jarza? Or Ludni?"

"They're *ten?*"

"They were when they joined. They're eleven or twelve now, I think."

That's so young … "Okay — but you still haven't answered my question," she reminded him. "I mean, point taken — but your aunt really let you join?"

"Yes. She wanted me to. *I* wanted to."

"That's not an answer."

Cor gave a frustrated sigh. "Fine. Then I'll give you a different answer. Tagg and I joined Fhír at the same time. I convinced him to come with me."

Chiara snorted. "So your entire friendship has been defined by making questionable decisions. Good to know."

"Hey, that's what makes him such a good spotter!" Cor countered. "He knows me better than practically anyone." He paused. "How did you meet Zelie?"

"She lived out behind my house. I found her one day and started bringing her food. We've been friends ever since." *The last three years notwithstanding.*

Cor laughed, and Chiara could feel it against her back. *I wonder if she ever talked about me.* That wouldn't be surprising, if Zelie's matchmaking efforts were anything to draw from.

She decided to risk the question. She cleared her throat. "Didn't she ever tell any of you about me?"

It was Cor's turn to laugh. "Did she ever! She wouldn't shut up about you! Said you were the best flier she'd ever seen. From day one, she was talking about how she wanted you to join us. Didn't she tell *you* about us?"

"Yes — I mean, not the arson part." Chiara tugged at the grass in front of her. "She always asked me to come meet you anytime Fhír was traveling through. But I didn't …" She trailed off.

"Why didn't you want to? I thought you said there wasn't a future for you in Belkar."

"There wasn't."

"So … what was the holdup? Didn't you want to escape?"

"Yes, but …" Frustration began to warm the pit of Chiara's stomach. "It was … complicated."

The little not-gravestone, the crepe myrtles.

I didn't want to leave him behind.

"Look, isn't it my turn to ask a question? Can you give me a real answer for why you joined Fhír?"

"Only if you give me a real answer for why you didn't leave Belkar until now."

"I already told you! It was complicated!"

"That's not an answer!" Cor sounded irritated. Chiara could feel the muscles tensing in his back.

She let out a frustrated sigh. "Okay … can we try this again? The whole point of this is that we practice trusting each other. So … let's look at this like it's part of our job."

It kind of is. She couldn't trust Cor to catch her if she couldn't even trust him to give her a straight answer.

"You're right." Cor exhaled softly. "I'm sorry." After a pause, he asked, "Can we agree to tell each other the truth?"

"Yeah."

"Okay."

She felt Cor's shoulders press against hers as he took a deep breath. "My parents died when I was a kid. Scatha raised me. She told me stories about them. She … she joined Fhír because of my mom — her sister. And … I think my parents would've wanted me to join," he finished, more quietly.

"Cor … I'm so sorry."

She felt his shoulders rise in a shrug. "I was really young. I don't really remember them at all. I don't even remember what they look like. Scatha never kept any photos. She was my only family, until Fhír."

He fell quiet, and Chiara knew he was waiting. She tilted her head up, watching a breeze stir the morning glories.

What do I say? Something true … not everything. Not yet.

"I didn't leave because … that was the only home I had. And I … don't like saying goodbye."

"I understand," Cor murmured. He sounded a little dispirited.

I think that's enough self-revelation for one day. "Come on." Chiara got to her feet and cast one more appreciative look around the clearing. "We've been here long enough. We should probably get back."

"You're right," Cor sighed. He stood up and began heading back toward the mouth of the tunnel.

"Hey, wait." Chiara jogged up to him. "Thanks for showing me this place."

"You're welcome." He smiled. "Nice breather, right? Ready for the return sprint?"

"Oh, no," she groaned. "I forgot we had to run back."

ଓ

Cor was indefatigable. Half a mile away from camp, he began picking up speed, shouting that the last one to camp had to report to Crovus.

No way. Sheer desperation propelled Chiara's legs forward until she was almost, *almost* close enough to touch him …

Just when she thought she was about to collapse, the trees began to thin out, and the camp clearing appeared beyond the trunks. Cor was still a foot ahead when they finally burst into the clearing.

More than half the circus was already there. Noon meal was in full swing.

Chiara collapsed on her hands and knees, heaving for breath. The idea of food was nauseating. All she wanted to do was completely submerge herself in water, but the idea of walking to the stream was torture.

"What … were … you … thinking?" she gasped, glaring up at Cor.

Cor was trotting in circles around her, hands above his head. "Don't stop moving! You'll be too stiff for our cool-down!" He was slick with sweat.

"Ugh," Chiara moaned, sitting upright. She staggered to her feet, ignoring her screaming joints. "I hate you."

A hoarse laugh escaped him. "Sore about losing?"

"Maybe." She put her hands on the back of her head and tilted her chin up, trying to remember what breathing felt like. The patches of sky above were completely clear, not a trace of a cloud in sight.

Then something large and blue flashed overhead. Chiara staggered backward, startled but too exhausted to cry aloud.

"Cor, what"—she gasped, pointing up—"what was that?"

"What? OH—!" He leapt backward as something plunged into the clearing.

People shouted and scrambled to their feet as a cloud of silver and blue unfurled itself a few feet in front of Chiara. She shied away as large, feathered wings filled her vision. *What in Arva …?*

And then she understood what she was seeing. She'd heard the stories, seen the *Encyclopedia* pictures, but in person … it was completely different.

A northern Tsuru. Dad used to tell stories about them, but never in a hundred years did she think she'd actually see one in person.

Until now.

He couldn't have been much taller than Zelie, but his massive wings arched up to the branches overhead — a riot of blues, flecked white and black. Feathers, not hair, grew from his head, framing his face and rising into a fierce crest at the back of his scalp.

"Kaito!" Cor exclaimed. Fleur and Leo ran forward, followed closely by Ludni and Kojni, and soon the Tsuru was surrounded. Noise flooded the clearing as two dozen voices rose in a clamor.

All Chiara could see of him now were his wings, lifted carefully above the crowd. They had to be at least eight or nine feet from shoulder to tip. She took a step forward, entranced.

Cor came back to her and leaned down to whisper, "That's Kaito Kimore. He's our courier from Crescor." He frowned. "He's a week early, which is weird."

"Skipper mentioned him," Chiara replied slowly, still fascinated by Kaito's wings. "He never said anything about a Tsuru!"

Cor grinned. "I'm glad he didn't. Your expression was priceless."

She elbowed him in the ribs.

"Hey!" he protested, laughing.

"Order in camp!" The roar was Mishkil's; everyone fell back as he stomped into the clearing. His face lit up as soon as he saw the new arrival. "Kaito! Vell met!"

He lumbered forward and shook the Tsuru's hand in a large claw. "How vas veather?"

"Good, I thank you. Where is the Skipper?" Kaito lifted a hawk-like nose. He held himself with dignity, addressing Mishkil as if they were standing eye to eye, and not at a distance of several feet.

"Here." Skipper's voice rang out. "Well met, old friend."

"Skipper." Kaito gave a flawless bow, wings sweeping upward elegantly behind him.

"You bring news, I hope?"

"Much."

There was a heartbeat's pause, and then Skipper said, "Clanmates, return to your duties. Kaito, with me." He crossed the clearing, heading south, and Kaito followed him closely.

Chiara watched until the blue wingtips were completely swallowed up by the leaves. Then she turned to Cor. "I thought Tsuru didn't like leaving the coasts. How did he get here?"

"He flew, obviously," said Cor, earning himself another elbow to the ribs. "Ow! What was that for?"

"You know what I mean!" she insisted. "How did he end up here? With you?"

"Well, he's been friends with Skipper longer than I've been alive. They met while Skipper was traveling down the Lassari Coast. I think they worked together to figure out more about the arson attacks. Kaito gets back and forth a lot faster than we do, so he's our courier."

Tagg jogged up to them. "Kaito's back." His mouth was grim. "That's not good."

"What? Why?" Chiara shot him a confused glance.

"It means—" Tagg looked around, eyeing the number of people still within earshot. He lowered his voice. "It means trouble. Can't say more. Talk at dinner."

☙

The dinner hour that evening was strangely subdued. Chiara could sense the tension from the moment she returned from sparring practice with Cor. Conversations were sparse, and some circus-mates didn't even appear.

She spotted a firepit where Zelie and Tagg were already eating, and hurried over, Cor just behind her.

"What's going on?" She kept her voice low as she slid onto the grass next to Zelie.

Zelie passed her a handful of cured meat. "Kaito's back."

"We know," Cor jumped in. "He met with Skipper — we saw them leave."

"Yeah, and then he called a Captains' meeting," Tagg interjected. "It lasted an *hour.*"

"An *hour?*" Cor's eyes flashed in alarm. He exchanged looks with Tagg.

Not for the last time, Chiara wished she had a Jeka's Gift. She would've given her dinner to know what they were thinking. "Why an hour?" she asked.

"It means something's definitely wrong." Zelie's tail twitched. Her ears were flatter than usual.

Tagg nodded curtly. His ears were twitching.

"Are you sure?" Chiara asked.

Cor scooted in closer and lowered his voice so that all of them had to lean in. "Kaito came back early, and the first thing he did was ask for Skipper. That doesn't happen unless Scatha's heard something."

"Something bad." Tagg's frown was even darker than usual.

"But we just finished at Belkar," Zelie argued. "What could she possibly have learned that changes things that much for the worse?"

Tagg sighed heavily. "Belkar didn't exactly go according to plan."

Chiara turned to him. "What do you mean?"

"We expected them to attack the Tower," Cor murmured. "We laid traps and everything — but even when the fire started, nobody showed. It was like it just … started on its own. It wasn't until the building was already ruined that we saw them running through the street. I practically had my hands on one of the bastards until—"

Zelie cleared her throat loudly, and he broke off.

Chiara looked at him, a twinge of unease in her stomach. He'd never cursed like that before. *Until …?* Then she realized. *That was when he found me.*

"Right," Tagg muttered. "They appeared, and then they vanished. In and out like it was nothing. Bakhita herself couldn't track them once they were gone."

Chiara's hands became heavy. Arsonists were horrible enough. Now they were dealing with phantom arsonists?

"Okay, so has anyone heard anything?" Zelie glanced around impatiently. "Tagg? Buzzing?"

"Lots," said Tagg, flicking an ear. "But that doesn't tell me much."

Cor pressed his lips together. "I might get some more details tonight. Skipper mentioned that Kaito had a message for me from Scatha. Maybe I can pull something from that."

The whole group fell silent as Rosc and Milio walked by. As soon as the two were out of earshot, Cor leaned in and hissed, "The sand pit. Noon meal tomorrow. Be there."

12

Chiara, Cor and Tagg stayed put at the sandpit after their morning practice. Zelie had enthusiastically volunteered to bring them noon meal, but Chiara vetoed that idea. Too much risk of dead rodents. Instead, they brought their meals with them.

A wise decision, considering that Zelie showed up several minutes late. "I'm here! What did I miss?"

"Bloody nice of you to join us," Tagg grumbled. He was sitting in the shade of the oak trees next to Chiara and Cor.

"Better late than never!" Zelie exclaimed. "And it took me longer because I was gathering important information."

"You mean eavesdropping," Tagg guessed. "You're not supposed to know any of this, are you?"

"Can't eavesdrop if there aren't any eaves!" Zelie crowed. "And that's beside the point. Do you want information or not?"

"Zelie, you're a scamp." Cor shook his head.

"You're just annoyed that I hear more than you," Zelie sniffed as she sat down. "I've been keeping an eye on the Captains' tent for the past day. They holed up there right after breakfast and didn't leave until just before noon meal."

She leaned in conspiratorially. "There was a debate — and a vote. Whatever it was, it had something to do with Kaito's news. Scatha found something about the Arsonists — something big."

"Big as in …?" Chiara prompted.

Cor cut in before Zelie could continue. "Big as in serious enough to cancel our performance at Riften."

"*What?*" Tagg exclaimed.

Chiara's breath hissed through her teeth. *So we aren't performing, then?*

"How is that possible?" Zelie demanded. "What could Scatha possibly know that requires us to *cancel?* Especially when we *know* that's where the Arsonists are going to be?"

"Maybe they aren't going to be there anymore," Cor countered. "We got that intel from Scatha, remember? That might have changed by now."

"But *why?*" Zelie exclaimed.

"Belkar," Tagg muttered. "You don't think … we're compromised?" He shot Cor a fierce look from beneath glowering eyebrows.

Cor shook his head. "No way. We were too careful."

"That's even more reason to stick with Riften!" Zelie added. "If they suspect we're onto them, and we cancel our show, then they'll *definitely* catch on!"

Cor sighed. "Look, I agree, but … whatever this is, it's got to be more important than Riften." He paused. "I think Skipper is taking us north."

"North?" said three voices in unison.

"Why north?" Chiara demanded.

"How do you know?" Tagg began firing off questions. "Did Skipper tell you?"

"He all but said it." Cor ran his hands through his hair. "I showed him Scatha's letter, and then he said something about leaving Vastil Forest tomorrow."

"Tell us about the letter!" Zelie piped up. "What did she say?"

"That's just it," Cor admitted with a frown. "There wasn't anything. It wasn't more than a few paragraphs."

"About what?" Zelie pressed.

Was it just Chiara's imagination? Or did Cor's cheeks turn slightly pinker? "You know. Political updates. Social things."

"Wait, isn't that important? Why else would she send it to you?" Chiara glanced between the other three, confused.

Cor was definitely pink. "Well—"

"He used to live there," Zelie cut in excitedly. "He didn't tell you?"

Chiara shot Cor a puzzled look. "No, I know that. We talked about that."

Zelie's mouth dropped. "You *didn't* tell her? Aren't you supposed to be doing trust exercises? That's the most interesting thing about you!"

"Gee, thanks," Cor muttered irritably. "I strongly disagree."

"He lived in Capitol Circle," Tagg said shortly.

"Capitol …" Chiara turned to Cor, open-mouthed. "You're *nobility*."

Cor's face was diffused with red. "Technically …"

"Technically? There's no *technically* about it!" Zelie's tail was flicking back and forth energetically. "His family is nobility!"

"It's not that important," Cor cut in. "Can we just get back on topic, please?"

"Wait a minute …" Chiara looked at Cor, putting the pieces together. "That's why Scatha stayed there, isn't it? Because her position helps her know more?"

"Yeah," he said tersely.

He clearly doesn't like talking about this. She decided to change tack. "Got it. Well, was there anything in the letter that might convince Skipper to take us north?"

Cor shook his head slowly. "Not that I could tell. Unless …"

He leaned forward, steepling tattooed hands in front of his mouth. Suddenly he looked up, eyes widening. "She mentioned Merik Orilan. She said he left Crescor for some kind of research project. Somewhere north — the Laustrul Mountains, I think."

Zelie frowned. "Who's Merik?"

Orilan. Chiara frowned, tugging at the grass. Where had she seen that name before? In big letters on some bronze plaque …

"He's that one rich historian," Cor said. "You know, the one who wrote those Tegid terrorism papers, the ones Scatha found."

Crescor. The plaque — a list of donors, hanging proudly in the lobby of Crescor East Gymnasium. She'd read Orilan's name that night, while they were waiting for Isak's performance.

"Right, yeah." Zelie was nodding, but she still looked like she had no idea who Cor was talking about.

Tagg made a face. "Real cheerful chap. So he's taking a walking tour. So what? Why's that so bally important?"

Cor's shoulders went up in a shrug. "I don't know. I mean … he hasn't traveled for research in a while, so … maybe she's expecting him to come back with something new?"

Zelie made a face. "Not very informative, if you ask me."

"I don't disagree," Cor sighed, "but either way, we'll find out soon enough. Skipper didn't seem too happy about it. I think he wants to leave as soon as possible."

"How soon is soon?" Zelie asked incredulously.

"Best guess? Day after tomorrow." Cor ran an agitated hand through his hair.

Tagg whistled. "That bad, eh? I wonder …"

"I don't know for sure, but …" Suddenly Cor's face lit up. "Maybe she found their base!"

"What?" Tagg narrowed his eyes. "You really think so?"

"How do you know they have a base?" Chiara broke in.

Cor pattered his hands on his knees excitedly. "They have to hide somewhere, right? Maybe it's more than one base; I don't know. But Scatha and Skipper know the risks of canceling a performance at the last minute. They wouldn't pull us unless it was vital—"

"—And finding the base sounds pretty vital to me," Zelie finished, tail flicking excitedly.

That sounds too good to be true. Sudden claws gripped Chiara's heart. "What if it's like Tagg said? What if we've been compromised? What if they know our location?"

"Another good reason for Skipper to pull us." Tagg was scowling darkly.

Zelie's eyes widened. "No way. They would've had to find us in all the tourists, and then track us all the way here. You know how many tourists left town after the fire? And the evacuees? And there's no *way* we wouldn't have noticed them track us here," she ended firmly.

"She's right," Tagg said. "They can't be that good."

"But *we're* that good," Cor said. "And we still couldn't beat them."

Chiara couldn't shake the creeping feeling that he was right.

Tagg glared at Cor. "No more of that. Your negativity is impeding the conspiratorial mood. We *are* good. We know that they were at Belkar. We know that Riften expects us to show up for the First Harvest Festival. They've been advertising our southern tour in the papers for months now. The best intel they have is that we'll be in Riften."

Zelie was nodding emphatically. "Exactly! Even if they were onto us, there's no way they'd expect us to go *north*."

"Right ..." Cor sounded less convinced.

Unless they already know where we are. Chiara didn't feel the same confidence as Zelie. "Where would we go, exactly?" she asked, trying to refocus. "Grede? Talin? Or a bigger city farther north?"

"No idea," Cor said. "I guess we'll find out tomorrow."

Chiara leaned back and heaved a sigh. Her mind was racing. *Leaving in a day* ... She glanced at Cor. "What about our routine?"

He shrugged. "Mission takes priority."

"Bold of you to assume Cor can't make a routine travel-sized." Tagg raised a wry eyebrow.

"Hey!" Cor shoved his arm. "As far as I'm concerned, that's an asset. We can't just go from dawn to dusk — the horses need a rest. We'll have plenty of time to practice," he said to Chiara, grinning. "Not to worry. Speaking of which ... we'd better get going, or we'll be late for Crovus."

"Well, that's our cue," Tagg said to Zelie. He rose to his feet and threw Chiara a mock salute.

"What? You're *leaving?* Things just got interesting!" Zelie exclaimed.

"Oh, no. We're not staying." Tagg nabbed her by the collar before she could dodge him. "You're supposed to be on hunting patrol today."

"You can't prove that!" Zelie protested, struggling as he began carrying her with him.

"I was standing right next to you when Bakhita told you …" Their voices quickly faded into the woods.

"So, what are we doing today?" Chiara sighed as she and Cor followed the other two.

"Bare-handed sparring!" Cor sounded far too excited.

"Oh, great," Chiara sighed. "Can I go hunting with Zelie instead?"

○੩

Breakfast was in full swing the next morning when Skipper walked out of the Captains' tent with a shout. The clearing fell silent.

Chiara exchanged glances with Cor. He lifted his eyebrows briefly at her before turning his eyes to Skipper.

"Kaito arrived yesterday from Crescor." Skipper's voice carried easily across the camp. "Scatha has updated her intel. There's been suspicious activity in Crescor …"

A buzz of whispers rose. Chiara's neck prickled.

Crescor. She never wanted to see that city again. *I guess I don't really have a choice now.*

Skipper continued, speaking above the noise. "… So we are canceling our Riften performance and following their trail. Break camp. We begin caravaning at noon — meal on the road. Finish your meals and then report to the Captains' tent for specific instructions."

He turned on his heel and strode back into the Captains' tent. Mishkil and Talia rose from their firepit and followed him. Kaito swooped down from the trees, close on their heels.

As soon as the Captains disappeared, the entire clearing erupted in chatter. A line was already forming in front of the tent. Ludni was practically leaping up and down in place, while Lopia and Milio exchanged nervous looks. Bakhita and the Dwyn were stone-faced, their expressions completely unreadable. But most of the circus members looked worried.

"Activity in Crescor," Cor murmured, relief in his voice. "*That's* why we're moving."

"See? I knew it!" Zelie exclaimed triumphantly. "I told you we weren't compromised!"

Tagg didn't reply. His face looked stormy. Chiara didn't have to read his mind to know what he was thinking.

The Arsonists weren't daft. Sooner or later, they would figure out who was following them.

"Right," he muttered. "Guess we'd better pack."

☙

Breaking camp was easier than Chiara expected. The hammocks, as it turned out, could be folded into packs, with clothing, blankets, and even food stored inside. The ties became shoulder straps.

While the circus broke camp, burying firepits and covering tracks, Tagg and the other tamers hitched the horses up to four of the wagons. And — to Chiara's surprise — Mishkil and Orek stood in front of the last two wagons, claws wrapped around the shafts. Apparently, the three Dwyn took turns pulling the wagons on two feet.

Rosc, Tara, and Nadia walked up and down the wagon line, ensuring that every person had some kind of weapon in functioning condition — saxes, swords, crossbows, even a few pistols.

All in all, it took less than an hour between Skipper's announcement and a caravan prepared for travel. The four tamers drove the four wagons. Mishkil and Orek needed no drivers. The rest of the circus was split evenly into groups of three or four per wagon, with six scouts on patrol around the caravan at all times.

Chiara was assigned to Tagg's wagon, along with Cor and Zelie. Theirs was the only wagon with only four members.

"It's because Kaito's not coming," Cor explained to the others. "Skipper's sending him out again to relay messages to some of our city contacts."

"Cheers." Tagg glanced around. "Well, aren't we a cozy little group? The trapeze crew and one questionably sane Kithsa."

"Hey!" Zelie griped. "Make that *no* questionably sane Kithsa. Not for now, anyway. I've got rear patrol with Yati and Fleur for the next three hours."

She scampered off as Leo, Nadir, and Zenith passed by, loping toward the head of the caravan — the front patrol.

Before the circus headed out, Skipper came to find Chiara. He brought Kaito with him.

They pulled Chiara aside as the wagons began lining up. Her heart began to beat strangely fast. She already had a guess about what Skipper would say.

Of course, he began with introductions first. "Kaito, this is Chiara, our new flier. She's working with Cor."

Kaito bowed low, and Chiara hesitantly copied him. "Well met, Captain."

Then Skipper explained. "Kaito has a few messages to deliver … one of which is from me to your father. He will have to fly to your family to deliver it …"

Chiara's heart leapt into her throat. She glanced from him to Kaito.

"Torin tells me that you wish to send a message to your family?" Kaito examined her with piercing, icy blue eyes.

"That's … yes, that's right." She twisted her fingers together. "I didn't write anything down yet …"

Kaito shook his head. "No need. I will remember it all."

"Oh … okay. Well …" She glanced back at Skipper.

He gave her a reassuring nod and stepped away. "Take your time." Then he strode off, calling instructions to the wagon drivers.

Chiara turned back to Kaito. "Tell them …" She tried to compose her thoughts. "Tell them I'm safe. I'm part of Fhír now. I'm a flier …" Tears sprang to her eyes. *If I could see them face to face …*

Kaito nodded. "There is more, yes?"

Chiara brushed her hands across her eyes. "Tell them I'm glad I'm here — and tell Dad—" *I didn't read his letter.* "—tell him I … I'll be glad to see him again."

Kaito nodded. "So I will. Arva guide your journey."

"And yours …" Chiara said as he bowed again.

"Skipper!" he called. "I fly!"

Skipper turned and lifted a hand. "Fly well!"

Then, with a running start, Kaito leapt into the air, sending a downdraft of wind, dust, and leaves rushing through the clearing. A few of the circus members shouted and waved farewell.

Chiara was still staring up at the sky when Cor walked up behind her. "Hey, flier!"

She turned to see him holding a long stave in his hand. Two short swords were strapped across his back, one hilt poking out over each of his shoulders.

"You've got your sax?" he asked.

She reached behind her to tap the handle. "Always."

"Great. Here." Cor handed over the stave with a grin. "You might want this — helps with hiking. Don't want you falling behind."

"I could also hit you with it, you know," Chiara replied calmly, examining the blunt end of the stave.

"Uh — no thanks," Cor said hurriedly. "Let's save that for practice when we stop."

❧

The caravan moved west through Vastil Forest at a steady clip. By midafternoon, they'd left the forest behind and struck northwest, winding through the hill country east of Belkar.

The landscape around them was a patchwork of fields, dotted with small farmhouses, tree groves, and the occasional cluster of buildings huddled together like hens — trading posts, too small to be villages.

Every so often, the hills parted to reveal the Tonitrus, a heavy green-grey band far to the north. Eventually, they'd reach the river and find a ford, but until then …

"Are we there yet?" Zelie piped up for the third time that day. She'd joined them next to Tagg's wagon as soon as she got off her shift. She and Ludni seemed to be the only ones not affected by the heat — they'd been wagon-hopping all afternoon.

"No, Zelie. We are not there yet." Cor didn't even bother to turn around.

Chiara didn't have to see his face to know that he was reaching the end of his rope. She didn't have the willpower to care much.

It was nearing evening, but the air was still thick and heavy. Conversation between the circus crew had faded hours ago as they all focused on conserving their energy.

"Ugh, you're no fun," Zelie muttered. "Okay … let's play a game." She rolled onto her back, hanging her head off the end of the wagon. "I spy with my hunter's eye—"

"An annoying Kithsa," Tagg interrupted from his seat at the front of the wagon. His ears were even droopier than normal.

Zelie made a face. "No!"

"An annoyed Nousk," Chiara said under her breath, but Tagg didn't seem to hear her.

Zelie snickered. "Nope! Close. It's something that is … blue."

"The sky." Cor sounded like he'd lost the will to live.

Zelie rolled onto her stomach and peered out the side of the wagon at him. "How'd you know?"

Wordlessly, he pointed up with a limp finger.

Chiara glanced at Zelie. "Not that hard. That's pretty much the only blue thing around here."

Zelie looked appalled. "How could you! My *eyes* are blue!" She opened them wide and blinked several times, as if demanding reparation for the insult.

"Right. Of course," Chiara sighed. "How could I forget?"

Tagg's voice carried back through the wagon, dry enough to choke a fish. "How the hell are you spying your own irises?"

"Irrelevant!" Zelie shot back. She leapt gracefully down from the moving wagon and trotted daintily past Ria. "Well, have fun doing nothing," she said airily. "I'm going ahead to scout. See you later."

"No rush," Tagg said as Zelie vanished into the grove of trees ahead.

Chiara picked up her pace until she came up beside Cor. "I think you offended her."

"A tragedy." Tagg looked completely unbothered.

"She'll be fine," Cor sighed. "Just wait 'til we get to the river. She'll have plenty to keep her occupied then."

"How long will that take?"

As soon as the question left her mouth, Chiara realized her mistake. Tagg shot her an annoyed glance. "Don't you start, too!"

"Sorry." She tried not to grin.

◌ঽ

The shadows lay long and black to their right by the time Skipper called a halt for the night. The wagons rolled slowly off the trail into a small cluster of hills. They set up camp in a small copse of trees. The Captains allowed small fires, but little noise.

Tagg, Chiara, and Cor sat around their small fire, eating in silence as they watched the flames. Zelie was nowhere to be seen — she'd find them eventually.

Chiara stared at it, mesmerized. The fierce sparks, the pulsing embers, the soft, musical crackling.

It's beautiful.

Even after all this time … after Isak … fire could still draw her in.

It was Tagg who broke the silence. "What if we were right?" he asked suddenly. "What if it really was the base?"

Cor shook his head. "There's no way. Skipper would've told us."

"Unless she wasn't sure herself," Tagg countered.

"Why would she be unsure?" asked Cor. "She's never been wrong before."

"But we've been searching for *years*, and we've found nothing — nothing that smells of Arsonists, anyway," Tagg argued. "Whoever they are, they're bloody good at going incognito. If we never even see their real faces, they could travel anywhere — *live* anywhere — without anyone being the wiser."

"And since they're Tegid, they blend in," Chiara added, rubbing at her eyes.

"Exactly," said Tagg. "All they have to do is show up at big events and buy a ticket. For all we know, there could be Arsonists …"

He trailed off, but Chiara knew what he was about to say.

There could be Arsonists in every city. A shudder ran down her spine. *I might've met one of them.* In Belkar. Or Crescor.

"Well, if that's the case, it leaves us with two possibilities," Cor said. "Either they've got residential status in the cities—"

"—Or they're breaking into the city secretly—" Tagg cut in.

"—Which is almost impossible for security reasons," Cor finished, "especially in Capitol Circle. And if they were really registered citizens, Scatha would've found some kind of record by now."

"Wait — there's three." Tagg's scowl had become fierce. "Three possibilities."

Cor tossed him a puzzled look. "What's the third?"

"A mole." Tagg's mouth was a dark line.

A prickle ran down Chiara's back. "You mean … a spy. A spy for the Arsonists?"

"Worse," Tagg growled. "If the Arsonists aren't just breaking in, and they don't actually live in the cities, then the only other option is they've got help. Someone on the inside is letting them in."

"Not just *someone*." Even in the dim firelight, Cor was visibly pale. "It would have to be someone in one of the High Councils. Someone who knows what kind of people"—he glanced at Chiara—"are the next targets."

Like Dad. Chills prickled across her skin.

Cor was drumming his fingertips on high speed now. "That means ... someone in the High Circle. But that's impossible. Scatha would have to be blind and deaf not to know about that."

The High Circle. Chiara's skin went clammy. The council of the Tegid republic, the ones who lived in Capitol Circle with their families and relatives — the Silver Class.

The council itself was one hundred elected Senators, each bound by a solemn oath of responsibility to uphold the good of Tegea's people. An oath that, when broken, was punished by public execution.

And now, there was a possibility that one of the Senators — or maybe more than one — was colluding with the Arsonists.

A Tegid Senator ... allowing Tegids ... to burn down Tegid cities.

The High Circle was far from immune to corruption. Chiara knew that as well as anyone. *But this ...?*

"This is insane." It burst out of Chiara in a laugh that was close to hysterical.

Eyes from other campfires drifted their way, and she went on more quietly. "The High Circle — I mean, this is ... we're talking about *treason* here." Her heart thudded in her ears as the words tumbled out. "The worst kind of treason — the kind that gets you killed and your family exiled."

Cor and Tagg both had worried looks on their faces.

Chiara tried to take a breath, stem the panic in her voice. "If someone in the High Circle was really getting away with that—"

"No," Cor said fiercely. "Tagg, there's *no way* Scatha wouldn't know about that."

"How can you be sure?" Chiara asked. "This is secrecy at the highest level. I know your aunt is good at what she does, but how much could she possibly discover about a *High Circle official* without being found out?"

Tagg shot her a puzzled frown. "Because she's—"

"Tagg." Cor's voice cut across him sharply.

Tagg lifted his hands in the air, exasperated. "Cor, *how* did this bloody not come up already?"

So he hasn't *told me everything about Crescor.* Chiara gave Cor a hard stare. "I thought we talked about this. What are you still not telling me? And better yet, why?"

"The fewer people who know, the better." Cor wasn't looking at either of them. He was carving lines in the dirt with his sax.

"Horse dung." Chiara glared at him. *I can't believe this.* "How are you *still* keeping secrets?"

"Keeping secrets?" Cor swung to face her, eyebrows shooting up. "If we're talking secrets, maybe we should start with you, huh? Why didn't you tell me about the extra seven years you spent as a flier?"

"How did you …?" Chiara began, but Cor wasn't finished. "If you got kicked out of the Academy, then who was your catcher all that time?"

Isak.

Chiara's ears were buzzing. She could hear the echo of hurt in Cor's voice as he stared at her, waiting for an answer.

But she didn't care.

Eyes stinging, she turned away from him. "You don't get to know that," she whispered.

Cor's face went stony. "Fine." He turned away. "I guess we're even, then."

"Holy Arva." Tagg's growl caused them both to start. "Would the two of you just give it a rest for *five bloody seconds?*"

I've never heard him that angry before. Chiara stared at him wide-eyed, her hands twitching nervously.

Cor lifted his chin slightly, but his attempt at bravado was lessened by the shadow of embarrassment crossing his face.

"Listen to yourselves! You're a disaster!" Tagg gave them both a scathing glare. "I thought we went over this back in Vastil! Bloody lot of good those trust exercises were, eh?"

Cor opened his mouth, but Tagg held up a finger. "Nope. Just shut up and listen, because if I have to hear you bicker one more time, I'll be *really* miffed."

He sounded like an angry parent chastising wayward cubs. "If you can't trust each other *off* the trapeze, then you'll never trust each other *on* it."

He continued, sounding slightly less irate. "Cor, she's your *flier*, mate. You need to trust her. Sooner or later, you'll have to talk about this."

Cor's mouth turned down, but he nodded.

"And Chiara …" Tagg's voice softened just a little as he turned to her. "I dunno what you've been through. And you don't need to tell me," he added, sounding unusually sympathetic. "But eventually, you need to tell *him*." He jerked his chin at Cor. "I already told you. Secrets are bad news in this line of work. They're the kind of thing that could land you in a real cock-up. Trust me on this one."

Chiara's shoulders sank. She knew, she *knew*, he was right. *But Cor has no reason to know, does he?* Couldn't she keep Isak and Fhír separate?

Keep them separate? The whole reason I joined was to find the people who killed Isak. There was no untangling those threads.

She bit her lip. "Alright."

"Now apologize." Tagg was insistent.

Cor sighed heavily. "Chiara … I'm sorry. That wasn't trusting of me, and it wasn't helpful."

No, it wasn't. But he also hadn't been wrong. Chiara's mouth twitched in an apologetic grimace. "I forgive you. And … I'm sorry about not talking about things."

Cor shook his head. "I'm guilty of that, too."

"So make it better now," Tagg interrupted. "Trust is give and give. You give, then she gives. Tell her about Scatha."

Cor's shoulders tensed. Then he nodded slowly. "Okay." He glanced at Chiara. "But you can't talk about this outside of the three of us. And Zelie. Otherwise … it could put Scatha in some serious trouble."

He didn't clarify, but Chiara got the idea that "trouble" meant the kind of thing that got people killed. "I swear I won't repeat it," she promised.

Cor inhaled deeply. "Okay." He glanced at Tagg. "Scatha is in the High Circle. She's a Senator."

13

Chiara blinked. Whatever she'd been expecting Cor to say, it wasn't that. "Wait … she's—?"

"Yes." Cor said quickly, eyeing Leo, who was passing by on his return from his shift. "She goes by a different title in Capitol Circle."

As soon as Leo was out of earshot, Chiara turned to Cor with the beginnings of an incredulous smile. "So if she's a Senator, that means you're—"

"Yes."

Was Cor turning pink? Or was it just her imagination?

"Wait." She was almost smiling now. "Seriously? You're—"

"Look, it really doesn't matter. It's just some dusty old title." Cor was *definitely* pink now.

"Just a title?" Chiara laughed. "Cor, you're"—she paused, lowering her voice—"you're not just nobility. You're part of the *Silver Class.*"

"We-ell—"

"No, don't give me that! You *are!*" She examined him with new eyes. "You're a silver spoon?"

Cor. The scrappy, rough-looking circus runaway?

"Yes, me," Cor grumbled. "Now can we move on? I'm not interested in being grouped with those insufferable, stuffy—"

"You're talking about your own family," Chiara pointed out with a smile.

"Scatha's different," Cor said quickly. "She wanted me to get out of that world. She started training me for Fhír when I was five."

The idea of a toddling Cor stretching up to grab a trapeze bar was so absurd that Chiara had to laugh aloud. "Okay. So you're a Tegid noble who spent his whole life being trained … for a traveling circus?"

"Are you saying Fhír's mission doesn't matter?" Cor lifted his chin proudly, staring her down.

"No. Of course it matters." There wasn't any doubt about that. Chiara gave him a curious look. "Why didn't you tell me sooner?"

"It … wasn't important," Cor managed. But his face was redder than it had been.

"What did I miss?" Suddenly Zelie was there, perched by the fire right next to Tagg. Cor's hands were already on his sword hilts before he got a good look at her.

"Nothing," Tagg sighed. "Just a fight, a lecture, and a theory that one of the High Circle senators is a traitor to the country."

Zelie's mouth dropped. She looked absolutely horrified. "It's only been an *hour*!" she cried. "How come I always miss the good stuff?"

ଓ

They started out early the next morning, curving on a vaguely northwestern tack. The ford was still a few days' journey away.

Chiara had more than enough to occupy her thoughts. She walked side by side with Cor as Tagg's wagon rolled along.

"You're Silver Class." She shook her head with a smile. "I still can't believe—"

"Hey!" Cor gave her arm a playful whack. "It's not like that, okay? I'm with Fhír now. No class or status. How many times do I have to say that this is so much better?"

"I don't disagree," Chiara murmured. "So … Scatha. She really wanted you here. Why didn't she come, too? I mean, she even founded it, right? So why become a Senator? Why not just leave Crescor and join Fhír?"

Cor didn't answer right away. "She had a lot of connections in the city. She's been in Crescor almost her whole life. By the time Fhír was founded, she'd already been elected as a Senator. She believed she could do more for Fhír in Crescor instead of leaving it. So"—he shrugged—"she stayed."

"I guess that makes sense."

"I wanted her to come." Cor rubbed his knuckles, a gentle look on his face. "I tried to convince her to come with me, once. But … she insisted."

"Did she want to come?"

"Badly." There was a smile on his face. "But she never admitted it. Not after being elected."

"Even though she founded it …" Chiara mused.

"She doesn't regret it," Cor added quickly. "She was able to find a lot of us after she was elected. She personally met with almost all of the original circus. And even after we started traveling farther away from Crescor, she'd inform us about potential candidates in different towns and cities. That's how we heard about Zelie … although I'm not sure that was exactly an advantage for us."

"How did she find …" Chiara glanced around. "… all of you?"

"She was looking for people with talent and … a past." Cor looked away, and the muscles in his jaw twitched.

"A past," Chiara repeated. "As in …"

"People who had seen the fires."

Chiara's heartbeat throbbed in her ears. *People who had seen the fires.*

Did Scatha know I was in Crescor?

And Cor. His parents had died when he was little. *Did they …?*

"Cor," she began hesitantly. *Will he even answer?* She changed her question … just slightly. "What about Scatha? Did she … have a past?"

Cor lifted his head, jaw tight. "She — yeah. She … lost a few people. Twenty-three years ago. It was one of the first attacks."

He glanced at her out of the corner of his eye, and he took a breath. "My … parents were some of them."

Chills trickled down her back.

She'd been right. Cor had lost family to the fires, too. *We're more alike than I realized …*

"Cor, I'm … I'm so sorry," she managed, trying to control the shaking in her voice.

Cor's eyes flicked down. "Can't undo it." He began walking faster. "Come on. We'll lose the caravan at this rate."

Chiara gazed after him, watching his shoulders, the green patterns of ink emerging from beneath his sleeveless shirt, lacing down his arms. Patterns she knew almost as well as her own scars by now.

He was her catcher. Practicing with him meant brought her almost closer than she'd ever been with any living soul. But what did she know about him?

His name. His job. His trapeze style. A few things about his past.

But not nearly enough.

What really happened to him?

&

The next few days brought a steady fall of rain. The last of the summer storms, passing through. Lopia and Milio passed out oiled hoods to everyone, and they kept trudging onward.

Soon, the drizzle became a constant downpour. The wagons were beginning to slow down. By day three, Chiara was sick of rain. Rain meant no fires, no dry clothes, and no comfortable place to sleep. Rothgar's gym was old, but it was paradise compared to this.

She watched dully as water dripped from the lip of her hood down to her boots. Beside her, Ria puffed out faint clouds of breath, plucking up her hooves with effort.

I miss Dad, and Mum. And Nani. Where was Kaito now? Was he anywhere near Belkar? Was her family anywhere near Belkar? *Maybe Dad took them away from all the cities entirely …*

Cor was walking on the other side of Ria. He lifted his head to examine the sky. "Clouds coming south. This won't stop anytime soon." The rain was so heavy that Chiara couldn't make out his expression.

Tagg grunted. "If we stay too close to the river, we could risk the wagons sinking. We'll be bloody sitting ducks." He was crouched in the wagon seat, dripping wet, his only attempt at keeping dry the hood over his head. Even his ears were sopping.

Talia appeared, walking through the rain, checking in on the wagon ahead of them. She must have heard Tagg, because she trotted up to Ria.

"Only one more day of this!" she said energetically. She seemed to be the only one who wasn't depressed by the rain. "Then we will arrive at Grede. It is a good town. Have you been?" she asked Chiara.

"Once, I think," Chiara said. "With my dad. But I was pretty young, so I don't remember most of it."

"Ah! Then you will be surprised. It has changed much. The ford has helped business."

"Is Grede close to the ford?"

Talia threw a hand in the air. "Close? Only a mile, or two. It is not far. First, we will rest and trade. Then we will cross the ford."

"Fording after all this rain?" Tagg shook his head. "Don't like that much." He sounded almost anxious.

"Mishkil says to me that the rain will stop by tomorrow," said Talia confidently. "His bones, they are never wrong. But we will have to be careful. The ford, it is dangerous if it floods."

Chiara frowned. "Isn't there still a bridge there?"

"There is," said Tagg, "and a ferry. But both of them have washed out before."

"Then we will find another ford. Farther north." Talia's optimism remained undefeated.

"Hooray," Tagg muttered.

Talia patted his leg. "I have faith in you."

"Thanks a lot."

☙

They reached the Tonitrus River the next day. The rain had lessened, but not soon enough. The river was flooding. The wagons stood in a single line, halted only a few yards away from where the overflowing water lapped vigorously at the grass.

"There's no way we can make it across this." Tagg glared at the thundering water.

"Is the bridge still there?" Chiara squinted, but it didn't help much. Most of the river was still lost in a haze of steam thanks to the noonday heat. The sun wasn't even out completely, but the air was as murky as ever.

"Yeah, it's there." Cor looked doubtful. "But I wouldn't trust it. The whole point of the ford is so wagons like ours can cross."

"But there are more fords upstream, right?" Zelie asked, peering cautiously out behind Tagg. She'd nested in the wagon bed while they were waiting. "Can't we go to one of those?"

"That makes the most sense," Cor said. "I'm not sure what the hold-up is …"

He trailed off as two figures approached the wagon — Oxys and Mykzi. Mykzi scampered back to Ness' wagon behind Tagg, and Oxys trotted up to Cor. "We're crossing the bridge. Everyone out of the wagons — take as much as you can carry."

"What?" Cor exclaimed. "Are you crazy? Why aren't we just fording farther north?"

Oxys shrugged. "Skipper's orders. Mykzi and I examined as much of the bridge as we could. We think it'll hold the weight … as long as we're careful." He kept on walking to the back of the line, passing on the news.

"This is insane." Cor ran his hands through his hair.

Tagg sighed and clambered down from the driver's seat. "Here goes nothing."

In about twenty minutes, every single person except the tamers was carrying something — hammocks, tents, bundles, boxes. The Telk were the ones transporting them across the river. Talia and Milio stood at one end of the bridge, bundles piling up around them, and lifted each load until it hovered at the middle of the bridge. Jarza and Nadia stood at the other, drawing every load from the middle of the bridge to the other side.

The whole process took almost an hour, and by the end of it, all four Telk looked drained from their telekinetic efforts. Then Skipper ordered the empty wagons across the bridge. One by one, the tamers drove their horses across, and Mishkil and Orek followed with the last two.

With every wagon that crossed, the bridge creaked and moaned louder. The sound was audible even above the rush of the swollen river. Chiara couldn't tear her eyes away from the support beams. They were mostly underwater now.

"When the water reaches the bottom of the bridge, we'll be in big trouble," Cor said grimly. There was still about a foot of space left when the last wagon finally crossed.

"Groups of two! Go, go, go!" Skipper yelled, and each pair began bolting across. The river was getting higher, lapping hungrily at the wood. Only half a foot — less than that — then finally it was Cor and Chiara's turn. Skipper and Talia were right behind them.

As soon as Chiara set foot on the bridge, she could feel the planks trembling beneath her feet. The bridge was becoming more unstable with every passing second.

She glanced nervously over the rail. *How much space is left …?*

"Don't look at the water." Cor was standing directly behind her. "Look straight ahead. Just keep going."

Chiara began to jog nervously as the bridge vibrated beneath her feet. It was definitely weakening — but they were nearly at the end. Only a few yards to go—

There was a harsh cracking sound, and something shifted under the bridge.

"RUN!" Cor yelled, and suddenly Chiara was sprinting — arms pumping — hearing the snap and splinter of wood behind her; the rush and roar of water—

—and then her feet were on firm soil. "Oh, thank Arva," she gasped, turning to Cor.

But Cor wasn't there.

He was still on the bridge, charging toward her as it collapsed beneath his feet.

14

"GOR!" Chiara would've plunged headfirst into the water if Tagg hadn't yanked her back.

Blood roaring in her ears, she struggled against his grip until he gave her a rough shake. "STAY HERE!" he roared in her ear. "I'll get him!"

The next instant, he was sprinting down the riverbank, eyes locked onto the ruthless water. The circus members gathered around the wagons, clamoring and shouting.

Then Chiara spotted a helpless figure tossing in the flood, still clinging to a slat of ruined wood. Her heart leapt into her mouth. *I'm not doing this again! Not again!* She ran wild hands through her hair, watching as Tagg froze several yards downstream.

"What's he doing?" she screamed to no one in particular. The river was so loud that nobody would've heard.

That was Cor. Her *catcher.* The strongest one here. Just … swallowed up by the water like an insect, another brittle twig swept along in the flood.

And she was standing there watching.

First fire … now water. *How many catchers?*

"No, no — stop it!"

Then Zelie was by her side. "Tagg's got him! See? He's lifting him out of the water!"

Sure enough, Tagg's arms were outstretched, and Cor's limp body was rising from the water. Chiara's legs were moving before she could even think. She sprinted over to Tagg's side, chest burning.

He was crouching down, examining Cor's pale face. Then he pressed an ear to Cor's chest.

"Is he okay? Is he alive?" Chiara demanded. *Please … please be alive … please don't be dead … please …*

Instead of answering, Tagg shot upright. "Where's Talia?" His skin had gone horribly white.

"Still across the river!" Zelie panted as she dashed up to them. Tagg took off, back toward the ruined bridge.

"What — what is he doing?" Chiara tumbled to her hands and knees, panic rising in her throat. "Why is he leaving him?"

Hesitantly, she tapped Cor's colorless cheeks; when that did nothing, she struck him in earnest. "Come on, Cor!"

His eyelashes fluttered, but he didn't respond.

Zelie crouched down, sniffing at his nose. "He's probably inhaled water! Didn't Rothgar teach you something about that?"

"I don't — I don't remember," Chiara sobbed. "Zelie, what if he—?" *I'm losing … I'm losing … Not fast enough—*

"Stop it!" Zelie snapped. "You learned this. You *know* this. Now tell me how it's done!"

"Okay." Chiara wiped wet, shaking hands on her pants. Rothgar had taught her, years ago. A few simple steps. "Tilt — tilt his chin up."

Zelie put a hand under Cor's chin and pushed his head back. "Now what?"

Rothgar's instructions were beginning to come back in full detail. "Now — now pinch his nose — open his mouth — and five small breaths."

Zelie promptly pulled open his mouth. "Well?" she demanded. "Do it! Now!" Her eyes crackled as she stared accusingly at Chiara.

"Okay — okay—" Heart pounding wildly in her chest, Chiara leaned down, pinched the bridge of Cor's nose, and lowered her mouth to his.

One … two … The river was deafening; or was that her own pulse? Pulse — pulse — did Cor have a pulse—?

… Three … four … Short breaths, small breaths, not too large; don't overexpand the lungs; breath? Was that breath?

… five. Chiara lifted her head and stared wildly at his face. "He's not breathing — he's not breathing—"

"Don't panic!" Zelie's voice cut through the rising fear. "What's next?"

"Thirty chest compressions …"

One … seven … thirteen … twenty-five … thirty.

"… And five more breaths."

One … two … three … four … five.

She'd never kissed anyone. Sometimes, when she was younger, she wondered what it would be like. But this — this crouching on a flooding riverbank, feeling the water seep through her clothes, his cold lips just beneath hers — praying desperately for some response — *this* was horrible.

Thirty more compressions. Five more breaths. *Cor, please … please, you can't do this … we didn't even get to perform …*

Tears were beginning to fall onto Cor's face.

Then suddenly he twitched and convulsed.

Chiara jerked backward as he doubled in half, legs folding up to his chest, hacking and gasping for breath. He rolled onto his side, retching.

Chiara and Zelie stumbled away, giving him space, just as Tagg and Talia arrived.

"What's going on?" Tagg yelled. "Is he okay?" He was clearly shaken — his skin was still blanched.

"Chiara did it!" Zelie cried. Tagg and Talia turned to stare at her.

Everything was numb. Chiara's hands were shaking. Her mouth felt cold. It wasn't until Cor sat up, still coughing for breath, that she believed it.

He's okay … he's fine … She nearly crumpled into the grass herself. Instead, she managed to throw her arms around Cor in a fierce hug.

Then, before he could react, she pulled away and struck his cheek.

"Ow!" He stared at her open-mouthed, nursing his face. "What the hell was that for?"

"Don't you *ever* tell me to go in front of you again!" Chiara snapped. "You almost *died*!"

"But he did not die." Talia knelt down beside him, examining his face. She placed a gentle hand on his chest. "Chiara, what did you do?"

Tagg was visibly shaking. Chiara gave him a worried glance. "I … they're called chest compressions. You …" She trailed off, realizing how much she didn't want to explain it. "It doesn't matter. Zelie can tell you about it."

Talia looked up at her with an expression of wonder. "The water — it is gone from his lungs. You have done well!"

"How do you know?" Chiara managed. Slowly, she got to her feet. Cor did the same, his eyes fixed on her face.

Talia lifted her hands. "Telk. I can sense the water."

Chiara glanced at Tagg. "You can do that?"

He shook his head, looking haggard. "I can't. It takes years of experience to manipulate something we can't actually see. Cor, I'm bloody sorry, mate," he said shakily, casting a desperate look at his friend. "I had no idea what to do … Getting Talia was the best thing I could think of. I had to lift her here from the other side of the river."

Zelie snorted. "Good thing she didn't wait on you. Cor would be a whole lot less alive right now."

Tagg winced, and Chiara glared at Zelie.

"It's okay, mate." Cor shook his head, looking up at Tagg. "I would've done the same." He glanced at Chiara, something like awe in his eyes. "Thank you."

The corner of her mouth twitched up. "You're welcome."

I didn't want to watch you die.

☙

Rain woke her that night — rain, and the sound of voices somewhere nearby. Chiara opened her eyes and stared up at the tarp slung above her hammock. The soft patter and drip on the roof of the tarp almost lulled her back to sleep, but then …

"… fine, Tagg. I promise."

"I should've been there."

Low whispers … two people. *Cor … and Tagg?*

"What were you gonna do? Watch me die?"

"No!" Tagg sounded frustrated. "That's the bally point! I'm your *spotter*! I'm not supposed to let you die!"

"Well, if it comes to that, *I'm* not supposed to let me die," Cor retorted. "I'm supposed to be invincible, and I almost drowned."

There was a pause before he went on. "You can't save me from everything. And I can't save you from everything."

I can't save you from everything … Isak's face blazed to life in her head.

"I could've done better." Tagg sounded almost bitter. Then there was a dull slap, and he gave a startled "Ow!"

"No, you couldn't!" Cor's tone was verging on annoyance now. "You did what you knew how to do. Chiara did what she knew how to do. I'm still alive, and honestly, that's pretty much all that matters to me. Now, please, for the sake of my sanity, can you just let it go?"

Tagg grumbled, but he seemed to comply. They lapsed into silence.

Weariness coaxed at Chiara's limbs …

"So, she saved your life. You gonna talk to her now?"

Tagg. Her eyes snapped open.

"I've talked to her before now!"

"I mean about *you*. What happened with you after your parents. All that?"

The seconds ticked by heavily — one, two — before Cor replied. "I … I will. We're getting there."

A flicker of resentment traveled through her … followed quickly by something like shame. *You expect him to tell you everything when you're the one causing problems with your secrets?* That smelled of hypocrisy, and she didn't like it.

"Not good enough, mate. I can hear the tension from a mile off. I know we won't be at Riften anymore, but you've still gotta finish sorting through things with her."

Cor gave a frustrated sigh. "I know. I just … It's like every time I start to ask, she pushes back. There's something she doesn't want me to know."

That's true. I don't.

So why did she feel so much more guilty about it now?

"I can't just force it out of her … and even if I could, I wouldn't. She has to *want* to trust me …"

"Do *you* want to trust her?"

Chiara's muscles tensed.

"… Yeah. Yeah, I do."

"That's what I thought." There was a note of triumph in Tagg's voice.

"… Do you think she wants to trust me?"

"I should bally well hope so! She saved your life. If she really didn't want you around, she wouldn't have run nearly so fast …"

"She ran?"

"Sprinted right to you."

"Oh …"

Chiara turned her head, tracing a finger along the inside of the hammock. Her skin felt warm.

"People don't just do that for anyone, mate. You've got something there. It's worth holding onto."

"… Yeah, alright." Was that embarrassment? Annoyance?

… Or something else …?

Worth holding onto. Something twinged in Chiara's chest. All traces of sleep had somehow disappeared …

℃

Rain came again the next day, but it wasn't entirely devoid of joy. They were past the river, and Grede was close.

"Grede in three miles!" Bakhita's voice cut through the sheeting rain. She appeared a second later, loping down the caravan. "Grede approaching! Keep your heads up!"

"Finally." Cor's hair was plastered to his forehead. "We can have a real meal."

"And a real shower." Chiara flicked rainwater out from under her eyes. Camping was exciting and all, but it wasn't much good for hygiene.

Cor grimaced. "No, thanks."

"What's the matter? Don't like bathing?" Chiara snorted.

"Are you kidding? After yesterday, I've had enough water to last me a year, believe me. That wasn't fun." He glanced away. "Thanks again. Zelie told me you did some kind of … compressure?" He shot her a confused frown.

"Chest compressions," Chiara said. *Please don't ask … please don't ask …*

"How does that work?"

"You, uh …" *Great. He asked.* She decided not to look at him. "You get the other person to breathe by … breathing into them. And pumping their chest."

"Breathing into — wait, mouth-to-mouth?"

Chiara shot him a surprised look. "You've heard of it?"

"Yeah, once or twice. I've never needed it." Most Tegids' lungs were strong enough to expel a significant amount of water before drowning. It figured that Cor didn't know how chest compressions worked.

"Well … you must have needed it yesterday," she said, trying to stem a nervous laugh.

"How'd you know about it?"

"Rothgar taught me, after I needed it once." Swimming in that same river … with Isak.

Cor lifted his eyebrows. "You're full of surprises."

"Thanks. I aim to impress."

"Well …" Cor almost laughed. "I think it's working. Do you know any ways to make us dry?"

"Can't help you there, sorry," Chiara snorted. "Guess you'll have to suffer until we're safe at Grede."

"You pulled me from the river, but you'll leave me to drown in the rain?" Cor made a mock sad face. "Cruel."

"You clown." She shoved him, and he trotted away, laughing.

There was a cough behind her, and she turned to see Tagg on the wagon seat, raising an eyebrow.

Awkward. Chiara tried to smooth her hair down and folded her arms, attempting a casual tone. "Well. He's in a good mood, isn't he?" *Please don't question it …*

Tagg snorted. "I'd say so. Glad you're finally getting along … although I can't say I'm chuffed about the dramatic circumstances," and he grimaced.

I'm not supposed to let you die. His words from last night floated back. Chiara glanced away. "Yeah." *Talk about a new perspective.*

"Are you gonna talk to him?"

She looked back to see Tagg watching her curiously.

"What do you mean?"

He shook his head. "Can't fool me with that. The conversation about Scatha? We got interrupted. You never gave him something back."

"Right …" She'd forgotten about that. "He knew about the Academy …"

"Zelie mentioned something about it." Tagg eyed her shrewdly. "I'm guessing you didn't ask her to keep that a secret?"

"No, I didn't," Chiara sighed. It wasn't Zelie's fault that Cor brought up the Academy. The argument could've been avoided altogether if she'd just trusted him from the start …

But the idea of talking about Isak — explaining all the training, the memories, the empty grave … It made Chiara's skin prickle.

Why? Why can't I trust him?

"Whoa." Tagg was frowning at her. "What's going on in there? You're starting to sound like you're about to fall off the bars."

She gave him a sideways glance. *How do I explain this …?* "There are some things that are just … hard to say out loud," she replied at last.

"Harder than falling out of the sky?"

Chiara winced. "Fair point."

"You trust him to save your life." There was a peculiar note in Tagg's voice. "Why not trust him with this?"

She bit her lip. It wasn't about trusting Cor … in fact, it wasn't really about Cor at all.

It was about Isak. Even after joining Fhír, it was about Isak.

I don't want to choose …

࿇

Three miles passed in a soggy blur. The caravan was beginning to pick up the pace. Chiara could hear voices through the rain, conversations rising as feet quickened. New energy was rippling through the line.

She stared ahead, trying to pick out any sign of civilization larger than the scattered farmsteads. Instead, she saw Zelie materialize out of the rain and hop up next to Tagg.

He gave a cry of protest, but she ignored him. "Ugh … a real room with a real fire," she complained. "Can you imagine being dry again?"

"Can you imagine being thrown off a wagon?" Tagg muttered, but Zelie leapt down before he could make good on the threat.

The rain was beginning to let up. Another half hour, and the walls of Grede loomed ahead. A smudged line of grey wound out of the walls, cutting through the plain to the left. The southern road.

Skipper called a halt, and they split the caravan. The two Dwyn wagons and their crews stayed behind and set up camp in one of the fields behind them. The other four wagons split into two pairs — Crovus and Ness, and then Tagg and Arli, with Skipper in Arli's wagon.

Then those teams headed for Grede, timing their arrivals at half an hour apart. "Safety measures," Cor called it. "So not all of us are tailed as one group."

"Or stuck in one spot in case Grede burns down," Tagg added. He said it so baldly that Chiara almost wondered if he was joking. When he didn't crack a smile, she decided not to ask. *If that actually happened … I don't really want to know.*

So, half an hour after Crovus' and Ness's wagons departed, Tagg and Arli started up. The two wagons curved and crossed slowly onto the pavement, Arli leading the way, and they began rolling toward the south gates.

Staring ahead, Chiara spotted a cluster of dark shapes just in front of the gates. A large group of travelers, maybe … only they weren't leaving the entrance.

She frowned. "What …?"

Then the caravan came to a halt. The gates remained shut. Curiosity overcame her, and she walked forward a few steps until their voices became audible.

Skipper and Talia stood a few yards ahead of the first wagon, face to face with the group of people at the gate.

"Guards," said Cor, coming up behind Chiara. She glanced over her shoulder to see a sharp scowl on his face. "Twenty-four of them. That's a lot for one gate, don't you think?"

Chiara turned back just as Skipper pulled something out of his belt. It looked like some kind of pamphlet. He handed it over to one of the guards.

"That can't be good." Cor sounded almost anxious.

Traveling papers. Chiara shifted uneasily on her feet. Tegid traders and caravans normally carried some form of documentation — a declaration of purpose, a list of merchandise, a record of their trade routes. Most of the time, official papers got little more than a perfunctory glance, especially with caravans smaller than three wagons.

Not this time, apparently.

The guard began leafing through the pamphlet. Finally, he looked up and waved a finger in the air. Ten of the guards began walking toward the two wagons.

"They're gonna *search* us?" Cor whispered in disbelief. He drew back to the wagon, fingering the ends of his scabbards.

Chiara followed suit. "Why? We're not smugglers …"

She fell silent as one of the guards passed her. A Tegid with a crossbow strapped to his back. He didn't acknowledge her — simply went to the back of the wagon.

She eyed him cautiously over her shoulder as he lifted the canvas flap. Then, after a terse moment, he dropped it and returned to Arli's wagon.

"What are they searching for?" Chiara whispered.

Cor's mouth was tight. "Trouble," he said at last.

Tagg dismounted silently and stood at Ria's head, stroking her nose. His ears were twitching.

Finally, the guards reassembled by the gate. A few more minutes. Chiara fidgeted quietly, trying to relieve the tension that was locking her muscles.

Then she saw the guard hand Skipper the pamphlet and signal to the rest of his platoon. They drew back to either side of the road.

Skipper turned around. "Onward!" he called.

The two wagons entered slowly through the gates, trudging past the guards on either side. Chiara forced herself to look ahead. As soon as the second wagon entered the walls, the gates slammed shut behind them with an echoing clap.

"Did you see their insignias?" Cor muttered in Chiara's ear as they walked.

"What? No. Where?"

"On their shoulders. It was the Crescor symbol."

Two firsts, clutching a hammer. Only the Tegea National Military wore that symbol. Chiara looked at Cor, wide-eyed. "Wait. Those were—?"

"—Tegid soldiers," he finished.

So those guards weren't employed by Grede. They'd been sent from the Crescor barracks.

But why?

"Something's happening in Grede, and I don't like it." Cor glanced around suspiciously, as if he expected more soldiers to show up at any minute. But the streets were mostly empty. The rain had likely driven everyone inside.

branded

The wagons rumbled slowly forward, following a road that curved along north and west. They passed shops, circles, marketplaces, even small private homes. Warm lights flickered in some of the windows, but most of the buildings were shuttered and dark.

"I don't remember Grede being like this." Chiara looked around nervously. She'd been very young when Dad brought her here. But she remembered the marketplace — big and loud and full of colors.

This was nothing like that.

"It's not," Cor said grimly. "We were just here a month ago. None of this was happening."

"Something must've happened, then." She gave him a curious glance. "Do you think …?"

"Whatever it is, it isn't good." He shook his head. "I guess we'll find out at the tavern."

℘

Their first stop was one of the shrines to Arva. Every Tegid city and town had at least four shrines: one for every point of the compass. Whether arriving or departing, it was Tegid custom to pass by a shrine to ask for blessing in travels.

The Tegids in their crew — Chiara, Cor, Ludni and Lopia — hopped off the wagons and ducked inside the tiny shrine, looking around curiously.

Vases of wildflowers perched in the alcoves. Glowworm lanterns swung from the ceiling, illuminating the small glass sculpture on the far side of the room — a pair of hands lifting a hammer and chisel, the symbol of the Maker.

The air was filled with the fragrance of scented oil. One by one, the four Tegids dipped their fingers in the dish of oil at the base of the sculpture. Murmured prayers echoed around the small space. Chiara's eyes lingered on the glass hammer. *Bring us through safely …*

A moment later, they filed back out into the grey street. "All aboard," Tagg called quietly. Cor and Chiara fell into step next to Ria, and Ludni and Lopia joined up with Arli. The wagons began rolling again, passing dripping eaves and clouded windows.

After about half an hour, they arrived at their destination: the trading yards. Huge, two-story buildings rose against the outer wall — firm sandstone, designed to resist fire and water damage.

The first floors were nothing but wide storage stalls, with enough space for goods, livestock, and wagons. The second and third floors were a two-story inn, designed for the merchants themselves. A large iron staircase led up to the wide wrap-around deck on the first floor of the inn.

The crew members pulled their bags and satchels out of the wagons. Then Tagg and Arli guided the horses and wagons into the first-floor bay. They made quick work of the harnesses, leading the horses into stalls farther back. Crovus' horse Toby and Ness's horse Norik were already in the stalls.

Chiara slung her bag over her shoulder. The others were already walking back across the courtyard. She trotted to catch up with her crew. "So, what's the plan? We don't stay here, do we?"

"Not us, alas," Zelie sighed. "Just the Captains, and sometimes the tamers. The rest of us peons stay at one of the regular old inns. But I vote we explore first!"

"I veto that," Tagg said immediately. "Inn first. Then we explore."

"Stick in the mud!" Zelie pointed ahead. "We're gonna be left out!"

Chiara followed her accusatory claw toward where Arli's crew was already out of the courtyard. Arli was walking with Rye the Vikur, deep in conversation, while Ludni and Lopia bolted off excitedly down a side street.

"So we just … go wherever?" Chiara asked, falling into step with Cor.

"Not wherever — the Golden Hand!" he exclaimed. "It's got the best food."

He began to walk faster, almost skipping along the pavement. Chiara tried not to smile.

"So *he* says," Zelie snorted, as Cor trotted on ahead, scanning the road signs. "I personally like the Gnarled Ink."

"Zelie, that's a *tattoo shop*!" Tagg gave her an exasperated glare.

She returned it with an innocent look. "So? It serves food!"

"Food? More like roadkill." Tagg made a face.

"You go where you like, and I go—" Zelie began, but Cor must have heard her.

He spun on his heel. "Absolutely not. You're banned from the Gnarled Ink, remember?"

Zelie frowned. "Technically—"

"Technically *nothing*." Cor narrowed his eyes at her. "Banned. Permanently. No." He made an *X* with his arms as if to emphasize his point.

"Why?" Chiara sighed. "Did she attack a patron again?"

"Attack?" Tagg repeated.

"*Again?*" Cor exclaimed.

"Friends, friends." Zelie skipped ahead and turned, holding her arms out dramatically. "Let's let bygones be bygones, shall we?"

"Absolutely not." Cor marched on her. "You've been living a double life, and I for one am ready for the worlds to collide."

Zelie gave a dramatic cry and began jogging away, Cor right on her tail.

Chiara and Tagg were slower walkers. "She attacked a patron?" Tagg asked.

"Yeah, at Rothgar's gym. Are you that surprised?"

He huffed. "Good point."

Chiara glanced at him. "What was the Gnarled Ink story?"

Tagg looked at her with eyes completely devoid of light. "I never want to think about it again."

"Okay, then …" *Guess I'm asking Cor about that one.*

☙

Three blocks later, they were out of the rain, nestled in a booth in the corner of the Golden Hand. The tavern was fairly busy, despite the weather. Chiara spotted some of their own among the flow of people — Milio and Tara from Ness' wagon; Rosc and Mykzi from Crovus' wagon. They exchanged nods with her, but little else was said — all part of keeping a low profile.

She examined the other bargoers curiously. Some were Nousk, and there were even a few Kithsa, but most were Tegids. She got a few odd looks from some of the Tegids, and it confused her … and then she remembered.

My scars. Suddenly self-conscious, she pulled her hair out of its bun and fluffed it around her face. One blessing of thick, frizzy curls — they did a good job hiding the burn marks.

She found herself walking closer to Cor, sidestepping the flow of patrons as they made their way toward the bar counter. Coming and going, greeting each other, talking, arguing, haggling. Grede was a relatively small town, which would explain why the locals were so familiar with each other.

Too familiar. Chiara drew back as a male Tegid who leaned over with a wink, gesturing to the empty seat beside him. "No thanks," she said distastefully.

Without missing a beat, Cor slid an arm around her shoulder. "This way, darling!" He completely ignored the other Tegid, marching Chiara toward the bar top.

As soon as they were out of earshot, Chiara turned to Cor. *"Darling?"*

"Sorry." He looked a little pink. "That was the first thing I thought of."

Chiara lifted her eyebrows. "Well …" *At least it worked.* "… thanks, I guess."

"Sure. What do you want to eat?" he asked abruptly, sliding her a small pouch.

"Money?"

He nodded. "Skipper normally gives us our cut *after* we've performed, but since we didn't make it to Riften this time, we got an early payday."

Chiara accepted it. "Thanks." What with arson and training and flooding rivers, the logistics of paying for food and lodging hadn't really crossed her mind.

She pulled open the bag and twitched a finger in it. *That much?* She squinted up at Cor. "Skipper pays this well?"

"Well … yes, sometimes. I can be very persuasive." Cor wiggled his eyebrows at her.

She rolled her eyes. "That's nice. How about you persuade them to lower the prices of their food?"

"Oh. Yeah." Cor glanced at the chalkboard menu with a frown. "It's more expensive than when we came last. I'll cover you."

"What? No!" Chiara folded her arms. "I just got my first real cut for this job, and you're not even gonna let me use it?"

In the end, they split. Cor got the food and Chiara got the drinks. They made their way through the crowded tavern to the corner booth, where Tagg and Zelie were already eating.

"Nice of you to join us," Zelie snickered into her fish. Chiara elbowed her.

Tagg leaned in. "We need to talk about the river yesterday."

Cor grimaced. "No, we don't. Can't I eat one meal in peace before you remind me about my near-death experience?"

"Not that." Tagg lowered his voice. "Why did Skipper have us cross the river yesterday?"

"To get to the other side." Zelie snorted at her own joke, but a sharp look from Tagg quieted her. "Sorry. I'm listening," she said hastily.

"He would never needlessly put us in danger — or risk losing supplies," Tagg said. "So why would he do it?"

Chiara reached over to the lamp at the center of the table. She tapped the frosted glass, stirring up the glowworms inside. From what she'd seen, Skipper definitely wasn't the reckless type. "Urgency?" she guessed at last.

Zelie lifted her eyebrows. "That's some sense of urgency. Even Ludni isn't that impatient."

"He has his reasons," Cor murmured, but his brow was furrowed.

"Oh, don't give us that," Tagg huffed. "What's really going on in there? What's all the buzzing about?" He pointed a limp finger toward Cor.

"Well … I wonder if—" Cor began, but he was interrupted when somebody stumbled against their table. All of them looked up, startled, at the female Tegid now keeling over the tabletop, laughing a little too loudly through her gaudy face paint.

A male Tegid was right behind her; he grabbed her as she wobbled forward. Chiara jerked back in alarm as the lady's drooping sleeve swung across the table, almost smacking Cor in the face. A tangy scent wafted in front of her — some kind of perfume.

"So sorry — didn't see you there — don't mind her—" The male was bowing profusely as he pulled the female away from their table. He practically had to drag her arm over his shoulder to get her to stand upright.

"No problem," said Cor with a tight smile as the pair stumbled away. Chiara caught a mutter of anger from the male as he scolded his partner.

"Too much to drink?" Zelie guessed, making a face.

But Tagg was staring after them with an alarmed glare, ears flicking. "That lady wasn't drunk," he hissed.

Then Cor began coughing — a terrible, choking cough, all too reminiscent of the riverbank yesterday. Shoulders shaking, he covered his mouth with his hands.

"Cor, what's wrong?" Chiara tried to calm her pounding heart. *It can't be water — it can't.* Talia had said his lungs were clear.

But he was still coughing.

People were beginning to notice. Heads were turning their way.

"We need to get out of here!" Tagg lifted Chiara and Zelie by the arms. "Go! Find the Gloria Inn! I'll be right behind you!" He all but shoved them out of the booth, and Zelie barely managed to snatch her fish.

They speedwalked out the door. Behind them, Tagg was making his excuses to the patrons as he pushed by. "So sorry; pardon us — food down the wrong pipe—"

What seemed like hours later, they found themselves standing a block down from the Gloria Inn. It was decided that Chiara and Zelie would check in first, while Cor and Tagg would time their arrival for a few minutes later. "No need to draw more attention to ourselves," Tagg whispered. "You two first. I'll stay with him."

Cor had stopped coughing, thank Arva — but he was rubbing his chest as though it hurt. Anytime they asked him what happened, he just shook his head. "I don't know … it felt like my throat was filling with cotton."

That didn't tell them anything. But it gave Chiara a bad feeling. *Tegids don't cough like that.* If something was wrong with Cor, she wanted to find out as soon as possible.

Unfortunately, there wasn't much she could do about it. Talia was several blocks away, and it probably wasn't worth the risk. Still … *I'm starting to like Grede less and less.*

So, she and Zelie left Tagg and Cor waiting in a nearby alleyway and began walking to the Gloria Inn.

It looked like a cheerful place. A few Tegids were scattered around the door, sitting on benches, talking quietly. One or two others were leading horses out behind the inn, presumably where the stables were. Faint music drifted out the door — some kind of fiddle.

Just as they were passing the alley that led back to the stables, somebody stormed out of the shadows. He shoved past them and struck Chiara's shoulder so forcefully that she lost her step and stumbled in the street.

"Hey—" She turned with a small cry of surprise, but the words died on her lips as the figure whipped around to face her.

She was staring at some kind of painted mask, so grotesque that she couldn't tell whether it was male or female.

No … A burning sensation flared up in her core, and she gasped, doubling over.

A second later, the figure turned away and strode off down the street.

"Hey! You—" Zelie leapt after him.

Chiara's ears were ringing. All of a sudden, a bad headache was splitting her skull in two. She winced as small hands gripped her arms, pulling her upright, and she looked up to see Zelie's face.

Zelie's eyes were snapping. "Are you okay? What was that? Did that guy hurt you?" She looked Chiara up and down.

"Fine … I'm fine." Chiara straightened slowly, rubbing her hands up and down her arms. Her head was still throbbing. "Who the heck was that?" She scanned the people around the entrance of the inn, feeling her heart pulsing erratically in her chest.

No sign of the cloaked figure.

"No idea," Zelie muttered. "I was gonna chase him, but …" She turned to Chiara. "Did you see his face? What did he look like?"

The image of his horrible, lifeless mask flashed through Chiara's head, sending another sliver of pain through her skull. She shuddered involuntarily. *I hate that … I hate that.*

"I … I don't even know if it was a he," she said quietly. "It had some kind of mask on — or paint, or something. It … wasn't pretty."

Where had she seen that before …? It was like the painted faces of Fhír at Belkar — only so much worse, like some kind of diabolical reflection, a grotesque parody.

"We've outstayed our welcome," Zelie stared around, ears pricked. The fur on her head and tail was standing on end. "Let's go inside and check in. Then I'm telling Tagg and Cor."

They wound up in a cozy room on one end of the second floor. As soon as they were settled, Zelie whisked away. "Stay here and lock the door," she instructed, and Chiara didn't argue.

Twenty minutes later, Zelie reappeared with a piece of paper clutched in her hand. She offered it to Chiara, who unfolded it.

We're across from you. —Tagodi

Chiara frowned. "Tagodi?"

"It's Tagg." Zelie grabbed the note, examining it. "He must've checked in using his formal name." She clucked her tongue. "You gotta forgive him. He's a little paranoid."

"He's not the only one." Chiara fidgeted with the paper in her hands. The windows were closed and locked, and the curtains were drawn, but she still felt like she was being watched.

15

Fire. Smoke. Ash. Clouding her vision, stinging her eyes, filling her mouth, her nose. Walls, crumbling down in front of her, collapsing, loud crashes swallowed by the dull roar behind.

The inferno.

Scrambling across the rubble, tearing apart her hands and knees, searching, searching. Throat raw. Screaming or smoke? Never breathe the free air again.

It should have been her … it should have been her … silent scream, tears from stinging eyelids.

It should have been her.

Wall of bricks, tilting drunkenly overhead — swaying — plunging down — she was crawling away, crawling across twisted wood and metal …

… Escape. No escape. Isak? What about Isak? Isak — Isak — she was turning — running back — winding through the clouds of smoke; over the fallen wall …

Shadow! Someone there. Isak. Isak! *Answer me!*

The figure turned … a twisted, painted face, hollow eye sockets, staring madly back at her—

Chiara jolted awake, scrambling to her hands and knees, sheets tangled around her legs. *"Isak!"*

Her heart was pounding in her ears, drowning out every other sound.

"Chiara, what is it?" Zelie was clutching her arm, looking scared.

Chiara was shaking uncontrollably; she glanced around, blinking in the early morning light from the window. "He was here — he was right here—"

But the room was empty.

"Who?" Zelie sounded utterly bewildered.

Just a nightmare. Chiara buried her hands in her face and took a deep, shuddering breath.

Calm … calm. She hadn't had that dream in over a year.

"Chiara, talk to me. What's going on?" Zelie sat at the end of the bed, watching her anxiously.

"Just … a bad dream." Chiara brushed her hands through her tangled hair. "I'm sorry I scared you."

"You're not the bad dream type. What happened?" Zelie asked softly.

"It was …" Chiara shook her head. "I dreamt I saw the person with the painted face again."

"Mask?" Zelie had already come up with a nickname for him.

Chiara nodded. "It's fine. I'm awake now." She disentangled herself from the sheets and climbed out of bed, stretching. "I'm sorry for waking you."

"Eh." Zelie shrugged. "We should probably get up now, anyway. We can get our trading done early and then head back out."

"Sounds good. Give me a minute to change."

Once Chiara was in the bathroom, she washed her face, and then leaned against the counter, thinking.

The fire was real. It really happened. And the face …?

It seemed so real … Did she really see someone else there, that night?

☙

Chiara couldn't shake the nightmare. Her headache didn't help things, either. It was like the dream had caused her head to physically ache. When the four of them arrived at the market that morning, armed with empty satchels for their purchases, she kept looking around for the same painted mask.

But nobody looked suspicious. The rain had finally stopped, and the streets were bright and cheerful, and the market was filled with travelers. Ludni, Lopia, and Milio were trotting past, arguing about prices, and even Skipper and Talia appeared briefly, haggling at a stall here or there.

Still, Chiara couldn't help looking over her shoulder.

"You alright?" Cor asked quietly.

"Fine. Just … jumpy."

"Tagg told me." He matched her step. "If you see anything, holler." His sentence ended in a rattling breath.

She gave him a worried glance. "How are you feeling?"

He winced. "Better."

But she knew him well enough to tell that he was lying. "You should see Talia."

"It's okay … I think it'll be fine. Maybe I'm still getting over the river."

That didn't satisfy the little nagging doubt in the back of Chiara's head. But she decided not to press it.

Zelie interrupted them, skipping past, tail lashing excitedly. "Alright, kits, brace yourselves for a professional at work." She rubbed her hands together eagerly, fixing an eye on a nearby dried fruit vendor.

"Professional?" Tagg sounded shocked. "You spent three hours last time haggling with that bloke!"

"You're just jealous you can't get the same bargains. Watch and learn." Zelie skipped over to the stand. Within seconds, she was engaged in a heated debate with the merchant.

Cor sighed. "He only puts up with her because we pay him ahead of time."

Chiara laughed. "Seriously?"

"No. But that's a brilliant idea." Tagg turned on his heel and kept walking down the street. "Come on. We've got work to do. She'll still be here when we get back."

ങ

They wove through the stalls, bargaining, chatting, even arguing. Cor was a good haggler. He could strike the right balance of cordial and insistent. Chiara wasn't too bad herself, and they got some pretty good deals.

"Let's see … cured meat, cheese, matches, soap …" Cor frowned. "What else was on the list—?"

He was interrupted by a musical squeal. Startled, Chiara turned and spotted a trio of buskers on the other side of the street. They'd stationed themselves between two booths, and they were testing their instruments.

The first young Tegid ran a bow across his fiddle. The second was piping at her whistle, and the third, a cub, was pattering quick fingers on a small drum.

A smile spread across Chiara's face. She hadn't heard music since the Festival at Belkar. Tegids loved to dance, and buskers were a common sight on the streets. Mum especially loved it — she always tried to get Chiara to dance.

She glanced at Cor. He was smiling, too. Then the trio of musicians began, striking up a cheerful jig. Tired of trailing after their parents, a few Tegid cubs drew close to the music, hopping in circles, crowing excitedly.

Cor slung the satchel over his shoulder with a laugh. "Wanna dance?" He held out a hand.

"What?" Chiara stared at him, a spark of alarm coursing through her. "I …"

She'd never danced in the street before — not without her scars covered.

"It'll be fun! Here." He took the satchel out of her hands and slung it onto his back next to his own.

"I'm not sure …" She lifted a self-conscious hand to the side of her face.

A look of confusion flitted across Cor's face — quickly replaced by understanding. "Nobody will see. I promise."

"You can't promise that!"

"Sure I can." His dimple flashed out at her. "I'll spin you so fast that nobody will notice!"

Chiara snorted. But the music grew louder, filling her limbs, coaxing her on.

She glanced around nervously. Most of the market-goers were still absorbed in their conversations.

"Well … okay …" She took Cor's hand, and he grinned at her.

They scampered over to the other side of the street, and Cor whirled her around with a laugh. They cavorted in a circle as the buskers' song filled the air.

They were trapeze partners, but dancing was a little different. Chiara didn't quite know what she was doing — but she knew *him*. She knew his balance, his height, his grip … and for some reason, that seemed to make it easier.

Not that she was much good at dancing. The whole thing would've been mortifying if Cor wasn't the one dancing with her. He must have done it before — he was good at it.

She twirled clumsily over the pavement, his hands guiding her through. "I'm glad this wasn't my path," she joked, wincing as her foot caught on a stone.

He balanced her out and sent her spinning in another circle. "You're doing great!"

"Sure," she snorted. "You're the only reason. Don't tell me — dance was your path before Fhír, right?"

"Not quite." He twisted her around again, but not before she caught a glimpse of the sheepish look on his face.

"Could've fooled me." She leaned out and he tugged her back to him again.

"Etiquette class," he admitted.

Chiara turned to look him in the face and stumbled again. *The Silver Class … dancing etiquette.* That explained it.

You never gave him something back. That was what Tagg had said, wasn't it? Cor *had* told her about Scatha.

Chiara glanced up at his face again, just as he flicked his gaze to her. Hazel eyes — long eyelashes. His mouth curved up in a half-smile.

Her hands grew warm. *Maybe I could tell him … something. Tell him Isak's name …? That would be good enough … wouldn't it?*

He spun her around, and back in again, and she took a breath. "Listen, Cor …"

With a last resounding chord, the song came to an end. Chiara's feet stumbled to a halt. The buskers were bowing to smattered applause from some of the bystanders.

"Yes?" Cor asked, looking at her expectantly. His hands were still in hers. She'd held them a hundred times, the callouses, the hard knuckles.

It's different this time.

"I …"

"There you are!" Tagg jogged up to them, and Chiara dropped Cor's hands.

Tagg didn't miss it. He shot Chiara a glance that set her face on fire. But he didn't comment on it. Instead, he said, "Cavorting around while Zelie's still on the loose?"

Cor looked pink. "We'd better find her." He glanced at Chiara. "Thanks. That was fun."

He didn't say, *What were you going to say?* Or *We can talk later.* But his eyes said it.

Chiara looked away. "'Course. You, too."

◌

Zelie was still at the dried fruit vendor an hour later. Apparently, she was just wrapping up her bargain by the time Cor and Chiara arrived. In the time they'd been gone, she had accumulated an audience. Ludni and

Milio were standing to the side, watching her with impressed looks on their faces.

Chiara was silently grateful that Zelie was such a tenacious customer. *I never would've danced if she'd been around to watch …*

"Is she done?" Cor sighed, walking over to Milio.

"Just about." Milio pointed as Zelie turned in triumph, a large bag of dried fruits clutched in her tiny paws.

"Success!" she crowed. Behind her, the vendor plopped himself on his stool, looking exhausted.

"Great." Cor crossed his arms. "Let's get back to the tavern, then."

Chiara scanned the crowded street, nervous again. "If we left Grede now, I wouldn't complain."

Tagg's face was dark. "Agreed. I've got a bad feeling that there's some kind of connection between Mask and … our mission."

Mask, an Arsonist …? Chiara shuddered. It was eerily close to her dream.

Cor pressed his lips together. "Normally, I'd call you paranoid. But with this, I'm open to exploring all avenues." He glanced around the market. "We can report to Skipper about Mask when we take our supplies back to the wagons. That's the kind of thing he'd want to know, whether it's fire-related or not."

"Will do," Chiara murmured. *Should I mention the nightmare?*

But what was the point? A bad dream wouldn't tell them anything. It was just a jumbled puzzle thrown together by her exhausted brain.

◌◦

They spent one more night in Grede, enjoying proper civilization while it lasted. But Chiara couldn't really enjoy it. The hours were nerve-wracking. She found herself jumping at the smallest things.

Before dawn the next day, the trading crews had left Grede and were trekking out to the tree line, a few miles east of the town walls. They had a staggered departure, just like their entrance, with two wagons leaving first, and then the other two leaving half an hour later. They'd bought enough supplies to restock six wagons, so the two wagons' worth of supplies had to be carried by the trading crew on foot.

The sun was just rising above the treetops when Chiara's crew finally reached camp.

"Velcome back, cubs!" Mishkil greeted each circus member with a hearty smile and a clap on the back. Chiara winced as he delivered hers with gusto.

"How vere the voods?" He extended a large claw, and she handed over the bulky satchels with a sigh of gratitude.

Mishkil lumbered through the trading crew, hauling bag after bag across his shoulders until he could hold no more, and then he turned and headed deeper into the trees.

"Thank Arva." Chiara stood and stretched her arms high above her head, wincing. The muscles had gone stiff in her back from carrying so much. "If I have to carry another bag, I'll drop dead."

"You'd better not!" Cor's voice sent her jumping like a startled mouse.

"Stars, was that necessary?" She turned, hand over her chest, trying to calm her beating heart.

Cor walked past her without a glance, carrying four other bags. "Yup. You keep me alive, I keep you alive."

She could see the smile in the corner of his mouth. "Oh, right. Of course. Thanks." She made a face at his receding back.

He wasn't carrying all that when he left town. She knew that for a fact. "Show-off." Still, four fewer bags for her to carry.

୧

They spent all that day and the next traveling northwest, weaving through hills and around small patches of woods and thickets. No more rain, but the ground was still damp, and once or twice a wagon would get stuck in a rut, and Mishkil or Orek would have to push it out. The Dwyn came in handy on a long journey.

… Unlike Zelie, who spent most of the afternoon trying to balance herself on Chiara's shoulders. "Your shoulders aren't very wide," she complained. "Cor's are much broader."

"Oh, no," Chiara deadpanned. "You mean I'm not quite the strapping young Tegid specimen you'd prefer for your seating arrangements?"

As soon as the words left her mouth, she regretted them. "Ooo, strapping?" Zelie cackled. "What a perfect word for him!" She leapt off Chiara's back and flicked her ears suggestively toward Cor. He was walking a few yards ahead of them, with long, loping strides, tattooed arms swinging by his sides.

"And why so scathing?" she chirped. "Don't pretend you don't like that!'"

Chiara eyed Cor critically. He did have good shoulders. But then again, of course he did. He was a Tegid. It would be unusual if he didn't.

And anyway, she'd rather die than admit that to Zelie.

"Come, now," Zelie purred. "You're telling me you *don't* find him attractive?"

Chiara snorted. "You little imp. We're in the middle of a serious mission."

"Exactly! How else am I supposed to be entertained?"

"Zelie! Anything that qualifies as a distraction should *not* be happening on a life-or-death mission!"

"Stick in the mud," Zelie griped, trotting by Chiara's side. "You're no fun."

"And you're being dramatic," Chiara laughed.

"Dramatic? Zelie?" Tagg chimed in from his seat on the wagon. "Never. We all know she's the paradigm of calm, logical thought."

"Hey!" Zelie protested.

Tagg ignored her. "What has inspired today's drama?"

Chiara could practically see Zelie's eyes light up as she began, "Ooo, it's—"

"—Not important," Chiara cut in quickly. "Don't encourage her, Tagg."

Tagg tilted his head to one side and raised his ears. "You're gonna lie to a Jeka, mate?"

"Not you, too." Chiara glared at him. *I don't have the patience for this.*

A shout came from the group ahead of them. "Break for evening meal!" A chorus of relieved voices followed. The entire caravan slowed to a halt and began clustering around the wagons.

Zelie trotted daintily away, heading for the Beast-skins at the front. Chiara watched her go with a sigh. Zelie was her oldest friend, but sometimes …

"Ah … I see." Tagg nodded slowly as he dismounted the wagon seat.

Chiara shot him a sharp glance. He was stroking Ria's side, carefully avoiding her eyes. "She's setting you up with him, isn't she?"

"Oh — no," Chiara began hastily. "It's not what you think. Zelie's just like that."

"Oh, believe me, I know," Tagg snorted. "She plays matchmaker anytime she gets bored. Half the bally crew's been set up at one point or another. You can't imagine the trouble she's caused."

"Oh, I can imagine it," Chiara grimaced. "I had to grow up with it."

"And what are your thoughts on her latest endeavor?" Tagg cocked an ear at her.

She rolled her eyes. "It's *ridiculous*. Arva forbid."

"Ridiculous, eh?" Tagg had a thoughtful look on his face. "Can't say I agree. I've never been more of a third wheel in my life — and I'd say that's a good sign."

Somehow, that made Chiara even more nervous than Zelie's wild fancies.

You've got something there. It's worth holding onto.

He'd said that to Cor the other night, when she was supposed to be asleep.

… And now this? What is he trying to say?

"A good sign?" Chiara tried to summon a warning tone. "Don't even think about it. You know how Zelie gets."

Tagg mimicked locking his mouth shut and throwing out the key. "Silent as the grave. … For the moment, anyway."

Now he was just teasing her.

"Troublemakers, the whole lot of you," Chiara grumbled. She ran her hands through her hair. *How'd we even get here?*

Zelie was nothing but saucy; Tagg clearly had a fair hand in mischief; and Cor …

Well.

Cor. Her catcher. *As if we didn't have enough drama there already.* Zelie did *not* need any more encouragement.

Suddenly, Chiara needed space. She should eat and rest with the others … but she didn't feel like eating, or resting. She drifted past the seated circles until she found herself on the far side of one of the hills.

It was covered with shrubby trees and vibrant yellow flowers, spots of gold scattered across the grass. She sat and stared west, watching as the sun dipped below the tree line, staining the sky crimson.

"Chiara?"

She practically leapt out of her boots as Skipper appeared from behind one of the trees. He was walking down the hill, taking the steep slope easily in stride.

"Oh … well met, sir." She dipped her head respectfully.

"I take it you've come to find some refuge here? Or is my guess incorrect?" His eyes were warm.

"Yes," she admitted. "I … needed some space to think."

"Hmm. A good place to come, no? The sunset is particularly beautiful. And the flowers."

"Yes, sir." Warm yellow … like butter in Mum's kitchen. *I miss her … I miss them.* Chiara let out a sigh. Where was Kaito now?

Skipper tsked. "You're too young to have that kind of sigh. What's on your mind?"

Chiara hesitated, searching for the easiest words. "I … think I'm restless, sir."

"After all this walking?"

She couldn't help a smile. "Yes, sir. It's not restlessness of the body. I've felt that before." *Too many times.* "It's … restlessness of the heart."

"I see," He nodded, looking thoughtful. "Come." He sat down on the grass and gestured next to him. "Tell me. Why restlessness of the heart?"

"Well …" Chiara sat near him and plucked a blade of grass, twisting it in her hand. "I miss my parents. I keep wondering if Kaito's reached them yet."

Was that a sad smile on Skipper's face? Or was she seeing things?

He replied without looking at her. "Kaito has never failed me yet. It's only right that you worry. Familial affection is a precious thing. I'm glad you're so close with them."

"You've known my father for three years, haven't you, sir?"

Skipper nodded. "Longer than that, as a matter of fact. We met when we were both still soldiers for hire — young and reckless. It was a mission outside of Crescor, and I've respected him ever since … although it wasn't until three years ago that we became closer friends."

He was smiling now. "He's a good fighter, your father. A good fighter with a good heart. He's always been so proud of you."

Chiara looked away. "Thank you, sir."

Proud of me … always proud of me. Me and Isak. Goosebumps prickled across her skin. Suddenly, it was hard to swallow.

"Are you worried about them?" Skipper's question caught her by surprise.

"Well … yes," Chiara said slowly. "And … no. I mean, of course, I worry. But Dad is the most capable Tegid I know. And Mum, too. I know they'll take care of each other."

"Your faith in them is well-placed." Skipper rose and dusted off his pants. "Come. It's time for food and rest."

Chiara leapt to her feet and fell into stride next to him as he began walking back around the hillside, still talking. "We still have a few more days before we reach Talin. Aren't you glad you joined the circus?"

Chiara smiled. "Happier than ever, sir. I wasn't doing much in Belkar." *Might as well make light of it.* She gave him a mock grimace — but to her surprise, it was met with a deeply compassionate look.

"Yes, you were. Zelie reminds me of that every day."

"Zelie? Really?"

"Believe it or not," he laughed. "Her wagging tongue is good for something, after all." His smile faded. "I'm proud of my heritage. But there are some things about our culture—" He broke off, and Chiara saw the muscles grow taut in his jaw.

"Stunted," she said, taking care to keep all the emotion out of her voice.

How strange was that? A whole lifetime of pain and tears — just … swallowed up by one insignificant word.

Skipper looked at her, and a chill ran down her spine. "Curse the heart that conceived that word. I know how far you've come, Chiara. They were wrong to call you that." His eyes were burning with hatred — thorough, unswaying hatred.

"No, they weren't." The words slipped out of her mouth before she could stop them.

"Your father told me what happened in Crescor."

Chiara froze in her tracks. She lifted her chin, hot anger already choking her. "What did he tell you?" she demanded tersely.

Did he tell you I was there? Did he tell you how I saw it happen? Did he tell you how I wasn't fast enough? Did he tell you that?

"He told me," said Skipper slowly, "that you ran in to save your brother. And he said that after all his years of fighting, he had never seen courage until he saw you that day. And I believe him."

Chiara clenched her teeth and looked away.

Never seen courage …

◌

The next few days passed in a blur, and Chiara didn't see much of Skipper. He was still at the front of the caravan. But she kept thinking about what he'd said.

He had never seen courage until he saw you that day.

Courage? Was it courage? She would've called it fear, desperation …
not courage. *Since when have I been brave?* That was probably the last time
she'd come close to bravery. She'd spent the past three years hiding …

"What's wrong?" Cor interrupted her train of thought one
afternoon. "You look like you've got a lot on your mind."

"It's—" Chiara was cut short when he started coughing again. She
clenched her jaw, watching as he tried to stifle it in the crook of his
elbow.

As soon as he was through, she said, "Go see Talia," in a tone that
brooked no argument.

"I—"

"Go! What excuse do you have? She's only a few wagons ahead, and
she has her supplies with her."

Cor gave her a protesting look, and she tried to propel him ahead
with a hand at his back. He was more solid than she'd anticipated,
though, and she only succeeded in sending him forward a step or two.

But it got him laughing, and that at least was better than coughing.
"You struggling there a little?"

"Shut up." But Chiara was stifling her own laugh.

"You gotta try harder," he joked, and she glanced at him, half-
amused, half-worried.

There was a pause, and then she kept on. "I'm serious, okay?" Her
heart sank again. "You're not supposed to be …"

Sick. Cor was a Tegid. He wasn't supposed to be sick — ever.
Unless—

She flicked her eyes to the ground, not even wanting to say the
word. Instead, she asked, "Has this ever … happened to you before?"

Cor pressed his lips together. "No," he said at last.

Chiara slid her fingers around his arm, slowing his steps, and he turned to look at her curiously.

"Please," she said. "For my sake, at least, if not yours."

He nodded. "Okay … I'll go." Slowly, and then picking up speed, he trotted ahead. Chiara watched him anxiously.

"Well, well," said Tagg from the wagon seat.

Chiara glanced at him, face heating. "Listen—"

His eyebrows were raised. "No, it's not that. I've just never seen him so docile."

"What do you mean?" Chiara frowned.

"He bally hates it when people try to take care of him for him," Tagg snorted. "Even I couldn't have talked him into that." He made a face at her. "Guess the flier position has special privileges."

"Maybe …" Chiara looked up ahead, watching as Cor kept stride with Talia's wagon.

"I mean it, mate," said Tagg, and she looked back to see that his gaze was still on her. "You've got something there."

Something? *What's* something? Her hands tingled nervously. *You've got something there.* First to Cor, now to her …

Tagg didn't clarify, and she wasn't quite brave enough to ask him to.

෪

It was midafternoon on the third or fourth day of travel when the scouts returned with news that Talin was ahead — still a few miles away, but close.

"Talin is bigger, isn't it?" Chiara had never been there before.

"Yep." Cor wasn't coughing today — in fact, he looked more chipper than usual. But that wasn't necessarily good news. Talia couldn't seem to find the source of his cough. She'd given him candied honey for a sore throat, but she hadn't been able to do much else.

Chiara glanced at him. "Do you think it'll be … like Grede?"

"You mean Mask?" Tagg asked quietly.

Zelie poked her head out from the wagon behind him. "Let's hope not!"

"He would've had to follow us all this way," Cor pointed out. "The scouts would've noticed something."

That wasn't as reassuring as Chiara wanted it to be. They'd told Skipper, of course, after they'd left Grede. But his reaction had instilled no confidence in her. And he hadn't dismissed the theory about a Mask-Arsonist connection when Cor brought it up.

That alone was reason enough to make Chiara anxious. *As if nightmares about Mask weren't bad enough …*

"Hey." Cor gave her a reassuring nudge. "He wouldn't have tracked us here. He doesn't even know who you are. We'll be okay."

"Thanks," Chiara murmured.

Finally, Talin was within spotting distance, and the Captains halted to split the caravan once again. This time, Tagg's wagon was with Talia, and the rest of the wagons were staying behind to camp.

"Gather 'round, clan!" Skipper called. The entire caravan came closer, forming a large, ragged circle around him. "In and out. No noise, no fires. Trading crew enters the city in an hour — no wagons. The rest of the circus camps out here. Prepare to leave an hour before dawn."

He began listing off names. "Rosc. Mykzi. Faye. Leo. Tagg. Chiara. Zelie. Nadia. Rye. Coren will be leading the crew. His orders are final."

Chiara frowned. *No wagons?* Only ten crewmates? She would've expected a larger group, since Talin was bigger than Grede.

"Crew to Talia!" Skipper instructed. "Everyone else, with me."

The trading crew split off, gathering around Talia. Cor stood by her side.

She picked up where Skipper left off. "You stay at a stable by the east gate. Skipper, he knows the owner." She looked around the circle carefully. "No trouble. Better to leave Talin early than risk drawing attention to yourselves."

Cor nodded.

The twisted mask flashed through Chiara's mind, and goosebumps prickled across her flesh.

Talia was still talking. "Make for the southern gate at dusk — one hour. Pack your bags. Cor, you discuss trading assignments on the way. Look lively!"

She turned and rejoined Skipper. Mishkil lumbered up to them, and immediately the three were involved in close conversation. Chiara watched them, anxiety growing like vines clinging to her ribs.

Then Zelie popped up beside her, startling her. "I bet I can get an even *better* dried fruit deal here!"

Chiara clutched at her chest. "Why must you do that?"

"I am a creature of stealth and the night," Zelie sniffed. "I appear and disappear at will."

"Which are excellent qualities for a nighttime sentry." Cor stepped in between them with a wide smile on his face.

"Guard duty?" Zelie exclaimed, looking dismayed.

"Do I detect ingratitude?" Cor fixed her with a stern look. "Need I remind you of your last escapade during a city foray?"

"No," she sighed.

"I'll trade places with you." Chiara attempted a smile. *Anything's better than another nightmare.* Mask's face was flittering around inside her head like some kind of phantom bat.

We won't see him. She wished she had Cor's confidence in saying that.

"You smell … nervous." Zelie was studying her carefully. "Are you okay?"

"Fine." Chiara rubbed her hands up her arms. "It's just … I'll be happy once we're on the move again. The Captains seem tense." She looked over Zelie's shoulder toward Skipper, Mishkil, and Talia.

Zelie followed her gaze. "Oh, I see! Don't worry — that's just them when they're more serious." Her optimism sounded slightly forced.

More serious … "Like at the ford," Chiara said quietly.

Zelie didn't reply, but her ears lowered.

So I was right. They are *tense.* Maybe Skipper suspected something. Maybe it was about Mask.

Please … don't let him be here.

ભ

Trading took most of the afternoon, thanks to the sprawling layout of the central market, and night had fallen by the time the crew was done. Then they split up into two groups, and each group met up with Skipper's contact.

Petrus was a tough-looking Tegid with a shaved head and rings in his ears. He met each group just outside the marketplace and then led them to his private barn on the outskirts of Talin.

It was a staggered trip, similar to Grede, to avoid any tails or suspicion. Unfortunately, instead of easing Chiara's fears, it made her more anxious.

Now they were gathered at the wide doors of the barn, looking inside at the double rows of stalls.

"Pick the empty stalls," Cor instructed, his voice barely audible. "Everybody gets their own."

The group went double-file down the walkway. Their footsteps crunched softly over hay and woodchips. The only light sources were a few ceiling lanterns, hanging several feet apart above the walkway. Soft nickering drifted in the air — horses, stirring from slumber.

"Didn't think we'd be back here so soon." Tagg glanced around at the darkened stalls as they passed.

"You've been here before?" Chiara breathed in deeply. The musky scent of animal filled her nose — strong, but not unpleasant.

"Two or three times, I'd say. Watch your step." Tagg sidestepped around a large drainage grate in the floor. "Last time was a bit before we came to Belkar for the Midsummer Festival. Time flies."

He stopped in front of a stall and peered inside. "This one's clean." He opened the lower door and gestured inside. "Go on. I'll find another one."

Chiara walked inside, breathing in the smell of fresh hay.

Tagg shut the door behind her. "'Night, Chiara."

"'Night," she called back, dropping her bag onto the ground.

She was shifting the hay into a pile when Cor stuck his head over the stall door, startling her. "Hey."

"Oh! Hi." She stood up, brushing hay off her pants. "What's wrong?"

"Nothing. Just—" He held up a blanket in his hand. "Brought you this." He tossed it onto the hay.

Chiara picked it up and immediately recognized the scent — dried rosemary. "Cor, this is your blanket."

He shrugged. "I don't need it."

"Are you sure?"

"Positive."

"Well …" She rubbed a finger over the blanket. "Thanks, I guess."

Cor's gaze flicked away. "I'm in the stall across from you. If anything happens …" He glanced toward the barn entrance and hesitated.

His hand was resting on the top of the door. Chiara noticed the tendons shift and tighten beneath the inky patterns.

He's worried.

"It'll be fine," she said, pretending like she wasn't bothered about the idea of Mask showing up.

"Just … call me if something happens, okay?" His eyes were liquid in the dim lantern glow.

"Promise." Chiara didn't know what possessed her to touch his hand, much less squeeze it quickly. But it happened, somehow, and then she was retreating into her stall.

And he looked so relieved that she didn't regret it.

"'Night, Chiara."

"'Night, Cor."

16

*F*ire. *Fire, all around, in her eyes, her mouth, burning along her skin … Isak! Soundless screaming … clawing over the smoldering wreckage …*

The shadow … appearing, moving toward her — reaching out a hand — the painted face—

Suddenly Chiara was awake, upright, gasping, staring up into the darkness outside her stall door.

He was touching me … Shuddering, she rubbed a hand over her scars. They were hot to the touch. Sweat had soaked her neckline.

Just a dream. Her shoulders sagged, and she slumped down, feeling the ache in her muscles.

Maybe I'd be better off sleeping next to Zelie. She glanced up—

—and Mask was there.

"Arva!"

Chiara leapt to her feet — she snatched up her knife — the Mask was coming closer — someone was screaming; there were shouts, thumping, lanterns flashing—

—and then Cor.

He was in the stall with her, one arm locked around her waist, a hand clamped over her mouth.

The scent of rosemary and honey filled her nose. "Chiara, you need to be quiet," he whispered urgently.

Only then did she realize that she'd been the one screaming. She went limp in his arms.

Lanterns flashed through the darkened barn; lowered voices, people passing her stall.

"Nod if I can let you go," he whispered again.

Chiara nodded vigorously. Cor released her, and she whirled around to face him.

"He was here," she gasped. "Mask — he was here — he was staring at me — right there—" She pointed a shaking finger to the top of her stall door.

"You were awake?" Cor asked quietly.

"Yes. I was already awake when I saw him. You saw him, too, right? He was *right there.*"

Cor shook his head. "I didn't see him. I heard you scream, and I came, but I didn't see anyone." He hesitated. "Are you sure …?"

"Yes! Yes, I'm sure. He was *here* — I *saw* him—" Chiara was shaking violently now, skin growing hot and clammy by turns. "I swear it was him …" *He was here … How did he find us …?*

Cor rubbed a gentle hand over her shoulder. "I believe you. I promise. It's just …" He shook his head. "Nobody saw anything. Zelie and Leo are on guard duty at the entrance. How could he get past them without being noticed?"

It wouldn't be the first time. Chiara shuddered. "Do you really think that could stop him?"

"What do you mean?" Cor sounded confused.

"I mean …" Chiara tried to collect her thoughts. "Remember Grede? He vanished as soon as Tagg went after him. Maybe — maybe he came in some other way."

"I'm not sure …"

Cor was interrupted when a tiny shadow leapt into the stall — Zelie. "Chiara! Are you okay?" She thrust her nose into Chiara's face, sniffing for harm.

"I'll … be fine," Chiara managed. "I'm not hurt."

"Did you see anything?" Cor asked Zelie.

"Not a thing." Zelie sounded worried. "I heard Chiara scream, and I turned around, and there was a lot of yelling and lanterns, and then—" She wrinkled her nose. "Oh, and I smelled something weird."

Chiara and Cor both turned on her. "Like what?" they asked at the same time, making Zelie jump.

"Well …" she said slowly. "It smelled like…like metal, or something. Like hot metal."

Hot metal. Like Belkar. Like Crescor.

"He was here," Chiara whispered under her breath.

"Hot metal …" Cor murmured. "You're sure it wasn't the lanterns?"

"No!" Zelie sounded indignant. "I know what lanterns smell like! This was *different*."

"He was here," Chiara repeated, louder now.

"He? Who?" Zelie asked, and then her ears sank. "Wait — Mask? How is that even possible? You ran into him *once*! How could he *possibly* have followed us all the way here? And for *what*? He has no idea who you are!"

"Maybe … maybe it wasn't him," Chiara muttered. "Maybe it was someone else."

That's … so much worse. Best-case scenario, it meant that there was more than one creepily masked figure lurking around their route.

And the worst-case scenario was that Mask was one of a group of people that could apparently appear and disappear at will … a group like the Arsonists.

The theory about Mask being one of them was gaining more and more credibility by the minute …

"I don't like that at all." Cor sounded dismal. "Okay. This happened twice in a row, and I'm not happy about it. Chiara, I'm taking you back out to camp."

"I'm coming with you," Zelie insisted.

"No," Cor said immediately. "Your nose is stronger than any of ours, and you've got his scent now. I need you to track him. It hasn't even been five minutes since he disappeared. He's got to be in Talin still. Find out what roads he took, any corners or buildings he might have lingered, anything."

Zelie's ears twitched. "Fine. You'd better take care of her." She was practically showing her teeth.

Cor didn't bat an eyelash. "I swear on my life that I will keep her safe tonight."

A prickle ran up the back of Chiara's spine.

"I take your word for it." Zelie turned and sprinted soundlessly down the walkway.

"Come on." Cor was already scooping up Chiara's bag and bedding. "I'll carry this. Get your sax. Ready? Good. Let's go." He herded her out of the stall and began striding toward the barn doors.

Chiara had to trot to keep up. "What about your things?"

He shook his head. "Don't need 'em. We've gotta get you to camp as fast as possible — no time to waste."

"So why did you take mine?" she insisted. Technically, the blanket was his, but—

"No more questions." He signaled to Leo as they passed through the entrance of the barn. "Reporting back to camp. Tell Nadia that she's leader in my absence."

Leo nodded, and Cor led Chiara out of the barn. They melted immediately into the shadows.

There he paused for a moment and turned around, leaning down so that his mouth was practically touching her ear. "No talking. Stay right behind me. Tug my hand if you see anything."

His hand slid into hers, fingers interlocking.

She nodded. Her skin was tingling … adrenaline, probably.

Dawn was still a few hours away. Every building was eerily silent. Cor led her down street after street, past darkened windows and locked doors and closed-up trading booths.

Around every corner, Chiara expected to see Mask lurking in some doorstep. But they saw nothing.

Cor's route was clever — he must have been around Talin a few times. They were cutting down alleys, vaulting over fences, even once or twice cat-walking on top of walls or rooftops. And all the time, he kept her hand in his, even pausing to tighten his grip.

He was so nimble that Chiara thought she might lose her footing behind him. But she didn't. *All Zelie's training is paying off.* She never thought she'd use it to escape a phantom arsonist in the middle of the night. *Thanks, Zelie.*

After about twenty minutes, they were squatting in the shrubbery just across the road from the East Gate. Two sentries with lanterns were posted on either side.

Chiara glanced sideways at Cor, who was watching the guards carefully. "Armed, but not heavily," he whispered. "Casual stances. City protocol, most likely. Come on — this way."

Hand still clutching hers, he led her in a wide circle until they were several yards away from the gate. Gnarled trees lined the inner wall, towering above the stone.

He pointed. "Ready?"

The whisper in her ear sent another prickle down her arms. Nodding, she released his hand, and even dared a joke. "Watch and learn."

She was up the tree and down on the other side of the wall in less than a minute.

Cor followed more slowly, and he paused for a moment in the tree and peered down into the sleeping streets. Then suddenly he leapt down, landing on his feet soundlessly next to her. "No one tailing us. Let's go." They struck out east.

Half an hour later, they arrived at the outskirts of camp. Talia met them. "I heard you coming." She wiggled her ears. "Something is wrong?"

Cor nodded. "I'll report later. Right now, Chiara needs a place to sleep — not the hammocks."

"She can stay in my wagon." Talia gestured over her shoulder.

"Fine. I'll sleep outside it."

Talia clucked approvingly. "You have great chivalry, Coren. But it is no need. I can take care of her."

"It's not about *can*," Cor said immediately. "It's about *should*. She's my flier. I'm taking care of her."

"You speak well, Coren." There was a note of pride in Talia's voice. "So be it."

Then she took Chiara's bag from Cor and led her to the wagon. A bulky shadow loomed beside it, huffing softly — Norik, dozing on all four legs.

Talia pulled aside the tent flap and guided Chiara inside. "You must stay here. I have guard duty. I will be back." Then she was gone.

Chiara pushed aside bundles and chests and laid out her bedding on the floor of the wagon. Cor's blanket was still inside.

She hesitated for a minute, and then she stretched it out over herself.

She kept seeing Mask's face flash in the darkness. She could almost picture the tent flap moving, the shadow appearing—

There was a crunch and a soft "Chiara."

She jumped. Cor — he must have been just outside the wagon canvas.

"Yes?" she whispered.

"I'm here."

"I know."

"Sleep. You'll need it."

"I'll try." She didn't think she'd ever sleep again.

"Good." There was another crunch, somewhere beneath her. Cor must have settled himself right next to the wagon wheels. She could practically hear his breathing. Steady, rhythmic …

Her heart rate began to slow. She breathed in deeply, inhaling the scent of his blanket.

I can trust him.

With her life. She knew that.

Then why wouldn't she trust him with Isak?

Isak was my brother. Protests rose, loud in her brain. *I can't replace him.* Cor was her catcher now, but …

I don't want to choose, I don't want to choose — the same battle since the very first day. *It hasn't come between us … has it?*

Only it had. It had, and she knew it. The whole reason they struggled as a duo was because she was still seeing Isak in her head, still remembering him in her muscles.

How much longer can I run from it?

ℭ

"Chiara."

She blinked awake. It was still dark outside, but a bird was twittering. She sat upright cautiously, blinking, realizing she was still in the back of Talia's wagon.

"Chiara. Are you up?" Cor. His voice sounded much raspier today. A pang of worry shot through her.

"I'm up," she croaked. Her voice wasn't much better.

The back flap of the wagon twitched and then grew still.

She laughed in spite of herself. "Take it easy. I swear I'm still in here."

"I know that!" Was that indignation in his tone? Or embarrassment? "I'm just … doing my job." The raspy voice became gruff. "Wash up. Breakfast in five minutes, and then we're heading out."

"Coming." She could already hear the rest of the camp stirring outside.

It was an hour before dawn, and camp takedown was already beginning. Just as the fourth wagon was being loaded, the trading crew arrived, laden with more supplies. As soon as everything was packed, the caravan set out north through the hills.

Chiara quickly saw for herself why Zelie was a liability on the trading crew — as if Grede wasn't enough proof of that. She'd brought back a tin flute, for no apparent purpose except to keep herself entertained while they traveled.

"You were supposed to track Mask," Cor rebuked her. "Not become a troubadour."

"I did track him!" Zelie protested from her perch behind Tagg. "I already told you — straight down the middle of the road, no turns, and then it vanished. No sign of the suspect himself. And how dare you imply that I couldn't excel at a musical instrument? I'll be the talk of the circus route." She put the flute to her lips.

One shrill, horrifying note later, Tagg pulled the flute out of her mouth. "Absolutely not. Play it again and I'll have to kill you."

Zelie looked offended. "It just needs some fine-tuning!"

Tagg snorted. "*You* need some fine-tuning. I'm not gonna spend the rest of this trip listening to you scandalize the birds. Talk of the circus, my ears. They'll talk, alright — they'll vote you right out of Fhír."

He stalked off, flute in hand, and Zelie leapt after him, protesting loudly.

"Thank Arva," Chiara sighed as soon as Zelie was out of earshot. "I would've taken it myself if Tagg hadn't."

Cor shot her an admiring look. "How did you manage not to kill her all these years?"

Chiara shrugged. "We're friends," she said with a laugh. "Would you kill Tagg?"

"Maybe," Tagg butted in as he rejoined them, "but not without me knowing first."

Chiara snorted. "And besides, her skills come in handy most of the time," she added.

Cor sighed. "Not this time, I guess. She didn't find a thing …"

"She said she found the trail." Chiara rubbed her hands over her face.

"Yeah, and that's the most confusing part," Cor said, exasperated. "How did his trail go right down the middle of the road? No dodging or weaving or cutting through alleys or *anything?* We should've seen something …"

He ran a hand through his hair, fluffing it into disheveled angles. "And yet somehow he appeared in the middle of a guarded barn."

"Straight down the middle of the road …" Chiara repeated softly. She chewed at her lip, picturing the streets from last night. Flat, wide, ordinary roads, with drainage grates and— "Holy Arva."

"What? What is it?" Cor exclaimed. He and Tagg looked at her, alarm written across both their faces.

She stared at Cor, wide-eyed. "The grate. The grate in the barn floor."

Sudden realization flashed across his face. "Fesht. We didn't even think of that."

"I bet whatever trail Zelie found went from one grate to the next," Chiara said, words flying as quickly as her thoughts. "Think about it. She picked up the trail a few blocks down, it went right down the middle of the streets, and then it disappeared again."

She glanced between them both, head buzzing. "I'm willing to bet anything that the trail appeared and disappeared at two different grates. That's how he must have disappeared in Grede — and last night. No wonder she couldn't find his scent!"

"He used the water drainage systems." Tagg's eyes widened. "And if he's even remotely connected to the Arsonists—"

"—Then maybe that's their method, too," Chiara finished. "Maybe that's how they get into buildings and then disappear. Fire burns upward. They could start right at the foundations somewhere, and the fire would do the rest of the work for them."

"Wait a minute — wait a minute." Cor frowned. "Those grates are welded. How could they *possibly* remove them without breaking them? There's no way we wouldn't notice a busted storm grate. And there's no way they could just weld them shut again."

"Maybe …" Chiara pursed her lips. "Don't they use some kind of accelerant? Do you think they could use that somehow? Or maybe they have some kind of tool? Something hot enough to burn through welded iron …?"

Even as she said it, she knew it was ridiculous. Tegids were strong, but even five or six fully-grown males couldn't tear off a properly welded iron storm grate without some kind of equipment. And welding a storm grate back in place …?

Cor looked skeptical. "I don't know. I've never heard of any tool that could weld a storm grate that efficiently — and it would have to have been soundless, too. His welding didn't wake us up, and it didn't alert Leo. Nobody was awake until we heard you."

Tagg was shaking his head. "I don't think your theory holds much water … storm drains notwithstanding."

Cor ignored his pun.

Chiara sighed. "I guess you're right." She was so sure she'd been onto something …

Cor was chewing his lip, looking thoughtful. "Still, I'd like to be sure I'm right before we move on from this entirely. I've got an idea — I'll be right back." He broke into a jog and peeled off, heading for the front of the caravan.

Chiara and Tagg watched him go.

Storm grates. That would explain how fast everything happened. How no one had seen anyone coming. How the fire traveled so quickly through the streets and buildings …

No trace of intentional arson, all the investigations had claimed. If the grates had been welded back …

She shuddered. *No wonder they look like accidents.* If the Arsonists really were out there, using the storm grates — using tools that could cut and weld iron without a sound …

… They're far more deadly than we ever could've guessed.

෪

Cor spent the next hour in close conversation with Skipper as the caravan wound slowly over the rolling hillsides. Tagg and Chiara kept an eye out for him, but before he came back to the wagon, they saw Bakhita peel off from the caravan.

Chiara turned to Tagg, wide-eyed. "She's heading back the way we came. You don't think …?"

Tagg raised a knowing eyebrow. "Skipper sent Bakhita. Well, I'd have done the same. She's the best tracker we have — and she's fast, too. I'm willing to bet that she went back to investigate."

"Are you sure?" Chiara felt a tingle of anticipation. Skipper must not be cutting any corners if he was willing to send someone back. *We might actually be onto something here.*

"We'll see, won't we?" Tagg said dryly. "We can't exactly go back to Talin *now*. That would look pretty suspicious, especially to Mask, if he's still lurking around. But Skipper might think the storm grate theory is weird enough to at least investigate."

Anything is better than nothing. Chiara's heart was pounding. "When do you think Bakhita will be back?"

Tagg shrugged again. "Dunno. Probably this time tomorrow — she'll have to cover the whole way we've come from Talin, plus however far we go after she left."

Tomorrow, then. Chiara breathed deeply, trying to relax the tension in her shoulders. Tomorrow.

17

But when the next afternoon came around, Bakhita still hadn't returned. That wasn't the only cause for worry. Cor's cough was worse today, and even though he kept eating candied honeys and swearing he would be fine, Chiara could see the anxiety in his eyes.

He was getting worse, and he knew it. The other circus members were noticing it, too. Most of them were used to sickness, but not sickness in a Tegid.

To top it all off, the Captains were taking the caravan off the beaten trail, back northeast, back toward the Tonitrus as it curved northward. Only, this wasn't a ford or a bridge. It was a narrow goat trail down the side of a gorge.

The road crumbled off into oblivion a few feet to their right, and the roar of the river hundreds of feet below echoed up the sides of the ravine. To their left rose sheer cliffs.

The path had forced the wagons into a single-file line, while those on foot walked two abreast. The horses picked their way carefully between the harsh rock face to the left and the deadly drop on the right. Trees hung thickly overhead, turning midday into a bizarre, otherworldly twilight.

The noise of the water was loud and constant.

"We might've been able to skip this if we hadn't stopped yesterday." Zelie's voice was barely audible over the roar.

As quiet as she was, Cor must have heard her. "No way." He dropped back to walk beside Chiara and gave Zelie a hard look. "Not with horses and wagons — we would've had to finish this in the dark. Not everyone has your nocturnal senses." His face was tense.

Zelie huffed. "Fair enough, I guess. Still … we could've made it to—" She broke off, staring at the cliffside, ears pricked.

Cor was looking in the same direction. His expression became uneasy.

"What? What is it?" Chiara watched him intently. The hairs on the back of her neck were already prickling.

Beside them, Ria was fidgeting restlessly. Chiara could hear Toby snorting behind them, Crovus trying to calm him.

What are they sensing?

"This is a bad place to get stuck." Cor was walking closer to her, close enough that his arm brushed against her shoulder.

Her heart skipped a beat. "What are you saying?"

"Look around." He tilted his head up. "No escape route for a caravan. We're all focusing on keeping our footing. The river drowns out most of the noise."

Suddenly she realized what he was saying. "We're birds on a wire."

His jaw was tight. "Perfect place for an ambush."

Chiara's skin wouldn't stop prickling. Whatever the horses were sensing, she was beginning to feel it, too … like something was up there, watching them.

She glanced upward. Was it the tossing branches? Or something else?

"Don't look," Cor hissed in her ear.

"What?"

"Don't look. If there's someone up there, we don't want to give away that we know. At least they won't have the advantage of surprise."

"Halt!" The whisper slid through the caravan from one wagon to the next, and the whole train came to a slow stop.

Zelie's ears went flat against her skull. Chiara exchanged an anxious glance with Cor. Even the river wasn't loud enough to drown out her heartbeat in her ears.

"Cliffside …" The whisper came winding back through the line. Chiara could feel Cor's body tense beside her. He hadn't touched the short swords at his back … yet. But he was ready.

"Chiara, behind me and to the side," he said under his breath. She unsheathed her sax and gripped it tightly.

A rush of panic was rising in the back of her throat. The sax was just a brittle piece of iron in her hands. She readjusted her grip. All the training in the world didn't change the fact that she felt she was about to find out how little she remembered.

I've never taken a life. Why, of all things — *why* was that the thought that crossed her mind? Standing there, heart in her mouth, seeing shadows move in all corners of her vision … She drew a soft, shuddering breath.

Moments stretched by. One … two … Her heartbeat was becoming more painful with every breath. Another horrible moment.

"Weapons up," Cor hissed, and suddenly his swords were in his hands. Chiara lifted her sax a few inches. On either side, she could just make out one or two metallic glints as the other circus members stood at the ready.

A piercing yell tore through the canyon, and dark shapes plummeted from the branches above. In a heartbeat, the gorge was filled with the deafening sounds of combat. The horses plunged wildly, rearing and striking out at anything that moved. Battle cries from Rosc, Crovus, the Dwyn — thundering through the canyon, almost overpowering the river.

"CUT THE ROPES!" Mishkil roared somewhere up ahead.

Attackers were crawling like lizards down the cliffside. Zelie snarled and launched herself through the air, latching onto one of the dark shapes. Suddenly the stone face of the gorge was crawling with Beast-skins — leaping, howling, clawing at their ambushers.

Bodies began to fall, cut loose from the lines, tossed down, thudding to the ground. The circus fighters made quick work of them. Cor disappeared as soon as the first body hit the ground, charging in to join the skirmish.

Chiara stood rooted in place, noise flooding her brain, until a flash and a rough shout brought her back to her senses. She whirled to the side just as a hooded figure brought his blade down.

She ducked, but the tip bit into her shoulder like red-hot teeth. With a cry, she charged forward, sax in both hands as she pressed him backward — there was an animal scream; a sickening thud — and he crumpled to the ground in front of her.

Ria had reared up behind him, kicking his head in. She screamed, rearing again, nostrils flaring red.

Dark liquid began to pool around the fallen body. Chiara's stomach turned, and she stumbled away — directly into another attacker. He shoved her aside, swinging a curved blade as he charged toward Ria.

The horses — they're targeting the horses— Instantly, her sax was swinging through the air, straight for his back. It connected solidly against his neck, and he staggered to the side.

Chiara cried out as pain splintered back up her arms. Before she could recover, he wheeled around and plunged toward her. She stumbled backward, panic roaring in her ears. It was all she could do to keep her footing. The hooded head loomed in front of her as he battered her backward.

He's trying to push me off the edge. Just as she guessed his strategy, he made a vicious swipe at her legs. She leapt to the side, feeling the blade slit through her pant leg, drawing blood.

She hissed at him; desperate energy coursed through her. Hands burning around her sax, she battered in a frenzy at his head — clumsy, vicious blows, nothing like the neat moves Crovus had taught her.

Her attacker danced backward, evading. Chiara swung at his legs, and he leapt back. Suddenly he cursed aloud, stumbling awkwardly to the side. A turned ankle.

Blood roared in Chiara's ears, and she lunged forward, both hands tight around the handle of her sax—

—and flesh gave way beneath the blade as it sank hilt-deep into his stomach.

He let out a gurgling breath, eyes going wide. "You …" he choked out hoarsely.

Chiara gave a sickened cry, releasing the sax. Her attacker staggered back and sank slowly to the ground, the weapon still lodged deep under his ribs.

Then he crumpled onto his side, shaking and twitching. Bloody foam began to drip from the corner of his mouth.

Chiara stumbled backward, away from him. The world was spinning around her head. She couldn't see — nothing except the body, still lying there, twitching.

Nausea rolled over her. She fell to her hands and knees and was sick on the ground. Shadows swarmed across her eyes when she finally lifted her head. Ria was plunging between the wagon shafts, still lashing out with her hooves.

Chiara crawled back to the wagon and slumped against the back wheel. *I just … I just …*

Movement, around her. Voices. The circus crew, shouting out names.

Tattoos. Cor. Cor was there, right in front of her. His mouth was moving. His eyes were locked on hers.

She blinked, trying to clear her vision. What was that … in his eyes?

Terror.

She'd never seen him look scared.

His mouth was moving. He was still speaking. Chiara frowned and shook her head. "What?" she asked thickly.

"Are you injured? Whose blood is this?" He was pointing to her hands.

Chiara looked down. Red — red, like ink, dripping down her hands and arms. She smeared it across her pants, then smeared it again. *Get it off — get it off me—*

"Chiara, is it yours?" Cor repeated more insistently.

"N-no," she shuddered. "Just my shoulder … I think. And … my leg."

Cor found her injuries in seconds. His shoulders slumped forward, tension draining from his face. "Oh, thank Arva — I thought—" and then he stopped.

"Cor … I don't think … I can stand," she managed faintly.

"That's alright. Here." He drew her in to him. "Just sit for a minute."

She rested her chin on his shoulder.

There, just behind Cor. The lifeless heap on the ground.

"Cor … I killed him," she whispered.

Cor glanced over his shoulder, and all the muscles in his arms went tight. He let her go gently, and he stood and stooped over the body, lifting an arm, pressing his fingers against the wrist.

Then he placed both hands on her sax handle, braced himself with a foot against the empty chest, and pulled.

"Ugh …" Chiara turned away, disgusted.

There was a soft scraping sound. Then something tapped her shoulder. She opened her eyes.

Cor. "Chiara … come on, Chiara. You can do this. Sit up for me … can you do that? There you go …"

He was talking to her in a low, soft voice, the way Tagg talked to Ria when she was spooked.

Her sax was in Cor's hand — mercifully clean. He must have wiped the blade.

Bile rose in her throat as she saw its cruel edge. She turned her head away.

"Chiara."

Something in Cor's voice drew her gaze to him. His eyes were dark. "What's going on?"

"I … I just killed someone …" She pointed a limp finger at the body. "He was alive — and I — I *felt* him die, Cor. I saw his face …" She swallowed, choking.

He knelt beside her and squeezed her hand. "It was self-defense, Chiara. You did exactly what I trained you to do."

"I know." *What difference does it make?*

She'd never taken a life before.

That old idea … how the opposite of innocence was knowledge … suddenly she began to understand.

I'll never un-know this.

"He would have killed you, Chiara." Cor's voice was low, hard. "Either stabbed you or sent you over the edge. You're only alive right now because you got to him faster."

"I've never — never—" Her breath was sobbing in her throat.

A spasm crossed his face — something incredibly painful — just for a moment. "I know," he whispered. "The first time. I'm sorry." And then he dropped her sax and his arms slid around her waist, and he was holding her.

She crouched against him awkwardly, burying her face in his shoulder. Tears were in her throat, in her nose and eyes … but they wouldn't come out.

"We can't stay." His breath was warm in her ear. "We have to leave as soon as we can. Can you stand?"

"… I think so."

He was right. But what did it matter?

He rose and lifted her with him. "Arm over my shoulder … there you go." He walked her to the back of the wagon. Then, in one swift motion, he scooped her up and set her in the back.

He hopped up beside her and pulled a satchel from out of the supplies. First aid. He patched up her leg first, then her shoulder, whispering small words of encouragement.

Chiara didn't hear. She didn't even see him — not really. Just the shape on the ground, the dead body, seared into her brain, behind her eyelids.

☙

Cor finished patching her up in minutes. "Stay here," he instructed as he hopped out of the wagon. "I'll be right back."

Chiara didn't argue. Her limbs felt like pudding. All the adrenaline had drained out of her, leaving her exhausted. She crawled to the front of the wagon and leaned against the back of Tagg's seat.

Around her, the circus members were weaving back and forth between the wagons — assessing damage, binding wounds, counting heads. They'd killed or driven off the ambushers, which were about a dozen in number.

But not without a cost. Many of them had been injured. Lopia, Ness, Oxys. And Kojni had the worst of it. Someone had stabbed him in the thigh. He was in his wagon with Talia now as she worked to clean and staunch the wound. His pained cries echoed off the rock walls.

They couldn't stay in the canyon. It was far too risky. After checking the horses — all of whom were miraculously unhurt — Skipper ordered the wagons to begin rolling again.

There was only about a mile or two left of the gorge, but it felt like an eternity. Every jolt was painful. Chiara closed her eyes, and all she could see was death's face appearing, burning behind her eyelids.

Cor walked behind the wagon, keeping a constant eye on her. He wouldn't let her get back out.

It took almost an hour before the dangerous path slowly rose uphill, turning gradually away from the Tonitrus. The gorge became a slope. Finally, the caravan spilled out in between two foothills. Just beyond those was an open plain. Far ahead, the river continued curving west, a smudged line against the horizon.

Then Skipper called a halt. The caravan would go no farther that day.

branded

◌ⳗ

Tagg and Cor were deep in conversation when she woke the next morning.

"Tegids. Not Arsonists," Tagg was saying. "They weren't nearly as skilled."

"We can't be sure." Then Cor began coughing again.

There was a thump, as though Tagg had clapped Cor across the back. "You good, mate?"

"… No," Cor said after a pause.

That brought Chiara awake.

"This is bad, mate. You're not supposed to be like this." Tagg sounded really worried.

"I'm the least of our problems. We can't be sure they weren't Arsonists—"

"No masks."

"We still don't know if the masks and the Arsonists are connected. And who's to say they wear the masks all the time?"

Chiara listened dully. Her body was aching, and her mouth felt like it was stuffed with cotton.

"They've probably been here before." Cor sounded as angry as he was hoarse. "That was the perfect place for an ambush."

I wish it hadn't happened … I wish it hadn't … Her hands were still shaking. She looked down, clenching and unclenching her fingers.

Was that blood on them? Was the blood still there?

Would it ever not be there?

Footsteps, and then the back flap of the wagon opened. Cor leapt easily inside, carrying a canteen. "You're awake. Here." He passed it to her.

She took a few sips, but the water tasted sour in her mouth. "Don't want it." She pushed the canteen away.

"What's wrong?"

What's wrong? She looked at him, anger and sorrow and terror all at once. *You're sick. We've been attacked. I just* … The lifeless body flashed through her head again.

"Chiara, look at me." Cor's voice was gentler than she'd ever heard it. "You did what you had to do. You're only here because he didn't kill you first. And I'm not sorry that you're still alive."

"I know. I just didn't"—she swallowed—"didn't think it would be like this."

"No one ever does." Cor touched a finger to his hand. She looked up. His eyes—

Tagg poked his head into the back of the wagon. "Caravan's moving out." He lifted his ears at Chiara, a sympathetic look on his face.

She couldn't imagine how much he must be hearing right now … from everyone in the caravan.

He turned and disappeared.

"Don't be sorry." Cor looked at her closely. "You're alive." He turned and leapt back out of the wagon.

But Chiara was sorry.

Sorry I'm still alive. Sorry to be alive when Isak was gone. Sorry that her life couldn't be more than that.

Was watching death new? Was it, really? After Isak? It was almost the same kind of thing.

Either way, she could never go back to before. She'd always have to live with it.

18

They made it several more miles northwest before night fell. It was a warm night, with no sign of rain. Skipper called a halt and announced their next stop: Daret, a small town farther northwest. He ordered fires. The circus members bunked down in the grass, inside wagons, up in trees.

Kojni's wound was serious. Talia hadn't left his side since the attack. It wasn't poisoned, but the risk of infection on the road was significant. Everyone seemed to know that. In the wake of that, even Cor's cough wasn't an immediate concern.

But that just kept getting worse, too.

There wasn't much conversation at dinner, and one or two anxious glances were cast toward Talia's wagon. Jarza was clearly very distressed. He hung around Yati's wagon, doing what he could to help Talia, wringing his hands silently. Fleur and Leo stayed with him, trying to console him.

Chiara didn't sleep. Somewhere nearby, she knew, Zelie was curled in a ball, snoring lightly among the roots of an old oak. She kept seeing faces …

Kojni's face. Cor's. Isak's. The death mask. The painted face.

They'd been attacked. Bakhita still wasn't back. And it felt like they weren't a step closer to deciphering the Arsonists' moves.

Even if the storm grate theory was true, that still left them with more questions than answers. Was Mask an Arsonist or not? If so, how did he keep finding them? Was there more than one of him? How did he break and repair the grates?

And if it wasn't the grates … they'd be right back where they started. No leads. No clues. No traces.

No meaning.

Chiara released a breath, letting it hiss through her teeth. She was trying to ignore Cor's wheezing breaths nearby, but it was hard. His hammock wasn't even close to hers, but she couldn't seem to ignore the noise.

If I don't sleep now, I'll regret it tomorrow.

The air was quiet … too quiet for her pounding thoughts. She wished she could pace, or run, or climb, or swing on the bars, or *something.*

… But what's the use? It wouldn't get her any closer to an answer.

A twig snapped somewhere out in the woods. Chiara lay still, listening. *That sounded big.* Too big to be a rabbit. *I didn't think any Felwen lived in these woods …*

branded

Something soft brushed against her arm. "Chiara!" Zelie hissed.

Chiara shot upright. "What is it?" She saw a black shape pacing nearby — Zelie. Her tail was curling back and forth.

"What is it?" Chiara repeated. "Can you smell anything?" Her whisper was almost soundless, but she knew Zelie could hear her easily.

Zelie didn't answer right away. She was still taking in the air. Suddenly she turned to Chiara, luminous eyes flashing in the dark. "Something's coming."

A cry and a sudden burst of footsteps scattered through the small clearing. "Up! Up, Fhír! Up, and be armed!"

"It's Bakhita!" Zelie sounded shocked. Chiara leapt to her feet, even as her stomach sank to her toes. *Something is wrong.*

All around, there was stirring as the circus members sprang up one by one, bundling bedding and unsheathing blades. Footsteps rustled through the grass and leaves.

"Light a fire," someone called, but Bakhita cut in. "No! No fires! No trace of light. Where is the Skipper?"

"Here." A tall, dark shape was striding up to her — Skipper, his voice low and calm. "Report."

"Talin is in flames," Bakhita panted. "I saw it — three miles out. Burning blood-red — the smoke will carry for miles." Her voice was ragged, like she'd been completely winded.

Chiara's body went numb.

The whole city … the trading market. The families. Skipper's friend Petrus …

Gone.

Fire blazed in her mind's eye — the same night, repeating itself endlessly, burned into her brain.

"Arsonists," someone hissed.

"There's more. Enemies coming," Bakhita went on, sounding less winded. "A party of six — hooded, mounted. Like what we've hunted in the cities. They found me in the woods — ten miles south of here. They gave chase. I ran—" She broke off, gasping for breath.

"Did they follow?"

"Yes. I tried to shake them, but …"

"How far out?" Skipper's voice was iron.

"Ten miles at best."

Skipper whirled around immediately. "Silence!"

The clearing went still. "Listen carefully. Your lives depend on it. They can track us in the dark. We split. Six groups. Yati, Ness, Arli, take your wagons now. Head north, east, or northeast. On for three days, until you're sure you haven't been followed. Then circle around east and rendezvous at Crescor."

"Aye, Skipper." The drivers sprang to life, summoning their horses, hitching up the wagons. Yati positioned herself between the shafts and stood motionless.

Skipper didn't miss a beat. "Orek, Tagg, Crovus, your wagons stay. Bakhita, stay with them. Gather leaves and make a bonfire in this clearing to buy us some time. They have nowhere to hide out here. Draw them to the fire, and then fight to kill." His teeth flashed in the dull moonlight.

Immediately the rest of the circus flew into action — all wagons hitched, people sprinting, drivers calling names. Then Bakhita's voice rang out. "Crovus' team! Orek's team! Tagg's team!"

They congregated around her. "Gather the loam and the leaf debris. Pile in the center. Rosc, Faye — dig a trench around the fire; fill it with as many stones as you can find. Tagg, you have matches?"

"Always."

"Light it up as soon as the wagons are clear."

"Yes, ma'am."

Hands shaking, Chiara wrapped up her blanket, thrust it into her pack, and threw it over her shoulders. She began digging up the layer of oak leaves with both hands, carrying heaping handfuls to the center of the clearing. Thank Arva it hadn't rained recently — the leaves were as dry as old bones.

They kept piling up the kindling, leaves and branches and anything else flammable, until it was a few feet across. Cor and Rosc stood by, snapping broken limbs in half, stacking the pile, shaping the whole thing into a tent-like structure.

Yati's wagon began creaking away north, still bearing Kojni and Talia inside. Then Arli, heading east. Then Ness. Slowly, and then picking up speed, they disappeared into the night.

Bakhita was watching them go. As soon as the last wagon vanished into the shadows, she turned. "Tagg! Fire!"

"Cheers!" A small spark, then a flare that lit up Tagg's face in an eerie underworldly red. The tiny flame was plunged into the foot of the pile. For a moment, there was nothing. And then—

Chiara could almost see it catch. A smolder, a bright blaze within the leaves, the stabbing song. Hungry flames sprang to life, licking along the wood and branches. She practically cried out in triumph. Tagg was already on the other side of the bonfire, striking another match, stoking the fire.

"Keep gathering!" Bakhita shouted. Chiara was trembling all over; she barely knew what she was doing. Dark tree roots — leaves crunching in her palms — the fire's glare in her eyes — heat and smoke — and then tossing in her kindling, seeing it devoured in lurid flames, like offerings at some ungodly altar. Over and over again, until her arms and back were stiff from bending and carrying.

"Enough!" Bakhita called. "Now we wait. Beast-skins, to the trees. First line of ambush. Tegids, Nousk, to me. Ring the south side of the fire."

She stood in front of the fire, facing southward, completely motionless. Cor stood beside her. The Beast-skins split away, Orek lumbering across the ground while Leo, Zelie, Nadir, and Zenith leapt up the nearby trunks, disappearing like liquid into the shadowed branches. Everybody else gathered on either side of Bakhita, forming a semicircle around the fire's edge, eyes fixed on the forest.

Time, turning to stone; moments stretching into hours; standing still and stiff; heart beating so painfully that every breath was labored. It couldn't have been more than five minutes since they'd kindled the fire … but it could've been five hours just the same.

Chiara shifted on the balls of her feet, gripping her sax. The face of death flashed before her again, an unshakeable ghost. *I can't hide from it.* She might have to take another life before this was all over.

Please, Arva — please, let my blade strike true. The prayer sprang suddenly to her lips; she was almost whispering it aloud, staring with eyes burning into the darkness.

"They're coming," Zelie announced quietly from her perch somewhere overhead. Chiara's heart pounded even faster.

"How many?" Bakhita whispered.

"Five or six."

"It's them. Stand ready."

Weapons were lifted. Chiara took a shuddering breath. The fire had worked. The Arsonists hadn't split off to follow the first wagons — their attention was on the main group.

Hopefully it stays that way … She strained her ears to listen, to catch any sound of their approach.

Was that her own heart, hammering in her ears? Or was it—

Hoofbeats. Thundering. Closer, closer …

Snarls in the trees — the Beast-skins, pouncing. Screams of terrified horses, heavy bodies thudding to earth. Every muscle stretched taught in Chiara's body. She tried to swallow, but her throat was too dry.

Suddenly a hooded figure burst into the clearing. A wild scream ripped from Bakhita's throat; she leapt forward, claws flashing blood-red in the firelight. He fell beneath her fangs.

Chiara barely had a moment to think — another figure was dashing out of the woods directly toward her.

Her vision went dark; she was sprinting forward, blade swinging wildly — all thoughts thrown to the wind, except one.

Murderer.

The edge of her knife caught something solid, bit in; she gave a shout — and suddenly she was choking.

A viselike hand clamped around her neck; heat tore into her arm; she was bucking, kicking her feet; spots appearing in her eyes; heat flaming up her spine—

"CHIARA!" A roar; a scream; something warm spattering across her face — suddenly she could breathe; she was on the ground, gasping, coughing, heaving for air.

Then something gripped her arm, dragging her sideways. She screamed, clawing at exposed skin.

"Fesht, Chiara, it's *me!*" Cor's face appeared in front of hers. He was the one holding her arm, lifting her upright, pulling her away from the battle, away from the limp form on the ground.

"Are you alright? Are you injured?" he practically shouted in her face.

"Not badly," she choked out. Her arm felt like it was on fire.

"Good." He pushed her into the shadows of the oak. "Stay here."

"I'm coming with you!" she rasped angrily.

"I said stay!"

"Try and stop me!" she snapped at him, nose to nose.

"Fine," he hissed. "Stay right behind me." He turned and dashed back to the fight, Chiara right on his heels.

Two lifeless shapes lay sprawled across the ground. Bakhita and the others were scattered across the clearing, still locked in fierce combat with two more Arsonists.

Cor charged forward, lunging at the knot of fighters as Bakhita struggled against both enemies at once. He thrust his blade forward just as Bakhita clawed at one of the Arsonist's swords.

Chiara's eyes squeezed shut; her limbs turned to stone. *Not again — not again—*

There was a sickening *schlock* and a strangled cry. She heard the body crumple to the ground. Moments later, there was another scream — the final Arsonist.

Shaking, Chiara finally opened her eyes and stared around. Cor came up to her, double swords still out. The blades were stained.

"Where are the others?" she asked, biting her tongue as pain shot up her arm again.

"Beast-skins got 'em." Cor pointed. Orek and the Vikur were prowling out of the woods, eyes glowing in the dull red firelight. Orek was carrying two large bundles in his jaws. He shuffled over to Bakhita, dropping the bodies at her feet.

She was panting. "Their horses?"

"Three killed," said Orek. "Two injured. One escaped."

"Broken legs?"

"No."

"Then leave the injured ones alive. Bury the others. No trace."

Orek nodded. "What about these ones?" He nudged one of the fallen Arsonists.

"Burn them." There was a cold, calm fury in Cor's voice, like a sheer wall of ice.

Chiara shuddered.

Orek looked to Bakhita, who gave a nod. "No trace. The horses might run, but they won't find the bodies."

"Aye." Orek nodded and turned toward the woods, followed by the other Beast-skins.

Cor strode forward and gripped one of the bodies.

"Wait!" Bakhita grabbed his arm. "Take off his hood."

Cor turned the body over and pulled the hood away — then drew back with a soft gasp.

"What? What is it?" Chiara came forward almost reluctantly.

"It's Mask," he said in a horrified whisper.

"What?" Chiara ran to his side and stared down.

The painted mask. Blood dripped from a cut in the forehead, making the twisted paint even more macabre.

"Check the others." Bakhita squatted down and began turning over the bodies and pulling away hoods.

All six Arsonists had identical painted faces.

Cor sat back on his heels with an expression of disbelief. "So we were right …"

A wave of nausea rose in Chiara's throat. She turned and stumbled away. A few paces in front of the oak tree, she knelt and was sick in the grass.

The painted faces … the painted faces.

It wasn't just a nightmare.

One of them had been really there. That night.

Her arm was still burning. She was rubbing the side of her neck. The divots in her scarred skin were hot to the touch, sore from the choking fingers.

"Chiara?" Cor walked up behind her.

She spat in the grass and sat upright. "Fine — I'm fine."

"Sick?"

She nodded wearily. Twice in two days.

"Happens to the best of us." He squatted next to her. "Are you sure you're okay?"

"My arm …" she admitted. "I think I got cut."

He saw it at once. "Here—" He dashed off to the nearest wagon and returned with a bundle of gauze. He cut her sleeve away, dumped his canteen on the wound, and began binding it tightly.

Chiara watched him. The stab was painful, but it didn't matter as much as the paint. "Cor …"

They were there that night. She almost, almost said it. The words were on the tip of her tongue.

The nightmares became more real the closer they got to Crescor. *What will we find when we get there …?* She shuddered again, uncontrollably.

"Chiara, what is it?" She could feel Cor's eyes on her.

I can't do it. Not now.

And it wasn't like it mattered, anyway. What difference would it make to tell him about the nightmares? They knew for a fact now that the Arsonists had painted faces. What would she say? *I was in a city that burned and I saw someone with a painted face?* That wouldn't get them any closer to knowing who the Arsonists were, or how they were starting the fires.

"I just … I hate it. The paint, I mean."

"Yeah, I hate it, too. It's eerie." Cor's arm twitched, as though he was about to lift his hand to her shoulder.

I wish he would. Then Chiara blinked, surprised. … *What was that? Why should it matter if he touches me?*

"Do you need a minute?" he asked. For someone who had sounded so hateful a few moments before, his voice was weirdly gentle now.

"I'll … I'll be right there," she murmured. He stood wordlessly, and she could've sworn his fingers brushed her shoulder — but then he was gone.

They burned the bodies, and then the last three wagons went their separate ways. Tagg's wagon headed northeast through the night. By sunrise, when Cor called a halt, all that was left of the attack was a thin blue line of smoke drifting up from the treetops far behind.

∝

Zelie found the stream right after they called a halt to pitch camp. Tagg stayed behind to tend to Ria, and the others went to wash and refill their canteens.

Chiara plunged cupped hands into the cold water, feeling tingles run up her arms.

"Praise Arva for running water," Cor gasped exuberantly, splashing it across his face. Zelie gave a startled *mrow* as he flicked it at her.

"Someone's in a good mood," Chiara remarked from her vantage point a few feet upstream. She stuck her canteen into the water, waiting for it to fill.

"Streams are good. They mean we're getting closer to the mountains," Cor said. He was still hoarse, but his tone was surprisingly optimistic, considering what they'd been through in the past few days.

Chiara didn't share his enthusiasm. Her arm was still throbbing. She nodded and swirled Tagg's canteen in the stream, watching the water eddy as it was sucked in.

Cor rose, ruffling his damp hair, and walked over to her. "Still shaken?"

"… Yeah." She pulled out Tagg's canteen and screwed on the cap.

He crouched beside her and pulled out his own canteen. "We still need to talk."

"About what?" she asked carefully. If he asked about the painted faces again …

"About how you insisted on fighting with me." Cor plunged his canteen into the water.

She shot him a look out of the corner of her eye.

"I needed you to stay by the oak tree. I didn't say anything last night, since there was no time to argue. But in future, I need you to listen to me." His eyes were somber.

"Why? So I can sit around until I get killed?" Chiara's mouth went tight.

"No. I need you to trust me," he said insistently, pulling his canteen back out. "Listen, Chiara — we didn't even get to finish your basic combat training before we had to pack up and leave. A last-minute nighttime ambush is hardly a good opportunity for me to put you out in the front and expect you to take a life."

"What are you saying here?" Chiara set down her canteen and looked at him, puzzled. *Is he … sorry?*

"What I'm saying is I shouldn't have put you in that position, and I'm sor—" He broke off, inhaling sharply. "Chiara, did that paintface injure you last night?"

"What?" Alarmed, she turned to face him. "You mean my arm? You were the one who bandaged it …"

He was scowling … staring at her neck.

Self-conscious, she lifted a hand, covering her scar. "He tried to choke me, but then — you were there. I'm fine."

Cor shook his head. "He did something to you." He lifted a hand.

Chiara flinched away instinctively. *Don't touch it* … "What do you mean?" she demanded, trying not to panic, trying to ignore the confusion on his face.

"It's your neck," he said worriedly. "It looks—"

"I know," she interrupted. "They're just burn scars. You know that," she added, more quietly. *It's not like you've never seen them before.*

"They look different."

Her heart stopped for a moment. "*Different?* Different *how?*"

"They're … bigger."

"Chiara!" Zelie bounded up to them. "I've filled the water bottles and — ooh, am I interrupting something?" She plopped onto the ground, wiggling her eyebrows.

Chiara became suddenly aware of how close Cor's face was to hers. She pulled away and glared at Zelie. "No, of course not! We're just talking."

"Right, right. I see." Zelie gave an exaggerated wink.

Cor was still staring at Chiara's neck. "Zelie, come here. I need you to look at this — does it look any different?" He pointed.

Chiara hesitated, then dropped her hand. Zelie had definitely seen the scars enough times to know if something was wrong.

Zelie skipped over to him. As soon as she saw what he was pointing at, her ears went down. "They're just burn marks, Cor." Her tone was guarded. "She's had those for a long time."

"No — they're different," Cor insisted. "They're bigger now — I swear. I've looked at them every day—"

Chiara flinched.

Zelie glared at him. "*Cor!* What are you even saying? Apologize!"

"It's fine, Zelie." Chiara gave Cor a harsh glance. "Thanks for letting me know."

Cor ran a hand through his hair. "Zelie, can you give us a minute?"

"I—"

"Please."

Something about Cor's tone made Zelie hesitate. "Alright," she said at last. "But I won't be too far off. And I'll be able to see everything." She turned with a sniff and stalked away upstream.

Chiara turned away and fixed her eyes on the water, watching it swirl. Its soft babble was soothing.

I've looked at them every day. The words stung in the back of her brain.

"Chiara." Cor's voice was low.

She didn't answer right away. Out of the corner of her eye, she saw him stand, fiddling with the buttons on his shirt.

"Chiara, look at me." Then his shirt fell to the ground, right next to her leg.

"Cor, what the he—what are you doing?" she exclaimed, scrambling to her feet.

He was standing face to face with her, bare-chested now. Green-inked tattoos swirled across his tanned skin, curving along the hard muscles — symbols, markings, years' worth of feats, broken records, victories in competition … or combat.

Chiara's neck prickled uncomfortably. "What are you doing?" She kept her eyes on his face, attempting to sound calm.

"I need to … show you something."

"You're kind of doing that already, no?" Her sentence ended in a nervous laugh. *What am I even saying?* Her face felt uncomfortably warm.

The corner of his mouth turned up in the ghost of a smile. "No. I mean … just … look."

He turned around, and Chiara's breath stuck in her throat.

His back had no tattoos — and she was close enough now to see why.

Burn marks. Ridges of raw reddish-pink flesh, running across his shoulders and upper back, like he'd been torched alive. What unharmed skin was left was pulled tight around the edges of the scars.

No tattoos. Not even a First Tattoo. No Tegid would tattoo over a burn. Bad luck.

So Cor didn't have his First Tattoo — or if he did, it wasn't on his back.

My parents died when I was little.

People who've seen the fires.

Cor hadn't just lost his parents to the fire. He'd been *in* the fires … hadn't he? Maybe even the one that had killed them …

Her hand lifted slowly, fingers outstretched—

"I know what burns look like," Cor said. "I know yours looks different now."

Chiara checked herself, fingers inches away from his blasted skin. She drew back, heartbeat pounding in her ears.

She'd almost — *almost* — touched him.

"It …" She licked dry lips, trying to get the words out. "It was the Arsonists … wasn't it?"

"Yes. It was." His tone was flat, hard. "I was only a toddler when they came. They took …" His voice rasped slightly. "… a lot of people."

"But … not you."

"No. They left me alive." He turned to face her, a bitter edge in his voice now. "Alive and strong … strong enough to survive, hunt them down one day." His jaw was tight, and his eyes were stormy, the lively spark completely snuffed out.

That's the reason. That's why he joined Fhir. Chiara was unable to tear her eyes away from him. "I'm … so sorry."

And was she any different? Refusing to put Isak's ghost to rest?

Cor shook his head.

She tried to think of something to say. "Have you ever … I mean, the scars — they're still there. You never got your First Tattoo …?"

"No." His eyes bored into her, adamant. She drew back slightly.

"No," he repeated. "I know what they say about me. I know they shun us. But I don't give a damn."

He went on, fiercely, eyes looking past her. "They weren't there. I was. I survived that day. I'm still alive. I'm still hunting. The scars are proof of that. Why would I tattoo over them? They're tattoos enough for me."

He turned his eyes back to her, and they were burning now.

Her skin prickled. She could practically feel heat radiating off his body. Funny thing … that lively spark of his. Sparks became fire, when pressed hard enough.

"I'm glad you didn't cover them." The words tumbled out of her mouth before she knew what she was saying.

Cor's shoulders relaxed, and he looked almost surprised. Then his mouth twitched upward. The fire in his eyes died down as he looked at her.

How long …? How many years had he told himself that; told anyone that? As though he'd been rehearsing it since the day it all happened …

And she would know, wouldn't she? She'd done the same.

They were both scarred.

"I'm glad you didn't cover them," she repeated. "It … wouldn't be the truth."

He smiled in earnest now. "I'm glad you didn't cover yours." Then he bent and picked up his shirt, tugging it back over his shoulders.

"What's the point?" Chiara muttered softly. She'd only ever gotten the one tattoo — her First Tattoo.

Her palms were tingling. *Proof.* Proof of survival.

For Cor, the scars were marks of triumph.

Not for me.

"Listen, Chiara. I, um—" Cor looked down, face reddening. "About earlier — when I said I looked at your scars every day …"

"I understand — well, now I do," she broke in, forcing herself to smile.

"I just … I'm sorry. It didn't come out like I meant it. What I meant was … I know burn marks. Yours looks worse now."

She sighed, rubbing at her neck. "Maybe you're right, but how is that possible? It's not like he …"

Pain lanced through her skull. Images flashing — *white-hot hands — fingers digging in — branding her—*

A short gasp burst out of her, and she clutched at her head.

"What's wrong?" Cor stepped forward, one hand already under her elbow.

Chiara squeezed her eyes shut, shaking her head. "Nothing — it's nothing. Just …" She blinked, trying to stand straighter. "Just … a headache." She lifted her head slowly, wincing.

Cor didn't look convinced. "Are you sure?"

"I'm sure." She looked him in the eye. *Believe it — believe it …*

He eyed her carefully. "… Okay. I trust you. But … tell me, will you? If something is wrong? About the burn, or …?" He gave her a concerned look.

He's figuring it out. Sooner or later, he would know — he would ask—

"I will. I promise." She bent down and scooped up the filled canteens. "We need to hurry up here. We've already stayed too long."

"Right. Zelie?" he shouted.

Zelie materialized out of the woods, looking rather pleased with herself.

"Hunting?" Cor laughed.

Chiara raised an eyebrow. She'd seen that expression on Zelie before. Hunting … but not for food. *She saw the whole thing, I bet.* Shirtless Cor and all.

"You could say that," Zelie replied cryptically. "Nice chat?"

"Fine," Chiara said forcefully, handing Zelie more canteens. "How about you make yourself useful now?"

"I'm just curious," Zelie grumbled as Cor walked past her, heading back toward the campsite.

Chiara took up the rear. Pain was still twitching through her head, dancing around her brain. She closed her eyes again.

The glow was still there … burning behind her eyelids.

A hand, reaching out toward her, glowing white-hot … almost as if it was on fire.

branded

There's no way. He couldn't have burned her with his own hand. He must have coated his glove in some kind of accelerant. *Maybe the thing they used to weld iron …?*

She was still walking when one final memory cracked through her head, and she stopped dead in her tracks.

The figure that attacked her that night … she'd seen him first. Then … then he'd spotted her — he was coming toward her, stalking through the smoke — she was turning, trying to run, turning to see—

—and he took off his gloves.

19

He took off his gloves first ... he took them off first. The next several days blurred together for Chiara — exhaustion, tension, weariness. The pain in her arm was a dull constant. Glowing hands haunted every waking moment. She was always so tired, but sleep was no relief. The painted faces followed her everywhere, even in nightmares, bringing more headaches.

"What's wrong?" Cor kept asking.

"Bad dreams." Chiara rarely said more than that. Between his cough and her nightmares, they added up to about one completely dysfunctional Tegid. *We don't need to add any more bizarre to the mix.*

If the Arsonist really had taken off his glove … But how was that even possible? What kind of accelerant could coat someone's *hands*?

The clusters of dense forest around them made it difficult to see far in any direction. Once or twice, Cor or Zelie would climb a tree and report that the Ondural Mountains were just visible to their right. As long as they kept heading straight north, eventually they'd get far enough to turn west and make it out of the woods.

They traveled mostly under the cover of darkness, one driving the wagon and one guarding while the other two slept in fits and spurts. Zelie, nocturnal by nature, had adapted well. As for the other three …

"We're supposed to be heading north*west* by now." Cor jabbed a finger ahead of them. His voice was sounding more and more hoarse with every passing day, and he kept rubbing his chest as though he was in pain.

Chiara squinted as she followed the line of Cor's finger and grasped the reins more tightly. She'd only been driving the wagon for a few hours, but the sun was already setting. It would be less than an hour before nightfall. After that, she'd surrender the reins to someone else with better night sense.

"The plan was to circle around back to Crescor. Remember? Circles?" Cor drew an exaggerated shape in the air with his finger. "We have to go *back* to where we were originally headed!"

"We can't head northwest yet." Tagg had been adamant. For days, he'd insisted they continue northeast. "We don't know if we're being followed or not. We can't risk leading the Arsonists back to everyone else."

"I can say with certainty—" Zelie began, but Tagg cut her off.

"No, Zelie. This is uncharted territory," he snapped. "We have no idea what's out here."

"Oh, yes, we do," Cor said immediately. "We know the Felwen clans are out here. It's bad enough that we're deep in their territory by now.

I'd like to avoid any confrontations." Storm-faced, he lifted his head to scan their surroundings.

Chiara could see the tightness in his shoulders. Anxiety … not in his eyes, but in his body.

What does he know?

She decided to probe. "If the Felwen are territorial," she began, "and we haven't encountered them yet, then how do we know if we're in their territory?"

"I can smell them," Zelie volunteered. "The scent here is faint, and stale. They might have come through weeks ago, but there isn't a tribe living nearby."

Cor was shaking his head. "That doesn't matter. They're nomadic, and they move fast. Even if a tribe was several miles away from us, they could cover that ground in less than an hour — especially if they see us as a threat. Which they *will*," he added with an accusing look at Tagg, "if we're just wandering willy-nilly through their territory without any coherent explanation for what we're doing."

"Which is worse?" Tagg wasn't giving an inch. "Felwen or the Arsonists?"

"I don't know; which do you think?" Cor shot back. "A *possible* attack from the Arsonists? Or a near-guarantee of a Felwen run-in?"

Tagg's frown had turned into a formidable glare. "The Arsonists will kill us if they find us! At least we'll have a chance at negotiation with Felwen!"

Chiara massaged her temples. The headaches were becoming worse. Ever since the night in Talin — and the nightmares after that—

"Cor's got a point," Zelie said hesitantly. "Maybe—"

Tagg wheeled on her. "D'you want a repeat of that bloody ambush? *Any* bloody ambush?"

"No, of course not!" Zelie's eyes were beginning to spark now. "But the more immediate threat is the Felwen! If we—"

"We won't give a damn about Felwen if we're burned alive, Zelie!"

Burned alive.

Heat rushed across Chiara's skin as fury blazed up in the pit of her stomach. *"Enough!"* She yanked back on the reins and the wagon came to a grinding halt.

Then she swiveled in her seat, glaring. All three of them were staring back at her, wide eyed.

"This is supposed to be a *professional operation!* And all you've done"—she stared at Cor, then Tagg—"for the past half an hour is bicker like *cubs!*" Her tone was scathing, unforgiving. "I will not be spending the rest of our trip listening to you quibble!"

Ria tossed her head, agitated, and Chiara lowered her voice. "It is your *responsibility* to keep us all alive and get us back to Crescor. We need to find the least risky and most efficient way to do that. So make up your minds, or Zelie and I will be leaving you here in the woods!" she finished savagely.

Their expressions went from surprised, to defensive, to defeated.

She let out a long, shaking breath, trying to release the tension in her muscles. *I'm so tired …*

"'Course. You're right," Tagg admitted gruffly. Hesitantly, he turned and offered a hand to Cor. "Apologies, mate."

Cor shook his hand. "Apologies accepted. And … please accept mine. You have good instincts." His eyes flew to Chiara's face for a moment.

"As do you," Tagg replied.

"Thank you." Zelie shot a grateful look at Chiara.

Chiara sighed. "Wonderful. Now, can we agree on a direction before we start moving again?" The sunset was long-gone by now, and stars were already beginning to peer out overhead. *We have to get a move on.*

"I have a proposition," Zelie piped up. "Cor was in favor of heading northwest, and Tagg for northeast. Let's just head north for the next few days. Maybe we could toe the line between Felwen territory and any Arsonists on our tail."

Cor looked slightly doubtful. "It's a thin line, but we might be able to make it work."

Tagg sighed through his nose. "I agree — on one condition. Two of us need to be on guard duty at all times. One in front, one in the back. That'll be our best possible buffer against attackers."

Cor nodded. "In that case, our shifts should be shorter, so we can still get enough rest."

"Agreed," said Tagg. "Hourly?"

"That works for me. Chiara? Zelie?" Cor waited for nods before continuing. "Great. It's getting dark," and he glanced around, "so we should switch now. Zelie, in front, smelling for Felwen. Tagg behind, covering our tracks and keeping an eye out for any tails. Chiara, go sleep. I'll drive."

She opened her mouth to protest, but he shook his head vigorously. "No. You're exhausted, and you've already been driving almost three hours. Sleep. We won't argue again … I promise." A flicker of shame crossed his face.

I don't want to sleep. Anything was better than reliving the glowing hands. And Cor was clearly not feeling his best. But he was already stepping up into the wagon, scooting Chiara over gently.

Defeated, she crawled down into the bed of the wagon and slumped against the side. She unstrapped the sax and belt from her waist and tossed it next to her, within arm's reach.

Cor leaned over the back of his seat and snatched up his blanket. "Use it," he insisted, tossing it into her lap.

She was too tired to protest. She lay down on her side and curled up under the blanket, resting her head on a bundle of banners.

Sleep was already tugging at her lids when Cor's voice drifted over her. Or did it? He sounded so quiet …

"Chiara."

He was saying her name.

"Yeah … yeah, I'm awake," she mumbled. *Barely* …

"I'm sorry for fighting. I know better. I let you down."

"Forgive you …" It was like talking through a heavy veil …

"Thank you."

He might've said something else … something like, "It means a lot."

But she didn't know for sure … she was already dreaming.

୧

Cor's voice was the only good thing about falling asleep. Nothing but nightmares came after that.

Glowing hands. Screaming. Searing pain as fingers clutched at her neck, branding her.

Painted faces, leering around corners, chasing her — chasing her into the inferno, cutting off all escape.

Circles, circles. Always coming back to the same building … the same end.

The same fire. Always, always fire … fire, surrounding her, in her eyes, in her nose and mouth … fire in her lungs … in her stomach … burning alive … burning, burning—

"Chiara. *Chiara!*" Someone was hissing her name, shaking her awake.

She shot upright, gasping heavily, pain rattling in between her eyes. Another headache. Her temples were damp with sweat. It was pitch-black inside the wagon, but she could tell they'd stopped moving.

Something moved next to her. "Chiara!"

"Cor?" she whispered hopefully.

"No, Zelie."

"Oh …" She felt vaguely disappointed. "What's wrong?" Gradually, her eyes adjusted, and she saw the vague outline of Zelie's face.

"We're stopping for a break in an hour. You're front guard next, though."

"Got it." Chiara leaned back. Every muscle was sore from sleeping in the wooden bed of the wagon. She tried to stretch the stiffness out of her limbs, but it didn't do much good.

Come on. Up we go. She reached out, feeling for her belt, and then she strapped it around her waist.

She clambered awkwardly out of the back of the wagon and came around to the front.

Tagg's silhouette was just visible on the wagon seat. "Evening." His voice was low.

"Chiara?" Cor appeared suddenly, a hand brushing her arm.

Her skin warmed where he'd touched her. "I'm here." She stifled a yawn. "Front guard?"

"Yes. But after that, we're all going to rest. Ria, too. She's been walking all day."

Sleep fell away, and tension came again to perch on Chiara's shoulder. "Rest where? I thought this was Felwen territory."

"Well … it could be. But Zelie's been scouting ahead, and she hasn't picked up a real scent for miles. We figured it was best to stop where there's no sign of Felwen."

"Okay." Chiara stretched her arms above her head. "I'll be going ahead. Just call when you want to stop."

"I'll come find you." That was definitely worry in Cor's voice.

You'll come find me?

"Raised voices could give away our position. I'm not taking that chance."

Of course. Practicality. Survival. Chiara shook her head. *I need more sleep* … Her thoughts were getting a little too close to delusional for her liking.

"Right. Got it." She trudged ahead several paces before she heard the wagon creak to life behind her.

It was slow moving. The ground was becoming rough and uneven. Clusters of trees sprang up suddenly on either side, almost invisible in the dark. Every now and then, she'd scrape up against solid rock — broken pieces of hillside, protruding from the grass like exposed bone.

Minutes stretched into eternity. One foot in front of the other. Again. And again. Eyes peering, ears pricked.

A lot of good I can do. Chiara cursed silently as she jammed her foot against a tree root. She knew her senses weren't nearly as good as the others. Even Tagg could pick up on a buzz of mental noise when other creatures were nearby.

But here and now, in the middle of the night in some star-forsaken valley … it was painfully clear how much duller her own senses were.

Maybe even enough to be the difference between life and death.

She shoved that aside, breath hissing through her teeth as a branch whipped against her face. She dabbed a finger to it and felt something wet.

I'm bleeding. Briefly, she wondered how strong the Felwen sense of smell was. *I hope they can't smell blood from miles away* …

She knew they were deadly hunters. They were forest- or mountain-dwellers, living off whatever game they could find in the woods. And they didn't like outsiders.

She'd only seen a Felwen once. She and Dad were on a ferry, heading up north on the Tonitrus, and she spotted it. Far away, running across the plains alongside the river.

"A scout," Dad had said, but he couldn't tell her much else. Felwen were secretive and viciously protective of their own clans, and they rarely interacted with the other species, even other Beast-skins.

She'd heard enough to know that some tribes had a reputation for killing outsiders. But those tribes lived farther north.

We are also farther north. Anxiety tightened the muscles in her chest. She did her best to breathe in deeply. Farther, yes … but not that much farther. Maybe—

Leaves crackled nearby. Chiara crouched, eyes darting toward the sound as her heart hammered in her chest. She couldn't make anything out. She stayed frozen in place.

There it was again. Something coming toward her … something that sounded large.

Felwen. Chiara tried to swallow the panic that was rising in her throat. As quietly as possible, she drew the sax from her belt, holding it out to the side, ready to strike.

Something darted past her leg, and it was all she could do to keep from squealing. A tiny shape — far too small for a Felwen. She made out the long ears right before it disappeared into the brush on the other side.

A rabbit. She almost laughed at herself. That's what had made all that noise. Small things always sounded so much bigger in the dark …

She was just standing up, blade lowered, when it occurred to her that rabbits weren't nocturnal. The only reason a rabbit would be running for its life in the middle of the night was if—

"It's being hunted," she muttered.

Suddenly, she heard something much larger plunging through the trees, coming toward her. Adrenaline spiked in Chiara's chest, but she couldn't even lift her blade in time — a solid mass crashed into her chest, sending her hurtling down.

The back of her head cracked on the ground so hard that stars burst behind her eyelids. "Ufhh …" A moan escaped her, but it was quickly stifled as two enormous weights pinned her shoulders down.

Stars were still dancing across Chiara's vision, blocking her view of the attacker. But the prick of claws in her skin brought her to painful awareness of her situation.

A Felwen.

She'd been pinned — easily. She hadn't even had time to call a warning … and now the others could be dead.

Fear raked through her stomach. Her hands were empty — she must've dropped the sax when she fell. Her fingers scrabbled on either side, grasping for anything — a rock, a stick—

"Misplaced something?" hissed a heavy female voice. Chiara froze. The claws stabbed deeper into her shoulder, and something metallic rattled across the ground. Her sax — the Felwen must have kicked it away.

Chiara shook her head, blinking, trying to get rid of the yellow lights in front of her eyes—

Oh, no. Those weren't glowing spots.

A pair of lemon-yellow eyes weas staring at her. She could just make out a soft gleam of teeth below them. Canines, bared in a savage grin.

"Cor," she croaked. "Cor—"

"Now, now." The Felwen traced a claw softly across Chiara's throat. "Let's not do that, shall we?"

"GET OFF HER!" Cor. Furious.

There was a loud "OOF!" and suddenly, the weight on top of Chiara vanished.

She scrambled to her feet, gasping for breath, staring in disbelief at the tussle just in front of her.

Cor, arms locked against the female Felwen as they grappled with each other, rolling across the ground, spitting and yelling. She couldn't see much in the dark, but she could see enough. The two combatants looked almost evenly matched.

She'd never seen Cor wrestle before, but he clearly knew what he was doing. Every time the Felwen's claws or teeth got near him, he was thrusting her away, rearing on top of her again, pinning her back.

They rolled toward Chiara, a ball of twisted limbs and faces; she stumbled back and her heel landed on something hard. Metal scraped against the ground — the sax. She swooped to pick it up.

As soon as her fingers wrapped around the hilt, a terrified bestial scream split the air behind her.

Ria. Chiara whirled on her heel and charged toward the noise. "TAGG!" she yelled at the top of her lungs. Staying quiet didn't matter if they were already being attacked.

"Here!" he roared, the sound almost next to her. She sprinted past a few more trees and spotted him in front of Ria, gripping the reins as she tossed her head savagely.

A dark shape flew through the air toward the plunging horse — those terrible hooves struck out; there was a dull blow and a heavy thud as the injured Felwen was thrown to the ground.

Chiara stumbled aside as it struggled to rise, squealing in pain. Ria flung up her hooves again, and the Felwen bolted back into the trees.

"Take Ria's reins!" Tagg yelled. "I've got to find Zelie!" He tossed them to Chiara and bolted away.

She caught them and mounted Ria breathlessly, tugging back, urging the horse's head to the side. Then she dug her heels in and Ria leapt forward, dragging the wagon behind her, charging back in the direction where Cor had been fighting the Felwen.

Please don't be dead, please don't be dead, please don't be dead … The mantra kept time with Ria's pounding hooves.

"Cor!" she yelled, straining for any response. Grunts and snarls were the only thing she could hear. "Tell me you're alive!"

"Alive!" His shout shattered the air, echoing through the tree trunks. Chiara almost collapsed in relief. *Thank Arva.*

Then a bloodcurdling screech erupted somewhere off to her right. Another dark shape came bolting through the woods. Ria reared under Chiara; she snatched at her mane, barely managing to keep her seating.

A third Felwen — but this one was followed by a much smaller dark shape.

Zelie. Chiara would've known that screech anywhere. The little Kithsa darted after the Felwen, hissing and spitting, right on its tail as it made for the woods on the left.

Seconds before it reached the cluster of trees, Zelie leapt onto its back and latched on, relentless. The Felwen let out a pained cry, jumping and tossing, trying to dislodge its vicious rider, but Zelie wasn't budging.

"Chiara! Where's Cor?" Suddenly Tagg was beside her, snatching at Ria's reins, bringing her back to earth.

Chiara pointed. "Fighting! Still alive!"

"Bloody Arva — he's gonna get himself killed!" Tagg sounded absolutely furious. "Wait here. I'll—"

He was cut off by a long, ear-splitting howl … utterly feral, devoid of feeling.

"Fesht." Cor — cursing. The noise of the tussle had ceased. There was another cry as Zelie was thrown from her Felwen. She tumbled across the ground and darted to Tagg's side, teeth still fully bared.

"Now, then." A new voice; masculine, rough, almost a snarl. Fire flared to life somewhere nearby, floating through the clearing.

A torch.

Then Cor appeared, backing slowly out of the trees in front of them, both swords raised in a defensive position.

Stepping out after him was a Felwen … the biggest one by far. He towered head and shoulders above Cor. He advanced weaponless, holding the torch. The firelight cast bizarre shapes across the ground, the trees, the faces.

His pace was slow, almost leisurely, as he forced Cor to the center of the clearing. Chiara lifted her chin, a cold wave crashing across her body. Tagg squared his shoulders next to her.

A soft hiss escaped Zelie as other Felwen began to emerge from the woods. Chiara dared a glance around them. Three, four … five Felwen. Her hand went to the sax at her back.

Zelie's victim rose to his feet and limped over to join them, making six. Plus the one in front … at least seven Felwen. *Maybe more to come …*

They were surrounded.

The large Felwen brought Cor to the center of the circle. Then he gave him a shove. Cor didn't stumble. He pivoted and whirled around, backing up slowly until he stood just in front of Tagg.

"Jumped me." He didn't take his eyes off the Felwen. "Should've seen it coming. Anyone hurt?"

"Nothing serious," Tagg replied, also watching carefully as the Felwen handed off the torch to one of his packmates.

"Sorry." Cor spoke through gritted teeth.

"Not your fault," Zelie said quickly.

"So, tell me, packmates." The large Felwen — clearly some kind of leader — was stalking in lazy circles around the ring of bodies. His words vibrated around them, powerful, dangerous.

A long mane of hair tumbled down his back. As he turned, Chiara could pick out a strong, chiseled face and nose. He looked like some kind of archaic marble statue. "What kind of travelers would dare trespass on Felwen territory?"

"Disrespectful," growled one — the female who had attacked her, Chiara realized.

"Or ignorant," hissed another from his crouch on the ground. He was favoring a paw — possibly Ria's doing.

"Well said," the Felwen chuckled appreciatively. He pivoted on his heel, turning sharply toward them. "They'd be fools, either way." He stalked quickly up to Cor, who stepped forward without flinching.

"Fools who nearly handed your tails to you," he shot back, sheathing his swords. "That was the sloppiest ambush I've ever seen. Too bad you still don't live up to the Felwen name, Fenris."

Chiara froze. *Fenris?* Cor *knew* him?

The circle around them broke out in snarls. But to Chiara's greater shock, the Felwen — Fenris — threw back his head with a hearty laugh. "Ah … Coren Ascolta." He bared his teeth in a savage grin. "It's been a while. I'd almost forgotten your sharp tongue."

"Always happy to jog your memory." Cor folded his arms defiantly.

Fenris clucked his tongue against his teeth. "Dangerous words for someone who's completely surrounded."

"Surrounded?" Cor took another step forward. His body was completely relaxed, as if he was in control of the situation. "Let me guess … hunting party, judging by the numbers, and the fact that you were completely unprepared for us to fight back."

Chiara's eyebrows shot up. *I can't believe him.* They were outnumbered and surrounded. *What's he gonna do? Talk them out of killing us? Is he an idiot?*

Or extremely brave? She couldn't decide. She also couldn't decide if she was more annoyed or impressed.

Whatever Cor was, he wasn't a coward. "I suggest we avoid further injury and go our separate ways," he said, spreading his hands wide disarmingly.

Fenris's eyes flashed green in the torchlight. "Not so fast. You're trespassers on Tivore's territory. That kind of decision has consequences … wouldn't you say?"

Growls of agreement echoed him.

Cor shrugged. "Very well. If you insist …" He broke eye contact and turned his head, scanning the circle. "… then you should take us straight to your Chieftain."

Tagg inhaled sharply.

Cor seemed not to hear. He was facing Fenris now, his words clipped. "See, for all you know, we might just be innocent travelers who got lost at night. I'm sure he would want to avoid any …" He paused. "… misunderstanding."

Fenris's ears went flat against his skull. For one tense moment, nothing happened. Then he turned away, arms flung wide in a leisurely gesture. "So be it! If they insist on visiting our Chieftain, then who am I to deny them hospitality?"

A chorus of snarling laughter broke out around them. A shudder ran down Chiara's spine. Cor turned and locked eyes with her. His gaze was searching, earnest.

She knew that look. After all those weeks practicing …

Do you trust me?

"Come, now — let's give our guests a proper escort!" Fenris called. The Felwen fell to all fours, surrounding them with barking voices.

Ria pounded her hooves anxiously, sending tremors through Chiara's body. "Oh, Cor," she sighed under her breath. "I really, really hope you know what you're doing."

20

For hours, the Felwen ran alongside the wagon, steering it east into the thick woods. Chiara guessed that they must be in the northernmost arm of the Vastil Forest, but she didn't know for sure.

Cor seemed to be the only one who really knew where they were headed. He'd insisted on taking the reins, and no one was willing to argue. He drove, stifling his cough, while the rest of them rode in silence in the back of the wagon. Every so often, the silence would be broken by the occasional crackle or thump as their escort navigated through the trees.

Chiara sat at the back of the wagon, staring out at the path behind them. Shadows crowded close, blotting out most of the light. All she could make out were patches of dark and less-dark. Not even fireflies lived in these woods. Every now and then, a flash of sky peered through overhead, its faint star scatter the only sign that the trees had parted.

How much farther? They'd been traveling for two, maybe three hours at this point. Surely dawn would come soon. After that … she didn't know. How far could Felwen travel? How big was a territory?

I never needed to know this kind of thing before. She felt a pang as the streets of Belkar flashed in her mind. The rattle of trains; the vendors' voices; the whirr of the ziplines overhead … the life of the city, pulsing just outside the gymnasium doors.

Chiara blinked. *What was that … fondness?* She tucked her knees against her chest, trying to warm herself. *What a weird thing to miss.*

"Chiara." Tagg was whispering her name.

She turned. "What is it?"

"You should probably sleep." His words were punctuated by soft, puffing breaths from Zelie, who was already curled up asleep.

"Why?" Chiara whispered back.

There was a pause before he answered. "I don't think we'll be getting to their Chieftain anytime soon."

Anxiety slid a sharp claw under her ribs. "What do you mean?" *Is this all a trap?*

"Felwen territories can be bally huge. There's no way for us to know how far away they are from the main pack."

Chiara leaned closer. "Are they leading us somewhere to kill us?"

"Of course not!" replied a low, growling huff.

Chiara almost bit her tongue to keep from screaming.

It was Fenris. He must have been right there outside the canvas, jogging alongside the wagon. She could just make out his soft panting.

"Why should I trust you?" She lifted her voice just slightly, trying to keep it from shaking.

Tagg squeezed her wrist silently in a warning, but Fenris was already talking.

"Ah … I'm wounded." Was that a *smile* in his tone? "Didn't Coren tell you … I always keep my word?"

"No, he didn't," she responded stubbornly. "And even if he did, *I* don't know anything about you except that you're Felwen. So why should I trust you?"

To her surprise, he gave a breathless chuckle. *What in Arva …?*

"So fiery! I like…your attitude," he said through labored breaths. "If we wanted … to kill you … we would've done it … already. Otherwise … why escort you … all this way?"

He had a point. But Chiara wasn't willing to admit that. "You might decide to kill us on the way," she argued. "What would we do about it?"

Another laugh. "Oh, no, no, sweetheart. I might be … dangerous … but I'm not about … to kill you."

"Call me sweetheart again and I'll give you a trim with my sax," she replied savagely. Danger be damned.

"Oo … she *is* feisty! As you wish … How's Snapdragon?"

"I hate it. Why should I believe you're not going to kill us?"

"You underestimate … your value!" His tone was chiding. "Cor is … a formidable fighter … even if he does … occasionally trespass." He ended in a playfully accusatory note.

Chiara frowned. For someone leading a clandestine hunting-party-turned-escort, he was weirdly nonchalant.

"Underestimate our value?" she repeated, probing. "I mean … I agree with you. Cor isn't the kind of person I'd want as my enemy—"

"Exactly!" Fenris panted. "We'd … much rather have … a civil arrangement. I personally … am not a fan … of unnecessary bloodshed," he added with distaste.

"And we're all so grateful for that," she said, more to herself than him.

But she had a weird feeling that he was telling the truth. None of the Felwen had drawn blood. Even the one that pinned her down was simply holding her there.

"So you … can rest assured … that we won't do you … any harm," he finished.

A civil arrangement … A line from the *Encyclopedia of Vanha* popped into her head. *Felwen are generally mistrustful of outsiders unless a civil arrangement or a mutual benefit can be established.*

A civil arrangement. That must have been why Cor insisted on seeing the Chieftain. If Cor knew Fenris, maybe it was because he'd worked out some kind of bargain with them before.

And maybe he can do it again.

He *had* to do it again. Otherwise … well, she wasn't actually sure what happened to trespassers on Felwen territory. Possibly because no one had ever lived to tell the story.

Small wonder Cor was so insistent on avoiding the Felwen. If he'd run into them before, he knew how dangerous this was. They had no choice but to trust him.

Can we trust him with this? Chiara's fingers drummed anxiously on her knees.

He'd shown up. In Grede. In Talin, when Mask found her. At the ambush in the gorge. And then tonight. She could still hear the raw anger in his shout.

GET OFF HER!

Chiara exhaled softly. *I do* trust him. She leaned against the wagon's side and closed her eyes.

જી

"Wakey, wakey!" Zelie … shaking her.

Eyes still closed, Chiara sighed. "Why?" She could already feel the ache in her neck. She'd fallen asleep at an awkward angle.

"We're here," Zelie murmured.

Chiara's eyes fluttered open. It was light out — that much she could tell. Tagg was already gone. She sat up and stretched out her arms.

"Come on!" Zelie whisked out the back of the wagon. Chiara followed more slowly, breathing in the cool, moist air. She stepped down into the grass next to Zelie and got her first good look at a Felwen camp.

It wasn't much of a camp. They were in some kind of clearing, only it hadn't really been cleared. Tumbled boulders lay across the grass like marbles. Uneven pillars of stone protruded at drunken angles from the ground. There were even fallen trees, forest giants collapsed long ago, their decaying trunks ending in knotted nests of roots.

Haphazard tarps were stretched out between every remotely vertical object, creating the shabbiest makeshift shelters she'd ever seen. Crouched beneath them were Felwen — at least a dozen, maybe more, some asleep, some awake. Fenris was nowhere to be seen.

Crowning the whole scene was a cluster of stone outcroppings, jutting several feet above its surroundings.

"*This* is their camp?" Zelie muttered, looking around skeptically. "What kind of …?"

"Temporary camp," Cor rasped behind them. Chiara turned to see him walking out of the nearby trees, Tagg on his heels.

Cor joined Chiara and Zelie, leaning up against the side of the wagon. Tagg went to Ria's nose. She was snorting and skittish.

Understandably so. The camp made *Chiara* uneasy, and she wasn't even prey.

"Why? Where's their real camp?" Chiara asked.

Cor shrugged. "Wherever they decide to spend the next season. They're traveling between hunting grounds." He ran a hand through messy hair, and another cough rattled in his chest.

A flash of alarm went through her. The Felwen could probably tell that Cor was sick — another distinct disadvantage.

"Okay, so what does that all have to do with us?" Zelie crossed her arms, eyeing a nearby Felwen with suspicion. He saw her glare and hurried past, refusing to make eye contact.

Chiara glanced around and noticed more than a few Felwen shooting odd looks in Zelie's direction.

Weird. Zelie was by far the smallest one here. So why …?

"Looks like you'll make lots of friends, Zelie," Tagg murmured.

Zelie folded her arms across her chest. "What's their problem?"

"They probably don't like Kithsa very much." Cor shot her a glance out of the corner of his eye. "You're tiny … but you're also a predator. As you demonstrated last night."

Zelie's teeth flashed. "I sure hope I did! They shouldn't have attacked us!"

"Actually, I think *we* drove through the middle of one of *their* hunting trails," Tagg supplied. "So, here we are, come to pay our respects to the Chieftain."

"Okay … " Chiara glanced around. "So where is he, then?"

"No idea." Cor had unsheathed one of his knives and was examining the blade. "Fenris told us to wait here, and then he left camp. Some kind of dawn patrol or something."

Zelie sniffed. "We're here to see him and he isn't even around? Rude!"

"Zelie!" Cor's tone was a cold warning. "Never insult the leader of a Felwen clan when you're already in his—" He stiffened and lifted his head.

Chiara followed his gaze to the top of the outcropping and almost jumped out of her skin.

Standing at the crest of the stone was an enormous male Felwen, glaring down at them from a harsh, bearded face. Muscular arms, thick with fur, were folded across his chest, and dark hair tumbled around his shoulders.

He was dressed simply, bare-armed and barefoot, and he was weaponless. The formidable claws at the end of each finger were weapon enough.

"Coren Ascolta." The Chieftain's voice rumbled through the air.

Goosebumps rippled across Chiara's skin. His voice was like steel in velvet — deceptively elegant.

He's killed people before. She had no reason to think that. But she was sure of it.

Coren made a low bow. "Chieftain Yari Tivore." As he rose, he whispered, "Stay quiet. I'll do all the talking."

Zelie opened her mouth to protest, but Tagg caught her arm in a death grip, fixing her with such a fierce look that she immediately clamped her mouth shut.

The Chieftain crouched and leaped headlong off the outcrop. Chiara stifled a gasp as he hurtled toward them, and then suddenly he landed: neatly, on all fours, before rising gracefully to his feet. He stood only a few paces away.

"Forgive my absence." Chief Tivore's voice was less a sound, more a sonorous vibration. "My deputy Fenris delivered his report on his way to dawn patrol." He narrowed his eyes at Cor. "You look unwell. Surely my deputy treated you with courtesy?"

"We have no complaints," Cor replied calmly. The rattle seemed to have disappeared from his voice. He must be hiding it … for now.

Chiara's gaze slid back to the Chieftain. *He looks … vaguely familiar.* Tivore's hair and beard were streaked with silver, and he scanned them with a fierce yellow eye … his left eye. His right eye was a murky gray, sliced through by an angry red scar that cleaved the right side of his face from forehead to chin.

Cataracts. The Chieftain was blind in one eye.

He turned his gaze on Chiara, and all the hair on her arms stood on end. *This is what rabbits must feel like.* She'd never cared much about exploring the psychology of prey animals … and she really didn't like experiencing it herself.

"We're happy to wait," Cor said graciously, stepping forward. The motion drew Chief Tivore's eyes away, and Chiara began breathing again.

"Well, as you see, I have returned," the Chieftain rumbled. "Fenris tells me that you were found trespassing on our territory … after which you promptly requested a meeting?" His good eye narrowed. "An interesting proposition … considering that *you're* the one proposing it, Coren."

Chiara's eyes went to Cor. *So he was* definitely *here before.*

Cor looked slightly paler, but he seemed to completely disregard the Chieftain's last remark. "Far be it from me to cause the Tivore clan any offense. We were clumsy enough to disrupt one of your nighttime hunts. I asked the favor of meeting with you in person in hopes of amending our mistake."

The Chieftain rocked back on his heels, examining Cor's face. "I smell no deception," he said at last. "Tell me, what brings one circus wagon, a horse, and a motley group of armed fighters to these parts?"

Next to Chiara, Zelie was bristling at the word "motley," but Cor didn't betray any sign of irritation.

"A simple misdirection." His voice was completely even. It was the same tone he used with Chiara when she was anxious during a routine. It meant that they were in danger.

Chief Tivore's scowl deepened. "A misdirection? I thought Coren Ascolta was wise enough to avoid such an amateurish mistake." His lip curled up, revealing a long, white canine.

"Traveling under cover of darkness has its challenges," Cor replied smoothly. "We found ourselves off-course last night."

The Chieftain released a slow breath. "I see. And then you crossed paths with my hunting party. I hear there was some struggle?"

"A minor altercation." Cor's shoulders relaxed slightly. "We withdrew as soon as we recognized your pack."

That wasn't the entire truth … but it was true. Chiara held her breath, waiting for Tivore's reply.

"And then you proposed a meeting." Tivore's eye was glowing. "Remarkably honest. I am impressed."

"We wanted to formally request safe passage in your territory. It was the least we could do." Cor sounded far too sincere to be sincere.

"So it was," the Chieftain agreed, and something in his voice made Chiara's stomach drop. "You saved me the trouble of finding you myself."

Finding? As in hunting? That was definitely threatening. Chiara's palms were tingling. She wanted to bounce on the balls of her feet, relieve the tension, but her sense of danger kept her rooted to the spot.

Cor lifted his chin. "Now that we're here, I'd like to negotiate a deal. Safe passage, in exchange for some favor I can perform for you. Considering it was my responsibility to lead us rightly, I will take on whatever task you deem fit."

Tivore flashed his teeth in a smile, and somehow that was more unnerving than anything else. "Very good. Follow me. We shall discuss terms in my tent." He turned, gesturing to the outcrop, and began walking back the way he'd come.

"With all due respect …" Cor began, and the Chieftain froze on his heel.

Slowly, he turned, and once again Chiara felt like prey, anxiety crawling up her spine.

She glanced at Tagg nervously. His mouth was tight. He was probably just as anxious as she was. Zelie still hadn't said anything, but her hair and tail were practically standing on end.

"I trust my companions with my life." Cor aimed an intentional look at each of them. "Please, do not feel burdened to speak in their presence as well as mine."

The Chieftain's ears drifted backward, closer to his skull. "The presence of your horse in this camp worries me … as does your Kithsa."

Chiara winced. A snarl tugged at Zelie's lips, but another warning look from Tagg and she remained mercifully silent.

Cor had stiffened again. "Must I doubt your courtesy?" The way he said *courtesy* made it sound more like *hostage situation*, which didn't do anything to calm Chiara's nerves.

Tivore's ears pulled back. "Do not doubt my *courtesy*, boy," he growled. "Especially considering how well it served you … last time."

Okay, what happened *last time?* But only a tiny part of Chiara's brain was asking that. Everything else was screaming, *Run!* The Chieftain looked like an animal ready to attack.

"Chief Tivore …" Cor was taking his life into his own hands at this point. "Your deputy and his hunting patrol can confirm that the four of us possess formidable skills. We might be able to perform you some great service in exchange for our safe passage."

Cor, what are you doing? Chiara wanted to scream, but she didn't. Her heartbeat was so loud that she was surprised anyone else couldn't hear it.

Tivore's good eye flamed as he stared down at Cor. But then his ears began to lift. "So you could." His eye narrowed. "Very well. We shall discuss terms here in camp."

☙

As Cor and the Chieftain finished talking, Chiara became gradually aware of movement out of the corner of her eye. She risked a quick look around, and the pounding in her chest kicked up a notch.

They were completely surrounded by Felwen — crouched beneath tarps, leaning against boulders, peering around nearby trunks. There had to be at least thirty Felwen gathered in the camp, and more were appearing every minute.

They were all ages. Chiara spotted an elderly female Felwen being guided under a tarp by a much younger male. Half-grown cubs poked small heads from behind their mothers. Weirdly enough, much of their attention seemed to be on Zelie. They eyed her with flattening ears and curling lips.

But as soon as Tivore agreed to discuss terms in camp, all eyes turned to him. Chiara tried to swallow, but her mouth felt like sand. *I'm not a rabbit … I'm not a rabbit … We're not rabbits …*

"Coren Ascolta and companions," Tivore announced, lifting his voice slightly. He never took his eyes from Cor's face. "You have been discovered trespassing on Tivore Clan territory without permission. Your leader is one who has been here before, and who left on unpleasant terms."

Some of the Felwen bared their teeth. All of them were looking at Cor now.

"Yet, at your own request, you desire to obtain safe passage through our territory." The Chieftain's eye was glittering angrily. "As you know, such a request can be negotiated … in exchange for a service from you. This, then, is my proposition."

Chiara tried to breathe deeply, but invisible fingers were wrapping tightly around her chest, constricting her lungs. *How horrible will this be?*

"There is a safehouse, several miles northeast of here," Tivore began, and suddenly the ears of every Felwen swiveled in his direction. "It was once a small Tegid outpost, abandoned nearly a decade ago. For many seasons now, we have used that outpost to store several caches of food, water, and other goods."

Caches? Chiara frowned. Felwen were supposed to be extremely secretive. *Why is he telling us where his caches are?*

The Chieftain continued with a growl that was almost a purr. "A few weeks ago, right before we left for new hunting grounds, we discovered a few raiders at our cache. They had broken into one of the buildings, and they were scouring it out."

Why didn't you fight them, then?

Cor was nodding. "Was that pack punished for its offense?"

Tivore's eye flickered at him. "They had only discovered one cache. We had no intention of exposing the rest of our stores. However, the raiders have taken up residence in that house, and they do not appear to be leaving anytime soon."

Cor's eyes narrowed. He must have guessed it at the same time as Chiara. *They're using us to clean out the place.*

Tivore began pacing back and forth, every movement filled with a dangerous elegance. "I was unwilling to begin outright war so close to our journey. But it is in the best interests of my pack to regain control of that outpost. As soon as possible."

He stalked toward Cor. "Should you desire safe passage through our land, you must retake the outpost." His lip curled up. "Should you fail to complete the task, or fail to do so on the terms I have stated, then our agreement is null and void, and you place yourself subject to the justice of Felwen law and custom." He began to circle slowly around Cor. "What say you?"

Cor kept his gaze forward. "How many raiders?"

"We spotted four."

Cor gave a sharp nod. "And how far is the outpost from here?"

"About two weeks' journey on foot. With your beast and wagon … I'd estimate a week."

"Where is its exact location?" Cor pressed.

Tivore curled his lip. "That I will reveal *after* you agree to my terms."

Don't do it. Heat surged through Chiara's body. If Tivore hadn't been right there, she would've reached out to catch Cor's arm. *It's not worth it.*

"Allow me to consult with my companions," Cor announced.

"Very well," Tivore snarled. "You have twenty minutes. After that … I'll need a decision."

21

"It's a trap," Tagg said flatly, as soon as they'd walked far enough from the camp. "The whole journey will take us too far out of the way. The risk is too dangerous. We could be followed by Tivore, or found by another Felwen pack … or worse."

Chiara glanced around them cautiously, looking for any movement in the trees. Tivore had given his word that none of his pack would eavesdrop, but she didn't trust that as far as she could spit.

"Believe me … I am *aware* that it's a trap." Cor leaned against a tree trunk, massaging his temples. His eyes were closed. "The question is—"

"The question is, why are we even agreeing to this in the first place?" Zelie demanded from her seat on a dead stump. "Why can't we just leave? Go back the way we came, head right out of their precious territory?" She swiped viciously at the bark beneath her.

"We can't." Tagg's expression was black. "If we try to leave now, they'll hunt us down and then punish us. If we agree to the terms and *then* try to escape, they'll hunt us down and then kill us. The only reason we aren't experiencing indescribable suffering right now is because Cor demanded a deal. We don't really have a choice."

"So … so what, then?" Zelie threw her hands in the air. "We're supposed to just play butler? Kick out the unwelcome guests? Do you know how risky that is? That takes us *miles* away from our original course! Anything could go wrong!"

"I *know!*" Cor snapped angrily, thrusting himself off the trunk. "I get it!" He ran both hands through his hair in a desperate swipe. "That's not even the worst—" He cut himself off. His eyes looked haggard.

There was a pang in Chiara's chest. *There's something else going on here.* She chewed her lip, and then she risked the question. "Cor, before we agree to anything, I'd like to know what happened the last time you were here."

What with the fight last night, and confronting Tivore today, there had to be some kind of disagreement between Cor and Tivore. The real question was, how bad was it?

Cor pressed his lips together. "I was traveling solo two years ago. I … found myself in Tivore's territory. I had to negotiate a deal with him. It was something similar to this — performing a task in exchange for safe passage."

"So what happened?" Zelie snorted. "Because he clearly hates your guts now."

Cor shook his head. "He … didn't like the outcome."

"So …" Chiara prompted. "You still did it, didn't you? Is he just sour that he didn't get to kill you or something?"

"Or something." Cor ran his hands through his hair again. "I don't think we can trust him."

"You don't say!" Zelie exclaimed sarcastically.

But Tagg was scowling viciously. "You think we can't trust him to keep his word?"

Cor shook his head. "No. I mean … it's the whole deal I don't trust. I thought …" He hesitated. "Look, based on how my last visit went down, I expected him to keep me hostage in camp — use me as some kind of leverage to make you all finish the task. But it sounds like he'll let *all* of us go—"

"Okay, so why is that a problem?" Zelie interrupted. "He's not being a sourpuss now! We already have to accept this crummy deal — it doesn't need to be any more complicated!" She was clawing again at the stump.

Cor turned glaring eyes on her, but Tagg interrupted the impending tirade. "Zelie. Let's take a walk. We need to talk about more effective techniques for when you're fighting Felwen." He plucked Zelie up by the back of her shirt, ignoring her protests. "Come on."

When they disappeared between the trees, Chiara walked over to Cor.

He was sitting down now, rubbing his hands across his eyes.

"Hey," she said softly, sitting next to him so that their shoulders brushed.

Cor looked up, and his eyes were so tired. The breath rattled in his chest. No need to keep up the façade now.

She studied the moss at her feet, trying desperately to come up with something encouraging to say. Zelie had always been better at that. "Listen, you're — you're doing great."

Cor let out a disbelieving laugh. "Yeah, right." He buried his face in his hands again. "I was on guard duty when they came through."

He lifted his head. "I've been here before. I should've known the signs. We might've been killed. You almost—" He broke off.

"But I wasn't," Chiara said, as gently as possible. "You were there. You came through. Thank you." Hesitantly, she placed a hand on his back. The ridges of his scars were hard and unyielding beneath his shirt. "I … didn't get a chance to say it earlier."

Cor shook his head. He gave her a tortured glance, and to her shock, his eyes were glittering wetly. "She could've killed you, Chiara," he whispered. "She could've snapped your neck like a twig."

Something in his voice … Chiara swallowed.

He kept going, still looking at the ground. "You would've been gone … and there would've been nothing I could do about it."

She didn't know what came over her. Maybe it was the horrible, wounded look in his eyes, or the feel of his shudder beneath her touch.

What did it matter why? She slid an arm around his back and gave him a rough squeeze. "I'm here." She pressed her forehead against his shoulder. "I'm here. I'm alive. You got us this far. I trust you."

I trust you. Three words. Just … tumbling out of her mouth. Just like that.

Suddenly his arms were around her, and he was crushing her in a bear hug — and then just as suddenly, he pulled away, and he was swiping at his face, not looking at her. "Thank you."

Chiara blinked rapidly. *What … what's happening right now?* Butterflies tickled her stomach, making her uncomfortably warm. She closed her eyes, trying to push it away. "Can — can I ask you a question?"

Cor gave a small, amused huff. "Sure."

"What … happened, exactly? Between you and Tivore?" she asked, watching his face carefully. "Was there a fight, or something?"

She waited, but when he didn't respond, she went on. "It really seemed like Tivore had it out for you personally. I mean, I know he doesn't love outsiders," she added quickly. "But if you fulfilled your end of the deal, then why does he hate you? What really happened?"

Cor's fists were clenching and unclenching. He shook his head, a bitter smile crawling up his face. "I came here once. On my own — not with Fhír." His jaw worked silently.

"Why?" she asked, after a pause.

"I …" He took a deep breath.

Please trust me … please.

"I'd heard something about … about the fire at my town. A clue. Something tied to the Arsonists. I wanted to investigate it on my own, so …" He made a helpless gesture. "I ended up cutting through here."

"And?" Chiara prompted.

Cor snorted. "Fenris found me. He was also on his own. Anyway, he caught me, and I knew it was bad news, but I'd heard something about how you could sometimes negotiate a deal with Felwen to get their permission to cross their land."

"So you tried it."

Cor nodded. "I told Fenris I wanted to speak to his Chieftain. We made a deal. I was supposed to help them with a mission — something simple. An in-and-out kind of job. It … went sideways."

He took a shuddering breath. "The only reason I survived was because of Fenris. He wasn't even supposed to be there, but he followed me. I guess he suspected foul play." His expression became bitter. "I'm glad he did. Anyway, I got out alive."

"Where exactly did Tivore send you?" Chiara asked slowly. *Why is he avoiding this?*

Cor's eyes flicked to her face. "It doesn't matter."

"Horse dung." Chiara folded her arms. "Fine. If you won't tell me what happened, at least tell me *why* you won't tell me."

Cor turned away. "I don't want you to know."

"That's not a reason. Try again." She stared at him stubbornly.

He glanced at her again, jaw working. "I don't want you to think …
differently of me."

Chiara stared at him, baffled. There was something in his face …
something like shame. *What's going on here?* "Think differently of you?
Why would I ever think differently of you?"

"I'm not …" Cor sounded like he was choking on his own words.
"… the best … person. Okay?"

"Okay. And?" Chiara shrugged. "Neither am I. I'm tempted to kill
my best friend on a daily basis." *And I've been keeping secrets from you …
and I couldn't save Isak …*

Cor turned to her. "Promise—" he began, and then he cut himself
off. "No. Don't promise." He took a shaky breath. "I'll tell you, and I'll
take whatever comes."

"I'm listening."

He nodded. "Tivore sent me to kill someone."

"He — sorry, *what?*" Chiara's ears were ringing. *Kill someone?*

"That's not what he told me when we made the deal," Cor said
hurriedly. "He told me to track down one of his clan members. He
claimed the Felwen had been lost in the woods."

"Okay? And then what happened?"

Cor licked dry lips. "It wasn't just a lost Felwen. Tivore had him
driven out of the pack. A traitor. He'd killed one of their clan — he was
dangerous. They were trying to hunt him down. I found out later from
Fenris that Tivore had planned for me to be the bait."

Anger flared in Chiara's stomach. "So Tivore's style is sending
outsiders to do his dirty work for him." *What a stinking dungheap.* "What
did you do?"

"Well … I tracked him down, and I was about to confront him when Fenris appeared. He told me that Tivore wasn't coming. He said the whole thing was a setup and Tivore had sent me there to die. But the other Felwen heard us. He came at me—" He broke off and swallowed hard.

"You killed him?"

Cor nodded. "Me and Fenris. If he hadn't been there, I would've died. I mean, I'm strong, but …" He trailed off and stared at the ground. "I was never supposed to live. Tivore knew that."

"So … what did you do?"

"Fenris swore he'd never tell anyone he helped me. I guess he thought I didn't deserve to die like that." The corner of his mouth twitched up. "Then he left, and I took the body back to Tivore and accused him of cowardice."

Chiara almost choked. "Come again?" Tivore was terrifying enough when Cor had been bowing and scraping for a deal. *Calling him a coward to his face …?* "How are you still alive? That's the real miracle here."

Cor laughed softly. "I guess so. Anyway, Tivore was furious. He probably would've killed me then … I don't know. But it would've been in cold blood, and Felwen have some pretty strict laws about that." He sighed. "He let me go, but he swore he'd punish me if I ever crossed paths with him again."

"And now you're back."

"Yeah." Cor looked up at her. "The only reason I got away with being here again is because I'm with you. He might hate my guts, but he's not going to risk breaking Felwen law by taking other innocent lives just for a grudge."

"Some silver lining," Chiara muttered. She ran her fingers through her hair. "So … we can say for sure that this whole thing is a trap."

"Oh, it definitely is. And I don't know how yet — maybe there are more than four raiders, or maybe there's something else going on. But if it's anything like last time …" His jaw went tight.

He didn't need to finish his sentence.

… This isn't a negotiation. It's an execution.

"I really wish you were wrong." Chiara dragged her hands through her hair.

Cor shrugged and rubbed at his chest again.

"You alright?" Chiara gave him a concerned look.

"Yeah." He glanced around. "We're running out of time. Tagg!"

"Here — we're here!" Tagg marched out of the trees.

Zelie was skipping behind him. "Good talk?" She winked as she passed Chiara.

Chiara rubbed her face in her hands. *What did I do to deserve this …?*

Zelie went straight up to Cor. "I'm sorry for getting up in my hackles about this," she said sincerely. "I don't like this place at all, and this whole situation is making me anxious. But I trust you."

"Thanks, Zelie." Cor offered her a smile.

Chiara heard movement in the trees. Their time was running out. She turned to the others. "We've got to make a decision."

"Okay." Cor folded his arms. "Here's the deal. I don't know what's at that outpost. If I could, I'd march us right out of here and we'd never come back again. But we don't have a choice. Either we try to run and get captured for sure, or we take our chances with the outpost."

Tagg opened his mouth to protest, but Cor stopped him. "This is the wiser risk. You know that as well as I do."

Tagg looked extremely displeased, but he nodded.

"Okay. Second thing … this is definitely some kind of trap. And we won't be getting any help from any of the Felwen," Cor added, with a quick glance at Chiara. "We're on our own, and we'll be going in essentially blind. I'm not even sure there's a real outpost, except for the fact that our skill sets are probably too valuable for Tivore to send us on a total wild goose chase."

"So we'll assume — at least for now — that there is some kind of outpost? In the mountains?" Tagg lifted his eyebrows. "A mountain outpost?"

"Exactly."

"Okay, so what's there to decide?" Zelie demanded. "We're obviously going to do this together."

Cor shook his head. "Technically, it only needs to be me."

"What?" Chiara exclaimed. "Are you insane? Why in Arva would we stay behind and let you do this alone?"

"I'm the one who's negotiating the deal with Tivore." Cor set his hands on his hips. "I refuse to take any one of you with me unless you explicitly agree to come."

"You'd have to kill me to stop me." Zelie flashed needle-sharp teeth.

Tagg snorted. "Mate, you've really lost it if you think I'm letting you off on some bloody wild goose chase without me. Nice try, but if we die, we're gonna die together."

Cor looked at Chiara and she folded her arms. "What do you think I am? Some kind of chump? We're trapeze partners, for Arva's sake. I'm contractually forbidden from abandoning you."

"True," he sighed. "Alright, then."

"Wait," Zelie said. "How do we know he won't kill us himself?"

Cor shook his head. "He won't. If we survive this"—he emphasized the "if" a little too much—"then he can't kill us, no matter how much he wants to. A deal like this is binding on pain of death under Felwen law. And he's honor-bound to let us pass safely through his territory this time, regardless of how long it takes us."

Chiara scrunched up her face. "So — hypothetically, of course — we could just wander around in here for years? And as long as we didn't set foot outside his territory, he wouldn't be able to do anything about it?"

"Don't tempt me with a good time," Zelie snickered.

"Thanks, but I'm sick and tired of Felwen." Cor's mouth was grim. "Let's get this done."

ଓଃ

It was midmorning by the time they returned to camp. Tivore was leaning against the base of the outcrop, arms folded across his chest. As soon as they reentered the clearing, he straightened and began walking toward them.

Cor took the lead, chin up, shoulders squared. Chiara never would've believed he was worried if she hadn't seen him herself just minutes ago.

"We've come to our decision," he announced. "All four of us are doing this."

Tivore lifted his eyebrows. "What excellent news. In that case, keep in mind that once we shake, you are bound to keep your end of the bargain. And we, ours, of course."

His good eye glittered. "I must also add that you are never to reveal the location of the cache … under pain of death. I hope I need not remind you that my entire pack has your scents now."

He gestured to the Felwen gathered around. "Should we discover that news of our cache has spread, then … well. It would not be difficult for us to find you."

Cor stuck out his hand almost aggressively.

Tivore shook it. "Now, listen carefully. You must travel exactly forty miles east of here — a straight line, do you hear? Not a yard north or south."

"Understood," said Cor.

"Good. Once you've traveled forty miles east, you'll strike the Ondural River at the foot of the mountains. Follow the river north until it curves sharply west — another forty miles or so. The outpost was built just upstream of that curve."

Chiara narrowed her eyes. *That sounds … deceptively easy.* Then again, the real difficulty might be getting the wagon through the woods. No trail ever ran directly east or directly north.

"Alright." Cor turned around. "To the wagon."

"Oh — one moment!" Tivore exclaimed. "I'd almost forgotten. Your wagon won't be much use to you in the woods. In fact, it would never be able to take you along that straight line I mentioned earlier. We'd be happy to look after it for you."

Cor didn't face him right away. His face went stormy, and his chest swelled. He turned on his heel. "We have shaken. That was not part of our bargain."

"Of course not. I'm simply hoping to make your trip easier." Tivore spread his arms wide in a gesture that pantomimed harmlessness.

Chiara stared at him, repulsed and fascinated. She was beginning to understand what Cor must have experienced the first time around.

Tivore was manipulative and incredibly clever. He knew that taking a caravan wagon straight through the woods was next to impossible, so he'd phrased his wishes as an offer of hospitality, instead of a demand for leverage.

Which it is. Arva knew what the Felwen would do to their possessions. They might not have much use for circus equipment now, but a wagon belonging to Fhír was a really terrible clue to leave behind for Arsonists to find.

Tagg and Zelie had drawn back, standing close by the wagon. Their eyes were on Cor. Even from behind, Chiara could tell that his jaw was working.

"So be it," he managed at last, forcing the words out. "But I insist that we bring our necessary supplies with us — as well as our horse. We cannot afford to lose her."

Tivore's expression hardened slightly when Cor mentioned Ria. But he didn't hesitate in his response. "Of course! Take whatever you deem necessary for the journey."

Cor spun on his heel and gestured sharply. Chiara and the other two followed him to the back of the wagon. Stone-faced, he began tying up the back flaps of the canvas cover.

The only reason he's not yelling is because we're still in the enemy camp. Chiara stepped closer to him. "What do we do?"

"Grab your packs." He was already pulling bundles out of the back of the wagon. "Take all the food, the extra weapons, and anything you consider valuable. Leave the equipment and costumes."

"Right." Tagg clambered into the back, stooping down to avoid hitting his head. "I'll grab Ria's saddlebags." Zelie leapt in after him and began handing out their packs. Crossbow and bolts for Tagg, swords for Cor, the sax and a stave for Chiara.

Twenty minutes later, they'd unloaded everything they needed and repacked it into traveling kits. There was about a week's worth of supplies. After that, they'd have to figure it out on their own.

Ria stood patiently as Tagg loaded her saddlebags. Only the occasional twitch of a tail betrayed her anxiety. Chiara didn't blame her one bit.

Most of the Felwen were still watching them. Her hands couldn't seem to move fast enough. Finally, she buckled down the last strap and swung her bag onto her back.

Tagg swung easily onto Ria's back and held out a hand to Zelie. She took it, leaping up behind him.

When Chiara turned around, Cor was already up, pack in hand, facing Tivore. "We'll be back."

"I certainly hope so." All traces of Tivore's smile had disappeared.

22

As soon as they were three miles out from the Felwen camp, Cor called Ria to a halt. "We're not doing this Tivore's way," he said bluntly.

"You think he's lying about the outpost?" Tagg asked cautiously.

"Not necessarily. But I'd wager a lot of money that he's lying about the directions. I mean, who goes directly east? And then directly north?" Cor folded his arms.

"So you're saying this whole 'forty miles east, forty miles north' thing is just supposed to get us lost somewhere?" Zelie flexed her claws impatiently. "Ooh, that makes me mad!"

"I mean … it's possible." Tagg looked skeptical. "I heard a lot of buzzing in Tivore's camp. He's telling the truth about the caches existing, but I didn't like what I heard when he gave us the instructions."

"Why would he tell us to go east and then north when we could just cut northeast?" Chiara asked. "Why was he so insistent that we not set foot off this trail?"

Zelie inhaled excitedly. "You mean, there might be something he doesn't want us to know?"

"Exactly!" Chiara pointed at her. "What do you think, Tagg?"

"I know we *can't* trust him, no matter what he says," Tagg huffed. "Maybe there're a dozen raiders at the cache. Maybe the cache itself doesn't really exist anymore, and he's sending us to a pile of rubbish. Maybe this trail is safe, and maybe it's not."

"Okay, but why was he so specific?" Chiara pressed. "Come on. Don't you think it was a little weird that he gave us almost no details about the outpost itself, but knew the exact number of miles we'd have to go?"

"That is a little weird," Tagg admitted slowly.

"Look, if he wants us dead, he's going to assume we'll end up dead," Cor reasoned. "There wasn't any *reason* for him to be that specific about how we wound up dead. Unless …"

Tagg clicked his tongue thoughtfully. "If there *is* something he doesn't want us to find, that might make sense. I was hearing a constant buzz the whole time Tivore was talking, and it got way louder once he started the instructions. Thoughts don't sound like that unless they're being deliberately withheld. I don't know exactly what he's lying about, but he's lying about something."

"So he *is* hiding something," Chiara finished with a grin.

"Cor, I think you're right," Zelie crowed. "Let's go northeast tomorrow and see what we can find."

branded

℈

They covered a lot of ground the first day, something like fifteen miles, and Cor filled the others in on what had happened the first time he met Tivore. Tagg and Zelie roundly cursed Tivore's name, and Chiara agreed with the sentiment, although she refrained from the more colorful language.

Ria was an excellent trail horse, picking out the slimmest paths with ease. They considered taking turns riding her, but ultimately it was decided that she would carry their bags while they walked freely through the woods, keeping an eye out for danger.

"The only downside is that if she bolts, we're out of all our supplies," Tagg grumbled.

Cor clapped him on the shoulder. "That's where you come in, mate. Don't let her bolt."

Afternoon quickly became twilight beneath the dense tree cover. Soon they were inching along in near-total darkness. Every sound seemed to be amplified in the air — snapped twigs, rustling leaves, even the owls' hoots.

Chiara was following closely behind Zelie, who had taken the lead and was practically skipping along, clearly unbothered by the dark.

Chiara wasn't so confident. Every crinkle of a leaf sent her heart into double-time. It was all too easy to imagine another Felwen ambush. She started as something shuffled through the leaves nearby. "What was that?" she whispered.

Zelie put her nose in the air and sniffed. "Oh … badger."

"It seems a lot bigger in the dark."

"Really?" Zelie sounded surprised. "Isn't that what all badgers sound like in the dark?"

"I wouldn't know," Chiara snorted. "I don't hunt things at night. But yeah, small things sound a lot bigger in the dark."

"So what about big things, then? Are they much, much louder? Or really quiet?"

That was a nasty thought. Something huge in the dark that didn't make a sound? *I don't like that at all.* Chiara shuddered. "Let's hope big things are louder."

Or maybe ... they aren't. "The Felwen weren't loud last night," she realized.

"They don't have to be loud for me to find them," Zelie said scathingly. "A few hours in that camp was too long. I'd know that scent anywhere."

Chiara fell quiet. *Hopefully she's right.* Maybe next time, Zelie would smell the attackers *before* the attack.

"Hey, Zelie." Cor's voice came out of the darkness, followed by Cor himself. He fell into stride with Chiara.

"What's up?" Zelie slowed her pace.

"We need to bed down for the night. Can you run ahead and find a good place? Preferably somewhere off the trail?" He broke off in a loud cough, and Zelie and Chiara exchanged nervous looks.

"Sure thing." Zelie disappeared into the shadows ahead.

Chiara slowed her pace. "You don't sound great."

Cor didn't respond right away. When he did, his voice was subdued. "That's the least of my worries. We made it pretty far today, but we've still got miles to go before we even get to the river. This is going to take us at least a week, and that's just getting there. Who knows what we'll find ... and then we'll have to come back."

Chiara sighed. He was right. At best, the whole trip there and back would take them fifteen days. At worst, it could be almost a month before they finally made it back to their original course.

Or … no. *At worst, there won't be any "making it back."* Another cheerful thought to add to the list. If the raiders didn't do them in, there was no telling what Tivore might do if they returned in one piece.

ʘ

After another fitful night's rest, they struck out northeast as soon as light began to filter through the branches. Chiara immediately noticed a difference in the terrain. The trail seemed to flatten and widen out, and the trees became sparse.

They made it another ten miles or so before Cor finally called a halt for noon meal. Zelie found a dip in the ground a few yards away from the trail and they settled down to eat there.

"We're making way better time than we would've otherwise," Cor said as he sat down. "Curse Tivore. He even kept the wagon. He probably wanted us to take the most difficult route possible."

"Figures," Zelie snorted, chewing on a piece of jerky. "Everybody knows forest trails don't run that straight."

"No, but this one does," Tagg said suddenly. The others paused eating and looked up at him.

"What do you mean?" Cor asked, swallowing a mouthful of food.

"Ria has been walking in a straight line ever since we changed course this morning." Tagg looked around at them. "And have you noticed that there aren't as many trees? There's a ton of brush — but not as many trees. It's almost like—"

"Someone cleared a real trail here," Cor finished. "You're right. I wonder who?"

"Not the Tivore clan?" Chiara asked curiously.

Tagg shook his head. "Not really their style. Fewer trees means less cover for hunting. They're more likely to travel within the forest, not remove it entirely."

"So, someone else must've done it?" Zelie swallowed, looking extremely nervous. "Like what, exactly?"

Tagg shrugged. "I don't think it matters. Whoever it was, they've clearly been gone a while. That path hasn't been cleared up in at least a decade."

They finished their meal and headed back to the trail. Cor took the lead, Chiara and Tagg walked beside Ria, and Zelie took up the rear.

They'd only gone about a mile when there was a dull *thunk* and Cor doubled over with a cry of pain. "Fesht!"

"What's wrong?" Chiara jogged up to him. He was bent over, clutching his right foot. His face was pale.

"Sorry," he gasped. "Didn't mean to curse."

Chiara waved him off. "Forget about that. How's your foot?"

He winced. "… Possibly broken. But it's already healing. Give me a few minutes."

"Ah, the conveniences of being a Tegid," Tagg remarked, leading Ria over to them. "What's broken this time? Hopefully nothing important."

Zelie scampered up. "What'd you find?" Suddenly she froze, sniffing the air.

"What is it?" Chiara gripped the hilt of her sax, immediately alert. "What are you smelling?"

Zelie shook her head and plunged into the underbrush in front of Cor. A second later, there was a surprised squeal, and her head poked out of the bushes. "It's a train track!"

"What?" Tagg strode forward and stooped, pushing aside the brush. There was a metallic rapping sound. Then he turned around, his mouth a small *O* of surprise. "Yep. That's steel, alright. How's your foot, mate?"

Cor groaned. "I knew it wasn't a tree."

Chiara came to squat next to Tagg. Just at his fingertips, a rusted steel railroad tie protruded from the ground. It was partially covered by dead leaves. She shoved aside the brush to her left and spotted its twin, also rusting, half-buried in dirt.

"Somebody cleared this … for a railroad track?" She squinted ahead. Sure enough, there seemed to be something of a tunnel through the trees, albeit largely overgrown by vines and brush.

"Ugh." Cor leaned back, gingerly extending his leg. "No wonder he sent us straight through the woods. He didn't want us to have a choice about leaving the wagon." He clambered over to examine the offending railroad tie.

"We could've easily taken it with us," Chiara realized.

Tagg folded his arms. "Now that's just bally rotten."

"Well," Zelie said cheerfully, "at least we've got a clear trail. And if we're lucky, it might even be a straight shot to the outpost!"

"I bet it is." Cor sat upright suddenly. "This is Tegid-made."

"How do you know?" Tagg demanded.

"Mark on the metal. I mean, it's nearly rusted away — but that's definitely the Tegea Rail Company."

Chiara's heart began to pound faster. "And the outpost is a Tegid outpost. You don't think—?"

The base. It would've been the perfect location for the Arsonists' base. Remote, unused in years, concealed in Felwen territory—

"Let's not get ahead of ourselves." Cor rose stiffly to his feet, dusting himself off. "We have no idea what's going on at that outpost, if anything. Besides," he muttered, picking his way carefully around the ties, "I don't love the odds of only four of us against the Arsonists. That'd be a real nice way for Tivore's wishes to come true."

The brief flare of excitement collapsed in on itself. Chiara stood by Ria, her hands jittery. If it really was the Arsonists' headquarters …

What could we even do about it? They could never attack it — not when it was just the four of them and one highly-trained horse. They'd have to go back to Crescor first; find the rest of Fhír. *And by the time we come back, who knows how much more damage they could do?*

Whatever was at the end of these railroad tracks, she probably wasn't going to like it.

☙

Three more days passed. The weather was getting colder. The farther northeast they went, more color began bleeding through the leaves overhead. And there were more evergreens, too.

Every hour, Chiara expected Zelie to come dashing out of the woods yelling, "Felwen!" or Tagg to whisper, "Someone's nearby." But that never happened, and they were already several miles into a journey that was nearly done — at least by Cor's estimation.

Still, Chiara couldn't seem to shake the feeling that something was coming. It was beginning to haunt every waking moment. *The Felwen? The Arsonists?* Tossing shadows turned into leering masks. Her arm was slowly healing, but her mind …

When they finally bedded down for their fourth night in the woods, she was so tense that she lay awake in her hammock, ears strained for some unusual sound …

… And she was still awake in the middle of the night when Cor came to get her for her guard shift.

"Chiara," he whispered, touching her shoulder.

She sprang upright, and he started back with a gasp. "Holy Arva, that was terrifying."

"Sorry." She extracted herself from her hammock.

"Were you already awake?"

"… Yes." She tugged her boots over her cold toes.

"You need sleep." His voice was raw. "Go back to bed. I'll wake up Zelie." He coughed again, and the sound sent a sliver of panic through Chiara.

She grabbed at his hand. "No, don't. I'm awake anyway."

He turned, and she could feel the tension in his arm. But then he sighed. "Alright. Holler if something happens."

"I will," Chiara promised. Then she crept over to the edge of their meager campsite and settled herself against a tree, peering out into the woods.

I can barely see a thing. One or two stars peeped through the leaves overhead, but the shadows of the trees lay thick and dense, hiding the rest of the sky.

Exhaustion stole over her as the minutes dragged by. Her eyes remained open, but her mind …

Where are we going? What's waiting for us at the outpost? When will we make it back to Fhír?

A wave of homesickness enveloped her, and she folded her arms closer to her chest. *I miss home.*

Belkar. With its crowds of people and clouds of train smoke, the heat from the cobblestones, the stale city smells in the air.

Why would I miss it there? She'd never exactly had a home in the city. Not besides Mum and Dad, and the gym.

Was it really home? Split between her family and the gymnasium? Isak gone, either way?

I wish you were here. She turned her face to the sky, searching for a glimpse of the stars. *You'd love it … Just imagine, me joining the circus, leaving home …* She almost laughed aloud at the idea of telling him that.

I guess this is where life has taken me. Sleeping in hammocks, no hot showers, hours of hiking through strange forests … The world of gymnasiums and assessments felt like another lifetime.

No … not another lifetime. Her fingers brushed against the scars on her neck.

No matter where I go …

☙

"Alright, everyone up!"

Tagg's voice stirred Chiara from sleep. He'd taken the guard shift after her, three hours ago.

Three hours … Chiara groaned. Despite her best attempts at keeping warm, every part of her body was still cold. She clambered out of the hammock, whimpering as she put her boots on again.

"Pack up! Let's go, mates! Brekky on the road!" Tagg was walking in small circles, clapping his hands softly together.

Ria snorted and pawed the ground. Beneath Chiara's hammock, Zelie gave a mewling yawn.

"Get a move on, Cor!" Tagg exclaimed, slapping the motionless lump of Cor's hammock.

One arm emerged, waving limply in the air, followed by Cor's muffled voice. "Working on it …" He sounded terrible. His voice was hoarse and scratchy.

"Why so early?" Zelie sighed, handing him her bag.

"We've only got a few miles left of this thing," Tagg said, strapping the bag onto Ria's back. "Let's finish it as soon as possible, and maybe we can get this job done by nightfall."

"That's optimistic of you." Cor walked up with his bag. His voice was ragged, and his hair was a mess.

"Need I remind you that this was *your* idea?" Tagg lifted his eyebrows and snatched Cor's bag out of his hands.

"Ugh …" Cor rubbed his face. "That was last night's me. This morning's me realizes his mistake." There were dark circles under his eyes.

Chiara's chest tightened with worry. *He looks even worse today …*

What kind of world was this, where a sick Tegid was the least of their worries?

☙

They packed up quickly and headed out to the railroad tracks again. Tagg moved about a mile or so ahead, scouting the terrain. It was a chilly morning. Dew coated the edge of every blade and leaf. Spiderwebs materialized in the branches, beaded with water droplets. A bird chirruped somewhere overhead.

It was almost noon when Tagg suddenly reappeared, loping back down the path. Chiara put a hand to Ria's halter and gave a gentle tug, leading her away from the tracks. Cor and Zelie followed. They clustered together among the trees, out of sight of the trail.

"It's about half a mile ahead." Tagg crossed his arms. "The train tracks veer off left and go north a few yards from here. Then the trees thin out, and you can hear the river."

"What about the outpost?" Cor interrupted, cracking his knuckles. "The layout? Any guards?"

Tagg wrinkled his face. "Not much of a layout, if you ask me. Half the place is in pieces, and the rest isn't much better. And there aren't any guards, either. Whole thing looks like it's been abandoned."

"Are you sure?" Cor scowled.

"Positive." Tagg's ears lifted in emphasis. "Nothing I could hear."

"Maybe they're really gone," Zelie suggested hopefully. "Maybe they used up the whole cache and then left."

"Well, Tivore didn't lie," Tagg muttered. "I mean, he didn't tell us everything. But what he said out loud was technically true. For now, we have to assume that the caches are here, and that the four Felwen are here." He gave Cor a doubtful look. "Maybe they're all out hunting?"

"Without a guard?" Chiara frowned.

"The whole place probably reeks of Felwen," Zelie said with a shudder. "Once the raiders get back, any creature stupid enough to trespass wouldn't last very long."

Including us. Uneasy prickles crawled up Chiara's arms. "There's no way it's this simple. It's supposed to be a trial. This is supposed to be a trade-off for Cor's life."

"You're right." There was a shadow on Cor's face. "Whatever this is, it's definitely some kind of trap. My biggest worry …" He trailed off, but Chiara knew what he was thinking.

Tivore wouldn't have let Cor go unless he believed the trial would kill him.

"So what do we do now?" she asked after a moment. "We can't turn around now, can we?"

Tagg grimaced. "Not unless we want Tivore to slit our throats."

"Not an option." Cor ran a hand through his hair. "Only way out of this is forward. Any ideas?"

"Well …" Chiara began thinking aloud. "If they aren't there, and we seize the outpost before they come back, wouldn't that give us an advantage?"

"Wait a minute," Tagg said suddenly. "We're a bunch of idiots. I'm a Telk. I could try pulling down the rest of it. Then they'd have nothing to come back to."

Zelie snapped her fingers. "*There's* an idea."

"I don't like that idea," Cor said at the same time. "How much is that going to drain you? And what if they come back, and we get into a fight? Will you even be able to fight?"

"There's not much left of this place," Tagg argued back. "And gravity's on my side. As long as you've got my back—"

"Wait a minute," Chiara interrupted. "Won't Tivore kill us for destroying his cache?"

A wicked grin spread across Cor's face. "Actually, he wanted us to retake the outpost. He never said a thing about preserving the caches."

Tagg snorted. "I'll be damned. You're right. You missed your calling in the court of law, mate. Spot on, though. If Tivore wanted the caches intact, he should've specified that in the deal."

"Alright, then." Cor clapped his hands together. "Let's figure this out."

Fifteen minutes later, they had a half-decent plan of how to destroy the outpost without getting themselves killed. Zelie would go ahead, keeping alert for any sign of returning Felwen. Cor and Tagg would follow her, and Chiara would ride Ria behind them. Then Cor and Tagg would sneak inside the outpost and tear down any standing buildings, while Chiara and Zelie circled around the perimeter to keep an eye out for trouble.

"Let's hope this works," Chiara said half to herself as she mounted Ria.

They walked the final half mile in silence, eyes and ears peeled for any sign of Felwen. True to Tagg's report, the railroad track curved north, so they left the track and headed into the underbrush. Finally, the trees thinned out and fanned away. The river's rumble filled the air.

In front of them sprawled a huge open space about a mile long, marching from their feet down to the nearby riverbank. Tagg was right — there wasn't much left of the place. Crumbled walls and toppled stone studded the ground. A handful of partial buildings rose in the air. Rotting wood and cracked stones, the crippled remains of what was once an outpost. Only on the opposite bank were there a few pitiful structures that vaguely resembled shelter.

Zelie had taken the lead; she poked her nose in the air, sniffing cautiously. "I'll be back." She slid across the grass and disappeared into the ruins, just another shadow under the thin sunlight. The others waited, crouching just inside the tree line.

Chiara's heart was pounding in her ears. Except for the river, the whole place was eerily still. She was beginning to pick out darker patches beneath the clumps of weeds and clinging ivy.

Ashes.

No … she couldn't be sure from here.

What if it's them? What if they're here? But the Arsonists had never left a building standing. Not much of this place could qualify as "standing," but it was better than what the fires had done in the past.

Strained minutes dragged by. Cor's mouth was moving in a silent count. Finally, he looked up. "That's time. We're going in. We'll be back as soon as possible."

Suddenly, Zelie emerged from the grass, a look of alarm on her face. "There's no Felwen scent here!" she hissed.

"What do you mean?" Tagg demanded.

"I mean Felwen haven't been here in months," she insisted. "Maybe years. The scent is so stale, I almost can't smell it at all. There's no way Felwen raiders have been living here."

Just then, a crackling sound floated through the trees behind them — something was charging through the underbrush.

Everyone spun around. Cor had both swords in hand. Zelie bared her teeth in a silent snarl.

Chiara slipped off Ria and whipped out her sax, scanning the trees. Whatever it was, it was large, and it was coming rapidly closer.

Then Zelie gave a hiss. "Felwen!" Her tail stuck out bristling behind her.

"Are you sure?" Chiara shifted back and forth on the balls of her feet, gripping her hilt. *They're awfully loud this time …*

"I'm telling you, it's Felwen!" Zelie dropped into a crouch. "I'm going in!"

"Zelie, NO!" Cor grabbed for her collar, but she was quicker. She shot off into the woods.

"Curse it!" Cor whirled on Tagg and Chiara. "Stay here! Watch the ruins! I'll be back!" He took off running into the woods.

"Like hell we will." Tagg leapt onto Ria's back and held out a hand. Chiara grabbed it, and he pulled her up behind him.

They plunged forward, following Cor's trail. It was all Chiara could do to keep from slicing one of her own fingers off as she tried to sheathe her weapon.

"Hold on!" Tagg shouted, and she gripped his waist fiercely as he urged Ria into a gallop.

"Coren!" A shout cut through the woods like a crossbolt — a familiar shout.

Tagg's entire body went rigid in Chiara's arms. "Come on, girl," he urged, and Ria charged forward faster, air whistling past them.

"Coren, LISTEN TO ME!"

The same voice — and then Chiara knew. "Fenris?"

Then she saw the three figures just ahead.

One was crouching on all fours — Fenris, apparently. Zelie was latched to his back, growling savagely as he pitched back and forth. Cor circled them, swords drawn, watching intently for an opening.

Just as Tagg reigned Ria in, Fenris bucked and twisted, throwing Zelie off. In the blink of an eye, Cor lunged in, and his blade was at Fenris's throat. Zelie drew back, chest heaving.

"There are consequences to breaking a deal, you know." Cor's voice was deadly soft.

"Oh, *can* it, will you?" Fenris shouted. The whites of his eyes flashed, almost as if he was afraid. "Listen to me. You need to get out of here right now!"

"What? Why?" Cor demanded. "Our deal with your pack is still binding!" His eyes narrowed. "What are you playing at? Getting me to break my word?"

"It's a trap, you numbskull!" Fenris exclaimed.

"Of course it's a trap!" Cor snarled. "Do we look stupid to you?"

"You'll look a lot stupider if you don't listen to me," Fenris shot back. "There's no point—"

And then the fire began.

☙

Chiara heard it before she saw it. High-pitched screaming, just like Crescor and the Festival. Only this time, it was much louder. Terror in her throat, she whipped around as a dull roar began to rise behind her.

Orange light flooded the sky as trees went up like torches. Fire, rushing like a plague, leaping from branch to branch. A wall of flames, ripping toward them; and just ahead of it, six black figures — running toward them, closer and closer, only yards away now, arms outspread as if they were pulling the wave of heat forward with them.

Arms outspread; why? Slowing themselves down, striking every trunk, and then—

—and then she knew. The accelerants — the storm drains — the glowing hands; the marks on her face; the nightmares.

"RIDE, TAGG! RIDE!" She was screaming at the top of her lungs.

It's them — it's them; *it's their own hands — their own* bodies—

"Arsonists!" Cor was yelling. "Back the way we came!" He snatched Zelie by the collar and began to run, but Fenris gave an ear-splitting cry.

"No!" It rang out above the inferno, stopping Cor in his tracks.

"Northwest!" Fenris roared in the same piercing voice. "Now, or we die!" He snatched Zelie up and threw her onto his back. Then he fell to all fours and bolted away through the woods, heading northwest. Cor sprinted forward, right on his tail.

"On, Ria!" Tagg was chanting, and somehow Ria was thundering forward, ears pinned to her skull, foam at her mouth; they reached Cor, then Fenris, then on, on into the woods, into the shadows, the roar of the fire and crashing trees behind them—

23

"**A**re you injured?" Cor sat her down at the base of a tree and scanned her carefully. He took her hands in his and lifted one, then the other, checking her limbs for wounds.

His face was shadowed, haggard, and he sounded like he'd swallowed sharp gravel.

Chiara shook her head.

They were alive. They'd made it out. They'd run for hours; hadn't stopped; until finally the sky grew dark. Fenris had taken them to the northwest corner of Vastil Forest, and they lay huddled just inside the treeline.

Ria was standing limply against a pine, her sides slick and heaving. Tagg stood next to her, brushing her down, whispering soft words. Zelie and Fenris were already curled up asleep around the fire they'd made.

Chiara stared past Cor, watching the flames. The soft, crackling song of the embers fell on indifferent ears.

It was them.

She knew. For the first time in three years, she knew. She remembered everything.

The screaming. The fire. The crumbling walls … the hooded shapes. The glowing hands. All of it … real. Even the thing that had burned her face.

Their own bodies …

"Are you okay?" Cor asked, softer.

"No," she whispered.

He squeezed her hand. A strangled sob escaped her, and she crawled forward, sliding her arms around his chest. He said nothing, just held her as her body shook.

"Cor," she managed, after a few moments.

He drew back; she could feel his eyes searching her face. "I'm here."

"The Arsonists. They're—"

"Lacar." His voice was horribly quiet. She couldn't see his face, but she could hear the soft puffs of breath through his nose. His shoulders were trembling.

Lacar. The fire-summoners.

But how is that even possible …? Lacar were forbidden by treaty to enter Tegea. Nobody ever would've guessed that they were the Arsonists.

They aren't supposed to be here at all.

Cor lifted a hand, and chills traveled down her spine as his fingers brushed the side of her face — her scars. "One of them touched you."

An uncontrollable shudder gripped her, and she reached up to touch her scars. "I thought"—she swallowed, nearly choking—"I thought it was a nightmare."

The thing in the Crescor fire … not a Tegid. A Lac. He really had grabbed her face … left the brand of his fingertips behind.

"How is this possible?" she whispered. "I thought they weren't allowed south of the Laustrul Mountains. How are they here?"

"This whole time …" Cor spoke through gritted teeth. "I should have known."

She frowned. "What do you mean? How could you have known?"

He didn't reply, just shook his head.

I wish I could see his face right now.

"You need rest," he said quietly.

"Rest?" Chiara rubbed her hands across her face. "My nightmares are real, and you expect me to *rest?*"

A quick huff of breath from him — a humorless laugh. "No. But I need you to try."

I'll never rest again.

Lacar. Lacar had killed Isak. And they'd left her alive … but not unmarked.

ॐ

"Lacar?" Fenris didn't even bother to hide his disbelief. "You want me to believe that those were *Lacar?* What, did you hit your head or something?" He stared back and forth between Tagg and Chiara.

"I know what I saw," Chiara insisted.

branded

It was the morning after the attack. Cor had woken everyone at dawn, and now they were sitting in a circle around the fire.

"So do I." Tagg's face was hollow. "They weren't carrying anything. No weapons, no torches, nothing. All they had to do was touch the trees to set them on fire."

"Their hands were *glowing*," Zelie said with a shudder. "I thought—"

An incredulous laugh burst out of Fenris. "How is that even possible? Isn't the Laustrul Treaty still around? Lacar haven't been allowed south of the Laustrul Mountains in *fifty years*! Maybe longer!"

"Almost a hundred." Cor wasn't looking at anyone else, just poking at the fire with a stick.

Fenris flung a hand toward him, as if in proof. "Exactly! If they're here, then they're here in violation of one of the most serious treaties in Arva. If they even still exist."

"Look, mate." Tagg folded his arms. "They exist. I dunno what you were looking at or seeing. But I know what *I* was seeing. And besides, how else d'you explain how quickly they got those fires going? You *live* in a forest. Have you ever seen a forest fire spring up like that?"

Fenris wasn't giving up so easily. "Okay, Ears, answer me this: how do you know they didn't have an accelerant—?"

Tagg cut him off. "We saw their hands glowing, and you're telling me you can't believe Lacar did it? You can still see the smoke!"

He pointed aggressively toward the sky. There was a gray smudge far overhead — smoke, blown northwest for miles.

Maybe it's still burning …

Fenris huffed impatiently. "Alright, fine. Let's assume you're right. Say those were Lacar—"

"They are." Cor was still eerily quiet.

Fenris continued. "—And they attacked us. Why? Why are they attacking us? Why are they even here?"

"Funny you should ask that," Cor said, turning on him, "seeing as that it was your *father* who sent us there."

Fenris's lips pulled back in almost a snarl. "Listen, Golden Boy. My *father* was the one who sent you, not me! If I'd been there, I would've negotiated a better deal for you!"

"Wait … your *father?*" Zelie scowled.

Chiara gasped. "*That's* why he looked familiar!" They had the same profile — the same nose, the same curve of the forehead. Without a beard, Tivore would have been a fifty-year-old Fenris.

Fenris shot her an approving glance. "Well done, Snapdragon. Tivore sired me. Hence my devilishly good looks. The only good thing he ever gave me," he added contemptuously.

"Tivore is your father," Chiara repeated, dozens of questions coming to mind. *Why did he help Cor? Why is he helping us now? Is he just leading us into another trap?*

"If Tivore's your father, how do we know we can trust *you?*" Zelie demanded, eyes blazing blue. "He sent us out here to die!"

"Listen, Pipsqueak, that wasn't my idea, and it wasn't my fault!" Fenris shot back. "I bolted as soon as I found out where you'd gone! I was trying to warn you about the fire!"

"You came a little late for that." Chiara fixed him with a cold stare. "Why should we trust you?"

"Because I'm telling the *truth!*" Fenris barked. "You're the ones with the Jeka! How about you ask Ears over there?"

All heads turned to Tagg, who lifted his eyebrows. "What do you want me to do, mate? Probe your mind?"

"Sure! I don't care, as long as it gets you to trust me!" Fenris threw his claws in the air.

"Alright." Tagg shrugged. "Shut your eyes."

Fenris obeyed, and Tagg closed his own eyes, too. After only a few moments, he opened his eyes again and looked around at them. "He's telling the truth."

"That's nice to know." Cor didn't look convinced at all. He crossed his arms, eyeing Fenris with suspicion. "If you want us to trust you, this is how it's gonna go. You're gonna tell us everything you know about that outpost — and why Tivore sent us there, and why you came to stop us. And Tagg is going to monitor everything you say, so if you even think about lying," and he crouched, staring Fenris down, "I'll kill you myself and leave you for the birds."

Fenris snorted. "Alright, have it your way. And you're welcome, by the way, for saving your lives," he added, glancing around the circle. "Twice, for Golden Boy."

"Why twice?" Chiara asked. "Why save us at all? Aren't you breaking your binding agreement?"

"What binding agreement?" Fenris's teeth appeared in a wicked grin. "My father made the deal. Not me."

Tagg lifted his eyebrows with a nod, but Zelie wasn't having it. "That doesn't matter. You're his son, and his deputy. You represent him."

"Oh, I do, do I?" Fenris spat on the ground. "Damn me to hell if I do. I came to warn you because Tivore is a bloodthirsty bastard, and I'm through with it. I'm leaving my pack."

Stunned silence followed.

"You're … you're what?" Cor asked slowly.

"You heard me, Golden Boy. I'm done with Tivore." Fenris lifted his chin, teeth flashing.

Cor glanced at Tagg, who gave a small nod. So far, so true.

"Why are you leaving?" Chiara demanded. Felwen never left their packs — not unless they were driven out or punished. That much she knew from the *Encyclopedia*.

Fenris's response was immediate. "Because I intend to challenge him. As a Chieftain."

Zelie snorted. "A Chieftain? With what pack? You don't have anyone else!"

"Not right now. But I will." Fenris sounded extremely confident.

"But … why leave?" Chiara asked. "You were in the same pack. Why not challenge him then and there?"

"Felwen law forbids a deputy from directly challenging his Chieftain's authority." Fenris shrugged. "Defecting and then challenging him as the Chieftain of a separate pack is my best option."

"So you're not deputy anymore?"

"Spot on, Snapdragon." Fenris pointed a claw at Chiara. "She's got some sharp brains behind those pretty eyes. Doesn't she, Cor?" he said, laughing.

"Shut up," said Cor. "Did Tivore know you were defecting?"

"No. And I doubt he'd care," Fenris added with a snarl. "I've never agreed with his way of running things. He's a tyrant — he's cruel, and all he cares about is ensuring the pack's survival. Even if it means bloodshed."

He shot a glance around the circle. "That's why I'm challenging him. I'd been planning on leaving for a while. Your crew provided me the perfect opportunity."

"You mean your father almost getting us killed? *That* opportunity?" Zelie glared at him accusingly.

Fenris looked hurt. "Like I said, I wasn't there when he made that deal. If I was, it would've gone down a lot better than this. I heard the story when my hunting party came back, and I left a day later."

"And you're positive you weren't followed?" Tagg narrowed his eyes.

Fenris shook his head. "Definitely not. Besides, after that little light show at the river, nobody who followed me would believe I was alive. They would've turned tail as soon as the first tree went up."

"Why?" Chiara's eyebrows knitted together. "Wouldn't Tivore want to kill you if he found out you were helping us?"

"That would be just like him," Fenris snorted. "But no. None of them would've followed me to the outpost. Tivore forbade us from ever going near it."

"So all that about caches was a cock-and-bull story." Zelie curled her lip. "What a dungheap. Why bother sending us, then? What would he get out of it?"

"Get out of it?" Fenris scoffed. "Nothing! He wanted Golden Boy dead. He never forgave you for that last little incident. He's sore like that. The rest of your team was a bonus."

"So he knew the Lacar were there?" Cor's eyes widened.

Chiara glanced at Zelie. If Tivore knew the Arsonists were there, and he set all of it up as a trap …

… *Is he working for them?*

"What? No!" Fenris scowled. "The caches *used* to be there. That much is true. A year ago, rogue Felwen discovered them and raided our supplies. Tivore wanted to ambush them. When I went to scout it out, there were more raiders. And the place looked even worse than before — scorch marks everywhere. I thought a new clan had moved in. I told Tivore to give it up or risk a clan war." His eyes darkened.

Chiara waited, breath coming shallow. Scorch marks …

"He wasn't interested in peace. He was interested in regaining power." Contempt was heavy in Fenris's voice. "The arrogant bastard got thirteen of our finest fighters killed. He came back alone, and he was badly wounded. He said nobody was ever allowed to return there, and he started leading us south the very next day."

"Badly wounded," Tagg repeated. "Let me guess — he was burned."

"Exactly," Fenris muttered. "He never said what hurt him, but there's no way he didn't know who attacked him. He never would've moved us if it was an ordinary threat."

"I thought he didn't care about bloodshed," Zelie accused.

Fenris's teeth showed. "Tivore would do anything to protect his pack. And I mean anything — including killing someone who broke his word," he said, with a pointed look at Cor.

The others exchanged grim looks. Chiara sat back, reeling.

Arsonists *had* taken over the outpost. Those were ashes that she'd seen. They'd probably burned the place down to flush out the Felwen raiders.

But why would they want an abandoned *outpost for a base?*

"And you're still gonna insist that Lacar have nothing to do with this?" Tagg raised a skeptical eyebrow.

Fenris let out a huff. "Fine. I'll grant you that the Lacar theory seems to be the most logical conclusion. Now what?"

"Well." Cor folded his arms. "Now we know the Ars—the Lacar are the ones at the outpost. And … Tivore probably thinks we're all dead. Is it safe to assume that we won't be followed? By the Felwen, at least?"

"I seriously doubt they'd follow us," Fenris snorted. "If Tivore knew I was running straight for the outpost, he'd let me. And if anyone else from my pack was following me, they'd turn around as soon as they realized where I was headed."

"What about our scents?" Zelie piped up. "We didn't bother masking those."

"Pretty bloody sure that the strongest scent in this forest right now is *fire*," Tagg pointed out.

"That's correct, Ears." Fenris nodded approvingly.

"It's pronounced *Tagg*," muttered Tagg.

But Fenris wasn't listening. "Besides, I took us northwest for a reason. It's way out of Tivore's territorial line. If we're getting chased, we're getting chased by a different clan — but that's a problem for another day."

Cor opened his mouth, probably ready to ask another question, but Fenris stopped him. "Oh, no. I've told you everything I know"—he shot a look at Tagg— "and I'm done talking. It's my turn to ask questions."

"Right, like we'd trust you," Zelie sniffed.

Cor looked to Tagg. "Well?" he asked tersely.

Tagg lifted his ears. "All clear."

"Perfect!" Fenris bared his teeth in a grin and leapt to his feet. "Now, here are my questions. What are four fighters and a single traveling circus wagon doing out here? Why were you heading deeper into the forest? And why"—he fixed them all with a keen look—"did all of you immediately assume that those were Lacar, and not something else? That seems like a pretty quick jump to make."

Chiara glanced at Tagg, then Zelie. *He could join us. He defected. Maybe he could help.*

Cor's jaw was working. He looked like he was trying to swallow a rock. "Fenris, I'd like a word with my team. Could you give us a minute?"

Fenris lifted his claws disarmingly. "By all means." He turned and sauntered back through the trees until he was nearly out of sight.

As soon as he was gone, Zelie said, "I don't trust him. He calls me Pipsqueak."

"I don't trust him, either," said Cor. "I know he's telling the truth, but pack loyalty runs a lot deeper than he's making it out to. I don't know if we can rely on him to have our backs if Tivore comes knocking."

"Well, he's definitely sincere about defecting," Tagg put in. "And he could be a great help to Fhír."

"*What?*" Zelie and Cor both stared at him.

"I agree," said Chiara. "Think about it," she argued as they turned on her. "We don't have to tell him everything about Fhír. We can just say we were separated from our circus and we need to get back to them in Crescor, and we can ask him for his help."

"Why his help?" Zelie demanded.

Chiara's mind was racing. "What's the point of letting him go off on his own? He knows there are Lacar at the outpost. If he leaves us, and he goes spreading that around, we'd lose the only lead we have on the Arsonists. If he sticks with us, he could help us."

Cor's face was grim. "I agree with what he said about Tivore being selfish, but I still don't trust him. He's spent his whole life living in Tivore's shadow, seeing Tivore's patterns of thinking. That's going to affect him, whether he admits it or not."

"He saved your life," Chiara argued.

"Twice," Tagg added.

"It wasn't as altruistic as it sounds, okay?" Cor glared at them. "He got me out of the way because *he* wanted to be the one to take out the clan traitor. It was his right as deputy. Apparently, Tivore thought it would be fun to pit us against each other — watch his son fume as some outsider usurped his birthright."

"But he got you out of the way first," Chiara said suddenly. "Why? Why didn't he just let you die? His father wanted you out of the way anyway. Wouldn't he have proven his point by letting you die *and* capturing the traitor?"

"Look, it doesn't matter that much," Cor huffed. "I don't think he's got what it takes to work with Fhír."

But Zelie looked a little less certain. "Maybe … but why would he bother saving the rest of us? That *definitely* wouldn't make him look good in Tivore's eyes."

Tagg's head went up. "Ask him."

"What? Why?" They all stared at him.

"Ask him," he repeated. "Look, we all got asked why we wanted to join Fhír. We all have our reasons. Let's ask him his. Tell him about Fhír — be honest — and then see what he says. If he's lying, we'll know."

Nobody could find a good enough reason to disagree, so they called Fenris back.

He reappeared with a jaunty swagger. "Return from banishment! How's the wind blowing?"

Cor still looked skeptical, but Chiara could tell he was trying his best. "What's the real reason you saved us? You could've just let us die."

"What, are you serious?" Fenris scoffed. But something in their faces must have reined him in. He cleared his throat. "Well … I figured I was damned anyway, so I might as well help you out."

"Really?" Chiara asked, narrowing her eyes at him.

"Yes, really! You think I like seeing my home burn? Or anything else, for that matter? No! And if it's really Lacar, I'd like to stop the bastards before they try it again."

Tagg raised his eyebrows and turned to Cor. "Clean." No lies.

"Fine … fine," Cor sighed. He turned to Fenris. "You agree that those were Lacar?"

"Yes!"

"And you don't want to let them do it again?"

"Yes!" Fenris insisted.

So far, so good. Chiara sighed through her nose. But Fenris still had to make it through the hardest part.

Cor folded his arms, speaking in a remarkably practical tone, which didn't at all match the words he was saying. "Would you believe me if I told you that our traveling circus is an underground espionage ring trying to hunt down Lacar?"

Fenris stared at him, shocked. Then he let out a barking laugh. "Seriously?"

No one laughed with him.

He looked around in disbelief. "You're … you're *serious*. You're not pulling my tail?"

Cor shook his head.

Fenris laughed again, louder this time. "You're telling me you're a kickass circus spy ring trying to take down a bunch of arsonists?" His tail was practically wagging. "That's insane! How do I sign up?"

Cor blinked. "You're … on board with that?" He frowned. "Are you being brutally honest?"

"Have I ever been anything else? Really, what do you take me for?" Fenris scoffed. "*Yes,* I'm in. As long as you don't make me juggle." He wrinkled his nose distastefully, and Chiara had to hold back a laugh.

"Noted." Cor sighed. "You have to promise to stick with us — with Fhír — until we've seen this thing through and the Lacar are permanently back on the other side of the Laustrul Mountains."

It wasn't quite Skipper's formal oath, but that was the gist of it. The rest of them looked expectantly at Fenris.

"Hell, yeah!" he exclaimed. "Ride or die."

Zelie winced. "Hopefully not *die,* but okay, sure."

Tagg shrugged. "Works for me," he said as he went over to untether Ria.

Cor sighed heavily through his nose. "Alright, then. Welcome to the clan."

24

By unanimous vote, their new heading was northwest. No point going anywhere else. East would take them back toward the outpost, and south was Tivore's territory. "Let's split the difference, then!" Fenris had suggested, and that seemed to be the wisest course of action.

He was a piece of work. Not once did he use anyone's real name. Cor was permanently "Golden Boy," and Zelie was "Pipsqueak." Chiara remained "Snapdragon" after the first failed attempt at "sweetheart." Tagg apparently had the short end of the stick. Fenris seemed to relish calling him "Ears."

"So what's the deal, Ears?" Fenris was cleaning his claws on the grass. He and Zelie had gone hunting for dinner, and now everyone was smoking rabbit meat over the fire. Stars began to flicker to life in the dark blue overhead.

Tagg grunted. "What's the deal about what?"

Fenris gestured toward his head. "Ears and thumbs? You're a mixed-blood?"

"We're called *doua*," Tagg said under his breath. "My mother was a Telk, and my father was a Jeka."

Chiara glanced at Tagg curiously. He'd never talked about his family. Until now, she wasn't even sure whether they were still alive.

"Sounds like the start of a very long and complicated backstory." Fenris wiggled his eyebrows. "Care to share?"

Cor snorted as he pried cooked meat off his stick. "Good luck with that."

Tagg shot Fenris a dirty look across the campfire. "No thanks, mate."

"Oh, come on." Fenris sprawled back on his elbows in the grass. "You already know mine."

"Still a no." Tagg scowled.

"Hey." Fenris lifted his claws disarmingly. "I wasn't the one who let me into Fhír. If we're all clanmates now, aren't we supposed to trust each other?"

He had a point. Chiara glanced at Zelie, who was curled up next to her gnawing on a piece of rabbit meat.

Tagg huffed through his nose. "Fine. You go first, then."

"Nice try." Fenris shook his head. "You already know about my father. But if you're so reluctant, then we'll start with Golden Boy first."

Cor, who was in the middle of eating, shot him a dirty look. He swallowed and said, "What do you need to know?"

"Your family drama, obviously." Fenris shrugged.

"I don't have family drama," Cor replied. "I was an orphan."

Fenris raised his eyebrows. "Sounds pretty dramatic to me."

Cor sighed. "I was raised in Crescor by my aunt. She's also part of Fhír." He looked at Zelie expectantly.

Zelie shrugged. "I don't know who my parents were. I was raised by other Kithsa on the streets in Belkar until I met Chiara."

"Arva, do any of us have decent relationships with our parents?" Fenris snorted.

"I do," said Chiara. "I mean — I was adopted. But that was when I was a baby. I've been with them my whole life. As far as I'm concerned, they're my real parents."

Fenris shrugged. "Borrowed is better than broken," he said, earning a harsh glare from Cor. "And they were fine with you joining the circus?"

"My father … knew about Fhír," Chiara said carefully. "He wanted me to join."

"Nice. Okay, Ears." Fenris turned to Tagg. "We've heard everyone else's stories. Your turn."

Tagg scowled. "My parents are traders. Their route was to and from Crescor. That's where I met Cor and his aunt. I joined Fhír when I was ten."

Fenris whistled. "And your parents were fine with that?"

A shadow crossed Tagg's face. "Not exactly."

Fenris gave an incredulous laugh. "Wait a minute — you're telling me you left home *against* your parents' will to join the circus?"

"What're you laughing about? You did the exact same thing, mate," Tagg shot back with a glare.

"Can't argue with that!" Fenris waved a claw in the air.

Chiara leaned back, staring into the fire. *So his parents are alive, then.* And from the sound of it, probably not happy about him fighting arsonists.

"How about you, Fenris?" Zelie stood and stretched lazily. "We know about your dad, but what about your mum?"

Something like rage flashed across Fenris's face … but it was gone so quickly.

Chiara blinked. *Maybe I imagined it …*

"Not around anymore," Fenris said quietly. "But that's a story for another day." The shadows flittered harshly across his features.

Chiara squinted up at the sky. It was almost completely dark now, hundreds of stars glimmering in the canopy overhead. "We should probably turn in."

"Agreed." Tagg rose to his feet. "I'll take first watch."

"I'll take second," Zelie said.

"Third." Fenris earned himself surprised looks from the others. "What? I'm a Felwen. We hunt at night half the time anyway."

Cor waved a hand in the air. "I'll take fourth." His voice sounded raw.

Chiara shook her head. "I don't think so. You sound terrible. You need sleep. I'll take fourth."

Cor stared at her like she'd just insulted his mother. "Are you kidding me? No! *You* need sleep. You and Tagg both. The rest of us can survive without it."

"Oo, a lover's quarrel," Fenris snickered, and they both glared at him. "What's the matter? Aren't you both Tegids? Why worry about sleep when you've got regeneration?"

"Not me," Chiara said shortly, rising to her feet.

Fenris blinked a few times. "Really? Damn. I'm sorry."

He sounded sincere. Chiara blinked, surprised. "Thanks, I guess."

"And that didn't stop you from joining Fhír?"

Chiara shrugged. "Best option, honestly. There's a lot more I can do out here."

"Really? Isn't fighting arson dangerous for you?"

"Not any more than it is for you," she pointed out. "Unless Felwen are flame-resistant."

Fenris shuddered. "Definitely not. And for what it's worth, we're in the same boat. I don't have regenerative powers, either."

So much for sincerity. Chiara threw her stick at him.

"Hey!" he protested. "I'm serious!"

She turned her back and threw a not-so-nice gesture over her shoulder as she headed to Ria for her bag.

Isn't fighting arson dangerous for you? The words kept repeating in her head as she set up her hammock.

Yes. But I don't care.

"Stunted" had taken a lot of things. But not everything.

For the first time in three years, she had a reason to go back into the fire.

෬

"How is it possible that out of the five of us here, not *one* of us thought to bring a map?" Tagg said for the hundredth time. He sounded like he was on his last nerve.

It had already been a week since their first night on the plains, and after the fifth plunging valley in a row, everyone was starting to get more than a little irritable. Cor had called a halt that afternoon, and now Zelie was scouting the terrain ahead while the rest of them argued.

"*You're* the intrepid traveling circus," Fenris snipped. He wasn't quite his jovial self. "Don't you have a map lying around somewhere?"

Tagg glared at him. "We did, actually! Funny you should ask. But we ended up leaving it behind in a wagon with a bunch of bloody Felwen."

Fenris ignored him. "Let's just vote on it — north or south."

"Don't we want to go west? That's where Crescor is." Chiara crossed her arms, leaning against Ria's shoulder. Her feet were aching, but she felt more mentally worn out than anything else.

"I don't think we're far enough north," Cor said slowly. He seemed more sluggish today, and he was speaking with effort. "If we strike west and we're still too far south, we risk running into the Arsonists again."

"If we go too far north, then we'll have to make up all that extra ground." Tagg sighed. "We'll lose even more time."

Chiara rubbed her face in her hands, trying to visualize the map on Dad's office wall. *I should've paid way more attention to geography.* Of course, she knew how far Crescor was from Belkar. But she had no idea how far Crescor was from their current position.

Dad's map. The one he used to teach her directions. Up north, there was Crescor, a smattering of surrounding towns, and—

"Wait a minute." Chiara lifted her head, thoughts racing. "Isn't there a whole string of Tegid outposts above Crescor?"

Cor squinted thoughtfully. "You mean the trade route? The one that goes west to east?"

"Yeah, that." Chiara straightened up and gestured energetically. "What if we made for that? If we keep going north, we're bound to stumble across an outpost or a road eventually. We can get our bearings there."

"Another outpost?" Tagg looked displeased. "I'm not exactly bonkers about that."

"There's no way the Arsonists are that close to Crescor." Cor was shaking his head decisively. "Scatha definitely would've told us."

"Maybe they are already, and we don't know it yet." Tagg was scowling.

Fenris looked between them worriedly. "I don't like the sound of that."

But Cor shook his head. "I don't think the Arsonists would risk staying in a well-populated area. More people would notice them. Their biggest asset right now is their secrecy. I don't think they'd be willing to exchange that for a well-visited outpost." He took a heavy breath.

Tagg's frown lessened. "That's a good point." He glanced around hesitantly. "We could try it. Thoughts?"

"Let's wait until Zelie gets back," said Cor. "Then we'll vote on it."

They didn't have to wait very long. Half an hour later, Zelie reappeared, racing down the side of the valley on all fours. She leapt to her feet and dusted off her paws. "What did I miss? Why do you all look so grumpy?" she added, glancing around.

"Never mind that. What's the report?" Fenris asked eagerly.

"Good news and bad news. Good news — some kind of building or town or something is about ten miles north of here. Bad news — I found out because there's some kind of smoke in the sky."

"That's it. We're going back south," Tagg muttered.

But Cor didn't seem satisfied. "What kind of smoke?"

Zelie gave him a puzzled look. "Um … light grey, I guess. I thought it was a wispy cloud at first. It kind of drifted away while I was watching it."

Cor turned to the others, relief in his eyes. "That's not the smoke a forest fire makes. That's the kind of smoke a chimney makes. I bet that's one of the outposts."

Tagg still didn't look thrilled. "Are you sure about the smoke?" He frowned at Zelie.

"Positive. I almost didn't notice it at first."

"Alright, then." Cor crossed his arms. "Let's put it to a vote. All in favor of cutting west?"

Tagg made a face, but nobody's hand went up.

"All in favor of going north?"

Slowly, all five hands were raised.

"North it is," Cor said, with a sharp nod.

"Let's hope it's still standing when we get there," Tagg muttered, earning himself a swat on the shoulder from Zelie.

☙

It *was* an outpost. The Tegid crest fluttering at the gate told them as much. They'd reached it after about a day's travel, and the distant paling came into view just as the sun was beginning to set.

Night lay darkly over everything by the time they were within shouting distance of the gate.

Cor called a halt in a nearby thicket of trees. "We need a plan," he said. "What's the move? Do we all go in?"

"What's their policy on Beast-skins?" Fenris joked.

But Zelie shook her head thoughtfully. "It probably isn't a good idea for you to go in there. Or me," she added. "We can stay out here and keep an eye on things."

Fenris began to protest, but Cor said, "She's right. Felwen don't normally come through here to trade. You'd stick out like a sore thumb, and that's the last thing we want."

"Fine," Fenris sighed.

"What do you think, Chiara?" Cor looked at her expectantly. "Did your dad ever come up here?"

Chiara frowned. "He's been up here a few times, but I only came with him once. I do remember that these places are small. There are a few frequent traders, and everyone remembers new faces. It might be best if Tagg stays out here, too."

"Not happening," Tagg said immediately. "I'm not sticking out here with these two clowns."

"Hey!" Zelie protested.

Fenris gave a snort. "You're in the circus, pal. Doesn't that make you a clown, too?"

Tagg shot him a dirty look.

"Knock it off, guys," Chiara interrupted, and she turned to Tagg. "Why not?"

"The Arsonists didn't burn this place down, but they might travel through it. They might even have spies." Tagg crossed his arms. "If there's anybody in there we can't trust, I'll be able to pick up on it."

Cor lifted his eyebrows. "That could be useful," he admitted.

"Alright, fine." Chiara leaned in, talking quickly. "Here's the deal. Cor, Tagg and I will go inside and see if we can figure out how far it is to Crescor. If there isn't any news of danger or anything else suspicious, we can just take the trade route back to Crescor. If there *is* bad news …well, at least we'll know." They were all used to roughing it by now.

"And what do we do if there's bad news?" Fenris cracked his knuckles. "How long should we wait before busting in to save you?"

"Nobody's busting in anywhere," Chiara said with a glare. "If there's danger, we'll find a way to slip out and meet back here. If not, we'll stay the night and leave in the morning. It's too late to travel much farther, anyway."

"Sounds good to me. Let's go." Cor leapt to his feet, but Tagg grabbed his arm.

"Wait a minute, mate. We need a cover story. People will ask, and we can't exactly waltz in and say we're part of Fhír — especially if there *are* spies in there."

"Good point," Chiara sighed. "We can't be traders, though. We've got nothing to trade."

In the end, they decided on travelers who'd been separated from their caravan. The trio slid out of the bushes and headed for the path to the gate, with whispers of "Good luck" following behind.

"We'll keep watch for you," Fenris promised.

"I hope those two know what they're doing," Tagg sighed.

☙

The only tavern in town was a dingy, worn-out set of rooms with suspiciously dark upstairs windows. Fortunately, the main bar area was decently crowded, and they didn't have to work too hard to blend in.

Chiara even spotted one or two Nousk sitting at different tables. *What a relief.* Tagg's Gift was an advantage, but not if it earned them unnecessary attention.

"We need to find a spot and an excuse to be here," Cor looked strangely pale, and Chiara gave him a worried glance. *Maybe he thinks there will be trouble.*

He went up to the bar and began ordering food for them. Chiara followed more slowly, glancing around. She half-expected to see someone turn around and reveal a painted mask, but no one there looked very suspicious. In fact, most of the bar patrons seemed relatively friendly, chatting with each other and exchanging handshakes.

She stood next to Cor, and Tagg stood on her other side. The bartender was a grizzled old Tegid with beefy inked arms and a strong jaw. He chatted with Cor as he dried a set of mugs. "Travelers, eh? Lost your way?"

"That's right," Cor agreed, leaning against the bar top. He winced slightly. "We figured we were close enough to the trade route that we'd stumble across you eventually. Get back on the trade routes until … we got back home." He didn't say *Crescor*.

"Home, eh?" The bartender lifted an eyebrow as he thumped the mugs down on the counter behind the bar. "Careful, now. Trade route's rough these days. Only last week, we had news of some kind of bandits jumping a caravan west of here." He squinted at them heavily. "Don't suppose you've got much to be stolen. Still, I'd be cautious, if I was you."

He was distracted by another patron shouting at the other end of the bar. "'Scuse me. Your food'll be out in a minute," he called back to Cor as he stumped away.

They found an empty table in the corner. Cor turned down the oil lamp on the table and sank his face in his hands.

He looks terrible. Chiara tried to bite back her worry. "What's going on?" she asked softly.

"It's just …" He sighed. "What are we doing? We're out here in the middle of nowhere. We don't even have a map. We don't have our wagon, and that'll be some very pretty evidence if the Arsonists get their hands on it."

"So, just another week for Fhír."

Cor laughed tiredly. "At least this trading post seems relatively normal."

Chiara glanced around. "It's a little rougher than the last time I was here, but that was years ago," she admitted.

"You came here?" Cor lifted his head. "Why?"

"With my dad." Chiara smiled a little. "Dad and"—*and Isak*—"and me. We went to Crescor first, but he always said the trading posts were just as important as the city. So he took us to visit them."

"Us?"

Belatedly, Chiara realized her mistake. "Me," she clarified.

Cor's brows furrowed. "Was it always … just you and your dad and mum?"

Chiara looked away, following the worn grain of the wooden table. "It's been like that …" *A while. Not forever.*

"Chiara." Cor leaned in, frowning in earnest now. "What's going on? I feel like—" He paused, and then went on, and every word felt like a stone against her chest. "I think there's still some stuff we haven't talked about."

Chiara twitched, staring out the window. "Sure," she said vaguely. "We've only known each other a few months."

"We're supposed to trust each other." He shifted in the seat across from her. "You said you did. Why don't you trust me with this?"

Chiara pressed her lips together. "It's not about you, Cor," she said at last. "It's just … personal."

"Personal."

She still wasn't looking at him, but she could hear his tone. Subdued. Nearly resentful. "So, we save each other's lives, but you won't tell me whatever you're hiding about your past? That kind of personal?"

He's figuring it out … he's figuring it out … Chiara chewed her lip fiercely. "I just can't talk about it, okay? It doesn't affect Fhír and it doesn't affect our performance, so …"

Liar. It affected both.

She'd never outright lied to Cor before. She fought off the guilt and shot a cautious glance in his direction.

He was drumming his fingers on the tabletop with a vengeance. "Glad we cleared that up," he said tightly, stone-faced. "Thanks for letting me know."

That wasn't good. Zelie would be disappointed. Dad would be disappointed.

I'm disappointed in myself.

The tiny voice was screaming. *Telling him means losing Isak!*

"You two fighting again?" Tagg came to sit down next to Cor.

Cor didn't answer the question. "Is the bartender clean?"

"Bartender's clean." Tagg tapped his fingers on the table. "I can't listen to much more than one person at a time. But most of the noise in here is relatively quiet."

Cor lifted his head. "If you're sure," he began, but his sentence quickly turned into a cough — a raw, hacking sound that grew uglier by the second. Shoulders shaking, he crouched over the table, covering his mouth with his hands.

Just like Grede. Only this sounded far worse. Chiara's skin turned clammy. "Cor, what's wrong?"

She tried to lift his shoulder to get a look at his face. He shook his head as though it was fine, but the cough was getting louder. People were starting to notice. Stray glances were drifting their way.

Panic began to rise in her chest. *Why is he coughing? Why is he coughing? He's Tegid ... He can't really be sick, can he?*

Cor's body was shaking now. "Get him outside," Tagg whispered in Chiara's ear. He slung one of Cor's arms over his shoulder and stood up with a grunt.

Chiara slid out of her seat and clung to Cor's other side. He felt almost weightless — Tagg must have been lifting him telekinetically.

Tagg slid a hand into his pocket and struggled for a moment, pulling out a handful of coins. He tossed them on the table. "Let's go!" He began walking toward the door, Cor still hacking out a lung next to him.

People were definitely looking now. Chiara's palms went clammy. They hadn't gone three paces before they ran into the bartender carrying a tray of food.

"Oi, what's this?" His face creased with concern. "Need a hand?"

"No need!" Tagg exclaimed. "Just some fresh air." Without waiting for a reply, he picked up the pace, dragging Chiara along now, too.

They couldn't get outside soon enough. Faint conversation drifted from the nearby lodging houses, but the street itself was mercifully empty. Cor's cough echoed strangely between the silent buildings.

Tagg didn't stop until they were a few streets away from the tavern. He dragged them both into a narrow alley and sat Cor down on an empty crate.

Cor was doubled over, still hacking. He spit on the ground, and it glistened darkly on the pavement. A small moan escaped him.

Chiara crouched in front of him and saw the whites of his eyes flashing. Ice gripped her chest. "Cor, what is it? What's wrong?"

"Blood?" He sounded groggy. "My head …"

"Tagg. Tagg, what do we do?" Chiara stared anxiously at Tagg. She couldn't keep the panic out of her voice.

"We need to get out of here." Tagg began to lift Cor to his feet, but Cor fought it.

"Not the gate — not safe." He began coughing again, and it sounded far too loud for any passersby not to notice them.

Tagg gave a frustrated snort and glanced around the alleyway. "Okay, fine. Listen carefully." He pointed to the building above him.

"I'm gonna climb the gutter pipe to that roof. Then I'm gonna lift you both over the paling. Got it?"

Chiara turned and spotted the dimly lit wall of trunks on the far end of the alley. "Okay."

Her heart hammered in her chest as she watched Tagg scale the wall as easily as any Kithsa. Moments later, he was perched on the roof, one more shadow among the rest.

"Arms around each other," he called softly. "It's just like rehearsal."

Just like rehearsal … Chiara was trembling. This was so, so much worse. She locked her arms around Cor's neck.

He was still coughing; his shoulders were shaking beneath her arms. He made an effort to lift his head away from her face. "Sorry," he gasped.

She could smell the blood on his breath, and her skin went cold.

"Don't be. Can you still carry me?"

His arms encircled her waist in an iron grip. "Even in my sleep."

A tingle ran down her spine.

"Ready?" Tagg lifted his hands.

"Hang tight," Cor grunted as a familiar tug pulled at Chiara's body. She hooked her legs around his and clung on for dear life.

They began to rise above the gutters of the houses on either side. Chiara's head was pressed against Cor's shoulder. She could hear his heartbeat pounding.

It's so loud … Is mine that loud?

In moments, they were floating through the air. Higher and higher, closer and closer to the rough spikes of the log wall — and suddenly darkness opened up beneath them.

Then gravity kicked in, and they descended far more quickly than they'd been lifted. Chiara almost lost her grip.

As soon as Cor's feet touched the ground, he began to crumple. Chiara released him and stumbled backward as he staggered down onto his knees. He was hacking again, a horrible grating sound, and he spit into the grass.

"Cor." She leaned over and put a hand on his shoulder.

He was shaking beneath her touch. He wiped his mouth with a hand and looked up at her. "It's blood … it's my blood." He sounded completely dazed. "What …?"

There was a crunch somewhere behind them, and a moment later, Tagg was at her side. "Can you walk?" he asked insistently, stooping to look at Cor.

"… I … think so," Cor croaked.

"Then let's go." Tagg hoisted him to his feet and threw an arm around him for support. "Chiara, other side."

He didn't have to tell her — she was already there. They began walking through the grass. Every few minutes, Cor would start coughing and bend over, and they'd have to stop.

Chiara prayed desperately that no one would overhear. *Please, Arva, let us get to the others without being stopped …*

They circled around the outer paling, eyes peeled for the gate. Finally, after several minutes— "There!" Tagg hissed. He struck out diagonally, aiming for the thicket of trees nearby.

They were still yards away when Fenris came bursting out of the trees and charged up to them.

"Why are you here? What's wrong?" Tagg demanded.

"What happened?" Fenris pointed a claw at Cor.

"Something's wrong with him," Chiara said breathlessly. "The cough—"

Together with Tagg, she lowered Cor onto the grass. He hunched over, still shaking.

"Great. We've got worse problems!" Fenris was hard to see in the dark, but Chiara could still hear panic in his voice. "Can Golden Boy walk?"

"Does he look like he can walk?" Tagg retorted. "What are the worse problems?"

"There's no time!" Fenris exclaimed, but he was interrupted by a crash in the trees. Ria sprang out, a tiny figure on her back — Zelie. She wheeled to a halt next to them.

"We have to go!" Then Zelie must have caught sight of Cor on the grass, because she gave a soft cry. "What's wrong with him?"

"No idea! Get off the horse!" Fenris crouched down and yanked Cor to his feet. "Can you ride?"

"Yes," Cor managed, still hacking.

Zelie slid down, her wide eyes reflecting in the dark.

"Then get up! We—"

There was a high-pitched screech, and orange light blazed up in the trees behind them.

25

"Bloody hell!" Tagg cursed and thrust out a hand, and in an instant, Cor was on Ria's back. "Chiara, hold on!" Suddenly, she was sitting behind Cor.

"Grab the reins!" Tagg yelled at her. Already the roar and screech of the fire was getting louder.

"What about Ria?" she screamed back. "She can't carry—"

"We don't have time!" He must have struck Ria's flank, because she bolted forward, almost sending Chiara tumbling off.

Heart in her mouth, she gripped the reins in tight hands, reaching awkwardly around Cor's body. He slumped in the saddle in front of her, still coughing.

Ria tore north, passing the outpost gates. The guards were yelling and pointing. Chiara risked a glance over her shoulder.

A wall of fire was sweeping across the field toward the outpost. Just in front of it, she could pick out two dark figures with glowing hands. Distant yells and screams were drifting up from the outpost.

Tagg, Fenris, and Zelie were nowhere in sight.

"No," she sobbed out. "Come on, Ria!"

Beneath her legs, Ria's sides were heaving. She was a powerful horse, and she was driven by terror — but she wouldn't be able to carry both of them at that pace for much longer.

Chiara stared ahead, eyes burning, trying to ignore the screeching in her ears. Up ahead, a dark line was beginning to appear across the horizon — a forest. It was still a few miles ahead.

We're never going to make it. Ria couldn't carry them that far. Chiara pulled back on the reins, but Ria only went faster. She plunged forward, ears pinned back against her skull, huffing loudly.

Then there was a blinding flash. Ria screamed and stumbled, throwing Cor and Chiara off over her shoulders. Chiara hit the ground hard, all the wind forced completely out of her lungs. Gasping for breath like a fish out of water, she managed to roll over.

"Cor," she croaked. "Cor …"

Somebody was walking through the grass toward them — somebody glowing.

No. NO!

But it wasn't the same vicious red glow. It was different … bluer. The figure strode past them and charged toward the inferno behind, blue light growing brighter by the second.

I'm losing my mind … Chiara rolled onto her back and stared up at the sky, stars and darkness swirling in her vision.

What kind of fire is blue …?

☙

She opened her eyes to an unfamiliar ceiling — wooden rafters, with dried plants hanging from them. Every inch of her skin felt like one massive bruise. With a groan, she sat slowly upright.

She was in a small, creaking bed with a patchwork quilt. There was a latticed window to the right.

The room was filled with odds and ends. A spinning wheel, old stuffed chairs, old mirrors, hanging lanterns. In one corner was a table laid out with a dozen china bowls; in another was a fireplace with a spit and a copper kettle; in another was a small shrine to Arva, decorated with bright flowers and incense sticks.

And a few feet to her left—

A bed. Another identical bed, with a tattooed arm stretched over the cover.

"Oh, no, no, no … please, no …" Chiara stumbled out of bed, barely able to stand on two legs. She knelt by the bedside and struggled to roll Cor's body to face her.

Cor awake was cumbersome enough. Unconscious, he was a dead weight she could barely move.

A gasp of exertion escaped her. "Come on, Cor, work with me here — come on — I need you to work with me—"

I never told him — I never told him about Isak — He can't be gone yet—

After a minute or two of straining, she managed to roll him out on his back. One look at his face, and her heart dropped into her toes.

Arva, no. Please, no.

He'd gone sheet white. His lips were a terrible purplish-blue, stained red by the blood now dripping from them.

Heart roaring in her ears, Chiara pressed her head to his chest and heard a harsh rattle echoing there. *Heartbeat — where's his heartbeat?* Her breath was coming faster in her throat.

Barely there … barely there. *No. No, no, no, no …*

Hands shaking, she snatched up his wrist, counting for the pulse. It was erratic, and slowing. Dread weighed down her limbs.

"No. Cor, do you hear me?" She grabbed his face in her hands and patted his cheeks firmly. "You're not allowed to do this! Are you listening to me? Can you hear me? You can't be doing this! Not now!"

His skin was clammy beneath her touch. "Come on — wake up — wake up—!"

His eyes didn't open.

She pressed her fingers to his wrist again. *Please … please … please …*

One heartbeat … another …

… Then another …

The room spun around Chiara's ears, blood rushing to her head like she was hanging upside down. She stared at his face, transfixed. *This isn't real. This isn't happening.*

He was alive … just seconds ago, he was alive and breathing. He was even joking with her. He was real, and whole, and solid, and alive; a living, breathing, tangible thing; a body full of motion and strength; as real as gravity, holding her feet to the earth.

Pain stabbed through her middle, sharp, cruel. She doubled over, sobbing with rage, gripping Cor's shoulder, shaking him a little. "Don't do this to me … don't do this … I can't lose someone else …"

Not again. Not like this. Not when she couldn't do a thing to save him. She pressed her forehead to his chest, hot tears flowing down her face.

He couldn't just die. He couldn't be sick. He couldn't stay hurt. He was *Cor.*

He was *right there.*

He couldn't be gone. It couldn't be over.

I don't want it to be over.

For the first time since Isak, there was a point to her life.

I don't want to lose that. I don't want to lose you. I don't want to lose … please, I don't want to lose you … please, pleas e…

"Oh, he looks terrible." A resonant, musical voice startled Chiara; she jerked her head up as someone appeared next to the bed. "Give him some space, my dear, and I'll get to work."

26

"W-what?" Dazed, Chiara wiped stiffly at her eyes as she peered at the person across from her.

It was a female — but she didn't look like any creature Chiara had ever seen before. Her hair was brilliant white, piled on top of her head in braided ropes and buns. Her skin was a shifting pattern of indigos, navies, and soft royal blues.

A Nousk …? But she had no horns, or ears, or double thumbs.

She looked older than Chiara … but not old. *Ageless* would've been a better word.

She stooped gracefully on the other side of Cor's bed, examining his face. Then she pressed her hands to his chest.

Chiara's heartbeat quickened, thumping against her ribs.

"Excuse me, my dear," she said, as she came to stand on Chiara's side. She moved like she was floating in water — liquid, ethereal. Her gypsy dress and bangled corset bore a vague resemblance to Talia's clothing.

But ... she's not a Nousk ...

Chiara clambered numbly to her feet. "I'm sorry ... who—?"

The lady turned with a smile, greeting Chiara with a pair of mesmerizing chameleon eyes that morphed from green, to blue, to purple, to pink, and back again. The freckles across her cheeks looked almost silvery in the light.

"My name is Ora. This is my home." She gestured around the tiny attic. "I heard your cry for help, and I came. Your other friends are downstairs. This one"—she gestured to Cor—"he is ill. He can still be saved, but we do not have much time. You must save your questions until he is well."

"What could you possibly do for him?" Chiara's voice was raw in her throat. "He's ..."

Gone.

She couldn't say it. Saying it would make it real.

Ora shook her head, placing a finger to Chiara's mouth. "No questions. Just ... breathe." She took a deep breath.

In ... and out. Air stirred around the room.

A weight lifted off Chiara's shoulders.

Ora looked her in the eyes. "I swear by Arva's Name that you can trust me. Your friend, what is his name?"

"Cor."

Ora nodded. "Cor. He is not dead. But he is dying. Now, listen to me very carefully."

She had Chiara stand at the table in the corner. The bowls on top were filled with different dried herbs, powders, and flowers. Chiara was instructed to stuff a cheesecloth bag with a pinch from every bowl.

Ora took a handful of powder from one of the bowls and tossed it into the fireplace. The flames flared purplish-pink, and the room was filled with a cool, clean scent.

Then she moved to Cor, chafing his wrists, whispering softly, almost like she was praying.

Please ... please, if she knows what she's doing ... please ...

Chiara's fingers moved clumsily. She couldn't seem to stuff the bag fast enough. As soon as she finished the last pinch, she tied the bag tightly and spun around. "Here!"

"Very good." Ora took it from her and placed it inside the kettle on the fire. "Now ... we wait." She returned to Cor's bedside.

"What are you going to do?" Chiara whispered, hovering over Ora's shoulder anxiously. "What's wrong with him?"

Ora turned luminous eyes on her. "You must sit." She gestured to one of the chairs.

Chiara dragged it to the foot of the bed and sat.

"He is sick." Ora gazed down at Cor's face. "He has been sick for many weeks."

I knew something was wrong ... "How is that even possible?" Chiara almost sobbed. "He's a Tegid! He's not supposed to be sick!"

Ora shook her head. "I have seen this before. His body is strong. He has fought it off long, but no longer." She sighed. "Normally, I would not do this, but I must make an exception for him."

"You've seen this before?" Chiara repeated, almost rising from her chair. "You mean ... sick Tegids? You've *healed* Stunted Tegids before?"

The floor was spinning under her feet. *If Cor is really Stunted, and Ora can heal him, then—*

"He — he has scars, too." The words were tumbling out of her faster than she could manage. "Could you fix those? Could you make him better again?"

Ora shook her head. "I'm afraid not."

The desperate hope faded out like dandelions in the wind. Chiara's heart came crashing down into her feet. "Why not?" she whispered.

"He does not need to be fixed."

Chiara's eyes stung. "What … what do you mean?" she whispered. "Are you saying it's fine that he's broken?" The palms of her hands grew hot.

Ora inhaled softly. "Of course not." She leaned toward Chiara. "Things are not always as we think they are. You believe a Tegid may never be broken, yes?"

The breath hissed from between Chiara's teeth. "Tegids aren't supposed to break."

"And you?" Ora fixed her with a piercing gaze. "Do you think *you* are broken?"

"Yes!" Chiara burst out angrily, clutching at the bedpost.

Yes. Yes, even after all this time.

Ora tilted her head. "Why?" she asked calmly.

"Because I couldn't save him!" Chiara yelled. "I couldn't save them! I — I wasn't fast enough …"

Her throat closed up. Her whole body was shaking now — rage, and bitterness, and despair. "And I never told him …"

Not fast enough. Not strong enough. Not enough. The scar was still on her face, and Cor was dying, and Isak was dead.

And there wasn't a thing she could do to stop it.

"I couldn't save him," she whispered. "And I'm still here …" Her fingers brushed the scar along her jaw. "And I never told him …"

"Never told him what?" Ora asked softly.

There was a desperate twist in Chiara's mouth. "I never … I never said I was sorry. I didn't tell him …"

"Tell me." No musical voice now, but a deep, echoing boom, washing through the room like waves against cliffsides. "*Tell me the truth.*"

The command rushed over Chiara, relentless, bringing with it memories that sliced like blades across her skin.

Isak, getting the letter, charging home. Screaming at the top of his lungs, telling Mum and Dad he'd made it to Nationals.

The long train ride to Crescor, sitting next to Isak as they pressed their faces to the window, watching hills and forests and rivers flash by.

Crowded streets and flapping banners, hundreds of competitors streaming toward the wide gates of Crescor's East Gymnasium.

Packed together, Mum on one side, Dad on the other, staring up at the stage. Isak soaring through the air, weightless, a bird in flight, frozen in time.

Screams of triumph as he stood, lifting the golden wreath above his head, eyes fixed on them.

And then the fire.

Fire, behind the curtains. Fire, climbing up the wall like a demon, consuming the stage. Fire, roaring toward them, the mad rush, the crush of bodies, the screams.

Isak's name, ripping from her throat.

Fighting, fighting for every inch, just to get closer to the stage. Fire, deafening her ears. Isak's face — he was tearing out of the backstage doors, just a few feet away. Fire, leaping after him.

Fire from glowing hands. Isak screaming; the muscles in Chiara's body freezing; the painted face; the brand on her skin.

And then … gone.

Chiara was sobbing, sobbing, striking the bedpost, all the heat in her melting away, taken by her tears.

Ora waited quietly.

Finally Chiara lifted her head, eyes and nose streaming. She wiped roughly at her face. "Isak," she choked out. "My brother ... my catcher. There was a fire ... I couldn't get to him ..."

Breathe — breathe—

"It was ... three years ago. And I thought ... I thought I was done grieving ... and then I joined Fhír—"

She was rambling now, words flooding, tears flooding. "—And Cor's my catcher now — but I'll forget Isak — I don't want to lose ..."

And now I'm losing them both.

Slowly, Ora extended a hand and placed her palm flat on Chiara's forehead.

Somewhere inside Chiara's body, the knot came undone. She went limp, a soft gasp escaping her.

What ...? Her chest was heaving. It was like she had never breathed until that moment.

Ora stooped in front of her, looking her in the eyes. "You think you are broken because you could not save them?"

"Yes," Chiara whispered. *I confess .... I confess ... I confess ... I couldn't save him ... I saw him fall ... I couldn't get to him ...*

"No." Ora shook her head. Her voice was calm and utterly unyielding. "That does not make you broken."

"How can you say that?" Chiara managed through tears.

Ora's gaze was inescapable. "Who told you that you had to save him?"

Her question lashed through the air like a whip, taking the breath right out of Chiara's lungs.

"What?" she gasped. "What do you mean, *who*? No one! He's my *brother*! I had to—"

"And Cor?"

"He's my … my friend." Chiara stared at the motionless heap on the bed, goosebumps rippling up her arms. "Why …?"

Ora was nodding. "You see? *That* is how I know you are not broken. Even after all this …" She glanced at Cor. "… you are still fighting for something. Your *heart* was broken. But *you* are not. *You* are still here. You fight with a broken heart. It means there is still a reason. You have a reason to be here."

"A … a reason?" Chiara swallowed, wiping her face clean.

Ora didn't say anything else. Instead, she went to one of the bowls on the table. She plucked a pinch of dried purple petals from one of the bowls and rolled it between her palms, crushing the petals. A fresh, sweet scent filled the air.

Then she stooped over Cor and rubbed the crushed petals across his forehead, leaving purplish stains on his skin. Her soft whispers drifted through the room…

… And then a different light began to glow, honey-gold, stronger by the second.

A light that came from Cor's own body.

Shudders ran down Chiara's spine. She watched transfixed as every vein beneath his skin lit up, rushing from his head down to the tip of every limb.

And then, a heartbeat later, it faded completely away.

Cor lay there just as before.

Ora folded her arms, watching him. "Come, now, Master Cor," she murmured.

Chiara gripped the coverlet with white knuckles. "What did you—?"

Suddenly, Cor's chest was heaving; he was choking, gasping for air.

Chiara leapt to her feet with a small scream. She was at his side in an instant, touching his face, throwing her arms around his shoulders, laughing and crying.

Cor began struggling to sit up. His skin was hot to the touch. "Chiara—" he choked out. "Can't — breathe—"

"Sorry!" She pulled away and stared at his face, beaming. "You're *alive*! Praise Arva! How do you feel?"

Cor was panting. He tried to return her smile, but he looked completely dazed. "I'm … fine …?" He glanced around the room, confused. "Where …?"

Then his eyes landed on Ora, and his mouth opened. "Oh, stars."

Ora's mouth twitched in a smile. "Not quite, Master Cor. You may call me Ora." She rose to her feet and gave a deep curtsey.

"What happened?" He rubbed a hand along his forehead, which was still smeared with purple.

He must have felt the petals. "Oh …" He pulled his fingers away, frowning at the stains that now decorated his palms. "What is this stuff?"

"Mountain lavender," Ora answered, and then the kettle began to whistle. "Ah — there we are." She smiled at Chiara. "I said we must wait, yes? And now it is ready."

"Wait …" Chiara looked at her, confused. "You never used the herbs. Why …?" She glanced from Ora to Cor.

Ora laughed; it filled the room, making Chiara jump. "Herbs for what? Healing Cor? No. It is tea." She went to the fire and took off the kettle.

"I helped you … make tea," Chiara repeated slowly. *What in Arva—?*

"Yes." Ora poured out three steaming cups. "Tea is good for the body. That is why I had you make it." She took one of the cups and sipped it calmly.

"Then how …?" Chiara stared at Ora. *What did she do to him?*

"Golden Boy?" The door was flung open, and Fenris appeared, stooping to enter beneath the doorframe. He folded his arms at the foot of Cor's bed, looking impressed. "Damn! I guess I lost the bet, huh, Snapdragon?"

Cor glanced at Chiara with a puzzled frown. "What? What bet?"

"Ignore him," Chiara said, rolling her eyes. She couldn't stop smiling. "You're fine now. That's all that matters."

"You're … sure?" Cor asked slowly. He rubbed a hand across his chest, as though he was searching for any remnant of sickness.

Ora nodded. "You are no longer in danger of death, but your body will need a few days to recover."

"Cor!" Zelie charged into the room with a squeal. She rocketed onto the bed and leapt bodily on top of him, knocking him back onto the pillows. "Praise Arva! You're alive!"

"Barely," he wheezed. Chiara and Fenris were both laughing.

"Well, well, well." Tagg pushed past Fenris and came to stand next to Chiara. He crossed his arms. "Look who had the bally decency to wake up."

"Nice to see you, too," Cor said. He sat up with a soft groan, and Zelie tumbled off the bed.

"You must let him rest." Ora was moving around the room, handing cups of tea to everyone. "Go. Downstairs. He must sleep. You too," she added to Chiara, as the others filed out reluctantly.

Chiara glanced back at Cor.

You're alive … Words were on the tip of her tongue, but she didn't quite know what to say.

"You sure you're alright?" she whispered at last.

Cor nodded. "I feel … a lot better than I've been." He gave her a warm smile. "I'll be fine. I promise."

"Don't," she whispered, searching his eyes. *Don't make me promises. Just … stay better.*

Ora clicked her tongue gently from the doorway. "He must rest." She turned and disappeared silently into the hall.

"Right. Sorry. Coming." Chiara stood, brushing her fingers across the top of Cor's hand. He looked up at her, but she turned away before he could meet her eyes.

She made her way down a creaking wooden staircase and found herself in a tiny kitchen with a tile floor, a small icebox, and overgrown flowerpots in latticed windows.

Ora stood at the sink, watering pots of flowers. Everyone else was crammed around the small circular table in the center of the kitchen.

As soon as Chiara stepped into the kitchen, Zelie immediately came over and gave her hand a squeeze. "I'm so glad you're awake."

"What happened?" Chiara rubbed a hand across her face. "I mean … before we got here?"

"You're gonna have a bally hard time believing this—" Tagg began, but Fenris interrupted him.

"It was the *craziest f*—"

Tagg cleared his throat loudly and glared at Fenris. "Oi! Watch your mouth, mate," he said, with a sharp jerk of his head toward Ora.

"You were saying?" Chiara sighed.

"You and Cor were way ahead of us," Tagg began. "And I'd lost sight of you, but I could still hear your thoughts. We were running, and we were barely past the outpost, and they lit it up—"

"They were so close. I could *hear* their breathing." Zelie shuddered.

Fenris curled his lip, exposing savage teeth.

"Then what happened?" Chiara said.

"Well …" Tagg looked over at Ora. She glanced over her shoulder but remained quiet.

"There was this … this light," he continued. "Out on the plains in front of us. I thought …" He pressed his lips together, looking pale. "At first, I thought they'd circled out in front of us somehow. But the light was all wrong."

Ora still hadn't turned around. She was assembling potted plants on the counter, pouring cups of water into each.

"Wrong how?" Chiara asked, eyes drawn to Ora's shifting braids, the clouds of dark color across her skin.

"It was this bluish-white glow." Tagg was staring at Ora, too. "It just … blazed out in the dark. And then I heard Ria. She sounded terrified."

"We thought they got you for sure." Zelie's ears drooped at Chiara.

"Yeah, and then Pipsqueak here took off like a shot in the dark," Fenris added. "It was all I could do to keep up with her."

"I was mad," Zelie confessed.

"Mad? Try *livid*," Fenris shot back. "I've never seen any Kithsa sprint that fast."

Zelie turned a shade redder, but she lifted her head proudly, and Chiara shot her a grateful look.

"By the time we all got there," Tagg went on, "you and Cor were both on the ground. But Ria was standing there — just standing next to Ora, as calm as you please."

Ora turned around, still holding a flowerpot. "She was very afraid. I did what I could."

"What about the Lacar?" Chiara asked.

"That's the weirdest part," Zelie said with a frown. "We turned around — I was sure they'd catch up to us by then. But they were gone. The fires were still there, but the Lacar were gone."

"Ora told us to take you both and keep going straight north," Fenris chimed in. "Until we got to a cottage in the woods. And then she left us here and went south — the same direction they'd come from."

Chiara turned wondering eyes on Ora. "You … gave chase?"

Ora's face was enigmatic. "I simply ensured that they had not followed." She turned to the counter again and switched out flowerpots.

"And then we ended up here," said Zelie, "and Ora got back a few hours after we did. That was just last night."

"You saved us." Chiara stared at Ora. "And then you saved Cor."

Ora nodded. "As I said. I heard your call. I came to help."

"Thank you," Chiara breathed. Ora gave her a nod and a smile before turning back to the plants on the counter.

"So … Golden Boy," Fenris began, glancing around the table with raised eyebrows. "Sickness? Poison? Can poison even kill a Tegid?"

Tagg shook his head adamantly. "It wasn't poison."

"How do you know that?" Zelie flicked her ears curiously. "Poison can kill Tegids — at least, sometimes. Right, Chiara?"

Chiara pressed her lips together. "Technically, yes … but the dose would have to be potent enough to kill us instantly. That didn't happen with Cor."

Ora lifted another large flowerpot out of the sink and set it dripping on one of the windowsills. "It was not poison." She turned to face the table, all eyes on her.

"Are you sure?" Zelie asked.

Ora nodded. "Yes. It was sickness, not poison. I have seen it before. It is airborne."

"You said he was sick for weeks," Chiara recalled. "If it's airborne, how did *I* not get sick? There's no way he'd catch something and not spread it to me."

Ora shook her head. "This is an unusual case," she said slowly. "That is all I can say. Do any of you feel sick now?"

She scanned the room as each of them shook their heads. "Good. Then you will not get sick."

"Do you have any idea what caused it?" Tagg's forehead was creased.

"You said it's airborne?" Zelie asked.

Airborne … sick for weeks … Something clicked in Chiara's brain. "Wait …" She spun to face Cor. "Grede. That Tegid lady—?"

"The perfume." Tagg's eyes went wide. Ora turned chameleon eyes on him.

"What perfume?" Fenris demanded.

"We were at a tavern," Chiara explained quickly. "There was some Tegid lady with this really heavy perfume …" *It still doesn't make sense.* "How did it not get *her* sick?"

All eyes turned to Ora. She lifted her hands in the air. "As I told Chiara. Cor is a special case."

Special case.

So Cor *was* Stunted …?

"I don't understand …" Chiara whispered, burying her face in her hands. "Why did he get sick and I didn't?"

"There are many reasons," Ora said calmly. "It is as the Maker has designed. It was to be that Cor should fall ill and you should not. Had he not, you would not be here right now, and many things would be different."

"What?" There was a skeptical twist in Fenris's mouth.

Tagg shot him a warning glance. "What if Cor gets sick again?" he asked, diverting the conversation. "How do we stop it?"

"What about the perfume?" Zelie chimed in.

Ora breathed in deeply. "He will not get sick again."

"How do you *know?*" Fenris asked. He still looked somewhat skeptical.

"It only infects once. Now his body has learned." Ora laced her fingers together. "He will not get sick again."

"Well … that's good to know, I guess," Zelie sighed.

That wasn't consoling at all to Chiara. Cor was healed, but it didn't make any sense. What was in the perfume? How did it immediately affect him and not her? *How do I have more questions than answers?*

Ora lifted her chin. "Now I must share my own news for you. There is much to tell. I came to find you because Tivore's clan was attacked."

"What?" Fenris shot to his feet, trembling. Ora gave him a steady look and he sank back into his chair, eyes fixed on her.

"Attacked by the people of fire," she said softly.

"The Lacar." Tagg's face went dark.

Ora nodded. "Yes. The Lacar found Tivore's clan and attacked it. Then they moved on. They were tracking five — five young travelers and a horse. They are trying to kill you. I followed them. That was when I found you."

"So we've been found out." Tagg slumped wearily in his chair.

Ora tilted her head to the side. "Yes … but I do not think they know as much as you think. I drove them off."

"And Tagg thought you were one of them …" Zelie glanced at Tagg, who frowned back at her.

Ora shook her head. "No. Not one of them. I know them … but I am not one of them. I have only bought you some time. You must stay here for now. Your friend, Cor"—she pointed to the ceiling—"he must rest. Stay three days. Allow your horse to recover. You all must sleep."

"With all due respect, ma'am," Tagg said, rising from his chair, "I don't think we can afford to wait much longer."

Ora gazed back at him, unflinching. "You must. I have sent the people of fire on a detour. You must give them time to take that detour. You must rest." She spread her hands. "It is settled."

"But where will we go now?" Zelie watched her, bewildered.

Ora looked thoughtful. "My advice? Go west. You are headed west already, no?"

"To Crescor," Chiara supplied. "We're meeting … friends there."

Ora nodded slowly. "Yes. Crescor. I have sent the Lacar south and east. Back to the forests and rivers. So you must go west. Follow the trading posts. Cut southwest when you reach the third trading post from here — seven days' journey. Once you cut southwest, you will reach Crescor in a week."

"Well …" Tagg said tiredly. "That … sounds like a good enough plan to me."

Everyone else was too exhausted to argue.

❧

That night, while the others went to bed, Chiara lingered in the kitchen, watching Ora put away the last dishes.

"You are worried?" Ora spoke without turning.

"I lied to him." The ugly words slipped out, too loud, too jarring in that lovely kitchen.

"Then you must tell him. Apologize." Ora faced her. "Tell him the truth. That heals many wounds. Will you do that?"

Were her eyes really glowing? Or was that Chiara's imagination?

She nodded hesitantly. "What … what if he almost dies again? Or what if something worse happens? What if the Arsonists find us?"

"Mm." Ora began trimming leaves from the potted plant on the table. "That is a good question. You ask my advice?"

"Yes."

Ora eyed her critically over the vase. "You think you are Stunted. There is more to you than meets the eye." There was a knowing look on her face. "You will know, in time. Very soon, I think. Then you will want to know more. I may have some answers. Travel north and east."

"Okay …" Chiara scowled. "That's awfully cryptic."

Ora looked at her sympathetically. "It is all I can do. Knowledge given before its time is the cause of much grief."

Well, that clears things up nicely. Chiara sighed. "What happens when we need answers? Should we come back here to find you?"

Ora shook her head. "No. North and east. Keep traveling north and east. I will find you. Now go. Sleep."

Chiara blinked tiredly. *Maybe it'll make sense when I'm not exhausted …*

As she stumbled up the stairs, Ora's voice followed her. "Remember, you must tell him the truth — the *whole* truth."

27

After three days at Ora's home, Cor was well enough to travel. He wasn't great — he was still hot to the touch, and he still looked like he'd been dug out of a grave. But they couldn't afford to wait any longer.

On the fourth morning, they said goodbye to Ora. She repeated her instructions, including the ones for Chiara. "Tell him the whole truth. Travel north and east," she whispered in Chiara's ear as she bid her farewell.

Then west. West, walking parallel to the trade road, praying they wouldn't run into anyone else. And, thank Arva, they didn't.

Cor was in good spirits, but he was clearly exhausted. He spent most of the time slumped over on Ria.

They halted at sundown both times. Both times, Cor collapsed into his hammock, asleep before his head hit the canvas. The other four took night watch in turns.

The minutes scraped by for Chiara. She alternated between straining her eyes for movement on the road and straining her ears for Cor's breathing.

It only infects once. Ora had said that, and Chiara believed it. But she didn't understand it. And she didn't like that she didn't understand it.

She still hadn't told the others what she'd seen, the way Cor's body had glowed. Whatever Ora had done to heal him, it wasn't like anything she'd heard of before — the glowing, the lavender, none of it.

But I know for a fact that I won't be able to replicate it. And that was what worried her the most.

You will want to know more. What if that was what Ora meant? What if she knew the kinds of sicknesses that a Stunted Tegid could contract?

That would have been useful information. If only Chiara had known there was a healer specializing in Stunted illnesses. *My life might have been a lot simpler …*

But none of this was simple. Not Isak, not Fhír, not the Arsonists … none of it.

It was late afternoon on the second day when the trading post came into sight. "We need to get there before dark," Cor insisted, and he wouldn't listen to anyone's protests. "I'll jog there if I have to. I don't care. But we can't spend any more time out here."

He was right, and they knew it. So before the last sliver of sunset disappeared behind the hills, they were standing at the gate.

"So, what's the drill?" Fenris asked. "Are Zelie and I outside again?"

Cor gave him a sympathetic look. "Looks like it. I'm sorry."

"Eh." Zelie shrugged. "I'd take that over Arsonists finding us. Sleeping in the grass is better than roasting alive."

Fenris winced. "Well, when you put it like that …"

This outpost was much smaller than the last one. It was simply one long street, lined with a handful of taverns, a few warehouses, and several trading booths toward the center. There weren't even stables — the horses were kept under long, low sheds, with communal troughs and water barrels.

They picked the largest tavern. Cor and Chiara went inside while Tagg haggled with the self-proclaimed stablemaster outside.

It was fairly busy still, despite the late hour, with Tegids of all ages chatting, swapping stories, negotiating bargains and deals. Chiara spotted an empty booth by a side window. She went to save their seats while Cor went up to the bar to order food for the three of them.

Chiara settled into the back of the booth and peered out the narrow window. She spotted Tagg under the light of the horse shed, still arguing with the stablemaster, Ria's reins in hand. He was getting a few strange looks from passersby.

An uneasy chill slid over Chiara's neck. She hadn't seen any other Nousk here. It was a smaller outpost. Maybe they didn't get Nousk very often.

… Or maybe news of the incident at the last outpost had traveled faster than they did. *I really, really hope not …*

Cor walked up with a large tray in one hand and three mugs in the other. "Ta da!" He set them down on the table with a flourish. "You think Tagg will mind if I sip his drink?"

"Don't," Chiara chided. "He won't take long." She scooted over to make room.

He sat beside her with a glance out the window. "He's a great haggler," he grinned.

Chiara sighed and buried her face in her hands. "Maybe too good."

"What do you mean?"

She glanced around before leaning in a little closer. "I think we're drawing too much attention to ourselves. Have you seen any other Nousk here?"

"Sure." Cor tipped his head toward the other end of the tavern. "There's a pair of Ensyth at one of the tables over there."

Chiara followed his gesture. There they were.

She still didn't like it.

Cor leaned over and sniffed the food. "If he takes any longer, I'll—"

"Don't even think about it." Tagg's voice made them both jump. He was standing at the table, arms crossed. "I could hear you from out there." His ears flicked lightly.

Cor made a face as he picked up one of the mugs. "You're no fun. How'd the bargain go?"

"I got us a deal," Tagg continued, snatching the drink out of Cor's hand, "so we've got a little extra for food."

"First of all, I'm deeply wounded," Cor complained, picking up another mug. "Secondly, that's great, but can you work your magic there?" He gestured to the bar, where a patron was arguing loudly with one of the bartenders. "The prices are pretty steep."

"See if you've heard anything," Chiara added, lifting her eyebrows pointedly.

Tagg turned with a wink. "I'll see what I can do. Don't touch my food," he added over his shoulder, just as Cor reached for a plate.

"He never misses a thing," Cor grumbled, passing Chiara the plate.

"I should hope not." She picked at her food, keeping a cautious eye on the bar.

Tagg was deep in conversation with a few of the patrons. People came and went. Some stayed longer than others. The atmosphere seemed generally relaxed.

But Chiara's uneasy feeling wasn't leaving. It had settled in her gut … the same feeling she'd had at Grede and Talin. Her heartbeat kicked up a notch, and she glanced around, anxious. *Something isn't right …*

"What's on your mind?" Cor's question interrupted her train of thought.

Surprised, she glanced up to see him looking at her with a thoughtful expression as he chewed.

"Oh … I don't know." She traced patterns on the tabletop with a finger.

Cor swallowed another mouthful. "Liar. You think I can't tell by now?" His tone was playful, but Chiara couldn't bring herself to laugh.

"Sorry. You're right," she admitted with a shrug. "It's just …" She cast a quick look around them. "I still feel like something's off."

"Uh, yeah?" Cor gave a sarcastic snort. He started ticking things off on his fingers. "We've been separated from Fhír; we're a misfit circus not-quite-troupe that sticks out like a sore thumb; we're being chased by lunatic arsonists — who *we're* supposed to be chasing — who might know about Fhír already; and we've caused a disaster everywhere we've been, so anyone with one eyeball and half a working brain could probably track us down. Did I forget anything? Oh, right — I almost died before some kind of miracle-working Tegid resurrected me."

"Tegid?" Chiara frowned.

"Yeah." He gave her a confused look. "What did you think she was?"

"Her skin — I thought—?"

Cor was frowning now. "What about it? She had tattoos — some pretty impressive ones, too."

"*What?*" Chiara stared at him. "No, she didn't. Her skin was indigo — all these different colors of blue … You didn't see that?"

"No!" Cor looked almost worried now. "Are you sure?"

"Yes!" she insisted. "It kept changing colors. I thought she was a Nousk at first, only she didn't have the horns or ears or anything."

Cor gave a nervous laugh. "Look, I know I was sick, but I'm pretty sure I know what I saw."

"And I know what *I* saw!" Chiara repeated. "How are we seeing two different things?"

What was weirder, Cor's glowing body or Ora's changing skin?

The blue glow in the field. The miraculous healing. The cryptic instructions …

Then it hit her. *What if she's not …?*

Chiara phrased it carefully. "Maybe she isn't … like us."

"What do you mean, not *like* us?" Cor asked. "You think she's a different species?"

"No …" Chiara went on hesitantly. "I think … she's more than that. The way she saved us. The way she healed you. The way she seemed to know all the answers. What if …?"

"… She's a spirit?" Cor lifted his eyebrows slowly. "A goddess, or something like that?"

Chiara shrugged helplessly. "Is there a better explanation?" She knew the Nousk and some of the Beast-skins believed in guardian spirits, but she'd never heard of one that looked like Ora — or appeared as a Tegid.

"A goddess. Sure. Why not?" Cor sighed. "That's pretty consistent with what we've been dealing with recently." He paused and looked at Chiara. "What really happened when she healed me? What did she do? Was the lavender magical or something?"

The image of Cor's glowing body flashed through her head. "I don't really know," she admitted. "She smeared the lavender on your forehead. And she was whispering something — some kind of prayer, I think. I couldn't really hear her."

"And … that was it?" There was a puzzled frown on Cor's face.

"Well …"

Ora's words still echoed. *You must tell him the truth.*

Chiara sighed. *He's going to think I'm insane* … But at this point, there wasn't much that could outdo the goddess theory.

So she said it. "Your body started to glow."

Cor stared at her strangely. "Glow?" he repeated, almost in disbelief. "As in … glowworm glow? Moon glow? A lantern?"

"As in … your-veins-looked-like-fireflies glow. Only for a minute or two," Chiara added hurriedly. "Then you went back to normal."

"Holy Arva." Cor leaned back in his seat. "So that's what it was …"

"You remember it?" Chiara shot him a curious glance. "I thought you were unconscious."

"I was. It was some kind of dream." His brow knitted. "I was swimming … in water, I think. Only it was gold. And I opened my mouth, like I was trying to — to swallow it or something. And then … I woke up." He looked at her nervously, as though he was hoping for answers.

"And you were fine," she finished.

"… Yeah. I guess so."

"I dunno …" Chiara shrugged. "Sounds like divine power to me."

"Maybe." Cor's eyes had grown distant.

"Well, let's hope you stay fine," she said, trying to joke. "I'm not a goddess, so I can't glow you back to life."

"Your lack of preparedness is a disgrace to the outfit."

Chiara rolled her eyes and pushed his shoulder. "Knock it off." At least he was taking it lightly.

"Seriously, though. Ora said I'd be fine." He grinned and took another sip from his drink.

She looked at him, and that same surreal feeling clouded her head … the fact that he was really alive, really sitting there.

Really right there.

You must tell him the truth.

Chiara cleared her throat. "Um … Cor, listen. There's … something I need to tell you."

He cocked his head to the side, an expectant look on his face.

"It's … something I talked about with Ora." She was twisting her fingers in her lap, unable to look at him. "While you were still unconscious. I … I lied to you." Heat diffused in her cheeks. "That night you got sick … at the trading post."

Cor's eyebrows went up slowly. "When we talked about …?"

"My family. Yeah." Chiara swallowed. "I should never have lied to you. I'm … I'm really sorry. You almost — that might've been our last—" She bit her lip.

Cor's face softened. "I forgive you."

"Thanks." Chiara almost couldn't look at him, she was so ashamed. "Well, after all that … I thought I should tell you … everything. So, this is … the truth. About … my family."

Cor leaned in, eyes locked on her face. "I'm listening."

"My … my parents adopted me." She had to force the words out.

"I remember."

"Right, yes," she laughed nervously. *Great. Now I just sound like an idiot.* "Well … it wasn't just me." She took a deep breath and looked up at him. "They … they also adopted my brother."

28

"You have a brother?" Cor exclaimed. "How could I possibly not know this by now? What's his name?"

Chiara winced. "Um … yeah. His name's Isak. He wasn't my brother by blood. At least, I don't think so. Dad adopted us both when we were still infants."

"He adopted *two* Tegids?" Cor's eyes went round. "How did that even happen?"

Chiara sighed softly. "He promised a friend he would take care of us."

"What friend?"

She shrugged. "He never told us. But I always thought it sounded like our biological parents were already dead, and someone else was taking care of us by the time Dad and Mum adopted us. Honestly … it was probably best that he kept it private. For all our sakes."

Cor nodded slowly. "I guess I could see that." He paused. "So … Isak."

Isak's blue eyes came back to her, so clear it stung.

"Isak." She exhaled through her nose. "Well, he was around my age, maybe a few months younger. He … wasn't Stunted."

He was incredible.

"We … we started the Academy at the same time. We were going to be trapeze artists together. I mean, that was before …" She waved a hand.

Cor leaned back in his chair, realization dawning on his face. "He was your catcher."

"Yes … that was him." Her face was burning. She rubbed a hand across her knuckles. *Please don't hate me … please don't hate me …*

"I had no idea," Cor murmured. "Torva never mentioned …" He looked at her, and there was sadness in his eyes. "And you practiced together, all those years? What happened?"

"Um …" Chiara's hands shook. *Don't cry … please don't cry …*

But her eyes were already stinging. "He, uh …" she began hoarsely, looking down at her lap. "Three years ago, we were at Crescor. My whole family. Isak made it to Nationals." A shaking smile broke out. "He — he won gold in his division. But …"

She practically had to bite her lip to keep a sob from slipping out. *Not here — not now.*

"The Crescor fire," Cor realized aloud. "Three years ago?"

She lifted her eyes to see his face darken. "Chiara … I'm so sorry." He placed a soft hand on her shoulder. "I had no idea …"

She shook her head. "No, it's — I should've told you. A while ago. I mean — we did all those trust exercises, and then you were almost dead, and—" She swallowed again, waving a helpless hand. "—and — I should've told you. I just … I didn't … I mean, we've been practicing — you and I — and being a flier was always my dream, but …"

Cor was silent. She couldn't bring herself to look at him.

"Trapeze was all I had left of him," she choked out. "I didn't … want to lose that."

"Chiara …" His voice was low.

She dared a glance at him.

"I'm sorry. About … about fighting." His eyes darkened. "Back at the outpost, before I got sick … I shouldn't have said what I said. I understand why you didn't want to talk about that. You don't have to tell me everything if you don't want to."

She was shaking her head. "See — see, that's the thing. I do — I should've. We're partners, and — and there's more …"

Cor was frowning. He looked so confused.

His face was turning blurry.

"I—" Chiara swiped desperately at her tears. "I was there … I saw him … I almost had him; and then—"

A sob slipped out, then another, and then Cor slid into the seat next to her, and his arms were around her. And she cried.

"It's not your fault. It's not your fault," he kept murmuring in her ear.

"I could've — could've saved him — if I was — fast enough—" She felt like she was choking.

"No … no, that's not how that works. Listen to me, okay?" His voice was so soft. "That's not how that works. I used to think — I used to think I could've saved my parents, somehow. But that's not how it works. You need to let him rest, Chiara."

"I can't—"

"Yes, you can. I promise," he whispered, and his arms tightened around her. "I promise. He must have loved you. He must have wanted the best for you. He wouldn't have wanted you to carry this your whole life."

"How can I not?" she gasped out. "The scars — my scars — I got them that night—"

"Mine, too." He drew back and looked her in the eyes. "But that's not who you are. You're not a scar. You're not just Stunted."

"But—"

"Chiara, you're *not*! You're a lot of things — you're intense and you're brave, and you're a fighter, and you never stop getting up ..." There was a smile in his voice, even though she couldn't really see him through the tears. "But Stunted isn't one of them. It just isn't. You're too much to be just that."

She almost laughed. "Thank you," she whispered, wiping at her warm face. "I'm sorry. I should've told you sooner — and I'm sorry about what I said—"

Cor was shaking his head. "I know why you did it. You shouldn't forget him. Even if you could, I wouldn't want you to. Just because I'm your catcher now doesn't mean that I'm taking his place. I'm not. I never could," he added in a low voice.

Chiara took a shuddering breath. "I know ... I know. I was just scared."

"I don't blame you."

She blinked, trying to regain what little composure she had left. "Can ... can we make a promise?"

"I'm all ears."

"No more secrets between partners?"

"No more secrets," he repeated earnestly.

They *were* partners, after all. Secrets got in the way of that. They had to start telling each other the truth … the whole truth.

Even if that was hard. Even if it meant she had something to lose now.

"Can we make a second promise?" There was a small twinkle in Cor's eye.

"Yes?"

"Can we both promise to be there for each other on the bars?"

Chiara bit her lip, and a teary laugh escaped her. "Yes — yes."

I want you to live. I want you to live. That's what he would've told her if he could be here.

She had to try.

"Lovely job all around, I'd say." Tagg walked up to the booth, a pleased look on his face.

Chiara groaned and rubbed her palms across her eyes. "How much of that did you hear?"

He looked offended. "None of it! As if I bally well couldn't interpret body language!"

Cor snorted, but Chiara's face became warm. *How many people saw us?* She glanced at Cor awkwardly, but he was still making a face at Tagg.

Tagg was ignoring him. "Would you look at that?" He pointed out the window. "It's raining again. Shocking."

Chiara turned around to see rain pouring down into the street. Thunder crackled quietly overhead. She sniffled, watching droplets trickle down the window. The lamplight was still blazing strong, despite the storm.

"That's some lantern," Cor said, sounding impressed. "Wonder what kind of light source they use."

Then a high-pitched keening grated across Chiara's ears.

Her heart stopped in her chest. "No." She shot to her feet, jostling the table.

"Chiara? What's wrong?" Cor was standing up behind her just as she turned around, nearly slamming into him.

"We have to get out of here," she muttered, looking at him with wide eyes. Panic was roaring in her ears.

"What? Why?" Cor sidestepped out of the booth, and she pushed past him.

"Right now," she hissed, putting on a false smile as she began brushing past other patrons.

Cor and Tagg hurried behind her, tugging up their hoods. Just as they reached the door, Tagg grabbed her shoulder. "What's going on?"

"That isn't a lantern! It's—"

Then someone burst through the doors with a yell that sealed all her worst fears.

"FIRE!"

29

"Ria!" Cor yelled. They shot out of the booth and bolted into the street, but a stream of Tegids began pouring out of the tavern, thrusting them aside.

Rain was still sheeting down; the street was pitch black. Chiara stared around wildly, trying to pinpoint the source of the screeching.

Shouts and cries filled the air.

"Where's the fire?"

"I can't see anything!"

"Over there!"

A dull, reddish glow erupted far to their left.

"Over there!" The cry was repeated. Fingers were pointing down the street. Flames were raging on the roofs of the first few buildings — flames too bloody, too hellish to be normal fire.

The Arsonists.

Chiara's breath came in short, bursting gasps. "Cor — they're here — they found us—" Any moment, the painted faces would appear; the glowing hands—

"The warehouses!" someone screamed; suddenly a stampede of traders and merchants was flooding the streets, charging toward the blaze in a desperate rush to save their cargo.

"Stick together! I'll get Ria!" Tagg turned to run.

Cor grabbed his arm, stopping him. "Other side of the outpost!" he shouted.

Tagg nodded and dashed toward the corner, elbowing his way through the crowd.

Cor snatched Chiara's hand and began shoving his way against the crush, leading her after him. Inch by inch, they pushed away from the fire, battling the chaos of bodies every step of the way as the storm thundered overhead.

They'd only made it a few yards farther when fresh cries sliced through the air — screams of agony.

They're coming — they're coming — they're coming— Chiara whipped around, eyes straining through the dark.

"Don't stop running!" Cor yanked at her arm.

"They're killing people!" she screamed. "We have to stop them! We have to do something!"

She turned toward the fires just as a cluster of people burst out of the crowd in her direction, nearly running her down.

The next moment, Cor was tugging her to the side, pulling her into an alleyway away from the rush.

They crouched in the shadows against the wall. Cor's hands clamped onto her shoulders, compelling her to face him. "Chiara, listen to me!"

It was too dark to see his face, but she could hear the desperate edge to his voice. "We don't have our weapons, and we have no idea how many of them are here!"

"But—"

He gave her a shake. "We can't save this place!"

She was shaking; she was starting to cry. "They're dying because of *us!*"

Cor was silent, but he lifted his head, eyes fixed on the street.

"What is it?" Chiara turned. Rain was still hammering down from the dark sky. She could see the road from where she sat. Black shapes were swarming like ants in both directions. A murky orange glow was beginning to flash in the puddles on the ground.

She turned back to Cor. She could just make out the grim line of his mouth. "If they're here for us," he said slowly, "then we can give them what they want."

"What?"

"Listen to me very carefully." He held her shoulders again, pulling her face close to his. "On my count, we run out of this alleyway. I need to you run as far and as fast as possible. Get away from the fire. Find Tagg."

"What about you?"

"Don't worry about me," he began, but she cut him off.

"No, don't give me that! What are you thinking? You're gonna be some kind of decoy? Are you insane?" The wail of the flames was beginning to flood her senses, driving up her panic.

"If they want us, they'll come and get us!" Cor argued. "Nobody else has to die!"

Anger flared in her chest. "*You* don't have to die, either!"

The orange glow was becoming stronger.

She could see his eyes now, darting across her face. "I promise you I'm not going to d—"

"No!" she snapped, getting up in his face. "Don't you dare promise me that! *Especially* not after what happened with Ora!"

Another scream pierced the veil of rain and darkness. Cor gave a snarl of frustration and turned his head away, running a hand through his hair. "Look, we don't have time for this! Either I find them and lead them off, or a lot more people are going to die! Can you please just trust me?"

"Trust you?" she screamed back. "Trust the guy who almost got himself killed a few days ago? And now you want me to trust that you won't do it again? No! I *don't* trust you!" There was a note of hysteria in her voice.

Cor brought his face within an inch of hers. "I'm not asking you to trust *that* Cor! I'm asking you to trust the Cor who pulled you out of the fire at Belkar! What about *him*? Can you trust *him*?"

Chiara drew back, heart pounding in her ears.

"Can you trust that Cor?" he repeated more insistently.

That Cor.

That Cor. That Cor, with the hands that caught her over and over again, the hands that never let her fall. The hands that had carried her out of the pyre.

Chiara's chest grew tight. "Yes," she whispered.

Footsteps were thundering closer. Cries of panic echoed between the buildings — the tide of people was turning now, stampeding away from the fire.

"Okay, then." Cor stood and darted a quick look around the corner. "On my count," he instructed as Chiara stood next to him. "Ready … ready … NOW!"

They sprang out of the alleyway in unison, right into the herd of bodies. "GO, Chiara!" Cor was shouting behind her. "Find Tagg!"

She plunged forward blindly, jostling and elbowing, following the rush away from the flames. Once or twice, she dared a glance over her shoulder, but Cor had already been swallowed up by the noise and the crowd. She thought she heard him yelling somewhere behind.

"Tagg!" She began screaming at the top of her lungs, arms pumping faster as she looked for any sign of a rider on a horse. A few mounted figures rushed past, hooves clattering on the pavement — but none of them were tall enough to be Ria.

Her lungs were burning. The screeching fire was nearly unbearable now.

Then she had an idea. It was stupid, and wild, but she couldn't think of anything better.

TAGG! She made it as loud a thought as she could muster.

"CHIARA!" Suddenly the rain-slicked flanks of a horse appeared in her peripheral, and Ria cantered past her. A familiar pull tugged her off the ground, and she found herself sitting behind Tagg.

"Hup!" He urged Ria into a gallop; Chiara laced her arms around his waist as they charged down the street, dodging the other panicked runners.

"Where's Cor?" he called back to her, just as the far gates came into view.

Chiara didn't feel like explaining. "He'll find us! Keep going!" She couldn't quite say *He said so himself.* That would have to be good enough for Tagg.

"Tell me he didn't stay behind for some noble sacrifice!"

Chiara didn't reply.

"Bloody idiot." Tagg cursed under his breath, but he didn't stop. He spurred Ria on faster, and they began picking up speed. Rain rushed into Chiara's face, running down her head, soaking her clothes.

"Come on, come on," Tagg urged. The gateway was still several yards ahead; both gates were flung open, and people were rushing out of the burning outpost into the night.

Suddenly there was a dull roar; a burst of heat and flaring orange light flooded over them from behind, sending long black shadows in front of them.

"COR!" Tagg hollered; Chiara whipped her head around.

There — there he was, sprinting down the street, mouth open, screaming something; and behind him … three dark shapes with glowing hands.

"Cor!" she screamed; cold fingers of dread gripped her heart as she watched him stop and turn.

He was taking a stance, right there in the street.

"*No!*" Her own scream sounded tinny in her ears. "Cor, just *run!*"

Buildings began to flash by as Ria leapt into a gallop; they were leaving him behind; they were leaving him alone—

"Tagg, stop!" she cried in his ear. *"Cor!"*

They were a few yards away from the mouth of the gate when two figures appeared inside it, white-hot palms extended.

Ria clattered to a halt, forelegs lifting to strike; a guttural scream ripped from her throat.

Chiara was sliding off; she was falling; her feet hit the ground hard. Searing pain shot up her leg as her left ankle twisted awkwardly beneath her.

She fell with a cry of pain, rolling away from Ria's massive hooves in the nick of time. Completely winded, she tried to stand, but her ankle burned and she buckled to her knees again.

Just then, Tagg gave an enraged shout. Ria's roar dissolved into a shrill scream of panic. Chiara whirled around just in time to see the massive horse bolt forward, Tagg clinging to her back as she plowed forward toward her two would-be attackers.

They leapt aside just as Ria vanished into the darkness beyond the gate. One of them shouted to the other, and they both spun and charged after her.

Chiara turned back to the combatants behind her. *"Cor!"*

She could see him now. He was planted in the middle of the street several yards behind her, a silhouette against the inferno, swords out, screaming threats at the three Arsonists in front of him.

She tried to run toward him, but her ankle felt like it was on fire, and the most she could manage was a lame trot. She limped forward, cursing incessantly under her breath. *Arva, why this? Anything but this. Please …*

Lurid orange light filled the street as the building fires crawled closer. Rain hissed and sizzled, turning into steam as it fell.

The three figures approached Cor slowly, hands alight. His furious cry drifted back to Chiara. "Come on! Come get some, you stinking cowards!"

"Cor, stop!" Chiara licked dry lips. Her voice was far too hoarse. *He's going to get himself killed …*

Then a horrible cracking sound split the air. The Arsonists spun around, and Cor darted backward as one of the warehouses collapsed heavily into the street with a deafening crash. Clouds of debris flew into the air.

"Chiara, run!" Cor was sprinting up, nearly crashing into her. "Let's go!"

He grabbed her arm and turned to charge toward the gate as angry shouts rose behind them. But one step brought Chiara to her knees. "My ankle!" she gasped as red-hot pain stabbed up through her thigh.

In an instant, Cor swung her arm over his shoulder and began charging forward, practically dragging her along at his side.

The shouts were getting nearer. Another deafening crash, a hot wave of air, choking with steam and smoke and ash. Chiara's breath burned in her lungs.

Cor slowed and glanced over his shoulder. "Can't see 'em," he panted. "Building must've blocked the street."

"Keep running!" Chiara pointed. "Almost there!"

They were so close — just yards away from the entrance.

Then a dark shape materialized in the shadowy gateway. Fiery hands illuminated a painted face. He began pacing slowly toward them.

Terror froze Chiara's limbs, choking her in the back of her throat. The scars on her flesh were burning.

She knew the touch of those hands; knew what they could do.

Cor lowered her onto the road where they stood. "Stay here! Use your sax!" he yelled, and then he turned and began advancing on the Arsonist, twin blades glittering. "Try burning me again, you bastard!"

The enemy's hands blossomed into a swirling ball of flames.

"Cor, NO!" Chiara screamed as he charged, swords upraised.

She was struggling to her feet; she was moving forward; ankle be damned—

Monster — monster with its painted face — screams; the smell of burned flesh — Cor, burning just like Isak — not fast enough, not fast enough—!

Cor struck; there was a *woosh*; his enemy ducked and rolled — and then the painted face turned on her, rushing forward.

Her foot caught on a crack in the street, and she collapsed to her knees.

"NO!" Screams sliced through her skull; her scream, Cor's scream, in her ears, in her head, the same desperate cry.

The Arsonist reared up in front of her, fists upraised. White-hot fear burned through her limbs; her eyes shut; she lifted her arms helplessly as blistering heat rolled over her body.

Not fast enough.

There was a squeal of agony, and Chiara opened her eyes. Fire was consuming her vision.

Her arms were on fire … fire that wasn't burning her.

She opened her mouth, but no scream came out. Flames blazed across her untouched skin, all over her hands …

… Hands that were glowing white.

Blood roared in her ears. "Oh, Arva …" *No. No, no, no … no …*

Her hands were shaking; she was shaking them, trying to put them out—

In front of her, the Arsonist crumpled onto the pavement, still screaming.

Standing behind him was Cor … Cor, a look of horror on his face as he stared down at her glowing hands.

acknowledgements

HIIII! Sorry about that. Just wanted to be sure you'd read the next book. Hope you'll forgive me one day!

Anyway, first and foremost, a lifelong thank you to Mom and Dad. I don't know how many other parents would be as thrilled as you that their daughter was majoring in English and becoming a freelance editor, let alone deciding to self-publish a fantasy novel. But you were. You never doubted my abilities, and you have no idea how much that means to me. After all those hours I spent staring at a blinking cursor on a blank page, questioning my existence and my life choices, what brought me back from the metaphorical edge was remembering that you truly believe that my work has meaning. And after remembering that, I would start typing again. I'll never be famous, but I'll always have parents who care about how I'm doing what I love. Thank you for having faith in me even when I didn't have faith in myself. You are incredible, and I owe you so much. (Unfortunately, fantasy novels aren't a good get-rich-quick scheme … I'll have to repay you in goodwill and acts of service … Hope that's fine …)

Thanks to Bridget, Michael, Mary, Eleanor, Patrick, Kilian and Keenan, who endured months of hearing me talk to myself as I typed frantically at a computer and somehow still wanted to read my book when it was done. Thank you for beta reading, talking, arguing, designing cover art, sharing your ideas, and calling me out on dumb plot holes. Each of you truly ~~annoyed~~ motivated me enough to finish. And if you see yourselves in some of my characters … well, I don't know what to tell you about that. If you weren't so funny, you wouldn't be in my book. Keep reading for your individual thank yous.

Hi, Bridget! Thanks for asking me "Are you done yet?" every day for four weeks while I struggled through my first and second drafts. If it hadn't been for you, I never would've almost lost my mind. I also never would've finished the manuscript. You're the greatest almost-Irish-twin anyone could ask for.

Thanks to Michael, who mocked me ruthlessly anytime I said "Almost done! Almost done!" and helpfully pointed out that I went between "This is amazing!!" and "This is total garbage" four times in as many days while I was finishing the first draft. Truly motivating. Don't know what I'd do without you, bro. (In all seriousness, thanks for the prayers.)

Thank you so much to Mary Virginia, my sister, who worked with me on character designs that absolutely SLAPPED. You brought my characters to life, and you have NO IDEA how EXCITED I AM ABOUT IT!!! Do you KNOW how BEAUTIFUL IT IS?? To see ART?? that is EXACTLY how you PICTURED IT in your HEAD???? You deserve *all* the medals. Sadly, I do not have any to give you (yet), but I owe you infinite chocolate.

Thank you to Eleanor, the most vigorous advocate for me to finish this book … ever since 2017, when she read the first terrible chapters of the first terrible version of what this book would eventually become (yikes). Thank you for the endless theories, plot twists, character arcs, and story development, and for being my digital design genius on Canva. The Instagram posts would be in a truly sorry state if I had to figure it all out on my own. You're the world's best beta reader, and I can't praise you highly enough. (P.S. Mathew made it into the final story. You're welcome.)

Thank you to Patrick, whose sense of humor leaves me in stitches and provided inspiration for some of the best quotes in this book. In addition to being the funniest person I know, you were also my very first illustrator back in 2017 (remember the Gwaelkwen? I still have those drawings!). No, the book wasn't published on July 31, and I didn't intend for it to be published then … but I appreciate how even though you thought that was the case, you didn't want to poke the bear by asking me in August why it wasn't already published. Thanks, man!

Thank you to Kilian and Keenan, who *definitely* appear as characters in this book. Thanks especially to Kilian, whose persistence in asking "Have you gotten to my character yet?" was frankly inspiring. Even George Washington could learn a few things about your perseverance, my dude. You were very motivating. (Sorry about threatening to kill off your character. I still love you.)

I hate the phrase "a tremendous thank you" because it really doesn't do justice to the amount of time, patience, and care that my friends and mentors have put into this — as beta readers, as advice-givers, as impromptu editors, as soundboards … so I will try to thank you each personally.

Thank you, Fr. Pollard, for all those evenings in the office and on the back porch where you showed such patience and attention to detail as I went on and on about character motivations and plot twists and villain arcs. The story and I were both a bit of a mess at that point, and your advice prompted character growth in more ways than one. I can happily credit my villain to you, and I mean that as the sincerest compliment, because that was possibly the biggest development (plot-wise and personally) of the entire writing process. I can't say I'd be doing much better than the villain if it wasn't for your wisdom and prayers. Thank you for being one of the greatest mentors I'll ever have.

Thank you, Kathleen, for your constant joy and investment in my growth as a writer. I'll always remember the day I understood for the first time why authors keep writing, because it was the day you said that you read my first draft the entire way through without putting it down. I will never forget that. Your "Deo gratias!" isn't just a phrase — you truly live in gratitude, and you inspire me to do the same. My experience of working on my senior thesis and my experience of actually writing this book were one and the same — both times, I couldn't put it down, and both times, you encouraged me to lean into that passion and run with it. Thank you so much for all your time and prayers over the last five years. This book wouldn't exist without you.

Thank you, Mary Grace, for believing in this story when it was still just a weird idea about a girl and an eclipse and setting stuff on fire. You had the singular misfortune of being that one friend who kept getting the first five chapters of various unfinished stories, for which I am profoundly sorry. (If it's any consolation, *The Rose of Auraveil* may yet be a reality …) The day I finally sent you that email with the first full-length novel manuscript was a day that will be celebrated on the calendars. Thank you for your unabashed enthusiasm, your attention to the smallest details, and your dedication to seeing my book become a reality.

Thank you, Maria, for all the years of back-and-forth emails, swapping story ideas and talking about books that might one day be published. I was so excited to read your beta feedback (even the criticism!!) because I knew it was coming from someone who had spent just as much time forging her way through one unfinished draft after another, searching for the perfect word. Constructive criticism is generally terrifying, but yours was inspiring — enough for me to be excited about draft three.

Thank you, Rachel P., for being the staunchest PR friend I never realized I needed. Every time we were at a social function together, you would drag me over to introduce me to people and then shout, "SHE'S WRITING A BOOK!!!" And it took me a while, but I finally realized that writing a novel is something worth telling people about. (I know, I'm kinda dumb.) Thanks for your relentless enthusiasm about books and boys. I'd say the Tea Chat will go down in history, but I hope it doesn't, for all our sakes.

Thank you, Abby, for stopping in the middle of lunch with your now-fiancé (soon-to-be-husband) when you got the beta manuscript and then insisting on reading it aloud to him. I can't quite explain the euphoria I got when I heard that, but be assured that it was significant. I'm so grateful that you voluntarily slogged through the first draft and then gave such amazing feedback (the pink tablet pen on the beta questionnaire made my day!). Thank you for your investment in both the story and the Tea Chat with Rachel. Your encouragement means the world to me!

Thank you, Grace, for your friendship and your joy. You are such a gift, and I am so sorry about that time you came to visit in November 2023 and I made you sit down for three hours while I scribbled plotlines on the dry erase board like someone who belonged in a mental institution. If it's any consolation, you're the reason I have a series and not just one or two books. Thank you so, so much. Here's to decades of stories to come (although maybe without the crazy whiteboard antics).

Thank you, Jennifer, because you weren't even on the original beta reader list, but I was thrilled that you wanted to read it — and I was EVEN MORE THRILLED by your feedback!! Girl, you SERVED. You need to do this professionally. You gave some of the most thorough constructive criticism on my character development that I think I've ever read … and I literally edit books for a living. 10/10. You're amazing. Thank you so much!

Thank you, Hayley and Rachel C., for patiently answering all my questions about self-publishing, hiring an editor, buying ISBNs, social media advertising … the list goes on. I don't know where I'd be without your help. Probably buried miles deep in Google searches and YouTube tutorials with no way out. You saved me a lot of tears when I didn't have many to spare. Thank you both so much!!

Thank you to Chrissy, Katie, Anna, Mim, Suzanne, Monica, Ellie, and Emilie, for wanting to read my first draft when it was still only a sad little lump of word glop. I won't lie — there were times I wondered if maybe I should put off publishing until December 2024, or even 2025. But then I remembered that each of you genuinely cared about reading it, and I knew I couldn't let you down. So thanks for pulling me through some of the most frustrating hours of my life. Even now, as I write this during Hell Week with four days left until publication, I think about how you all still want to read it, and I get really excited.

Thank you, Sophia, for being my Zelie. There's so much more I could say, but I don't know any better ways to say it except that. You'll always be part of my stories. Here's to many more years of chaos. I love you!

Thank you, Andrew, for listening very attentively to my half-hour explanation of the character design for every single one of my species, and then promptly calling them furries. Your devil's advocate perspective was an excellent test of how well my worldbuilding could stand up to the fleeting impressions of the uneducated masses (not to imply that you're one of them, of course … but if that makes you mad, stay mad). I genuinely appreciate it, because it reinforced my belief that writing good stories matters, even if some people don't quite get the details. You have the singular honor of being my only *almost*-beta-reader (alas, Quantico was an insurmountable inconvenience).

Thank you to Egil Thorsson, who has no idea who I am but made one of the world's best YouTube videos about Viking seaxes. Everybody knows about fantasy broadswords; I wanted something different; and he delivered. His knowledge of all things Norse is paralleled only by his amazing mustache and accent. Sir, I don't know if you'll ever read this book, but I'm thanking you anyway. That was one of the most enjoyable research rabbit holes I've ever explored, and it gave me some much-needed confidence in my fantasy weaponry. Keep making videos!

And thank you to all the personal friends, family friends, relatives, professors, mentors, fellow students, and even fellow conversationalists who were invested in my book, prayed for me, followed my Instagram, asked about my progress, and shared it all with their friends and family. I know I probably can't fit most of your names in here, but words can't explain how grateful I am that this mattered to you. Thank you for reading. Thank you for sharing. Thank you for praying. Don't stop! Keep going! The rest of the series is still in the making!

And last but not least, thank you to that one guy (we'll call him Phil) from that one self-publishing company (we'll call it the Book Company). Look, Phil, I know you were doing your job, just trying to sell me a multi-thousand-dollar self-publishing program. And I won't deny that there were times when I was putting myself through the horrors of social media posts and KDP formatting and thought, *I could've avoided all of this if I'd listened to Phil.* But you know what? I don't regret it for a second. And I want to thank you in the most genuine way possible, because you changed my perspective on the entire process. The last question you ever asked me was, "Do you want to work with the Book Company, or do you want to spend another five years writing your novel?" And Phil, I took that personally. If you hadn't said anything, I probably wouldn't be here right now. You did a great thing that day, Phil. You made me realize, "You know what? I *can* do this myself." And…I did. No multi-thousand-dollar program needed. So, huge shout-out to Phil for doing his job of getting a book self-published without even needing to sell me his program.

And thank you to you, reader, whoever you are, for getting this far. I promise there's more to come, and I fully intend to finish this series before it finishes me. Maybe you and I know each other well, or maybe we've never met in person … but either way, I hope that Chiara's story is worth remembering.

about the author

Cat McCaughey has been an avid fiction reader since her first pair of glasses at eleven months old, and she's been a writer almost as long. Her first attempt at a novel was technically a self-insert Narnia AU fanfiction, but at the time, she had no idea that was what it was, because she was only eight and assumed that was just how you wrote stories. Needless to say, she's come a long way since then.

In addition to publishing *branded*, the first novel in her debut fantasy series, she runs her own freelance editing business, *Wordcraft Editorial*, which consists mostly of ranting at words on her computer screen. When she isn't frantically scribbling for some deadline, she's probably outside listening to Novo Amor, Noah Kahan, or Hozier while journaling with colored pens. You can find her at wordcraftnovels.com or on Instagram: @wordcraft_novels.

www.ingramcontent.com/pod-product-compliance
Lightning Source LLC
Chambersburg PA
CBHW070306310726
48976CB00005B/1594